Contents

In memoriam
Derek Marlowe (1938-96)

PENGUIN BOOKS
The Time Out Book of New York Short Stories

Nicholas Royle is the author of three novels – *Counterparts* (Penguin),
Saxophone Dreams (Penguin) and *The Matter of the Heart* (Abacus) –
and around a hundred short stories. He has edited five anthologies
including *A Book of Two Halves* (Indigo) and *The Tiger Garden: A Book
of Writers' Dreams* (Serpent's Tail). A regular contributor to the books
pages of *Time Out*, he also edits Time Out City Guides and is online
editor of *Time Out Net Books* (http://www.timeout.co.uk).

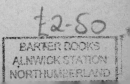

The Time Out Book of
New York Short Stories

Edited by Nicholas Royle

PENGUIN BOOKS

PENGUIN BOOKS

Published by the Penguin Group
Penguin Books Ltd, 27 Wrights Lane, London W8 5TZ, England
Penguin Putnam Inc., 375 Hudson Street, New York, New York 10014, USA
Penguin Books Australia Ltd, Ringwood, Victoria, Australia
Penguin Books Canada Ltd, 10 Alcorn Avenue, Toronto, Ontario, Canada M4V 3B2
Penguin Books (NZ) Ltd, 182–190 Wairau Road, Auckland 10, New Zealand

Penguin Books Ltd, Registered Offices: Harmondsworth, Middlesex, England

First published in Great Britain in Penguin Books 1997
3 5 7 9 10 8 6 4

Printed in England by Clays Ltd, St Ives plc

Contributors

Mark Amerika is the author of books and hypertexts including *The Kafka Chronicles*, *Sexual Blood* and *GRAMMATRON*. He is the director of the Alt-X Publishing Network located at http://www.altx.com.

Brooke Auchincloss was born in New York and moved to England in 1983. Her short stories have been published in *Border Lines* (Serpent's Tail) and *ABeSea* magazine, and broadcast on radio.

Thomas Beller was born in New York City in 1965. He has worked as a staff writer at the *New Yorker* and the *Cambodia Daily*. His fiction début was the short story collection *Seduction Theory*. One of the editors of the literary magazine *Open City*, he lives in Greenwich Village.

Christopher Burns is the author of five novels – *Snakewrist*, *The Flint Bed*, *The Condition of Ice*, *In the Houses of the West* and *Dust Raising* – and one short story collection, *About the Body*. He lives in Cumbria.

Jonathan Carroll is an American living in Vienna. His books include *The Land of Laughs*, *After Silence*, *From the Teeth of Angels*, *Voice of Our Shadow*, *Outside the Dog Museum*, *The Child Across the Sky* and a collection of short stories, *The Panic Hand*.

Born in Birmingham in 1961, **Jonathan Coe** is the author of *The Accidental Woman*, *A Touch of Love*, *The Dwarves of Death*, *What a Carve Up!* (which won the John Llewellyn Rhys Prize and the Prix du Meilleur Livre Etranger) and *The House of Sleep*.

Rikki Ducornet is the author of five novels – *The Stain*, *Entering Fire*, *The Fountains of Neptune*, *The Jade Cabinet* and *Phosphor in Dreamland*. A collection, *The Word 'Desire'*, is forthcoming. She lives in Denver, Colorado.

In addition to running his film promotion company, the Creative Partnership, **Christopher Fowler** is a prolific novelist – *Roofworld*, *Rune*, *Darkest Day*, *Spanky*, *Psychoville* – and short story writer, with collections including *City Jitters*, *The Bureau of Lost Souls* and *Sharper Knives*.

Edward Fox was born in New York in 1958 and now lives in London, where he works as a freelance journalist. He is the author of a number of short stories published in *London Magazine* and one non-fiction book, *Obscure Kingdoms: Journeys to Distant Royal Courts*.

Maureen Freely was born in Neptune, New Jersey in 1952 and grew up in Istanbul. She now lives in Bath with an industrial sociologist, has four children and two stepchildren. Her novels are *Mother's Helper*, *The Life of the Party*, *The Stork Club*, *Under the Vulcania* and *The Other Rebecca*.

Samantha Gillison was born in Melbourne, grew up in Papua New Guinea and New York City, and now lives in Brooklyn. She has published stories in *Open City, Paris Transcontinental, American Writing, Descant* and elsewhere, and has recently completed her first novel, *The Undiscovered Country*.

Executive editor of *Time Out*, **Steve Grant** writes regularly about arts and entertainment. His short stories have appeared in *The Time Out Book of London Short Stories* and *A Book of Two Halves*. He lives in London.

Charles Higson is a writer, producer and performer on the BBC comedy programme *The Fast Show*. Formerly a singer with the Higsons, in the early 1980s, he is now the author of four novels: *King of the Ants*, *Happy Now*, *Full Whack* and *Getting Rid of Mister Kitchen*.

Born in Oxfordshire, **Liz Jensen** lives in south London. Her first novel is *Egg Dancing*; her second, *Ark Baby*, is due early in 1998. She has also lived and worked in Hong Kong, Taiwan and France.

Russell Celyn Jones is the author of *Soldiers and Innocents* (which won the David Higham Prize), *Small Times* and *An Interference of Light*. He has held fellowships at the universities of Iowa, East Anglia and Western Cape.

Cris Mazza is the author of three collections – *Animal Acts*, *Is It Sexual Harassment Yet?* and *Revelation Countdown*. Her most recent novel is *Your Name Here: _____*. With Jeffrey DeShell she co-edited *Chick-Lit: Postfeminist Fiction* and (with DeShell and Elisabeth Sheffield) *Chick-Lit 2*. She teaches in the Program for Writers at the University of Illinois at Chicago.

Michael Moorcock was born in London and currently lives in Texas. A past winner of the *Guardian* Fiction Prize, the Nebula Award, the British Fantasy Award and the World Fantasy Award, his novels include *The Condition of Muzak, Behold the Man, Gloriana* and *Mother London.*

Kim Newman's short stories have been collected in *The Original Dr Shade and Other Stories* and *Famous Monsters*; his novels include *The Night Mayor, Bad Dreams, Jago, The Quorum* and *The Bloody Red Baron.* Born in Brixton in 1959, he lives in north London.

Joyce Carol Oates is the author, most recently, of *Foxfire: Confessions of a Girl Gang, What I Lived For, First Love: A Gothic Tale* and *Zombie.* Resident in New Jersey, she is the Roger S Berlind Distinguished Professor in the Humanities at Princeton University.

Lisa Natalie Pearson, a writer and performance artist, was born in Texas and now lives in Portland, Oregon. Currently working on a novel, *Neither Here Nor There*, she began writing fiction after several years of working in the theatre in the US and Europe. Her first published story appeared in *Chick-Lit: Postfeminist Fiction.*

Elisa Segrave is the author of a memoir, *The Diary of a Breast*, and a novel, *Ten Men.* Her short stories and journalism have been widely published. She lives in London.

Lynne Tillman is the author of three novels – *Haunted Houses, Motion Sickness, Cast in Doubt*; two short story collections – *Absence Makes the Heart, The Madame Realism Complex*; and two non-fiction books – *The Broad Picture, The Velvet Years: Warhol and the Factory 1965-1967.* She was born in New York City, where she still lives. A new novel, *No Lease on Life*, is forthcoming.

Born in Lagos, **Elizabeth Young** lives in London. She is the co-author of *Shopping in Space: Essays on American 'Blank Generation' Fiction.* Widely published as a literary journalist, her short stories have appeared in several anthologies and magazines. Her collected criticism and essays are due to be published as *Pandora's Handbag.*

Introduction

On a recent visit to New York I took a cab from Greenwich Village to Chinatown. My driver was Gabriel, a Romanian who stowed away on board ship in Constanta and was discovered *five times* before he finally managed to escape. Both his parents had been executed by the Ceausescu regime; he saw no reason to stick around. Gabriel jumped ship off Miami and made his way to New York where he married a French woman and ended up driving a yellow cab. The government which replaced Ceausescu, according to Gabriel, was almost as bad – it never lifted the conviction against him and others like him, so that if he'd returned to his country he'd have been arrested. It's only since the installation of the current regime that Gabriel's been free to go back.

But will he bother?

No. He's made his home in New York.

It's that kind of place.

It's the kind of place people dream about. The kind of place people have ideas about. Write stories about. The *idea* of New York can be as potent as New York itself. It's for this reason that we decided this anthology didn't have to consist exclusively of stories set in New York written by New Yorkers. We saw no good reason to exclude British authors – far from it. And for every piece which engages with the *concept* of New York, there are another two or three in which the Manhattan setting is so real you can smell the coffee, taste the pretzels, feel the bitter chill of Central Park in the middle of winter.

Time Out has a traditional involvement with innovative fiction and new writing. The magazine has published original short stories and profiles of up-and-coming writers – in addition to the weekly books pages which are packed with informed critical comment, author interviews and events listings. *Time Out New York* was launched in September 1995; by January 1996 (issue 19) it had already made a foray into fiction, publishing new stories by three New York writers. *The Time Out Book of London Short Stories*, edited by Maria Lexton and published in 1993 to celebrate the magazine's twenty-fifth birthday, proved enormously popular. In *Net Books* on *Time Out*'s web site (http://www.timeout.co.uk) we publish two new short stories in each online issue, along with reviews and features.

In a magazine-publishing world increasingly obsessed with printing novel extracts as marketing opportunities, it is vital to create and nurture genuine markets for short stories. Without them, writers, both new and established, are deprived of a proper outlet for their work, and readers are starved of one of their favourite forms.

This book is intended to be a composite picture of New York City, from twenty-three different angles, taken an eye-blink before the end of the millennium, and a reflection on the state of the art of the short story in Britain and America today.

Put simply, a cab ride through one of the world's most exciting cities.

Don't hang about about on the sidewalk. Let's go.

Nicholas Royle
Time Out
London
April 1997

THIS COULD BE THE FIRST DAY OF THE REST OF MY LIFE
Mark Amerika

The day that I was to be slaughtered was a very busy day. First I had to go meet my agent who wasn't really my agent any more but, rather, my gallery director. Well, not exactly my gallery director either. You see, we had decided that it would be better for me to completely forget about my publishing life and to take a leave of absence from my multi-media installation life and to just do the same thing my Modernist predecessors had done, that is, 'create an art that imitated life that had actually imitated art, in admittedly unexpected ways'. Or so that's how I had described it in the dissociative prose-rant I distributed via my Internet column which wasn't really an Internet column any more but a kind of performance art spectacle since it now incorporated what my personal critic called a 'hyperrhetorical display of iconographic typography' which, if you stop to think about it, is exactly what all my work has been about. Although who's to say what a work is 'about', I mean, the important question to ask nowadays is 'what is the artist trying to do?' Everybody knows that.

When I tried to explain this to my painter friend who kept telling me that 'every "system" is a seduction with all of the consequences of a seduction', I improvisationally stole some of his ideas which weren't really his ideas at all but something Robert Motherwell said in his Big Dada Book all those years ago, that is, I suggested that every God-like feature invented by Microsoft and built into their latest version of Word was an opportunity for artists to become independently wealthy and that what we needed was to create an expressive set of virtual forms that could relate to the various tribes of consumerism that, in toto, composed the mass market, and that playing to the interiorised logic of this mass market's desire to experience the consummate orgasm would be a phenomenon of public morality not seen since the days of Joe DiMaggio.

Actually, my painter friend isn't a painter at all, rather, he's a poet, or not a poet since he really hates poetry and says he would rather be a garbage man or a Web-designer than a starving poet with nothing new to say, but a kind of network programmer who uses verbal constructions to conjure up a spirit of superiority that certain people in his Rolodex are willing to pay big cash dollars for. Well, not really cash dollars. Digicash. A kind of simulation-crude that, when applied to the anal vortex, enables the butthole surfer to imagine what it's like to take part in a large-scale swindle. This, and the occasional foreign translation, not to mention participation in digital arts festivals and travelling exhibitions, has proven to be the key to his survival.

But this is all beside the point because I was stuck inside my apartment in Battery Park City and it was Sunday and all of the rich international financiers who usually troll through the neighbourhood due to their occupation of the various World Trade and Financial Centers were nowhere to be found and as I looked down from the advantageous perspective of my bedroom on the thirty-sixth floor I saw schools of yellow cabs transport whosoever wished to be brought into the heart of capitalism's immortal lock on the human race, whose winning gift-horse, a filly called Information Currency, was rounding the millennial bend with its intellectual cousin, the *New York Times*, who, it ends up, was now going to slaughter me in the most normal of ways.

You see, my girlfriend, who's not really my girlfriend but my common-law wife, had already received three e-mails from various friends of ours in the literary network that my new book was going to be reviewed in the *Times Book Review* and that it would be devastating and that it would effectively kill my career. None of them wanted to tell me directly because they knew that she'd have a way of preparing me for it that I myself could never come up with. And I must say, I found this honest distantiation of our friends to be perfectly legitimate.

Nonetheless, as I told my girlfriend/wife before she could even begin rolfing my ego, I had willed the end of my career myself, having started the process three years ago by refusing to publish anything in print again. I was adamant. 'The literary print world is totally useless,' I remember telling my editor, who was really not an editor but a marketing representative for a tobacco company that happened to be in the book business, 'and,' I continued, 'I'm quite content seeing it die its much-ballyhooed death.' But then my agent, if you could call this person who represented me an agent, sold the rights to what was at that time my collected Net columns and everyone thought that this acquisition was a total waste of time and money, which it was, yet the market can be funny sometimes, and now they were going to be my friend, yes, my good-cop bad-cop publicity buddy, in that they weren't going to ignore me any more, which is really worse than death itself, no, they weren't going to turn their heads away from me any more, they were just going to slaughter me and my anti-literary digerati arrogance in the most public way possible and, my girlfriend/wife kept reminding me, that's what friends are for.

My publishing friends had reason to slaughter me. First of all, I had already slaughtered them. My imported butcher knives cut through all of their pretensions and displayed their cronyistic innards in ways that I didn't even realise I had in me. The whole pathological deformation that passed itself off as The Publishing Industry was laid bare inside my operating system so that the sloppy mishmash of bleeding organs and twisted tubes leaking silvery rivulets of fatty acids and venereal diseases ate through my computer screen in an attempt to *become* me, but, alas, my utility programs were powerful enough to not only disinfect my desktop of the gargantuan grotesquerie it had rapidly morphed into, but even managed to clear my work-space of the corpse-like stench that filled my hairy nostrils. It was as if an undifferentiated Digital God of Endless Being had approximated my need to tear off the grubby hands that were feeding me – and by bypassing their deadwood paper-mill distribution system of eco-death and black desire, I could go out of my way to bury those cold, manicured *manos* in their own blood and bones and the contaminated dirt that filled their pockets.

As my friend the film theorist recently told me, although he's really not a film theorist but, rather, an underground comix artist whose periodical forays into avant-garde ventriloquy stubbornly resist psychological and linguistic categorisation, 'our bodies still retain the marks of the old bacterial freedoms, even when our institutions work busily to suppress them'.

Knowing this doesn't make things any better. Rather, knowing that you'll be butchered in ten minutes gives you a funny kind of feeling (the altruism of a girlfriend/wife's love) – until then, you never in your life know what it's like to play the leading role in a social play whose theme is animal sacrifice. It's like you have to totally grow up and learn to live beyond that sacrifice and even use the painful knowledge you associate with that sacrifice to build up the kind of inner-strength and self-confidence one needs if they plan on using their aesthetic positioning and network-armoury to slaughter others with. This is what 'being social' in a competitive environment is all about. And this isn't even really being social any more although it feels better than, say, taking smart-drugs while watching smart-bombs do dumb things on TV. It's much more REAL. Visceral. A kind of self-inflicted public execution where one is caught ripping out their organs and putting them on display as a kind of creative exhibitionism (my girlfriend/wife doesn't really like this). I'm not sure I'm making sense here but that's not the point.

Let me start over. The day that I was to be slaughtered was a very busy day. True, it was a Sunday, and in New York nothing really happens on Sunday, but it was a very busy Sunday for me because I had 15 deadlines to reach as a result of taking on too many freelance writing gigs which was a result of me being broke or so I perceived myself as being broke. All of my friends say that I'm not doing that bad but that's because all of my friends are artists or musicians or writers who live in New York and the first thing you learn when you move to New York is that if you're serious about being an artist or writer or musician you kind of have to tell white lies to all of your friends about how great things are going so that they'll think you're really up to something important and will want to spend more time with you which, if everything works out okay, will lead to more gigs which, when put through the multiplier effect, exponentially increases the amount of work you get, work you then can't say no to because you never ever want to be poor and have to ask someone who once offered you work and who you refused, that you'd now like to have work again. So that two weeks ago I had no gigs but then I got one gig, then three more gigs, then seven more and now I have 24 gigs. Twenty-four gigs and 15 deadlines. And meanwhile I'm going to be slaughtered and all of my friends tell me I'm doing great and my girl-friend/wife keeps telling me that it's important that they supply me with these necessary white lies, lies that insist that, first of all, the reviewer is stupid, that he doesn't know what he's talking about and that he has it out for me, and that the *Times* is the worst piece of crap ever published and that it keeps getting worse, just look at what they review.

'Yeah,' I'll say, 'they're reviewing me.'

'No,' they'll come back at me, 'they're not reviewing you – they're slaughtering you.'

THE COALMINER'S SCARF
Russell Celyn Jones

Where were you when Andy Warhol died? Let me tell you something. You wouldn't want to have been in my shoes.

For fifteen years I'd been a gardener in New York City. A gardener in Manhattan? I hear you say. *Cushy number.* So some people have no ambition, so what? I liked regularity. One year's experience fifteen times. When I did change jobs it was to a garden centre. Something more stable. Out of the rain. And it was around this time that I began to notice people staring at me, often with a wry smile. It was only when a woman stopped me in the street and said 'Mr Warhol…' that I realised. I ran home and looked in the mirror. I'd never had this trouble until now. I must have grown a late resemblance.

To look like someone famous anywhere else lends itself to comedy. In New York it's a tragedy. Fame is the product and not the art and my humiliation was index-linked to that other guy's ascendancy. Not a month passed without some ecstatic voyeur grinning at me though the foliage. A request for my autograph would rapidly degenerate into a bad-mouthing the moment I denied them: 'Do you really think Warhol would be up to his elbows in alkaline fertiliser?' The next second I'm looking into an empty space, with spent expletives ringing in my ears. I've seen more than my share of receding backs, let me tell you. The only friends I've ever made in New York are people who have never heard of Andy Warhol. And how many do you imagine that is? It is a lonely road until one of you dies. And even then it's no picnic.

We'd had an actor in the White House for several years when one evening I was walking on Lexington. I stopped outside a restaurant. It was an opening, a ribbon cutting. On the sidewalk was a television crew, their spotlights trained on to the windows. It was then I saw Warhol inside. He was dressed in black leather with a knapsack on his back. I wanted to ask him, my nemesis, did he realise the grief he was causing me?

I sidestepped the security at the door and idled up to him. But his atmosphere was so strong my legs buckled and I had to sit down. It was my face that did the talking. Warhol took my photograph with a Polaroid camera. Then without saying a word he wrote a phone number on the back of a ten dollar bill and handed it to me.

The next day I called the number. Warhol answered. 'How's it like to be me?' he asked.

'It sucks,' I replied.

'What if you were paid to be me?'

'That would suck less.'

And so began my five year tenure as Warhol's double. In New York City. Several times a week.

Everyone knows that Warhol liked a party, but even he could only attend so many. So he sent me out instead and caught up with sleep. I enhanced my Slavic, impish face with a grey rug and large-rimmed spectacles and his red silk scarf around my neck. Actually, his father's scarf – the very one he was wearing the day he died down a Pittsburgh coal mine.

I perfected an air of someone physically present, but in another world. A 'star' is only really an apparition anyway, existing in people's dreams and fantasies. When they talked to me I laughed, throwing my head back each time, like some dumb blond. Customers got their beatification. The proprietor got his celebrity. The only place it proved hard to maintain this conceit was in the john.

What I had to do, all that was required of me, was to turn up, cut a ribbon sometimes, then for the rest of the night enjoy star status. I met genuine celebrities who could only safely come out to play at such closed events as a restaurant opening, a launch of a new club. In the eighties they were opening and closing within the same week and this same crowd turned up each time, like a hired funeral cortege. Fame, beauty, power – what a mix, what bubbly! They weren't simply glamorous, these people, they were capable of miracles.

New York is a great idea, but it is not a real idea. Nobody understood that better than Warhol. He thought it was the coolest thing, having a double, and his fees reflected his enthusiasm. They were generous. One gig paid a month's rent on an apartment near the Natural History Museum, on West 84th and Columbus. Central Park was just over there.

If anyone suspected anything they didn't let on. Only in the blaze of a flash bulb with someone's bare arms around my shoulders would a few eyebrows be raised, but only for a moment, only for 1/60th of a second. In the gloaming of a restaurant or a nightclub I was the man they wanted me to be.

Fame has an interdependent relationship with light.

There was only one time, at a gallery preview, when I came close to being rumbled. A guy came over and said, 'Hey, you're not Andy. I don't know who you are, but you ain't Andy.'

I had to act fast, cause a diversion. The show was of Andy's own work. I started to wreck a Marilyn portrait, shouting, 'Yellow hair, pink face, turquoise eye shadow, red lipstick…'

Literal stuff, but you know, was I an art critic?

The security guards came bounding over and restrained me. At my side, a woman with tiny helium balloons for earrings shouted, 'It's his own work. He can destroy it if he wants. It's some kind of statement. Back off!'

Now she *was* an art critic.

I put a call through to the man that night. 'Andy,' I said, 'the game's over.' I told him exactly what had happened.

But he didn't seem fazed by what I'd done to his painting. 'It's only a silkscreen, dear.'

'Well maybe it's time for me to quit anyway.'

'Yeah?' Andy crackled down the phone. 'Where else are you going to earn a thousand bucks a gig?'

So I went back to work.

When people ask what you do for a living, it is designed to part you from information you'd probably rather not reveal. 'I'm a gardener.' 'Oh. See you around.' The beauty of being Warhol was that nobody needed to ask me that question. I rested on his laurels and drank for free. When I came off duty and the job question came up, in some bar, say, I'd confess to being a mere gardener, and had to buy my own drinks.

I became addicted to the game. Between parties I went into a sort of decline, cold turkey. I moped around the apartment all day and ordered in pizza. From the 27th floor I slid open the windows and tossed anchovies to the minnows toeing the sidewalk below, each one a Warhol vampire.

The night he went into hospital for routine gall bladder surgery I was in Studio 54, dancing with that writer with the skunk hair. Yeah, that's right, Susan Sontag. With her head resting on my neck, she said, 'I always thought the rhythms of baseball are like those of Jane Austen novels.'

I said something under-educated, something Gore told Andy about how he'd once tied Truman to a bedpost in his apartment, then went out to watch the New York Mets. My dancing partner liked that. She got off on that one.

It wasn't hard to mix, I didn't have to be profound. Andy was no philosopher. He threw yoghurt over women in the Factory then filmed himself licking it off.

At 4am I left the club and called Andy from the limo. He had his own phone by his bed in New York Hospital. But it was a nurse who picked up. As a protective gesture towards her patient, she wanted to know who I was. I said, 'I'd like to know that too.' This did the trick. I happened to be on the line to a woman who dug Andy's idiosyncrasies. But what she told me I wasn't prepared for. Andy had died during surgery. My first feeling, I'm ashamed to admit, was of relief to have got out of Studio 54 before all the world knew.

In the streets police car sirens were wailing like wolves. A big moon, for such a small place, hung in the sky. I looked down at my feet and saw my loafers were covered in silver dust.

I told Andy's chauffeur to drive me around for a while, as I sensed this was going to be my last ride. I sat numbly in the back as he cruised around the meat-packing warehouses on the Lower West Side. The transvestites crawled out of shadows and into the sodium street light as the limo inched by, the tyres hissing on the damp macadam. They were having a bad time of it too, pretending to be someone they weren't, on that cold desolate night.

Andy's funeral was strictly out of bounds for me, and that was painful. I had no one to mourn with. The period that followed was even worse. The future was looking bleak. There was no severance pay, I got no pension. I had to move apartment all the way up to the 120s. In a very short time I'd gone from being a proxy celeb to a lonely white nigger. No more fish-tank restaurants, Italian clothing stores, polite children on my block. My new apartment snuggled up to the projects and the crack houses. At night the streets became no-go areas. Stolen autos were set ablaze in the vacant lots. Traffic lights changed from red to green, green to red at silent, windswept junctions.

For months after Andy died I was still being asked, downtown, to sign his autograph.

I couldn't go back to work in a garden centre, there was no way. But at least I could become my own person, within reasonable limits. Yet after five years imitating Warhol I didn't know who I was. The solution lay in a change of scenery. Andy used to say, a shoe is a shoe but put it in an oven and it becomes something quite different. If I could transplant myself into another environment then maybe I'd become something quite different.

That environment came in the form of a jazz singer called Ilsa, three hundred pounds on the scales, an island among women. In dark shades and a beret I'd sit all alone at a table in the 92nd Street Y, and watch her exercise a feral grip on the audience. Her voice was monotonic but her big presence made up for it. At the end of her set she'd squeeze next to me at my table, the sweat beaded on her face, and claim me with a kiss.

We'd originally met at the permanent Rubens exhibit at the Tier. Warhol had liked Rubens and I used to go along whenever I felt like mourning him. This voluptuous woman was staring up at a painting of three nudes. In a long diaphanous dress she looked like she'd stepped down from the canvas.

Nearby a young couple were having a loud Manhattan argument, their backs to the paintings. 'I love Philip Johnson, don't you?' the girl said.

'Who is Philip Johnson?'

'You don't know who PJ is? Really, Michael.'

The couple moved on and the fat woman said to me, 'I bet she only found out who PJ is this morning. People like her read the *Times* book reviews but never the books.'

'Yeah,' I said. 'I know the type.'

'You're Andy Warhol, aren't you?'

'Warhol is dead.' I smiled.

'You've had a bit of surgery to the face, maybe, a demi-perm, but you can't fool me.'

'I'm not Warhol.'

'I'm impressed. I'm my own work of art also.'

'What you mean, *also*?'

'A singer can't leave her art at home any more than you can.'

Warhol told lies all the time and that was all right. Like the one about his father dying in a coal mine in Pittsburgh, when in fact he died from drinking poisoned water in West Virginia. And even when they knew they were phoney, people preferred to believe his lies. Lies enhanced the myth they projected on to him. It was a suspension of *belief*.

There was no persuading this woman with the truth either. 'Okay, I'm Warhol,' I indulged her. 'But don't let on.' I noticed Ilsa admiring the silk scarf around my neck. I said, fingering my prop, 'My daddy died in a coal mine with this scarf around his neck. It's a fetish. Protects me from too much reality.'

'Remember what you once said, that it would be glamorous to be reincarnated as a big ring on Pauline de Rothschild's finger? Well, I guess she's going to have to wait a while longer.'

She smiled and asked me if I'd like to go have a drink.

In Paddy Reilly's she ordered a Bloody Mary. I had a Scotch and Seven. She paid. 'What a stunt, to fake your own death! That's so cool.' She drank a whole glass of Bloody Mary in a single swallow, then ordered another. She needed the ballast.

I noticed that Ilsa had two voices, a New York accent and a South African one that curdled in her throat.

I asked her about her life. In 1976, she said, she'd come to NYC from Jo'burg to go to college. 'It was a protest move against Apartheid. Now like all exiles I don't know where I belong. Some days I think I'd like to go home, since the change, but I doubt whether I'd fit in there any more. I've been away too long.'

During the day (she worked at night) Ilsa and I would tour all the Irish bars in the village, getting lit up on Wild Turkey with Guinness backs. During one such session she asked, 'Do you like fat women, Andy?'

'Sure. Why not.'

'Then why haven't you tried to seduce me?'

'Courtesy?' I tried feebly.

'It's so hard to find a man who likes opulent women. They all want waifs. That's why I cruise the Rubens. You think I like Rubens? My hunch is any man who likes Rubens' women might want to ravish me.'

That afternoon we ended up on the observation deck of the World Trade Center. We were both drunk. Looking across at the quartz clusters, Ilsa said, 'You can always tell a tourist in New York because they look up as they walk. But here you can't tell them apart, who is who. It makes the Afrikaner in me insecure.'

The traffic below was backed up all the way down Broadway, pedestrians were like a million ants. I felt overwhelmed with sudden indignation. 'Christ turned the devil into a herd of swine and left them to wander through Manhattan,' I declared. 'He called them Legion, for they are many.'

Ilsa shouted back so angrily she made my ears ring. 'That's the most un-Warhol thing I've ever heard you say. Manhattan is grace personified!'

A security guard came over. 'On your bike you two. This ain't no cathedral.'

In the elevator Ilsa was close to tears. 'Here I am, with an all-American Wesleyan education and I get thrown out of the World Trade Center. Life sucks.'

The tension continued between us. I knew what the trouble was. She wanted me to say Warhol-type things. I said me-type things. They weren't the same. And I was probably too serious.

One night in late August we went to a free concert in Central Park. She brought a blanket. I brought the champagne. I had a plan I wanted to execute.

In the second act of *La Traviata* our glasses had toppled over so many times on the uneven grass that we ran dry sooner than I'd anticipated. It was time to pop the question. I asked Ilsa if she'd like to marry me.

This is what she said: 'Marriage and murder both carry mandatory life sentences. I have no intention of committing either.'

'Not even to Andy Warhol?' I said cowardly.

She sighed in a plaintive sort of way. 'I fell in love with you the instant I saw you, because you were Warhol. Yes, that's true. But now I know you, the man, I'm not sure that I do any more.'

She hauled herself up slowly and left. She moved through the crowd like a ship heading for open sea, abandoning me in my agony among 100,000 strangers.

Months passed before I plucked up the courage to go find her. I was going to suggest that we consummate this relationship. Things might then start to look up. I got a cab from Harlem to West 10th Street, where her band were playing Smalls. Ilsa was not among them. One of her sidemen stunned me with the news that Ilsa had left town with a Zulu chief who'd picked her up at the Rubens exhibit. I dropped into a chair, with every intention of throwing myself off the Brooklyn Bridge later. Then this musician waved a flag of hope. He'd recently received a letter from Ilsa. Apparently she'd not understood, back in New York, that she'd be sharing the chief with his eight wives. She objected so strongly that he gave her the dump, the big drop. Now she was stuck in the southern hemisphere in a town called Darling, a fool for love.

A man with an action knows who he is. Within twenty-four hours I was leaving for JFK with a small bag and a big mission: to go find Ilsa and tell her who I really was. I bought a seat at the airport on the next flight out to Cape Town.

That's all the geography you'll need to know.

For several kilometres the road follows the ocean. There is nothing between me and the Atlantic but a strip of hastily laid asphalt, awash with spent surf and seaweed. Spindrift falls through my open window like steam. I drive so fast I begin to aquaplane, floating free from gravity – the original sin.

Running alongside is an electric tram line. When, by and by, a tram appears I catch a glimpse of first-class passengers sedately reading newspapers. In the second-class carriages blacks hang out of open doors. If I put my arm out of the window now I could shake hands with them.

It is the last contact I have with society, as the road parts company with the ocean. I set keel for the interior. A land of no cities, the empty landscape shimmers in the heat. As I drive I can smell jasmine in the air. Or maybe it's just the idea of jasmine I smell.

Three hours later I see an old battered sign that says, Darling 11km. I can't believe my luck. What a break. This is too good to be true.

This is the longest journey I've ever made without encountering a single traffic light. And I've yet to see another car. The road becomes unsurfaced and passes through undulating scrub. Not a single tree breaks the skyline.

By late afternoon I resign myself to being lost. Losing your way in a foreign country may be the best way to discover that country, and maybe even yourself. But here it's a prelude to disaster. That's what the guy at the car hire company told me anyway. Keep the car filled with gas. The country is on the eve of reconstruction, but the old dangers still exist. You could disappear in the interior and nobody will ever find you again.

Suddenly I have to negotiate a sharp bend. In the next moment I'm stepping on the brakes. The road has terminated in a sand dune. A sand dune! Can you believe this? I turn off the engine and get out of the car. I climb the sand dune and take a look around. There is no more road, anywhere. This is as far as I can drive. I have no choice but to go back and see if there's not another way to Darling. It is now early evening and in a few hours will be dark. I don't want to be lost at night.

I turn over the engine but nothing happens. This Fiat Uno has absorbed all the punishment it can take from numerous rental drivers and has quit on me. An electrical fault.

This is a setback, but I refuse to think about it as such. I take my bag from the car and strike out on foot across the scrub to the hills stockpiled in the near distance. When you are feeling vulnerable it is the high ground you make for. I start whistling, refusing to give into fear.

Clouds of red dust rise around my knees. The wind grows colder as I gain altitude. I fall into a kind of trance, but that's okay, it actually helps. Now I don't care if I live or die.

The lower slopes are covered with wild flowers – fynbos. *Fine-bosh*. It's fynbos city up here, all the families, the daisies, ericas, vygies, irises, legumes, proteas. Proteas are the ones with sharp pink petals protecting a delicate violet stamen from the extremes of weather. A protea rarely survives a week in a Manhattan apartment. Don't like the air conditioning. Here I'm surrounded by hundreds blossoming in the wild and it fills me with heart.

But then, in the higher reaches all that remains of the fynbos are black charcoaled roots. A fire has destroyed acres of flowers. This would have killed me, had I not known that fynbos seed have 'learnt' how to survive fire. In fact they can now no longer live without a torching every ten years.

I reach the top of the hill. And there below is a sprawling township stretching for as far as the eye can see. The edges of the township are swollen with squatter camps of the refugees from war, famine, from this as well as neighbouring countries. I hear the babble of a million voices in the air.

I can see no way forward, no way back. I feel like weeping and collapse on to the ground. The wind chills my skin.

A solitary black figure arrives on the hilltop plateau a hundred yards away and frightens me. My instinct to survive releases adrenaline. I try to keep as still as a piece of nature. Half an hour passes. He grows less visible as the light fails.

It is what I see him doing that raises my hopes.

He is trying to fly a kite into the wind.

I approach the lonely figure. He is young, no more than a teenager. I may yet live through this day.

He doesn't seem to realise me at all, as though I were a ghost. He stays preoccupied with getting his kite airborne.

I get close enough to see why his kite won't fly. 'You need a tail on that,' I say, my voice sounding thin in the open air.

He spins round. In his hand he holds a knife. He shouts in a language that sounds like hooves clicking along cobblestones.

He is as frightened of me as I am of him. But fear kills the one without a weapon.

From around my neck I take Warhol's silk scarf. Very slowly I walk over and pick up his kite. As I am tying the scarf to the end he lays his weapon on the ground. It is a homemade knife fashioned from tin lashed to a length of wood.

With a tail on, the kite flies. It goes up fast. The boy runs over to where he's left a large spool and begins feeding out string. Soon the kite is high above us.

I lay on the ground with my hands behind my head as the boy continues to let out more line. Soon the kite is a tiny yellow dot with a red silk scarf drawing a curvy line behind. I feel the closest to contentment in years. I watch the kite grow even smaller until it finally disappears, lost among the developing stars.

SWALLOWS
Lisa Natalie Pearson

10

to pass (food, etc) from the mouth through the gullet or esophagus into the stomach, usually by a series of muscular actions in the throat.

He lies quite still, and she imagines once she falls in love with him, she will envy his restraint, the even keel of his words, *I'll make you coffee* in the same register as *I'll make you come*. She waits for him to open his eyes, see her – seize her, pull her so close she'd almost be afraid he'd never let go. She knows she'd never leave him, though the decay will soon set in. He might be the one.

Naked, he is stretched out flat, blanketed by a crisp white sheet. She can inspect him thoroughly; a sheen of light from the overhead fluorescents leaves none of him obscured, like a saint aglow with suffering awaiting beatification. Her finger traces a path from one temple to the other, brushing over the scruff of an eyebrow, skating over the thin sheath of an eyelid, over blonde eyelashes brittle like winter grasses. If she swiped her thumb over her tongue, she could, with a little saliva, rub away the creases on his forehead. His skin is cool, almost damp. It gives with the slightest pressure, leaving for a moment her fingerprints on his cheek, his chin. His lips are closed, tentatively, as if he wanted to whisper something to her but decided against it: he knows she will do anything for him but loves her so much he doesn't ask. It's true. Every minute she loves him even more. He will hold her captive. She will lose herself in his embrace, open her mouth, say nothing, let his foreign tongue press against her teeth. His face, a familiar intersection when she is lost. She will look at him and know where she is.

Grains of hair exploding on the surface of his skin bristle beneath her fingers. She touches his throat, traces a circle around his Adam's apple. A chunk of forbidden fruit on which he choked. She pushes down on it, but can't seem to make it disappear. Funny, she thinks, I don't know why women don't have one.

Reaching over him to take the sheet from his shoulders and tuck each fold under, she lets her cheek almost brush his hairless chest. A brown nipple erupts close to her eye. Her breath, she thinks, seems to blush his sallow skin, perhaps even bruise it. When she inhales, her throat fills with the scent of moist, rotting wood, talcum and brassy vinegar. Acid rises from her gut, she almost retches. But she pulls down the sheet, lets it slide down the precipice of his empty rib cage, over his sunken belly, following the tracks of a crudely stitched seam.

Erections on Greek vases, a bulge in blue jeans, a glimpse of a boy's balls beneath the loose folds of running shorts have always filled her with dread and excitement. Just the thought of penetration paralyses her, of something so deep inside her she wouldn't know where she ends and he begins, orgasms like fleeting epiphanies: an insatiable hunger, a constant stream of inarticulate thoughts. She has always feared sex because she knows she'll enjoy it.

Trembling, she puts her hand under the sheet that still drapes his groin and legs, gingerly weeding through the coarse tangle of hair until her fingers graze flesh. She knows this is only practice for when the real moment comes, when she looks the live one in the eyes. When she gives him everything. When he takes it.

She slips her hand beneath his cock, squeezes it, and a cold shock tears through her, every hair erect, her skin suddenly alive as if it were her first day in New York City all over again. Pores open, sweat pearls. The electricity of a slight breeze – from a taxi door slamming, a skittish pigeon aloft for three, four beats of its wings, strangers briskly walking by churning the air into tiny eddies, a newspaper slapping open, lights changing walk, don't walk, a shout from down the block – makes her shiver, regain her senses and career down the street, savouring each muscle giving and contracting, pretending to know where she's going to save her life. She is happy she was born somewhere else so she could come here and know what it must be like to lose one's virginity.

I could fall in love with you, she reaches down his legs for his toe tag, *Mr Jeremy Schwalbe* – she really could, she thinks, if he were alive, he might be hard to resist, then again, who knows how many pills he swallowed. She doesn't even know the colour of his eyes. She turns back toward his face, and when she puts her finger to his pale, dry lips – *sssshhh, don't say a thing* – they pop open.

She half-expects him suddenly to proclaim his love: she saw it in a movie once, a dead man still conscious but his body giving nothing away.

Damn, damn, damn.

She looks up, watches the doorknob to see if it turns. Already, a drop of sweat between her shoulder blades, a slight convulsion in her gut. She's not supposed to glue them, stitch or sew. Only make them up: bring a flush, a satisfied glow to their cheeks. With her palette of flesh tones and tubs of ochre, periwinkle, berry and blue, she can bring them all back to some semblance of life. She dips a tongue depressor in clear tacky glue, holds one hand in the other for precision, seals his lips shut, and prays no one will notice. When she leans in close to blow on his lips for the glue to set more quickly, his face is suddenly too close to focus on, his skin like spilt milk, and her eyes travel from the steel table to the tiled floor to the wall of drawers and then the door before she pulls back as if the last kiss is over. She does her best work when a little frightened; it holds her concentration. She has to make him up now. But just looking at him – her heart threatens to explode.

9

to perform the muscular actions characteristic of swallowing something, as in emotion.

Knock, bock and blutwurst, raw, smoked and boiled sausages, stuffed and knotted, tubs of livers and hearts line the deli case in precarious order. If the glass shattered, everything would spill out, a strange body with too many hearts and bowels, rib cage split, organs eviscerated. The case, however, remains intact, no matter how much weight she leans into it.

She is so hungry she thinks she'll vomit if she puts anything in her mouth, but she knows she has to eat or her hunger will subside into vague nausea and indecision. Her own faint stink of formaldehyde and almost sweet pressed powder clings to her nose. Sliding one hip against the steel frame, face close to the glass, she stumbles from case to case, drawing a little flight pattern in the steam of her breath, hoping she'll know what she wants when she sees it.

Hey, watch the hands, lady! shouts the man behind the counter, his apron string wrapped around his waist like a tourniquet.

Sorry, I was just looking.

You gonna look at the food until it winks at you or what? It's dead. You eat it. First you buy it, then you eat it. So whadda you want?

Order anything, she tells herself, *it doesn't matter, just order.*

Behind her the door opens, a bell clatters with a hard gust of rush hour noise, exhaust and breathless twilight. After it closes, a relative quiet settles in as if the city were just a barking dog in the distance. A small old woman in a tattered camel coat pushes past her, steps up to the counter, and, while digging in her pockets, orders a knish. The scent of sun-rotted roses and medicinal sage trails her in a flourish.

Potato today? the man asks.

The old woman nods and he wraps the knish in plain white paper, creasing each fold without thinking as if buttoning his shirt, zipping his fly. The old woman fingers a handful of pennies and nickels, sliding each one across the countertop to the cash register until her hand is empty and she has counted to sixty-five.

Eighty-nine cents, he says.

So take a little bite and the rest you give me for sixty-five.

He hesitates, then unfolds the paper and slices the knish into perfect quarters with two swift strokes of a large sharp knife. He places three pieces back on the paper and shakes his head.

Only for you. You know that, don'tcha? What the hell, take the whole thing. For me, you will warm it, yes?

She hands the knish back to him, standing almost on her toes, reaching her arm up over the deli case so that her wrist is bared from under the cuff of her coat. White skin laced with blue veins, ringed with a smudge, a scar, or the shadow of a tattoo, a bracelet of numbers, she must be a survivor.

Her face shows it, wrinkles like a well-marked book as if fright and joy were on the same page. Hiking herself up on a stool and settling on the cushion, she seems impatient with her own slow care, feet swinging slightly in thick brown shoes. Her bones are tiny, stiff, almost collapsible. The hot knish in front of her steams like breath in the cold, and she rubs her palms together over it before pinching a corner of the shiny first layer of dough. She peels it back and tears it off. Her mouth is full. Though she chews and chews, it is still too much to swallow, but she rolls the next sticky layer between her finger and thumb and licks it off. She strips the first quarter of the knish bare, layer by layer, until a small heap of potato is left to mash with the back of her fork.

To what lengths would she have gone for such a simple pleasure as a knish?

Maybe at night when it was darkest, she slipped out from her tiny hiding place beneath the stairs in a condemned apartment block. They'd been there with dogs and lights and batons, but never found her, perhaps didn't know that she was even there to look for. Outside, in the cement courtyard, four high walls of broken windows towered over heaps of trash – broken bicycles and china cups, rusted motors and shredded clothes. Sometimes she found something useful, a safety pin, a spoon, a corner of clean cloth, as if it were safe enough for the moment to look around a bit. After pulling herself between the loose wood slats that barricaded the door, she got herself with absolute precision to the grocer's: sliding her back against the cold stone wall until the first corner, rushing beneath the shadow of the old station and glancing behind her every few steps, then edging the rim of yellow light from an unavoidable streetlamp, trembling as if balancing high on her toes, afraid to fall, until she arrived exhausted two blocks away. She scratched her fingers lightly across the grain of wood, tapped on the window as if to attract the attention of an animal caged in glass. The door opened silently; he had oiled the hinges.

Inside, she wanted to linger in the warmth and light, but he hurried her down to the cellar, back into the dark. She stood still as he unbuttoned her coat, then she raised her arms in obeisance as he ripped off her layers of sweaters. When he leaned his head over her shoulder to unclasp her skirt, the stench of rancid butter and stale tobacco – the smell she always left with, that lingered in her small hutch, that she couldn't ever wash off – choked her. She pushed him away, let her skirt fall, and finished undressing herself. The coat she lay on the floor, its arms outstretched like wings; the sweaters she picked up and draped carefully over the wooden steps. Then she pulled him on top of her as if sweating with fever but knowing she still needed warmth. Between heaps of coal bricks, he thrusted, the heaving and swaying and stink like the ride on a crowded boxcar down miles of track to nowhere. There, an expanse of white with no edges, the snow, the sky, broken only by the sharp grid of thick wood poles and barbed wire, tatters of cloth, strands of hair caught on the twisted iron. She dreamed that once she arrived, she could never leave this place with no sun to show her east or west. Even if they let her go, she wouldn't know where to turn.

The old woman looks up as she wipes her mouth and sees her staring.

I never know why no one in this country wishes a good appetite. There's no American words for it, no? What are you going to eat, skinny girl? I got a little extra.

No, no thank you. I'm going to order something. I haven't decided yet.

What's to decide? Order what you like. For me, a knish is enough. Ach, I don't need so much no more. You have hunger, you eat. So simple it is.

This woman has known a fear she'll never know, a fear she's only seen feigned on a movie star's face. She wants to ask her when she first fell in love, but instead goes to the counter and orders a sandwich and a soda.

So, you don't want no mayo, mustard, tomato, no lettuce, no onion, no cheese. Lemme get this right. Meat and bread, that's it, am I right? Don't think you get no discount for just meat and bread.

The bell on the door clatters, and the old woman disappears outside. The bright lights inside the front window reflect the empty inside of the store. She can't see out. If someone pressed his face to the glass to look in, only then could she see him.

8
to put up with; to bear humbly; to tolerate.

A single token in her pocket, money buried in a zippered pouch, her bag strapped across her chest. She touches each part of her body to check that everything's in place the way some people cross themselves at the sight of sin or blood. Once a man seized the end of her scarf and almost choked her; now she takes pains not to wrap it around her throat. A friend told her she need only act a little crazy and she would get left alone. But she could never master the gibberish and facial tics: it required too much effort to seem out of control. She knows no matter what she does there's always an element of danger. At least her other safeguarding measures let her keep her fear in check.

Hearing the rush of the train, she takes two steps at a time down the subway stairs, fighting against the warm oil-stink wind that blows out from the tunnel. By the time she reaches the turnstile, the train is pulling away, like a movie grinding off the projector reel, a blur of bodies trapped in squares of light, blue sparks flashing from the tracks. She saw it once in a movie house, a scene between some husband and wife, the space between them churned as if in an earthquake: arms shaking violently, words stuttered, reaching for each other but never quite touching. The film finally stopped, both caught dead still, a white burn erasing them until the screen charred black. The train disappears into the tunnel and she surveys both ends of the platform. Empty, but for a small bird skittering from crumb to crumb.

The stench of urine and rotting food wafts on still air with an endearing foulness, tolerable like the odours of one's own body. She stands against the cold, tiled wall in the token booth's line of sight and waits. Something always happens. A drunk squats in a corner to take a shit. Some girl with bare feet and stringy hair dances in spirals too close to the tracks. Kids with clothes five sizes too big shove and shout at each other, strut by, always a little too close. A crazy lady with bows of yellow yarn tied in her hair, wearing ten layers of clothes, swears at god. The echoes in the tunnel amplify the shouts, the piercing laughter, the click of heels, fits of coughing, rustling of newspapers, a clatter of coins. Everything a little larger, louder than life. In the crowds, she searches for the men to avoid, waiting until she hears the train and positions herself several cars away. Once on the train, there is silence amidst a mass of bodies, jostling, rubbing, swaying, heaving against each other, one body beginning where another ends, some other man always with his leg pressed against her crotch or his hand on her ass, and she cannot move or get away. She would like to have the courage to grab his arm, raise it high and announce to the crowd: whose hand is this? it's not mine. But she is overcome with fear of what he might do then. She knows she should take the bus, but it lulls her to sleep and she forgets her stop.

Tonight just a few people trickle in, spacing themselves at regular intervals next to columns and on benches, faces buried in books and newspapers or staring into nothing on the platform across the tracks. The rumble of the train stirs a breeze. She watches the little bird hop high, spread its wings and take flight.

Gotta light? a man asks, suddenly close, holding his cigarette like a pencil.

First she fumbles in her pocket, then holds out the lighter to him, mesmerised by the bird darting and swerving as it nears walls, pillars or steel bar gates. When he doesn't take it, she looks up and sees him jutting his face toward her, cigarette in mouth, waiting for her to light it. The train gets louder, closer and the bird's chirps are pitched high and sharp. As the flame wavers, he holds his hands around hers and pulls himself toward her, head bowed, the tip of his cigarette hissing orange. His stubbly chin lightly scratches her knuckles. He doesn't let go, his eyes raised toward hers as if locking her in his stare. The brakes squeal and the bird flies faster and faster, wings scraping every solid edge. She pulls away and runs down the platform. When the train finally stops, the bird is still in the air, oblivious to all the exits out.

The car is almost empty. She takes a seat across from someone buried in a newspaper, catches her breath and strains to read. On the front page, treaty negotiations, an airplane crash, scandals. A smaller article on the back page announces the death of a famous writer. Died today at the hospital. Reportedly, fell out the window while trying to feed the birds. She wonders if the birds trapped in subway tunnels ever get enough to eat.

7

to receive or accept, as in opinions or beliefs, without examination or scruple; to believe gullibly; to drink in.

She reads the newspaper the way some people undress in front of the mirror: scrutinising every column inch for something about which to get hysterical. Everything in the news makes her quiver with distress, all the deceit, the greed, the blood, the bullet wounds, the accidents, the weather, almost but not quite enough to keep her satisfied. She has sometimes imagined an airplane, diving hard and out of control toward her apartment. Instead of bursting through the window and sending the building up in flames, the plane thumps the glass in midflight and drops stunned to the sidewalk, metal belly exposed, landing gear erect. There are sirens, the persistent flash of red and blue lights shrouded in black smoke, pockets of flames. On the street half-naked bodies strewn across the sidewalk, slick with blood, burns and oil, clothing ripped apart as if everyone in the plane was simultaneously overcome with brutal desire. On closer inspection, the bodies themselves mixed up, someone else's leg with another's arm. How do they identify them, she has always wondered. Front page news, headlines declaring tragedy. Names listed in the obituaries, suddenly all these people with remarkable lives only once they're lost. They don't write about the missing parts, what they couldn't put back together, but she keeps reading anyway.

On Sundays, her tiny living room is wall to wall words, each page opened wide, flattened on the floor with the palm of her hand. She kneels, then crawls across the paper to each story, running her index finger down the length of an article, tracing the musculature from story to story into the crevices of news briefs and around the broad backside of each section. Her fingers are dirty with newsprint, knees and palms stained with ink. She scratches the bridge of her nose, her brow, leaving a tiny illegible message as if written in ash. When she turns the page, the paper moves like a single beat of wings – *institutions are too fragile to allow – explosion a spillover of violence – without being thrown down at gunpoint, the first in a region plagued by civil wars – champagne flows and kisses mark the start – expect all of them to be freed by the end of the day – an object, a bargaining chip – posed a challenge of centrifugal proportions – more mistakenly freed – the very ideas stirred the fury and fear – they are particularly vulnerable to being whipsawed – a handful pleaded – and waded in warm water to extract its sugar –* and her eyes never leave the print as if she were navigating in unknown territory, as if she were looking for a home that she would know only when she's found it. When she's done, she squats in the middle of the room, surveying the world laid out before her. Like her body, the world supposedly has all its parts in place regardless of how foreign they might seem.

The only thing she knows how to do is fold up the paper neatly and tightly with that precise talent for returning maps to glove compartments – as if it had never been opened, never been read, as if she needn't know where she was going or could get there completely on instinct. I'm at the centre of the world, she always thinks, the safest place to be, in the eye of a storm buried on page twenty-two. It's the comfort of constant disaster, of expecting it, of recognising it again and again, of being inside it. A friend said once, you know you don't have to read the paper, what's so important about all these catastrophes so far away? But this is why I moved to New York City in the first place, it's always around the corner, you can't be complacent, how would you know what street to take home, she replied. Falling in love or being assaulted, what's the difference? Everyone's always waiting for both to happen eventually: one day when you turn the corner, one or the other will be waiting for you.

6
to take back (words said); to retract; to withdraw.

Girl, you gonna let her paint your face after she's been putting make-up on dead people all day?

The dressing room is cramped, lit with big round bulbs, loud with the chirping of nine or ten mostly half-naked women. Sequined skirts and bras, metallic gold g-strings, see-through shirts made of mesh armour, shiny pumps and scattered plumage hang from mirrors and racks. All of it easily untied, unclasped, unravelled, none of it holds anything in. She could never get away wearing things like these.

Most nights they just ignore her as she moves from face to face, and she buttons her lips, says nothing unless forced. With her toolbox of cosmetics next to her, she sits on the edge of the vanity – in front of her the girl whose face she's making up, behind her the mirror – as if ready to defend herself. With the palm of her hand, she pushes the girl's head back so she can line her eyes – *close them*, she says. The girl obeys like a child pleased with the fuss over her, smiling slightly in anticipation of inevitable compliments. She could make this girl into anything: when she looks in the mirror all made up, she'll believe she's seeing what she was meant to be.

After lining the crescent of the girl's eyelid with a brown kohl pencil, she instructs her again: *open your eyes, look up*. The light catches in the white blonde fuzz on the girl's cheeks, the wide open pores, the red capillaries broken in tiny nets on either side of her nose. If left to their own devices, most of the girls wear too much purple, blue, black as if bruised, attempting to compensate for the bad lighting on stage.

The girl says, hey, she knows what she's doing, I look good out there. I've got on – she reaches for the lipstick case – 'crimson cantata' and what're you wearing? Death kit purple?

She's a feminist, she's gonna make you look ugh-lee.

Feminism is just a dirty word for sexually liberated, another says. I'm a feminist, I'm not ashamed.

Whatcha doin' working here, bitch?

So miz feminist, I should wear whatever lipstick I want. Fuck it if they don't find me attractive, but then where's the fun? If they don't look at you, there's no action.

Show 'em your tits and they don't care what colour lipstick you wear.

I said feminist, not idealist.

We must all be feminists because we are Sex-u-ally Lib-er-at-ed.

They laugh and the girl in front of her shakes hard, her cheeks suddenly flushed pink, until tears run from the corners of her eyes, mascara and eye-liner like smudges of dirty brown coal.

Don't move.

The room quiets. She is caught with her mouth open, thumb wet with saliva, about to wipe off the girl's eyes and start all over.

Just how liberated are you, missy?

She stutters, feeling the bile rise from her gut, the acid taste of fear on her tongue that she swallows back down and it burns. They must know she's a virgin. They'll make her confess. She wants to close her legs, press her knees together, she can feel the sticky wet on her panties, a pulsing where the seams of her pants cross her cunt. Suddenly, all her muscles ache, her calves, her thighs, the whole curve of her back, her neck, even her wrists. She wants to stretch, but can't. She envies them all the ways their bodies move – a holding pattern of hips circling, diving and rising. Her skin feels tight like a grip she can't cut loose. She hears herself straining for air, panting.

I'm liberated. I love sex. I know there's almost nothing I wouldn't do.

That's not necessarily liberated, honey. You gotta know your limits.

With this man – Jeremy – I'm in love with him – he makes me so happy I forget myself.

Does he eat you out? I mean really put some effort into it.

I'm remembering all over when I come. Forget him.

Like does he put his tongue inside you or just lick a little around the edges, duty-like?

Yes. Always…

Yeah, I bet he makes you coffee every morning, too.

… Every time. Of course.

You lie, girl. You make him coffee, you let him come too quick. You're his little love slave.

I'm not. I don't give in. When you want so much you can't, right? I know what happens when you surrender.

Girl, the war is over. Give and take, a little diplomacy. They like to think they're heroes.

Yeah, like Mr What's-his-face in the movies. Terminator Man. Gotta love him.

5

to refrain from expressing; to hold back; to suppress.

So do you swallow?

God, they love it if you swallow. And you have to act like you like it.

I actually like to swallow. Someone told me it's good for you, your teeth. A lot of vitamins.

They think it's really intimate. You're taking him in, you know.

Aren't we always taking them in?

But it's power. You take some guy's dick in your mouth, you make him come, and he's not fucking you, you're doin' him and he's absolutely helpless. He may think he's in control. Who's ever in control when they're about to come?

I heard cum has a lot of calories.

Personally, I can't give a blow job without gagging.

You'll see it in his face, I'm telling you, you'll see a guy who fears you, fears what you can do to him, but not enough to say no. You know why?

You know what you do? You have to breathe in deeply through your nose on the upstroke, exhale when you're going down.

Because there's some kinda adrenaline rush. Pleasure's gotta have a fucking element of danger in it. Sex is about feeling alive.

I know how to do that – it's like breathing for yoga.

Jesus, who have you been sleeping with?

You know, you have to swallow. It's either that or get cum in your hair. I hate cum in my hair.

A lot of men who think they're in love with me.

So – they turn to her – do you or don't *you* swallow?

4

to take in, absorb, engulf, overwhelm; usually with up, as in swallowed up by the night.

Beneath the sidewalk at regular intervals, the subway rumbles the concrete with little tremors like a pronounced hunger. The sudden motion a reminder of the emptiness underneath. A burst of air through the grating, like breath between clenched teeth. The sun is rising somewhere unseen to her right. A glint of turbid yellow reflects like signals off shop windows and the rearview mirrors of parked cars. Catching the glass shavings and diamond dust poured into the sidewalk, the light crackles, always two steps ahead leading her forward. It splits and scatters when the air is disturbed by a single cab, a bicyclist, a jogger.

From above, one familiar city block seems an entire country – parked cars like lit pin dots to mark train stations and towns, the flat square rooftops, grey and brown like dead and turned fields, waterways between small hills a stream of piss snaking to the street, and telephone cables, electric wires and antennae drawn in an almost perfect grid. No matter how much movement will wake it up, it all seems to stay the same, the dream of a migratory bird or an impatient cartographer.

She takes the long route home in the very early morning so as maybe to catch a glimpse of the horizon. It's more dangerous – drunks, drug dealers, foul-mouthed garbage collectors, a pervert or a lunatic or two around every corner. Every day she survives it, she is all the more ecstatic when she arrives home. But there haven't been the encounters this morning she expected. Instead of feeling safer, she notices a shiver of sweat behind her knees, in the crook of her elbows. It's as if there was a war, apparent only from the occasional alarms and the seismic quivers of tanks in the distance. You never know if a bomb will fall or if you're already inside dead centre of surrender.

Across the street she thinks she sees the old woman from the delicatessen bending over the sidewalk, reaching out, her hand open to grasp something lost. A brisk current of air from the subway grating lifts her long skirt, revealing frail, thin legs, almost unable to bear any weight. She forgets what she was looking for, lets her skirt billow and float, while stretching her arms outward, palms open as if she is expecting either the wind to lift her up high or someone to embrace her. As if balancing on a high wire, she teeters, almost falling with the force of the wind until the train is past and her skirt settles around her ankles. She licks her fingers, preens, pressing a few loose silver strands of hair back in place, the only evidence of her flight.

3

as much as is swallowed at one time.

She cuts through the park for a few blocks of respite: there is so much activity even at this hour no one will pay her any mind. And if anything happens, there will be plenty of witnesses: a few old men reading the paper and sipping coffee from paper cups, ratty kids waking up on benches hugging skateboards like teddy bears, tipsy girls coming home from nightclubs smoking a last cigarette, a jogger or two. Sometimes she sees a small troupe of circus artists rehearsing. The clowns have no make-up, the girls aren't dressed in tights or sequins. They look like everyone else except for the fire-eating and gymnastics, unicycling and juggling, and other things like putting needles through their cheeks or bearing weights on their chests. She takes a seat on the concrete steps that circle the stage. Even as she watches the mistakes, she is mesmerised by the ease of their illusions. She feels giddy like a child stirred by the possibility of danger but believing unabashedly in the magic of invincibility: lion jaws, free falls, flames and sharp objects pose no real threat. The grease pencil make-up on a clown's face so thick he is always happy, though the grown-ups know he's probably drunk, like they know the ferocity of a caged tiger whipped to a frenzy is tempered with drugs. For all the explanations, the sword swallower still amazes her most, how he takes in the entire length of a thick sharp sword all the way down without slicing everything inside or letting it all spill out, how he knows it's gone far enough or if he knows only when it's already too much.

2

the act of swallowing.

Once inside the elevator almost home, she presses the 'close doors' button, not letting up until the view to the street narrows. When she sees a man running toward her, leaping for the slight gap, she slaps the knob again, holds her hand there, but he reaches in just in time to shove back the doors and slip between them. Suddenly the space is tight, air scarce. He is breathing hard and sinks into the opposite corner, resting his hands on bent knees. He looks up at the panel of buttons, punches 'ten' although it's already lit. The elevator begins to rattle like a cage hoisted on a string, and the numbers on the silver plate light up.

One slipping in through the vertical blinds and the crisscross of grates, the sunlight in her apartment will fall in a perfect grid on the hardwood floor. She will hover near the door, before latching the bolt which fits perfectly between her forefinger and thumb, as if her hand had evolved specifically to turn a lock. *Two* she could fall in bed with this man – whose breath is consistent and deep – as easily as one might forget one swallows or blinks, lose herself, let go. She might even fall in love with him, the ripe papaya stink wet on his sweatshirt, the way he wears his keyring like a jewel on his finger, his broken shoelaces mended with knots. *Three* through the peephole in her door the outside world always seems suddenly small, distant, contained. Inside, she walks to the middle of the room, the sun to her back, and she spreads out her arms, fingers almost reaching the walls. Her shadow darkens the floor like an eclipse hiding the sun from the city. *Four* he could do anything to her, she doesn't know who he is. He could strangle her with bare, sweaty hands, she has only her keys to jab at him as she struggles for breath, as her mouth fills with saliva unable to swallow. She waits for him to get too close, so she can knee him in the balls, hit the alarm button, pray someone will come. *Five* even without love, she could enjoy sex, she knows she would. That need.

Someone so close, inside you, you're wrapped around him like an extra layer of his skin or as if he were an extra piece of your body. *Six* she could be rescued. A hero in her own right for her resistance. And if he overwhelms her, she will have struggled. It would make a story that someone else could see herself in, maybe save her from the same fate somehow, take charge of her life. *Seven* she will ache with happiness. Home safe, intact, free, finally. Four solid walls, the constancy of a compass no matter at what angle she catches her reflection. *Eight* her love and devotion to him measured in proportion to the pleasure he brings her, the bombardment of her senses, every touch a liberation. *Nine* where will she be when she has nothing left to fear, left blind, deaf and dumb. *Ten* she will go to sit by the window, every inch of skin warmed by the sun falling on her face as if to map it, pleased she has faced the city again so that she could seek refuge from it.

1

any small swift-flying bird of the family Hirundinidae... known for its regular migrations.

The elevator doors open. His lips are slightly parted as if on the verge of words. She stiffens, waiting to see what he will do. Her eyes fix on him as if she were staring at a movie screen, waiting for the climax. Everything rises in her gut, a heat spreading inside her chest, up her throat, she bites her lip, her entire body poised on the cusp of swallowing. But he says nothing, wipes his hands on his sweatpants and smiles slightly without meeting her gaze. It suddenly occurs to her his thoughts have been elsewhere, he hasn't really seen her at all until now, as he decides whether it is proper to let her off the elevator first.

After you, she says.

He nods. She sees he has brown eyes, he is that close. With one easy step out of the elevator he is gone. With him he takes her fear like a thread from her clothes caught and unravelling with one long steady pull.

SUCK ON THIS

Charles Higson

Three men and a woman stood in the drizzle. A director, a producer, a designer and a PA. The smallest of the men, the director, was in the process of quoting from a Stevie Wonder song. His Oxford-educated voice making a mockery of the original American.

'There it is, New York, just like I always imagined it, skyscrapers and everything.'

The tallest of the three, the producer, laughed automatically, and the small man turned on him.

'You think it's funny, do you, Jerome? You think it's a joke.'

'No... Well, I thought you were making a joke. I didn't think the situation, as such, was necessarily a joke.'

'You think I'm a joke?'

'I think you made a joke.'

'I didn't make a joke.'

'I'm sorry, but it sounded like a joke.'

'It did sound like a joke,' said the third man, the designer. A dapper chap in his fifties, with a beard.

'Howard,' said the director. 'Maybe you can help me.'

'I'll try,' said Howard with a helpful smile.

'Yes, good. Maybe you can tell me what this is?'

'I'm sorry?'

'*This...*' said the director, gesturing down the street with a flailing arm. 'What is *this*? What is this SUPPOSED TO FUCKING BE?'

'New York.'

'New York? New York?' The director seized up and fell silent.

Bill Gavin was not a happy man. He wasn't ever *really* happy at the best of times – when things were going well and his girlfriend was being nice to him and there were large sums of money in his various accounts and the Jeep Cherokee was running properly and not blowing up every time he TURNED ON THE FUCKING AIR CONDITIONING, FOR FUCK'S SAKE. No, even when he was happy, he wasn't happy. And now, huddled here in the rain beneath the PA's umbrella, he wasn't happy on any level. There wasn't a single happy thought in his head and his insides felt poisoned. He was rigid with anger, vibrating slightly. He had lost the power of speech and become this senseless, spluttering, shaking, thing.

'I think it looks quite good,' said Jerome.

This statement caused Bill to get his voice back. 'Fuck off,' he said and turned to Howard. 'Howard,' he said quietly. 'I like you, Howard. You are a good designer. I've not had any problems with you before. BUT THIS IS NOT FUCKING NEW YORK! This is BOLTON.'

'Well,' said Howard calmly. 'With all due respect, Bill. Yes, it is Bolton. You knew it was going to be Bolton.'

'But I thought it was at least going to look like New York. Now, maybe that was foolish of me, do you think that was foolish of me, Howard?'

'It's the BBC,' said Jerome. 'And for the money we've got, I think Howard's done a pretty good job.'

'Oh you do, do you?' said Bill. 'You think this is a pretty good job. Look at it. How am I supposed to film the pivotal scene of the whole fucking film here today on this... THIS! This which is not New York. What have we got here? Let's study it, shall we? A couple of old brick warehouses, a shop which I can only describe as a greengrocer's, a clapped out yellow cab, two Fords with right-hand drive, six extras off *Emmerdale Farm*, a fruit stall, a road sign and a billboard advertising Coca fucking Cola...'

'It's not bad,' said Jerome. 'I've been on streets in New York that look like this...'

'Exactly,' said Howard. 'You know, there *are* ordinary streets in New York, not everywhere is...'

But Bill cut him off before he could go any further. 'Have you read the script, Howard? Have you? Have you read the fucking script?'

'Yes, of course.'

'Well, it doesn't call for an ordinary street, does it? It calls for NEW YORK! In your face, up your arse, all over you... NEW YORK!' Bill turned to Jo, the PA. 'Read me the script,' he said.

Jo had to hand the umbrella to Bill so that she could fish the script out of her waterproof bag. Then she nervously flicked through to the relevant page. 'Scene seventy-two. Ext, New York Street, night...' Reading quickly, her voice flat, neutral and business-like, pretending that nothing was wrong, that this was somebody else's problem, that she was just there to do what she did... 'Neon signs flash everywhere. Steam rises from vents in the road. The street is jammed with traffic. A subway car thunders overhead on a raised section of track. The sidewalk is jammed with crazies. A porno cinema marquee announces XXX hard-core. A Jewish deli is doing a roaring trade. Two men push a railing of clothes from a van into a clothing sweat-shop. An Italian storekeeper is throwing a drunk out of his brightly lit store. Another drunk is on the street preaching. A noisy black street gang dance around a huge beat-box, insulting passers-by. Two cops are frisking a young hood up against a wall. Two prostitutes in high heels and mini-dresses tout for work. Three old bums sit on the floor against a wall, fighting and arguing over their hooch. A mugger snatches a woman's purse and runs off.

'Martin and Naomi get out of a cab and push their way through the crowd on the sidewalk… Martin: "I didn't know, Naomi. How could I have known? You never once…"'

Bill snatched the script out of her hand. 'Thank you,' he snapped, then thrust the script at Jerome, slapping it against his chest. 'That,' he said, 'is New York… This…' he waved the script at the street, 'is Bolton.' Several pages flew out and landed on the wet ground. Jo picked them up and tried to dry them.

'You knew we didn't have the budget to film in New York, Bill,' said Jerome. 'We agreed that we couldn't afford a night shoot… And you saw the location…'

'We agreed on a lot of things,' said Bill. 'Or at least I accepted. No, I didn't accept… I allowed, under protest, that we wouldn't actually get to film New York in New York.'

'We agreed Bolton,' said Howard.

'I did not agree Bolton. I *allowed* Bolton. On the understanding, on the assurance, that you assured me that you could make it, at least partly, resemble what's written in the sodding script. I wanted the Big Apple, and you've given me the Big… Meat Pie.' Bill felt a hot flush. He realised he was making a fool of himself. He was not happy with 'the Big Meat Pie'. It was the first thing that had come into his mind and he really would have liked something stronger… The Big Chip Butty? The Big Fish Supper? No. The Big Cup of Tea? No…

'I have photos,' said Howard. 'As I said, there are a lot of streets in New York that look like this.'

'I don't want that, Howard. Listen to me, listen to what I'm saying here. I want what's in the script, I want the New York that when you get there for the first time, you say "I can't believe it! It looks just like it does in the movies…" Where's the steam? Where's the porno cinema? Where's the deli?'

'I can do you steam,' said Howard. 'The viz effects guys are standing by with smoke pellets…'

'Smoke pellets won't make this crap look like fucking New York. Look at it, look at this grey sky, this grey street…'

'With respect, Bill, there's nothing I can do about the weather…'

'We'll put a caption on the screen saying New York,' said Jerome. 'I mean, it's not a long sequence in the film.'

Peter Davies, the actor playing Martin, strolled over, sipping tea from a polystyrene cup. He looked at the set and sniffed. 'This doesn't look much like New York.'

'FUCK OFF!'

Peter looked shocked, then pissed off, then he turned and walked back the way he'd come, chucking his cup into the road. Jerome chased after him calling his name.

'What do you want me to do, Bill?' said Howard.

'I want you to kill yourself, Howard,' said Bill.

Sitting on the coach with the other extras, Vince Hayman watched what was going on outside. He could tell who the director was, he was the small man in the waxed jacket and flat cap. He'd just watched him give a note to Peter Davies, the lead actor. Vince felt of stab of jealousy mixed with excitement. One day he'd be a lead actor like Davies and he'd be given notes. He'd have his own caravan to sit in, instead of being stuck on this crappy bus with the sheep. They were driving him crazy with their whingeing and their gossip and their low expectations. They were so boring. They none of them wanted to be a proper actor like him. He knew what he had to do. He always did something, whatever scene he was in, he did something that would make the director notice him. Sooner or later it would pay off. Sooner or later a director would say, 'You, there, I like you, I want to give you more to do…' Today he was playing 'second gang member', and the wardrobe people had fitted him out in trainers, jeans and a baseball jacket and cap. Make-up had even given him some stubble. Not that he needed it. He had already become the part. He'd spent all weekend living it, really thinking himself into the mind of a vicious New York gang member. 'Method acting', they called it. He knew the important thing was to make it real. He'd even brought his own gun. A small Beretta. It was a shame it wasn't a .45, like they used in *Pulp*

Fiction, but it was the best he could get. A guy down the pub had sold it to him. He'd practised with it in front of the mirror.

'Hey, motherfucker, suck on this.'

He knew that he wouldn't get to use the gun, but just having it here, tucked into his waistband, made him feel good, made him feel right. He *was* second gang member. Yeah, he'd show 'em. He was 4 real.

Bill sat in the driver's seat of his Jeep and listened to the rain tap-tapping on his roof. Jerome knocked on the passenger door, opened it and climbed aboard.

'We've got to shoot something, Bill,' he said. 'I've spoken to John, and he doesn't see any real problems with filming in this rain, it's not heavy enough to...'

'Shoot what, exactly, Jerome? Martin and Naomi go to Bolton?'

'Look, Bill, I've tried to be patient. We all knew the problems. So just stop sulking and think how we can get round it...'

'I've had it with this fucking film. I've had it with this fucking pissy country. Why did I ever agree? You cannot shoot in England and make it look like America.'

'Kubrick does it,' said Jerome.

'Have you seen *Full Metal Jacket*, Howard? They might as well have shot it in Trafalgar Square for all it looks like America... And as for Vietnam...'

'The sets were amazing.'

'But it still looks like England. England looks like England, there's no getting away from it.'

'Maybe we could make the scene an interior. Use some stock footage for the exterior and...'

'The whole point of the fucking scene, Jerome, the whole point of the film... is that after the cosy claustrophobia of England, Martin is suddenly thrown into this incredible, vibrant, dangerous place... The whole screen explodes, his relationship with Naomi explodes. NEW YORK. It's big, it's brutal, it's alive, it's... It's NOT FUCKING BOLTON.'

'Actually,' said Jerome, 'since this zero tolerance initiative thing, the streets are much cleaner in New York, there's much less crime there, much less violence...'

'Oh, fuck off...'

'Look, this is a film for the BBC, it's not for Steven Spielberg, or Columbia, or something. It's a little romantic comedy, and it...'

'And it's going to be shit, and I'm never going to work again.'

'I know it's tough, Bill. I know what you really want to be doing is working in America making proper films. Right there on the streets of New York. But there'll be other problems, there are always problems, they'll just be different. Nothing's ever right, we just have to try to make the best of what we've got. You'll never be happy on set, and that's why you're so bloody good, because you won't give up. So don't give up on me now.'

'Is this a pep talk, Jerome?'

'How long have we been working together now, Bill?'

'Too bloody long.'

'Bill…'

'I don't want a fucking pep talk, Jerome. I'm fed up with hearing your whining encouragements every day on every shoot we've ever done. I just for once want to be allowed to make something good and not this shit.'

'It's not shit and you know it.'

'I know, I know, I know.'

'To tell you the truth, Bill, the only shit thing in this film is that New York stuff. Tony's a good writer, but he's never been there, it's clichéd, it's like a parody…'

'New York *is* a parody. That's what I wanted to shoot…'

Jerome shifted in his seat and shot a sly glance at Bill. 'This isn't what I came to talk to you about, actually,' he said. 'I didn't come to give you a pep talk. Perish the thought. I've had some news. Sally just phoned from Berlin. I'm sorry you couldn't be out there, but you're flying out at the weekend and…'

'We won?'

'We won.'

Bill grabbed Jerome and kissed him. Jerome grinned.

'Sally can't move for Yanks pestering her. Everyone wants you, Bill. You're the hottest thing on two legs at the moment. But… if you walk off this shoot, well, if word were to get around, then…'

'Are you blackmailing me?'

'Are you blackmailing me, Bill?'

'All right, so we're both a couple of bastards.'

'You don't have to make it the clichéd New York, you could make it the Bill Gavin New York…'

'Get me a fire engine,' said Bill.

'What?'

'I want rain.'

'You've got rain.'

'I want proper rain, not English rain, I want a biblical deluge. So you can't see anything, just this apocalyptic rain, and a few lost, drowned souls bobbing about. I'll get steam and rain and chaos and confusion…'

'Thanks, Bill.'

'Don't mention it… Just get me a fire engine.'

Vince was soaked, but he could handle it. They'd done this scene ten times now and he was freezing. The two old guys playing tramps had already bottled it and been sent home and it was only a matter of time before the rest of the extras mutinied. Between takes they stood in huddles and grumbled and plotted. But not him. He was an actor.

'Okay, okay,' said the director. 'Hold it. Cut the rain.'

The hoses were turned off and Vince watched the director come towards him.

He was going to talk to him. He was going to give him some notes, maybe ask him to get nearer the camera. He'd been trying to get noticed, but he was too far at the back, he had to keep going up on tiptoe and creeping forward during the take, looking for the camera to make sure that he didn't get blocked.

The director put a hand on his shoulder. 'Okay, mate, listen. Your job in this scene is to hide this post box for me, okay? Do you think you can remember that? I don't want you to move. And I need you to keep facing away from us, all right? So I don't see your face. No offence, but you look like a Yorkshire farmer.'

The director let go of him and strode off back towards the camera and his umbrella. 'Right,' he called out. 'Let's go for another one.'

The first assistant took over. 'Cue the rain, cue the first driver, cue the taxi, turn over…'

Vince stood there, the rain dripping down his neck, and he fingered the handle of his gun. Motherfucker. Motherfucker. He was no Yorkshire farmer… He had to show the director what he could do. He heard the taxi stop, the actors get out behind him.

Right. Go for it. He turned and pushed his way through the other extras.

'Hey, motherfucker,' he said, grabbing Davies by the collar of his jacket, and he went for his gun, but it got caught up and he couldn't get it out.

Davies looked startled, the actress playing Naomi was laughing. The director was yelling. The rain stopped.

Jerome sat on the bus which they were using as a mobile production office, trying to get warm. They'd got there in the end, and they'd got some good stuff. It had looked touch and go at one point, Bill was pushing everyone too hard, but then that bonkers extra had gone haywire and it had broken the tension. If it hadn't been for that nutcase Bill might have had a riot on his hands, but as it was everyone had enjoyed themselves after that. It had reminded Jerome of just why he'd stuck with Bill, why, when it came to it, he was a bloody good director. If anyone could have made this street look and feel like New York on a non-existent budget, it was Bill. All he had to do now was tell him that they hadn't won in Berlin, that they'd only got a special commendation from the critics. But he was still hot stuff and he would go on to direct in America, and Jerome would stay here and scrape the money together for small-scale, under-funded, well-respected little films, and Peter Davies would become a star, and he too would go over the pond...

He looked out of the window and saw Bill go past, and he knew that he'd never work with him again. Bill looked happy for a change and Jerome almost felt sad. Except that the man was a pig.

Vince stood in the alley where the cars were parked, checking and re-checking his gun, making sure that this time nothing would go wrong. This time he'd prove to that motherfucker of a director that he was no fucking Yorkshire farmer. He'd make the little bastard sorry he'd called him a fuckwit and thrown him off the set. Sooner or later the cocksucker had to come to his car, and then – wouldn't he be surprised?

Vince shifted his weight from foot to foot, back and forth, edgy, itchy, fresh from the streets of Brooklyn.

Motherfucker.

As he walked along, Bill whistled through his teeth. 'Singin' in the Rain'. He couldn't get the tune out of his head. Didn't matter. He was pleased. It would work, he could see it working, but already the day's events were fading away and being replaced with thoughts of tomorrow. The first set-up, the second, the whole intensive shebang. He sometimes wondered how he could fit it all in his head, concentrate on it and hold it all together. The problems that each shot would pose, how they'd work with each other, the camera movements, the...

There was somebody in his way, standing dead centre in the alleyway. Legs apart, head tilted provocatively.

It was that moron of an extra.

The moron pulled a gun out of his trousers and aimed it at Bill.

'Hey motherfucker,' he said, his northern accent making it sound more like fookah. 'Suck on this.'

'Oh, fuck off,' said Bill wearily.

Vince pulled the trigger, three times, blam, blam, blam.

The only thing that could have made the moment better would have been if the gun were real. But for Vince it was, he heard the shots in his head, he saw the blood spurt and the director fall dead. He heard the police sirens – maybe Sipowitz was coming after him, or Dirty Harry...

'Fucking New York,' said Bill and he walked on down the alley towards his car.

TOBY AND COLE

Samantha Gillison

It is dark then and cold when she walks home, carrying bags full of food for Toby. She has bought fresh pasta, pâté, tissue-wrapped pears from Dean & DeLuca and ten tiny lamb chops folded in orange butcher paper. She has cleaned her apartment, changed the sheets, wiped the dark hairs and dirt from behind her toilet – she even tidied her drawers, folding sweaters into neat piles and placing rolled balls of stockings into Ziploc bags.

Cole smokes as she puts the groceries away and then opens a tin of butter cookies and nibbles one as she surveys her apartment. It is too small: she is humiliated by its low ceilings and shabby, dirt-smudged walls. She lights two candles and places them on the mantel above the bricked-in fireplace. She imagines Toby walking in the door, his glance flickering over the familiar dinginess of her life. The two months that he has been in Europe, buying photographs, she has spent thinking about his life in expensive hotels. She saw him in the morning, waking up in neat, antique-filled rooms; lying in starched white sheets and then showering in marble bathrooms full of brass fixtures and steaming hot water. When he called her she could not imagine his face, only the expanse of pale carpet on hotel corridors, a single narcissus in a black vase on top of the television set, and the hushed shuffle of a bell boy taking the suitcases from his room to the lobby.

But when he does arrive at her apartment, full of the stale smell of the airplane cabin, he is exhausted and cannot stay awake for the dinner she has planned. He falls asleep on her bed with his face buried in the pillows. She cooks anyway, frying the lamb and spreading thick pâté on to Stoned Wheat Thins for herself. She is excited and nervous and even though Toby is asleep she is self-conscious.

Her hand drops to her groin unconsciously and she smoothes the wool felt of her expensive slacks. She has blown out her dark curly hair and clipped it up, away from her round face and she glances in the mirror now and likes the way her pink lipstick makes her mouth soft in the glimmering candlelight. Cole is short, with large breasts and thick muscular legs. She looks younger than she is and foreign. Toby said that when he first met her he felt like Odysseus, exhausted and mud-encrusted, washed up on the shore, gazing at

Nausicaa. He said that she looked as though she were born in a fishing village in Greece or a hamlet in the Andean mountains only to emerge fully grown, swathed in Agnès B, in the West Village. And now she stares at her reflection with satisfaction and thinks: this is how Toby saw me.

Even when Cole is with other men and Toby is on a different continent, in a different hemisphere, she thinks of him. The men she sleeps with are all friends of hers and sometimes even of Toby's, and although these affairs are never serious or passionate she enjoys them. Her lovers exist in a haze for her and sometimes, when she is in a bar, happy and flirting, drinking thick red wine and eating fried calamari with one of them she thinks about Toby and becomes morose.

Her mind becomes full and she imagines him walking along the waxed floors of a gallery, intent on the carefully matted photographs hung perfectly before him on white walls; she sees him pointing and buying endless grainy, black and white images. Toby's immersion in his work makes her sullen. She experiences his enormous capacity to look and buy and think about photographs (that aren't even his own work) as aggressive; she feels that next to him she is frivolous and agitated, too distracted to do her own work.

But she is pleased that he is there, now, in her apartment, and she hears him shift and mutter. Cole eats her dinner quickly, smoking, reading the paper and listening to Toby's restless, jet-lagged half-sleep. She makes a plate of food for him, carefully arranging the lamb chops and sliced Brussels sprouts under tin foil before she puts it in the refrigerator.

He has dropped two suitcases by the door and she moves them, lugging them to the far end of the couch so that they do not dominate the space and make it seem even smaller. Toby no longer has an apartment in New York, although he talks about buying a loft downtown. He rents a painting studio for Cole in Brooklyn and keeps some of his things there: boxes of books, file cabinets, skis and suitcases full of sweaters all stacked neatly under a drop cloth.

Cole's studio is small with a wall of frosted glass windows that open out on to roofs of empty factories and the blue-painted pilings of the Manhattan Bridge. There is a toilet and sink behind a sheet rock partition and Cole staples her oversized canvases to the acrylic-encrusted walls.

When Toby first rented the space for her she was embarrassed and unable to paint for two months. Slowly she began to realise how much money he had, and that her studio was a small expense for him and she wondered if he thought that she had been waiting for this all along. He always pays for his friends whenever they are with him. He buys meals and taxi rides and when he travels with people he pays for plane tickets and hotels without discussing it, ever. Cole understands that for Toby this is how he can stand to be close to people.

She knows that when her dour, expressionist paintings are exhibited he is uneasy, and she has not decided if this is because he does not like her work. Unconsciously, she blames Toby for her disappointing career, believing that somehow because she is with him she cannot have success.

And when she is angry with him about her painting or his ceaseless travelling she becomes confused about what it is that she wants from him. She does not want to keep him in New York and she does not want him to have sex with her more often, to express desire or touch her – she knows him too well for that. He is so familiar to her that when he is nude, when he returns from a run and his smell fills her small apartment he seems like a sickly child to her, covered in freckles with his mouth full of sour breath. No, she does not want more of him in that way. What is it then? she thinks.

Cole undresses in the bathroom and runs her fingers over her collarbone and breasts. She fills the bathtub and washes herself, shaving her legs, her armpits and the hairs that grow from her toes. She is menstruating and she inserts her diaphragm and carefully wipes the blood from her fingers and labia with a piece of toilet paper so that she can get in bed next to Toby, naked. She wraps a grey kimono around her pale, shaved, city-plump body and takes it off only after she has crawled into the sheets. She lies there uneasy, smoking and reading the *Vanity Fair* Toby has brought with him until he wakes up with a start at 3am, still drowsy from his disturbed circadian rhythms.

He gets out of bed, undresses quickly and then gets under the covers and pulls her to him. He does not speak and Cole is not sure if he is awake while they have sex. The contours of his body, the thin hair on his chest and arms, the belly that fills out his lean frame and the strong, sharp smell of him comforts her then. They lay awake together, not speaking as the dawn filters into her small apartment. She fantasises about talking to him, about unleashing her affairs, her fury about her unfinished, unfinishable paintings, her unending anger at him. But then, she senses that he already knows everything, that he does not need to hear it from her and she watches him as he falls asleep.

In the morning Toby is restless. He unzips his bags and spreads his clothes on to Cole's couch and sorts through them, making a pile for the dry cleaners and a pile for the laundry. While Cole is eating cereal, watching him, he tells her that he wants to drive up to the Catskills to fish for brook trout. He says that he thought about fishing the river on his friend Roger's property the whole time he was away.

'All right,' Cole says, annoyed.

She is irritated that he is wide awake, roaming around her apartment, organising his clothes, planning this day trip and she is still full of sleep, craving the smooth, clean sheets of her bed. She is offended because it is always like this with him: he cannot stand to be in her small apartment during the day.

He makes a picnic lunch while she dresses. He slices Cheddar cheese and tomatoes for sandwiches and he packs them with the pears, a few tins of sardines, and a six-pack of Harp into a Styrofoam cooler. They drive to her studio where Toby stores his fly rods and then they head out of the city, skirting Manhattan, speeding over the Bridge until they are on the New York State Thruway. He likes to drive with the windows and sunroof open and soon the cut grass and crushed leaf smell of the upstate highway floods Toby's Saab, filling Cole with a sharp nostalgic twinge.

Roger's family's property is past a summer camp on a dirt road. Their land is covered in dense, untrimmed pine and birch so that as soon as Toby and Cole drive past the rotted gate, they are covered by its cool, dark green canopy. There is no one there: Roger's family are at the Adirondack club for August. Their empty, locked-up house, a stacked log cabin, was built from thick Catskill beeches in the 1920s. Except for the sliding glass doors that Roger's mother installed 15 years ago the place looks deserted, as though it slipped away from an ancient memory.

Cole walks down the red dirt path that leads from the driveway to the house while Toby puts on his waders behind the car. He follows her, carrying his rods and the Styrofoam cooler and they walk past the house down the narrow footpath through a stand of pine trees to the winding, shallow river. Standing on the bank they are once again in the brilliant day – the sun is clear and it lights up the hundreds of grey rocks on the riverbed and coaxes an earthy pine smell from the ground.

Cole watches Toby walk into the water. She knows that although he does not talk to her he likes her to be there while he fishes; he likes her to see him dressed like this, casting for brook trout, squinting into the light. He fished with his father when he was young and he still does. Toby and his father fly to Alaska every July and charter a Cessna to search for salmon-packed waterways. They fish for days, standing in the freezing water, surrounded by the lush green landscape and discuss money. They talk about his portfolio, and the family trust, and how it will be if the coming year is good.

Cole eats one of the Cheddar cheese and tomato sandwiches and then opens a tin of sardines and scoops out the salty, oily fish with her fingers. She lies down on the ground, positioning herself so that she is out of the tree's shade, directly in the sun. Cole closes her eyes and feels the sun covering her face and body, penetrating her clothes, filling her blood with its strong, calming warmth. She thinks about how different she is from Toby and, right then, she is enormously proud that she is with him. She dozes then, listening to the flowing river and the tiny splash of Toby's line.

She hears Toby walking out of the water and when she opens her eyes to see him everything is covered in a blue wash. He has not caught any trout and she smiles at him and then sits up and lights a Camel. Toby is sweating and he wipes his forehead with his sleeve. Cole hands him a cheese sandwich and a Harp. He looks out at the water and then at the slope of mountain behind it.

'Do you think we should keep going, Cole?' he asks quietly. 'You know – do you think we should continue our relationship?'

'Yes,' she blurts out, instantly alert and scared. The sun-filled day retreats until she is only aware of Toby's being and the pine needles pressing into her palms.

'Why?' he asks. 'Don't you get restless when I am gone for so long? I mean,' he pauses, 'I'd still pay for the studio and everything.'

Cole starts crying. 'That is so ugly,' she says. 'Why are you doing this? Did you bring me up here just to do this?'

She can see how uncomfortable he is and she is humiliated, mortified that she must be another unpleasantness for him to manoeuvre around.

'No,' he says thoughtfully. He glances at her and then back at the water. 'All right. I just thought you were lonely. I thought – I don't know, that you might want to be with someone else, someone who could be more of a real boyfriend to you.'

'Well, I don't,' she says dismally, looking at the ground. 'I don't feel that way.'

Toby finishes his beer, shakes the last few drops out of the amber glass bottle, and carefully places it back in the cooler. And then, without saying anything, he walks back into the river and starts casting. Cole sits there, unhappy, feeling the adrenaline rush ebb out of her blood. She lights a cigarette and moves back under the elm tree's shade, so that she is out of the sun which has become unpleasantly hot. She looks around her and thinks about going back to the city with its summer stench and the endless rows of brownstones and pavement and buses that rumble over the cobblestone street outside her apartment window. She thinks of the brown Hudson with its decomposing piers and the transvestites who meander along the far end of the West Side Highway, surrounded by cement pylons and the purring cars that endlessly cruise them.

Cole looks out at the slow-moving river that envelops Toby's legs and the tiny blue birds that hop on the ground in front of her and warble into the quiet day. It occurs to her that this is what the city used to be, green and still, full of hills and forest and the smell of the sun-warmed earth. She thinks of the drive back and how they will speed along the West Side Highway, past the factories and warehouses on the banks of New Jersey.

It is too much then – her brain is beset by images of subway tunnels, steel and glass buildings and electricity buzzing light from streetlamps into the tired, polluted air. She closes her eyes and leans back into the elm's rough, ridge-filled bark. She stays like that, waiting for the sadness to pass through her until Toby walks out of the river, climbs up the bank and begins getting ready for the trip back home.

COASTAL CITY
Kim Newman

From the window of his 38th-floor office, Francis X Riordan could see the Statue of Freedom out in the bay, his torch held high; the Allied Nations HQ, reflecting the city like a giant black mirror; and the Imperial State Building, still the tallest skyscraper in the world.

In the rare moments when Coastal City was not in crisis, Chief Riordan liked to stand before his panoramic window and look out at the metropolis, at the thin mists drifting around the spires of the highest structures, at the blimps making doughnut-holes in low clouds, at the flying folk.

Riordan could remember when there were no flying folk.

He couldn't put a date on it, or even a decade, and his head buzzed a little if he tried. But there was a time before the miraculous. Some things had changed enormously, beyond belief in fact, but others, ordinary things you expected to change, had stayed the same.

He had no idea any more of his age.

At the beginning, he had been only a few years away from retirement. Somewhere in his late fifties, hair iron-grey, moustache white, pipe clamped in his teeth. He was still there, caught in that moment. Wars had come and gone, radio given way to television, books of mug shots and sketch artists replaced by tap-ins to the Federal Bureau of Inquiry's national database and interactive imaging computers, man had reached the moon and beyond. But Police Chief Frank Riordan still wasn't retired. He was a ticking clock, stuttering on a moment in personal time, straining forward but pulled back.

A golden jet shot across the sky. It was the first of the flying folk, the most beloved, Amazon Queen.

She had come to Coastal City before the War – WWII, the Big One – and declared her own war, on criminals and fifth columnists and other evildoers. Riordan remembered his first sight of her, after the aversion of a major elevated railway sabotage incident. She was a goddess in a golden cape and bathing suit, a streetcar lifted over her head, gently drifting downwards, tiara shining in the sunlight.

They coined a word for her, hyperhero.

Soon, there were others: some flew, some didn't. The Streak, who could run faster than sound. Green Masque, who dressed like a Ziegfeld girl and broke up rackets with high kicks. The Darkangel, who haunted the night in search of miscreants. Gecko Man, the wall-scaling, wise-cracking youth. Teensy Teen, the Shrinking Cheerleader, and her sidekick, Blubber Boy. The Outcasts, high-schoolers with hyperpowers and acne. Vindicator, the cyborg avenger remade in Vietnam as an implacable enemy of evil.

The hypers brought out the best and worst of Coastal City. They set an example, protected the innocent, kept the peace. But there were equally powerful, equally hyper, villains; gimmick gang bosses like Max Multiple, Circe and Mr Bones, mad scientists like Dr Megalomaniac and Comrade Atomic Man, freaks like Dead Thing and the Creech, mystery men like the Dealer and Shadowjack, flamboyant sociopaths like Pestilence and Hexfire. And that was only the more-or-less human ones.

Giant monsters from beneath the seas or the earth: Tentaclo, the ten-armed titanic octopus; Ssquarrq, the living earthquake; the Anti-Human Wave. Alien invaders from Mars, Mercury, Planet Q, Aldebaran, Dimension Terror and Zandorr. Demons from Hell: Asmodeus Jr, Lillyth, the Jibbenainosay.

Coastal City had been levelled more times than Riordan could count. It seemed each of the hyperheroes spent ten months of the year pairing up with a rotating succession of hypervillains, demolishing city blocks in their fights. Sometimes, hypers would form tag teams and knock down whole streets. And once a year, there would be a crossover free-for-all, frequently involving something enormously powerful from another galaxy, and all the hypers would destroy the city while saving the universe.

Chief Riordan, whom some called the city's heart and guts, had lived through mediaeval plagues, alien invasions, month-long nights, demonic manifestations, nuclear fires, transportation of the whole city back to the age of the dinosaurs or one of the moons of Zandorr, and a thousand one-man hyper-crimewaves. He had personally been possessed by Asmodeus Jr, temporarily granted all the powers of Gecko Man and had a million-dollar contract put on his head by Max Multiple. Always, he'd sustain a few bruises, wrap a bandage around his head or have his arm in a splint, then be back in his office and on the job.

The city could be rebuilt overnight, and often had been.

In the beginning, it wasn't even called Coastal City. For the briefest moment, during Amazon Queen's battle with Lady Nazi, it had been New York, and there had been a Statue of Liberty and a Brooklyn Bridge. Then, when the Streak came to town, the city was revised, the buildings had grown taller and shinier, the shadows become deeper and darker.

Amazon Queen saved President Roosevelt from Lady Nazi's poison kisses. And the Streak began his decades-long persecution of the crazy crime boss, Max Multiple. Suddenly, everyone was calling the place Coastal City and things became more hectic.

That must have been 1939 or '40.

Then, there had been a framed photograph in Riordan's office of him in France, posed by his biplane after his famous victory over Hans von Hellhund, the Demon Ace. Later, the picture showed him with the crew of the bomber Eudora Fae, after dropping the third atomic bomb on Samurai Satan's private army. Now, his younger self, flashing Nixon Vs, was beside his experimental hypersonic Stud Fighter on a carrier off the coast of Vietnam. He knew that if he sat here much longer, the picture would show him in the Gulf War.

Floating about twenty years in his past was a war. But that war kept pace with the present, always lagging the same distance behind him.

That was just one of the things that changed.

He had no real memories, he thought sometimes, just polished anecdotes, flashbacks that faded. If he concentrated on the framed photograph, he saw all the images at once, all the wars, all the planes. Only his face was always the same, albeit with different moustaches: from Douglas Fairbanks to Clark Gable to Dennis Hopper.

There were firebursts over the city.

Amazon Queen was dancing in the air with three small, swift, insect-like humans. Flameflowers blossomed and streamers fell towards the streets where people looked up and pointed. They were rarely hurt by falling debris. It was another typical day in Coastal City.

Only a moment ago, it had been the '30s. There was a Depression finishing and a War to come. That was always the moment in Coastal City, though the Depressions and the Wars changed.

Now, it was... what year was it?

It was always Next Year in Coastal City, just far enough ahead for the hyperinventions to be off the drawing board, but not so far that the President of the day was out of office.

A green shape flashed upwards across the building, crossing the window in a green flash, leaving those sucker-marks that were hell to wipe off.

Riordan craned to look, but Gecko Man was gone.

Riordan was more comfortable with Amazon Queen and the Streak, beyond human comprehension as they were, than youngsters like Gecko Man or the Outcasts. Amazon Queen and the Streak, the first generation of hypers, were of his vintage and had his attitudes. They were clean-cut, good-humoured, even-tempered, unswervingly confident in their own rectitude.

Gecko Man never seemed to take anything seriously but was plainly knotted with neurosis; he was just a mixed-up kid, though he had been around since the Brittles came out of Liverpool and Kennedy was shot by that alien in Dallas. And even Gecko Man was weirded out by the Vindicator, who had been a hypervillain the first time he showed up with his blockbustergun but become popular enough to be classed as one of the good guys. The old hypers always trussed up even the most powerful menaces and left them for the cops, but the Vindicator collected severed heads.

The department had cops, newer men and women, who understood the world of the Vindicator. But Chief Riordan would always be a New Deal man. Hyperheroes with capabilities that put them in the demigod class looked to him for fatherly advice, and accepted his judgments as final.

And the city rose and fell. Again and again.

Ginger, his assistant, brought in a report. The three creatures Amazon Queen was zapping were the latest conjurings of her arch-enemy, Lillyth. Amazon Queen could handle that.

Ginger had been with him since the beginning.

At first, she was a scatty secretary, and looked like Ginger Rogers. Now, she was Assistant Chief, and looked like Sharon Stone. Along the way, she had resembled Lauren Bacall, June Allyson, Jane Fonda and Meryl Streep. She had been an undercover femme fatale, a starched housewife, a counter-culture radical, a feminist overachiever.

But she was still stuck with a name from the '30s.

Riordan told Ginger to pass on a routine alert to Colonel Gritsby of COM-MAND (Central Operation to Maintain Massive American National Defense) that hyperhumans were engaged in a firefight over a populated area.

'Lillyth?' Ginger mused. 'Is she a supernatural entity or an extra-terrestrial being?'

'She's a demon sorceress from Dimension Terror. Check both boxes.'

Ginger shrugged, and left the office.

*

For decades, Coastal City had been almost cosy. Buildings might be destroyed, but innocent bystanders were rushed out of the way. Casualties were amazingly light, limited to hypervillains who unwisely made final stands on perches above the bay – the torch of the Statue of Freedom was very popular – and accidentally fell to their usually temporary deaths in the waters below.

Hyperheroes never so much as gave them a shove, though it was quietly agreed that no one should ever hold the Streak, who could accomplish anything in a fragment of a second, responsible for not darting out and saving Dr Megalomaniac from a fatal fall in the way he would if Ginger, on whom he was kind of sweet, were tottering on a ledge. As it happens, dozens of falls, fires, explosions, executions, banishments to Dimension Terror and Mittel European lynch mobs had failed to do any permanent harm to Dr Meggo.

A few months – years? – ago, that had started to change. A few minor hypers, mostly those who had not been heard of for a while, got killed in the odd big brawl. Peers gathered for funerals, though they could hardly be expected to remember much about the fallen.

At first, when Iridium Man was destroyed by Mr Bones, Riordan had expected I-Man to be back within the month, but it seemed his death was more permanent than most. In life, he hadn't been much of a name – just a second-stringer in a short-lived group, the Atom Age Teens, who had been around for a while before Gecko Man turned up. But, as a dead hyperhero, he took on a totemic position. If Iridium Man could die, so could anyone else.

About that time, Vindicator started seriously collecting heads. The mood of the city changed, even its look. Edges were sharper, shadows thicker. The Depression spread, affecting more than the picturesque and grateful orphans who received Christmas presents in the Streak's annual Santa Claus act. There were homeless persons, mentally ill veterans, even the odd teenage hooker. A few street cops turned out to be dirty.

Riordan couldn't understand it.

Once, he found himself picking up the phone and asking to speak with President Roosevelt.

Then, in his mind, he asked himself: which one?

The silver spires and the elegant dirigibles were still there, in the world of the flying folk. But down in the labyrinthine streets and alleys, the Darkangel kept the fragile peace through terror. Even Vindicator started to seem soft.

Nightgaunt, the city's newest 'hyperhero', was a demon turncoat who ate the entrails of slain foes.

Once, the city had been an American Ideal. All problems were solved quickly and with good cheer. Even the worst of the worst were like naughty children, sent to their rooms until the next scrape. And the hyperheroes were all big kids, enjoying themselves.

What had changed?

Now, Coastal City was America's Nightmare.

The old city was still there, if you looked.

Riordan realised the problem was in himself. Like Max Multiple, he hopped between personalities. He was different with different people: fatherly with Amazon Queen, irascible with Darkangel, a buffoon with Gecko Man, sad but stern with Vindicator, almost senile with Nightgaunt.

He was in everyone's world, and they were all inside him, tearing him apart.

Only months 'til retirement.

But months were eternal in Coastal City. It was just months since Watergate (when Dr Meggo replaced the President with an evil robot), since the Bay of Pigs, since Anzio.

Riordan wondered. I-Man was gone and even poor sweet dumb Teensy Teen was stomped flat by the Dealer. For a while, it seemed Amazon Queen had actually died, sucked into the Nevergone Void, but she came back, reborn and rejuvenated and with a more revealing costume, and a meaner streak. But Green Masque, who had been around almost as long as Amazon Queen, fell victim to a serial killer, Pestilence, and was actually gone from continuity, rarely seen even as a ghost.

It could happen.

He could die. Ironically, on the eve of retirement. He would be greatly mourned and swiftly avenged.

But he was an anachronism. The times would be served better if Coastal City's police chief were a woman or a psychopathic hypervillain or a black man. There was more potential in any of those, more chance for conflict or crisis.

It was all about stories, about plot material.

He wasn't one of the immortals.

Dr Megalomaniac was out there, a one-time nuisance reworked as a mass murderer. And so many others. With grudges, with hyperpowers.

Living through months that spanned decades, only noticing the gradual changes when they were well-established, always careening from crisis to crisis, Frank Riordan was wearing out. At first, slowly; now, rapidly.

How long would this go on?

He looked out of his office window as night fell. The torch of the Statue of Freedom burned bright, its fires reflected in the frontage of the Allied Nations HQ.

A giant, ten-armed octopus was pulling itself painfully up the Imperial State Building, tentacle by tentacle. Futile shellbursts were exploding all around. Crowds in the streets were running in panic.

Riordan forgot his troubles and used the gold phone. It was answered at the first ring, but as usual she didn't speak, just listened.

'There's a crisis in Coastal City,' he told the silent party. 'If ever we've needed you, we need you now.'

RECOVERING AT THE CHELSEA

Maureen Freely

It's the drink talking. Jimmy knows that. But for once, he has to admit it, the drink is right. He's asking a hell of a lot of himself, trying to work the program in this fleabag hotel. Since he's been gone, the pimp population on their hallway, it must have doubled. The one Stan's put next door, his radio's so loud, it's like the whole Motown Experience, it's right there in bed with them. Same goes for his welcome home presents – these lowlifes Evie has camping out on their living room floor. Jimmy doesn't care what she says. He's not impressed. So what if they're on the FBI's most wanted list. So what if they had once shaken hands with Ho Chi Minh or made some dumb Molotov Cocktail that blew up the wrong brownstone. If you ask him, the FBI should get its head screwed back on if it's wasting tax dollars running after this kind of garbage. These guys, they aren't going nowhere. They can't even put a wig on without getting it ass backwards. The only thing these clowns are threatening now, it's his serenity.

One thing he's learned from going through the rooms is, if you don't stick with the winners, the zombies get you in the end. He's told Evie this, how many times since he got back from St Vincents and found the three stooges snoring with their heads under the couch. It's gone in one ear, out the other, like he was trying to teach her how to say the rosary or sumpin. But this morning, even she's shaking her head, because it's a pigsty in that kitchenette – cockaroaches everywhere, dishes piled that high, and what was it about these guys and ashtrays? There was so much ash and hash on the floor even the cockaroaches couldn't walk straight.

There isn't a square inch of that living room floor where there isn't a lumped up sleeping bag with a hairmop hanging out of it, or a work boot that smells like someone left a Chinese take-out in it last Thursday. The stench is so thick it's like it's a real hand pushing him back into the bedroom. So while he's sitting there watching Evie hunt around for her clothes, he says, 'Honey, it's not fair. You're the one with the job, you're the one who has to go to night school, and this sublet is your responsibility. You can't let these dead end revolutionaries trash your life like this.'

She rolls her eyes and says, 'How many time do I have to tell you? They're not revolutionaries, they're radicals.'

As if that didn't mean the same thing. It really gets to him when she played Ms Library Lips with him, like just because he hadn't been to a fancy college, he's some kind of clunkhead who's never opened a book. He come this close to saying, let's get some things straight, who's the Wordsmith around here, who's the one Norman Mailer called the Noble Savage's Thesaurus, and by the way, which one of us was doing the running when we met, and which one the chasing? But he catches himself just in time, by using the satellite trick someone was talking about at the meeting yesterday. This was how you did it. You sent your words up to a satellite in space, and you waited for them to bounce back again before you said them, and this gave you enough time to ask yourself, how important is it? How much energy do I want to invest in this pointless conflict? Which took it out of you, but you had to think about the instant benefits, like right now, thanks to the satellite, he's not having to listen to Evie telling him how these no-hopers who never get up until four in the afternoon are fighting a war.

Except this time he fucks it up somehow. It's like he's beamed his inner-most thoughts straight into her head. Because even though he's kept his mouth shut, she gives him her Miss Superstar, Barnard summa cum laude class of 71 look, and says, 'Anyway, I'm not the only one working.' Pointing to the fattest, lumpiest sleeping bag on the floor, she says, 'Somehow, and typically, you've forgotten Louise.'

But he's still managing to keep his cool, and so he does not say, 'Hey, foxy baby, I don't count stripping as work.' He does not say, 'But you know what, if she keeps chomping on those chocolate bars like she's been doing lately, the only place they'll want her is in an elephant bar.' He does not say, 'And another thing, there's something fishy about her having two boyfriends. I just don't believe it.' And he does not say, 'Yeah, and while we're on the sub-ject, if she's a stripper, and her two boyfriends here are living off of her, assum-ing they are both her boyfriends, what does that make *them*?' Keeping these thoughts to himself is a good move, because that means she doesn't say, 'Right, and while we're on the subject, when's the last time *you* brought home a paycheck?' Which gives him no opportunity to say, 'That reminds me of something I've been meaning to ask you since I got back. What exactly do you do for yours?' Because this job of hers, he just doesn't get it. Since he got back, she's on his case if he even thinks the word chick, all he has to do is tell her she's looking foxy and it's checkout time, but somehow it's okay for her to do shitwork for that weirdo upstairs, the French guy, or is he German, who has got to have something seriously wrong with his head because he wore a fur hat all last summer. She says he's a respected international publisher, but ever since Jimmy took a look at that translation she's been doing for him, he's been wanting to ask, respected for what, exactly? The number of words he can come up with that rhyme with suck?

Another thought to keep to himself. As she heads out into the hallway with her briefcase under her arm, he imagines himself swallowing it, when the door slams shut behind her, he feels it turning in his stomach. When he closes his eyes, he feels it pumping through his bloodstream. And when he opens them up again, it's the drink talking again, and the drink is saying, look at me, I'm over here on the counter, I'm the bottle of Sauza tequila and depending on how you look at me, I'm half empty or half full, but let me tell you, one hit and you won't care which.

And Sauza, she says, why do you have to be the only one who has to try so hard? When everyone else gets to type porno for perverts and spend the whole morning crapped out on sleeping bags on the floor and live in darkness? He couldn't have put it better himself. And she almost gets the better of him, almost but not quite. He's halfway across the room and reaching for that Sauza before he catches himself, asks himself, is this stinking thinking, or is this stinking thinking? He has to let this go. If these people on his floor want to live like animals, that's their business. If Evie wants to make her living translating the words dick and cunt into every European language known to man, then that is her decision. What was it his mentor had said when he called him up to talk about it when he couldn't sleep at two in the morning? He had said so many wise things, it was hard to remember them all, but this was the one Jimmy wanted to engrave on his brain. It was 'never try to illuminate the unconscious'. Some things, you just had to leave for your Higher Power. Before you put yourself on someone else's slippery slope, his mentor had said, just ask yourself this question – when you see a rock rolling down a hill, what do you do, stand there shouting at it or remember that no way that rock can hear you and step out of the way?

'And it doesn't stop there. Remember, Jimmy, you've got to love those rocks, too, even when they're shooting right past you, racing each other to see who gets to the bottom first. There's no wrong time for remembering the good times,' his mentor had said, and so that's what the task is Jimmy sets himself next as he contemplates the human debris on the living room floor. He stops thinking what he'd like to do with these sleeping bags. Instead he remembers the way Evie curled up against him when she fell asleep last night. He remembers how her face lit up the first time she came to see him at St Vincents. He reminds himself how she kept on coming to see him, even when her face couldn't light up no more, or else he couldn't see it light up, because he was in darkness. But he can't think about that too long, not without remembering the bad parts. Every happy memory he dredges up these days, it's covered with barnacles. He's got to get back to the present, he's got to stop waiting for Evie and these animals to get it together first. He has to look around him and ask what can I do right now, even if I can't budge these scuzzbags, to make the world more beautiful?

That's when the floor, it says, start with me. And the windows. The crapped out john, it says, do me next or else. So, for the next two hours, Jimmy Wordsmith, aka the Noble Savage's Thesaurus, aka infamous author of Red Lines, Red Pome, Red Lites, Red Commershal, Red Liberry, and countless other unsigned street poems, who featured in an article in *New York* magazine called 'Twenty Faces to Watch out for in 1973', and who almost died four months ago, but is now hard at work on a fearless moral inventory that will help him put his life back together, for two hours he puts all head stuff to one side and he sweeps every last free square inch of floor, and does the sink and sends the cockaroaches scuttling for their lives, and zaps the bathtub and polishes the mirror and gets down on his hands and knees to get at the gunk oozing out between the tiles. He throws all the wigs and backpacks and hair dye kits into one big stinking pile. He puts new sheets on him and Evie's bed and plumps up the pillows while he's at it, and when he's through he sits down with a Benson and Hedges he found under the sink, surveying his work and feeling as serene as, hell, as serene as he felt that meeting that first time he handed over.

He feels so serene, he's almost ready to pick up a spray can and begin his new project, which he thinks should be called The Seventh Step and his mentor thinks he should call Mea Culpa, but then he remembers the promise he made, not to take on too much too soon. What was it his mentor had said when he had talked to him during their last phone call, it must have been around sunrise? 'Do what you can, with what you have, where you are. You don't have to paint the town red again to become a good person.'

Every time you feel yourself yearning to do something big in the distant future, he had said, do something small, in the present. Which is why, at eleven o'clock, after he's called his mentor and told him not to worry, he's turned the corner – when he's on his way to his day job, that's what he calls the chores he does for Dr Z in 802, he takes the stairs so he can stop by 611 first to check up on Assumpta, who's been lying low the last few days. Every time he says, hey, how about a meeting? she comes up with some new excuse. First it was a head cold, then it was a sore foot, then two days ago it was some painting she was doing. Yesterday it was a glass of turpentine she says she took a sip of by mistake that gave her a sore throat. What'll it be today? It'll be something, he's sure, because when he called her up at four in the morning, she said she couldn't talk, and when he tried to go see her at six-thirty when he couldn't get through to his mentor, she and Lars and God only knows who else were making such a racket no one heard him knocking. Even now, it takes Jimmy eight knocks to get her to the door, and her face, it looks like one of her self-portraits, a piece of paper someone just scrunched up and threw into a basket. The air that comes out with her, it's got to be a hundred proof.

But he's not going to judge her. His job is to be there for her. So he says, 'How's my favourite bag lady?' She says, 'I've seen better days.' He says, 'What were you and Lars up to last night, from the hallway it sounded like you was entertaining a whole shipload a sailors.' 'No such luck,' she says, and he waits for the joke but it doesn't come, which means she must a given herself some hammering. Every cell in his body wants to warn her about that slippery slope she's headed for. She's worth so much more than this! With her talent, she has so much to live for! He catches his words just in time, and just to keep the door open he says, 'How about coming with me to a meeting tonight?' She says, 'Okay, doll, it's a date. Let's talk about it later, though, when I'm feeling human.'

And shuts the door in his face. But he's too up to make the mistake of taking that personally. He heads up to 802, where the old guy takes his time answering the door, like he always does. There's some soprana scream-ing her head off on the radio, but when Doc finally hears the knocking, he turns her off, and while they're putting the cats in the bags, he says, 'So how you doing, Jimmy? You're looking a little peaky. That Evie feeding you okay? Maybe when you pick up that loafa bread for me, you should buy yourself a donut.'

'You're worse than my momma,' says Jimmy, even though the truth is, at the moment, he's about as likely to get a donut from her as a hole in the head.

Dr Z says, 'Here. Take this quarter. Have a nice one with coconut on top.' Like a donut was medicine or sumpin. Jimmy's still laughing about it in the elevator, but to himself, not out loud, which is a good thing, because the fucking cats they're already going wild by now in those bags of theirs, and he has Pimp O'Crazy in there with him, and he's wearing his biggest purple hat, and has this look like maybe the catfight's a hallucination, and the lady in the suit who's the other one in the elevator with them, she looks like she's about to report Jimmy to the management. But it's cool, she ends up with just giving him a dirty look, and when he passes through the lobby Stan the Man is too busy with some jailbait wearing last year's hot pants who says she's looking for someone Jimmy's never heard of she says is a famous drummer, and so no one notices the cats, not even when he's standing right there on the Hotel Chelsea doormat, putting on their leashes.

And the air, it's just that much warmer and sweeter than it was yesterday, you can tell spring is around the corner, so he decides to take the scenic route to Dr Z's bank, along 23rd, then up Fifth Avenue and over, even though that means he's taking the exact same route he did with The Pome That Rises Red in the West, which is taking a risk, because who knows how many store owners haven't forgiven him yet for what he did to their windows, and even though this route doesn't take him past the Greek restaurant where Gus the waiter is probably still interested in finding out when Jimmy can pay him the two grand he owes him from that poker game, and even though it takes him in the opposite direction from the bookie he hasn't seen since he made that dumb bet on the Knicks game, it does take him right past the OTB, which is bound to be packed by now with a lot of angry men with long memories and very short forgiving streaks and a lot of bars he's been avoiding since he got out of St Vincents. Which makes him nervous, because he's been eighty-sixed from every single one of them, and with some of these bartenders, the old ones like Abe and Larry and the wackos like Captain Bill, if you've been eighty-sixed they're going to come after you even if all you're doing is taking a couple of cats for a stroll down the sidewalk.

'Jimmy, you're going to have to try to keep this in proportion, and take one step at a time,' his mentor says when Jimmy calls him from a phone booth. 'Don't ask yourself why or how, just do the footwork.' And so he concentrates on putting one foot in front of the other, and as usual, his mentor is a hundred per cent right, which is why Jimmy's glad he's called him, because even though it's true what Evie says, that he talks in slogans, you have to be an expert to know exactly which motto to apply to a specific situation. The cats, they're such slow pokes he keeps having to pick them up and carry them like they was children, and he gets fed up with the looks he's getting, but remembering what his mentor said about his sense of proportion, he plants his mind on the funny side, he imagines how it looks to his old buddies on the benches, and the bottom feeders outside the OTB, him in his jeans and his mean leather jacket with these two Siamese cats on rhinestone leashes, he can't blame them.

But it wears him out, all this taking one step at a time, and seeing everybody else's side of it. He feels like a rag by the time he gets back up to the Chelsea, and Dr Z he picks up the vibes. 'You didn't have that donut, did you?' he says. 'You still look peaky.' And Jimmy says, 'Why should I lie?' Because it's true, if you've sat on a ledge with some guy for two, three hours like he did with Dr Z, and you've told him all the reasons why you want to jump, and he doesn't say a thing to hold you back, but doesn't take his big owl eyes off you neither, well, you know you're going to a place with that person where words can't reach.

So he sits down in the big armchair, right where he sat down yesterday which was when they had their last heart to heart. Where to begin? Jimmy thinks to himself as Dr Z sits down in the little armchair and clasps his hands. When you have as much on your chest as Jimmy does, and so many worries trying to drag you back into darkness, you could begin almost anywhere. It's finishing that's the problem. But before he can say one thing about Evie, or the three stooges, or Assumpta, or all those people out there he owes money to, Dr Z says, 'I'm a little busy right now, Jimmy, but let me tell you what I'm going to do for you. I'm getting on the phone now and I'm calling Jose downstairs and I'm telling him to make you one of those Spanish omelettes and there's no two ways about it, this one is on me.'

'Just don't sit near the bar and you'll be fine,' are his last words. And when Jimmy calls him up from the lobby, his mentor says the same thing, so Jimmy doesn't, but from his table in the corner, he can still hear the water behind the bar gurgling. What do they have back there, a sacred spring? It makes him so thirsty he drinks the whole jug of water they bring him, but the omelette it's the best thing he's eaten in weeks. As for the rest of it, it's not ideal. He's always thought El Quijote was too dark for daytime, and now he thinks the bottles behind the bar are too bright. The main problem, though, once his eyes are used to the gloom, is Evie's down here with Mr Fur Hat and a couple other baldies. She has her Miss Barnard '71 smile back on, until she sees him that is. Then it falls off real fast and the first thing she does is look at his glass, to see what he's drinking, and when she works out it's just water, it's almost like she's disappointed, and she gives him this glare as if he's so uncool he's going to give her a hard time in front of these assholes. He's not about to do that, though. If she wants to waste her lunch hour with those cruds she can go right ahead. He's focusing his energies on his omelette until he looks across the room and sees Evie and Fur Hat and co have gone and instead there's Al, the lawyer who got the New York Public Library to drop charges! He hasn't seen him since he returned to sobriety. He's about to go over and say hi but then he sees he's with that Miss Priss from his office, the one who was at the party that night Jimmy nearly checked out, who got so freaked out when he got out on the window ledge. The sight of her makes him change his mind about going over. Then one of the other guys at the table turns his head and Jimmy sees it's Mike the Mike, who he hasn't seen since he was on his radio show to talk about Red Sentense, and Joe the editor, who was going to collect the whole Red Series into a book, and so Jimmy says to himself, what the hell, I'll just say hello on my way out. But they invite him to sit down, even though Miss Priss winces when he offers her his hand, like he was going to hit her or sumpin.

The guys are all smiles. 'So Jimmy, long time no see,' Al says, and Mike the Mike says, 'Hey, you're looking great. I wouldn't a recognised you.' Joe says, 'What else you been up to besides maybe lifting weights?'

So Jimmy explains, how it's early days, which is why he's not up to much. How the business of the day is taking care of number one, how his mentor has said it's a bad idea to make any big changes in his life for six months. 'Sounds like good advice, Jimmy,' they say, nodding just a little too vigorously. 'Sounds like your mentor has a head on his shoulders.'

'He's a fucking genius,' Jimmy says. 'You wait and see, he's going to win the Nobel Prize some day.'

'Oh, really?' says Joe, perking up. 'What's his name?'

Jimmy tells him, and Joe goes, 'Oh, not him. He's history.'

Mike says, 'Yeah, I thought we got rid a him for good.'

'How can you say that?' Jimmy protests.

'Yes, but you tell me one good thing he's done since 1962.'

'Well wait till you read his life story,' Jimmy says.

'His life story?' says Joe. 'You mean after all those thousands of pages, there's something he left out?'

'Yes, there sure is,' Jimmy says, and now they're all looking at him with some interest. 'Yes,' he says, relishing the moment. 'You wait and see. You guys are going to be fighting over the new one like nobody's business.'

'Oh really,' says Al. 'What he confess to? Killing the Kennedys?'

'Listen to what I'm saying,' says Jimmy. 'This one's the one. I'm telling you, you're not going to believe it. His story, it's so good, they've got him going to meetings all over the city, even upstate. First time I heard him share, I'm telling you, he brought tears to my eyes. He has a beautiful spirit, Joe. He's a different man from the one you knew now that he's found sobriety, honest to God.'

But no one wants to hear any more about it. Everyone has to get somewhere all of a sudden. 'Great to see you, Jimmy,' Mike says with a big smile. Joe says, 'Drop by and see me when you have something new on paper.'

'You bet. I'll do that,' Jimmy says. He extends his hand to Miss Priss as she gets up, but she just looks at it, like he was offering her a dead rat. She doesn't even say goodbye. She just walks away.

'Don't mind her. She's like that with everybody,' says Al with another fake smile. He gives Jimmy's shoulder a punch and says, 'Keep up the good work, and oh yeah, how could I forget, same goes for that mentor of yours. It's pretty funny, you two ending up together. Who would have guessed?'

And Jimmy can tell, the guy's trying to smooth the waters, but it just isn't good enough. It tears Jimmy up to hear them call such a great man history. Five years ago, his mentor was Mr Front Page of the *Times Book Review*. What'd he do to suddenly go out of fashion, except to survive and hold his great hand out to others? It's okay for Jimmy, he's young, it's early days for him, but for your friends to abandon you when you're about to hit fifty… no wonder his mentor sounds so tired and beat up, Jimmy thinks, when he gets through to him on the phone in the lobby. And to think he's been suffering these indignities all this time when he's been better than a higher power to Jimmy and God knows how many other people…

Jimmy wants to tell him what a great man he is, he wants to get together a group of vigilantes to take out any asshole who tries to drag him down, but how is he supposed to say how mad he is to hear someone call him history without dragging him down even more? He chokes on his words when his mentor asks what's wrong, and when his mentor says, 'Then maybe we should wait until the meeting tomorrow before we talk again,' he tells himself his mentor knows what he couldn't say, and understands, and like the great man that he is, has found a gentle way of letting him off the hook.

'Remember, live and let live,' he says, his voice cracking with weariness. But Jimmy just can't let it stop there. Not when he sees that Al and co have not gone back to urgent business after all but regrouped outside the Oasis. This is his chance to tell them what he thinks of them for calling his mentor history, he tells himself as he heads across the street. It's not until he's followed them into the Oasis and over to the bar and looks around him that he remembers what Captain Bill, the wacko bartender, said he would do to him if he ever, ever set foot in this place again.

It was, Jimmy recalls, a very long and involved threat. Really more of a recipe, because it ended with Captain Bill eating him. Little snatches of it come back to him now as he looks down the bar, which is one, long, sickening blast from the past. There, on the other side of Al and Mike and Miss Priss, is Gus the waiter he owes the two grand to. Next to him is Evie and the three stooges, and yes, it turns out to be true. The three of them, they really are an item. Next to them is Assumpta, she's getting tanked up with Dr Z, and, what do you know, Pimp O'Crazy, and at the very end of the bar, talking to Captain Bill, who's looking extra red already, it's oh god, the bookie he hasn't seen since that Knicks game, and oh god, he has that calm look bookies have just before the guy they've hired to do you comes in to blow your head off.

And the first thing he thinks is, well, this is one more thing his mentor was right about. This is the big test, that one that happens to all recovering alcoholics, he said, no matter where they live, and just happens to you sooner if you do something truly dumbassed like try and recover at the Chelsea. Since there's no way he's going to get to a phone to find out if he's reading this one right, he knows that this time, he's going to have to be his own mentor. So he tells himself, Stay cool, and when he feels his resolve melting as Captain Bill lifts his bulk up off the bar and comes slowly towards him, he goes through all his slogans hunting for the one that will save him. He tells himself to live in the present, let go and let God, ask how important is it? listen and learn, keep it simple, keep an open mind, easy does it, just for today. He reminds himself, just like his mentor did last night, which time was it? that there are so many ways to a gift for words like he has, which means that he's not at the end of the road, just at the beginning of a new one, but they just can't hold up the lie this time. The whole house of words comes tumbling down as Captain Bill stops in front of him.

He can't see his face now. He's just one big shadow of a prince of darkness, and those rows of golden bottles behind him, they look so bright, it's like the sun's inside them, like every word he's ever written is shimmering inside, every hope and friend who ever smiled at him, and they're all saying the same thing – you really asked for it this time! – and they're all throwing those rays out so hard that Jimmy's hand shoots up without his willing it to shield his eyes.

And Captain Bill clears his throat, as if in acknowledgement of this sign of weakness. He wipes the bar with a cloth. The rest of the bar falls silent as if this is the show they bought the tickets for. Jimmy braces himself. Prepares himself for the worst. Then, in a bored, matter-of-fact voice that he'd use for anyone, any nobody he didn't know from Adam who'd just walked off the street, Captain Bill asks him, 'So. What'll it be?'

9TH AND 13TH
Jonathan Coe

I live on the corner of 9th and 13th, and I promise you, it's not a good place to be. It's not a place where you'd want to linger. It's the sort of place you pass through; the sort you move on from. Or at least, that's what it is for most people. For everybody but me.

I can't believe I've been living here for more than eighteen months now. I can't believe that every morning, for the last eighteen months, I've been woken up by the rolling of shutters at the Perky Pig Diner and BBQ just across from my apartment. Shortly after that happens, the noises will start downstairs: furniture being shifted, trucks driving in and out right underneath my bedroom, the throb of their revving engines so insistent that even when I try to block it out by putting on my headphones and turning the keyboard's volume up to Max, even then I can still feel it through my feet. I live above the business premises of the Watson Storage and Removal Company: which makes sense, in a way, because like I said, this is a transient place, a place for people on the move, a place for people who are getting ready to pack up and leave.

9th and 13th. Do you know what that sounds like? You can find out for yourself, if there's a piano anywhere nearby. Start with... start with a C, if you like. Way down on the keyboard, two octaves below middle C. Hold it down with your little finger, and now stretch your fingers, really stretch them, more than an octave, until your thumb is on a D. Now play the two notes, and listen to the interval. You've got your 9th. It's slightly rootless, already: those two bass notes that don't quite agree with one another. There's an audible sense of indecision. And now, with the thumb of your right hand, you play a B flat. This adds a kind of bluesy overtone, turns the ambiguous statement of those two notes into a question. It seems to ask: where are we heading? To which the next note – another D – adds nothing except emphasis. Now the question seems even more urgent, but when the F is introduced, it changes everything. All of a sudden the chord feels hopeful, aspiring. There's the hint of an upward movement, the sense that we might be about to arrive somewhere. And then, finally, we add the A, so that we have our 13th interval at last: and listen to how plangent it makes it sound, how wistful. This chord is aching to resolve, to settle on something: C major would be the most obvious place to go next, but it could be A minor, or F major seven, or… well, anything. It's so open. As open as a chord can get. Brimming with potential.

9th and 13th. The sound of possibility.

And how long is it since I played those chords, now? How long since she came into the bar and stood over the piano as I improvised, in the half-dark, after even the most hardened drinkers had finished up and gone home? I don't know. I lose track. All I remember is that for a few minutes we talked, swapped a few banalities, as my fingers wandered trance-like over the keyboard, tracing the usual patterns, the easy, familiar harmonies that I'm locked into, these days, like a series of bad habits. She was from Franklin, Indiana, she said, and had only pitched up in New York that afternoon. She said she'd given up her job in the local record store and had come to the city to write. To write books. And that's all I ever found out about her – not even her name, just that she was from Franklin and that she was going to write and that she had dark hair, pulled severely back from her face into a short ponytail, and tiny freckles on either side of her nose, and brown-green eyes that narrowed to a smile whenever I looked at her. Which wasn't very often, I have to say, hunched as I was over the keyboard, picking my way slowly through those well-worn chords, until my hands finally gave up; faltered, and came to rest; came to rest where they always did. The usual place.

9th and 13th.

At which point – at which precise point – she asked me a question.

'Listen,' she said. 'Is there anywhere… do you know of anywhere that I can stay tonight? I don't have anywhere to stay.'

The possibilities raised by that question, like the possibilities raised by that chord, hung in the air for as long as it took the notes to decay.

Infinite possibilities.

To take just one of them, for instance. Supposing I had resolved the chord. Supposing I had resolved it in the most obvious way, with a soft – soft but insistent – C major. Perhaps with an A natural in there somewhere, to make it just a little more eloquent. And suppose I had answered her question, by saying:

'Well, it's getting pretty late, and there aren't that many places around here. There's always my couch.'

What would have happened?

Where would I be now?

This is what would have happened:

Her eyes would have narrowed again, at first, in that warm, shy, smiling way she had, and then she would have looked away, gathering her thoughts for a moment or two, before turning back to me, and saying:

'Would that be OK? I mean, that's really nice of you...'

And I would have said: 'No problem. It's just a couple of blocks from here.'

'I don't want to put you to any trouble,' she would have said. 'It'll only be for one night.'

But it wouldn't only have been for one night. We both would have known that, even then.

I would have closed the lid of the piano and said goodnight to Andy at the bar, collecting my fee (a thin wad of dollar bills from the cash register), and then opening the door for her, warning her to mind her step on the narrow, dimly lit staircase that led up to the street. She would have had a bag with her, a black canvas hold-all, and I would have offered to carry it, slinging it over my shoulder as I followed her up the stairs, admiring the sway of her back and the shapeliness of the stockinged ankle I would have glimpsed between the bottom of her jeans and her neat brown shoes.

Once out in the street, she would have pulled her coat tightly around herself, and looked to me for guidance – only her eyes visible above the turned-up collar – and I would have taken her arm gently and led her off down West 4th Street, heading north towards 9th and 13th.

'Are you sure this is all right?' she would have asked. 'I hate to think I might be imposing.'

And I would have said: 'Not at all. It's good of you to trust me, really. I mean, a total stranger...'

'Oh, but I'd been listening to you play the piano.' She would have glanced at me, now. 'I'd been in there for a couple of hours, and... Well, anyone who plays the piano like that must be a good person.' Then a nervous laugh, before offering up the compliment. 'You play very nicely.'

I would have smiled at that: a practised, rueful smile. 'You should tell that to the guy who runs the bar. He might pay me a little more.' After which, almost immediately, I would have been anxious to change the subject. 'My name's David, by the way.'

'Oh. I'm Rachel.' We would have shaken hands, a little awkwardly, a little embarrassed at our own formality, and then hurried on to my apartment, because Rachel would have been looking cold, already: her breath steaming in the frosty air, the hint of a chatter in her teeth.

'You probably want to get straight to bed,' I would have said, as soon as we got inside, and I would have helped her off with her coat and hung it up in the hallway. I would have showed her where the bed was, and changed the sheets for her while she was in the bathroom. The old sheets and blankets I would have taken with me, using them to make up some sort of bed for myself on the couch. When she had finished in the bathroom I would have gone to check that she had everything she wanted, and then I would have said goodnight, but afterwards I would have lain on the couch for ten minutes or more, waiting for the light in her bedroom to be turned off. But she wouldn't have turned it off. Instead, her bedroom door would have been pulled slowly open, and I would have felt her looking at me, trying to work out if I had gone to sleep, before she tiptoed through into the hallway, and started searching through the pockets of her coat. A few seconds later she would have found what she was looking for and would have come back; and just as she was returning to the bedroom I would have said:

'Is everything OK?'

She would have started, and paused, before saying: 'Yes, I'm fine. I hope I didn't wake you.' And then: 'I forgot my notebook. I always try to write something in it, every night, before I go to bed. Wherever I am.'

'That's very disciplined of you,' I would have said. And she would have asked me:

'Don't you practise every night? Surely you must practise.'

'In the mornings, sometimes. By the time it gets this late, I'm too tired.'

She could have turned, and gone, at this point. The silence would have been long enough to allow it. But that wouldn't have happened. I would have sensed that she wanted to stay, and would have said:

'So what are you going to write now?'

'Just a few… thoughts, you know. Just a few thoughts about the day.'

'You mean like a diary?'

'I suppose.'

'I've never done anything like that. Never kept a diary. Have you always kept one?'

'Yes. Since I was a child. I remember, when I was about seven, or eight…'

We would have talked, then, for fifteen minutes or more. Or rather, I would have listened (because that's always how it is) while she talked; talked, and came closer – sitting on the arm of the couch, at first, then sitting beside me, after I had shifted over to make room for her, her bare thighs (because she would have been wearing only a T-shirt, and panties) in contact with my hips: only the sheets and blankets intervening.

I know, too, what would have happened at the end of those fifteen minutes. How she would have leaned towards me, leaned over me, the heaviness of her body against mine. How her hair, freed now from its ponytail, would have drifted across my face until she brushed it back, and how her lips would have touched mine: her lips dry with the cold. Dry at first. How I would have followed her into the bedroom. How there would have been a rapid, almost imperceptible shedding of our last remaining clothes. How I would have learned about her by touch, first of all, and by sight only later, when the bedclothes lay dishevelled, thrust aside, strewn across the floor. How willingly she would have given herself to me. And how beautiful she would have been, by the flashes of neon through the uncurtained window. How very beautiful.

How right for me.

That's what would have happened. And this is what would have happened next.

In the morning, we would have had breakfast together at the Perky Pig, and even that would have tasted good, for once. Over refills of coffee, we would have made plans. First of all, there would have been the question of accommodation: it would have been blindingly obvious that we could afford a bigger and better place if we pooled our resources, and moved in together. But that would have presented another problem: her parents, both Christian fundamentalists, would never have countenanced this arrangement. We would have to get married. The suggestion would have been made jokingly, at first, but it would only have taken a few seconds for our eyes to make contact and to shine with the sudden, instantaneous knowledge that it was what we both wanted. Three days later, man and wife, we would have spotted an advertisement in the *New York Review of Books* for a vacant apartment in the West Village, offered at a derisory rent to suitably Bohemian tenants. It would have been the property of a middle-aged academic couple, about to depart for a five-year sojourn in Europe. Arranged over three floors, it would have included an enormous studio room – at the centre of which would have stood a Steinway baby grand, sheened in winter sunshine from the skylight – and a small but adorable garret study with a view over the treetops of Washington Square. In this study, during the next few weeks, Rachel would have written the final chapters of her almost-completed novel. A novel which, after two regretful but encouraging rejections, would have been accepted for publication by Alfred A Knopf, and would have appeared the next September, becoming the sensation of that fall. Meanwhile, as her book climbed the bestseller lists and scooped up prizes, I would have finished my long-projected piano concerto, an early performance of which (at the Merkin Concert Hall, with myself both playing and conducting) would have caught the attention of Daniel Barenboim, who would have insisted on programming it as the chief item in his recital for the 'Great Performers' series at Lincoln Center.

Our son Thelonius would have been born a few months later. Followed, after another couple of years, by our daughter Emily.

Yes, by our daughter Emily...

Wait a minute, though: I can hear her crying. I can hear her crying downstairs.

No, it isn't her. It isn't Emily. It's the squeal of those big garage doors at the Watson Storage and Removal Company. Those rusty hinges. The first of the trucks has just arrived.

Do you want to know what I did say to her, instead? Do you want to know how I actually answered that question?

'Sure,' I said. 'There's an excellent B & B near here. Just around the corner. Halliwell's, on Bedford Street. It's just five minutes' walk.' And I looked away, to avoid glimpsing the disappointment that I knew would flare in her eyes, and I played the same two chords again, over and over, and I heard her thank me, and I kept on playing them, and she left, and I played them again, and two days later I went to Halliwell's to look for her, but they didn't know who I meant, and I said her name was Rachel but of course it wasn't, I made that up, I never knew her name, and I carried on playing those two chords and I'm still playing them now, this very moment, 9th and 13th, 9th and 13th, the sound of endless, infinite, unresolved possibilities. The most tantalising sound in the world.

I don't know what chord I should play next. I can't decide.

A MANHATTAN ROMANCE

Joyce Carol Oates

Your Daddy loves you, that's the one true thing.

Never forget, Princess: that's the one true thing in your life of mostly lies.

That wild day! I'd woken before it was even dawn, I seemed to know that a terrible happiness was in store.

I was five years old; I was feverish with excitement; when Daddy came to pick me up for our *Saturday adventure* as he called it, it had just begun to snow; Momma and I were standing at the tall windows of our eighteenth-floor apartment looking out across Central Park when the doorman rang; Momma whispered in my ear, 'If you said you were sick, you wouldn't have to go with – him.' For she could not utter the word *Daddy*, and even the words *your father* made her mouth twist. I said, 'Momma, I'm not sick! I'm not.' So the doorman sent Daddy up. Momma kept me with her at the window, her hands that sometimes trembled firm on my shoulders and her chin resting on the top of my head so I wanted to squirm away but did not dare, not wanting to hurt Momma's feelings or make her angry. So we stood watching the snowflakes – a thousand million snowflakes drifting downward out of the sky glinting like mica in the thin sunshine of early December. I was pointing and laughing, I was excited by the snow, and by Daddy coming for me. Momma said, 'Just look! Isn't it beautiful! The first snow of the season.' Most of the tall trees had lost their leaves, the wind had blown away their leaves that only a few days before had been such bright, beautiful colours, and you could see clearly now the roads curving and dipping through the park; you could see the streams of traffic – yellow taxis, cars, delivery vans, horse-drawn buggies, bicyclists; you could see the skaters at Wollman Rink, and you could see the outdoor cages of the Children's Zoo which was closed now; you could see the outcroppings of rock like miniature mountains; you could see the ponds glittering like mirrors laid flat; the park was still green, and seemed to go on forever; you could see to the very end at 110th Street (Momma told me the name of this distant street, which I had never seen close up); you could see the gleaming cross on the dome of the Cathedral of St John the Divine (Momma told me the name of this great cathedral, which I had never seen close up); our new apartment building was at 31 Central Park South and so we could see the Hudson River to the left, and the East River to the right; the sun appeared from the right, above the East River; the sun vanished to the left, below the Hudson River; we were floating above the street seventeen floors below; we were floating in the sky, Momma said; we were floating above Manhattan, Momma said; we were safe here, Momma said, and could not come to harm. But Momma was saying now in her sad angry voice, 'I wish you didn't have to go with – him. You won't cry, will you? You won't miss your Momma too much, will you?' I was staring at the thousand million snowflakes; I was excited waiting for Daddy to ring the bell at our front door; I was confused by Momma's questions because wasn't Momma me? so didn't Momma know? the answer to any question of Momma's, didn't Momma already know? 'I wish you didn't have to leave me, darling, but it's the terms of the agreement – it's the law.' These bitter words *It's the law* fell from Momma's lips each Saturday morning like something dropped in the apartment overhead! I waited to hear them, and I always did hear them. And then Momma leaned over me and kissed me; I loved Momma's sweet perfume and her soft-shining hair but I wanted to push away from her; I wanted to run to the door, to open it just as Daddy rang the bell; I wanted to surprise Daddy who took such happiness in being surprised; I wanted to say to Momma *I love Daddy better than I love you, let me go!* Because Momma was me, but Daddy was someone so different.

The doorbell rang. I ran to answer it. Momma remained in the front room at the window. Daddy hoisted me into his arms, 'How's my Princess? How's my Baby-Love?' and Daddy called out politely to Momma in the other room, whom he could not see, 'We're going to the Bronx Zoo, and we'll be back promptly at 5.30pm as agreed.' And Momma who was very dignified made no reply. Daddy called out, 'Goodbye! Remember us!' which was like Daddy, to say mysterious things, things to make you smile, and to make you wonder; things to make you confused, as if maybe you hadn't heard correctly but didn't want to ask. And Momma never asked. And in the elevator going down Daddy hugged me again saying how happy we were, just the two of us. He was the King, I was the Little Princess. Sometimes I was the Fairy Princess. Momma was the Ice Queen who never laughed. Daddy was saying this could be the happiest day of our lives if we had courage. A light shone in Daddy's eyes, there would never be a man so handsome and radiant as Daddy.

'Not the Bronx, after all. Not today, I don't think.'

Our driver that day was an Asian man in a smart visored cap, a neat dark uniform and gloves. The limousine was shiny black and larger than last week's and the windows dark-tinted so you could see *out* (but it was strange, a scary twilight even in the sun) but no one could see *in*. 'No plebeians knowing our business!' Daddy said, winking at me. 'No spies.' When we passed traffic policemen Daddy made faces at them, waggled his fingers at his ears and stuck out his tongue though they were only a few yards away; I giggled frightened Daddy would be seen and arrested but he couldn't be seen, of course – 'We're invisible, Princess! Don't worry.'

Daddy liked me to smile and laugh, not to worry; not ever, ever to cry. He'd had enough of crying, he said. He'd had it up to here (drawing a forefinger across his throat, like a knife blade) with crying, he said. He had older children, grown-up children I'd never met; I was his Little Princess, his Baby-Love, the only one of his children he did love, he said. Snatching my hand and kissing it, kiss-tickling so I'd squeal with laughter.

Now Daddy no longer drove his own car it was a time of rented cars. His enemies had taken his driver's licence from him to humiliate him in small, petty ways, he said. For they could not defeat him in any way that mattered. For he was too strong for them, and too smart.

It was a time of sudden reversals, changes of mind. I had been looking forward to the zoo, now we weren't going to the zoo but doing something else – 'you'll like just as much.' Other Saturdays, we'd driven through the park; the park had many surprises; the park went on forever; we would stop, and walk, run, play in the park; we'd fed the ducks and geese swimming on the ponds; we'd had lunch outdoors at Tavern on the Green; we'd had lunch outdoors at the boathouse; on a windy March day, Daddy had helped me fly a kite (which we'd lost – it broke, and blew away in shreds); there was the promise of skating at Wollman Rink sometime soon. Other Saturdays we'd driven north on Riverside Drive to the George Washington Bridge, and across the bridge, and back; we'd driven north to the Cloisters; we'd driven south to the very end of the island as Daddy called it – 'The great doomed island, Manhattan.' We'd crossed Manhattan Bridge into Brooklyn, we'd crossed the Brooklyn Bridge. We'd gazed up at the Statue of Liberty. We'd gone on a ferry ride in bouncy, choppy water. We'd had lunch at the top of the World Trade Center which was Daddy's favourite restaurant – 'Dining in the clouds! In heaven.' We'd gone to Radio City Music Hall, we'd seen *Beauty and the Beast* on Broadway; we'd seen the Big Apple Circus at Lincoln Center; we'd seen, the year before, the Christmas Spectacular at Radio City Music Hall. Our *Saturday adventures* left me dazed, giddy; one day I would realise that's what *intoxicated, high, drunk* means – I'd been drunk with happiness, with Daddy.

But no other *drunk*, ever afterward, could come near.

'Today, Princess, we'll buy presents. That's what we'll do – "store up riches".' Christmas presents? I asked.

'Sure. Christmas presents, any kind of presents. For you, and for me. Because we're special, you know.' Daddy smiled at me, and I waited for him to wink because sometimes (when he was on the car phone, for instance) he'd wink at me to indicate he was joking; for Daddy often joked; Daddy was a man who loved to laugh, as he described himself, and there wasn't enough to laugh at, unless he invented it. 'You know we are special, Princess, don't you? And all your life you'll remember your Daddy loves you? – that's the one true thing.'

Yes Daddy, I said. For of course it was so.

I should record how Daddy spoke on the phone, in the back seats of our rented cars.

How precise his words, how he enunciated his words, polite and cold and harsh; how, though he spoke calmly, his handsome face creased like a vase that has been cracked; his eyes squinted almost shut, and had no focus; a raw flush like sunburn rose from his throat. Then he would remember where he was, and remember *me*. And smile at me, winking and nodding, whispering to *me*; even as he continued his conversation with whoever was at the other end of the line, so remote from me, so unreal to me, these 'business associates' of Daddy's were not even mysterious to me but did not exist. And Daddy would say abruptly, 'That's enough!' and break the connection; Daddy would end the conversation when he was through, with no warning; Daddy would fit the plastic receiver back into the phone at the back of the seat, by the rear window; and forget completely whoever he'd been talking with, whatever their conversation, how urgent, how tense; 'That's enough!' were the magic words, the words I awaited; 'That's enough!' Daddy would say, and turn to *me*.

That wild day! Breakfast at the Plaza, and shopping at the Trump Tower, and a visit to the Museum of Modern Art where Daddy took me to see a painting precious to him, he said… We had been in the café at the Plaza before but this time Daddy couldn't get the table he requested, and something else was wrong – it wasn't clear to me what; I was nervous, and giggly; Daddy gave our orders to the waiter, but disappeared (to make another phone call?

to use the men's room? – if you asked Daddy where he went he'd say with a wink *That's for me to know, darlin', and you to find out*); a big plate of scrambled eggs and bacon was brought for me; eggs benedict was brought for Daddy; a stack of blueberry pancakes with warm syrup was brought for us to share; the silver pastry cart was pushed to our table; there were tiny jars of jams, jellies, marmalade for us to open; there were people at nearby tables observing us; I was accustomed, in Daddy's company, to being observed by strangers; I took such attention as my due, as Daddy's daughter; Daddy whispered, 'Let them get an eyeful, Princess.' Daddy ate quickly, hungrily; Daddy ate with a napkin tucked beneath his chin; Daddy saw that I wasn't eating much and asked was there something wrong with my breakfast; I told Daddy I wasn't hungry; Daddy asked if 'she' – meaning Momma – had made me eat, before he'd arrived; I told him no; I said I felt a little sickish; Daddy said, 'That's one of the Ice Queen's tactics – "sickish".' So I tried to eat, tiny pieces of pancakes that weren't soaked in syrup, and Daddy leaned his elbows on the table and watched me saying, 'And what if this is the last breakfast you'll ever have with your father, what then? Shame on you!' Waiters hovered near in their dazzling white uniforms. The mâitre d' was attentive, smiling. A call came for Daddy and he was gone for some time and when he returned flush-faced and distracted, his necktie loosened at his throat, it seemed that breakfast was over; hurriedly Daddy scattered $20 bills across the table, and hurriedly we left the café as everyone smiled and stared after us; we left the Plaza by the side entrance, on 58th Street, where the limousine awaited us; the silent Asian driver standing at the curb with the rear door open for Daddy to bundle me inside, and climb inside himself. We had hardly a block to go, to the elegant Trump Tower on Fifth Avenue; there we took escalators to the highest floor, where Daddy's eyes glistened with tears, everywhere he looked was so beautiful. Have I said my Daddy was smooth-shaven this morning, and smelled of a wintergreen cologne; he was wearing amber-tinted sunglasses, new to me; he was wearing a dark pinstriped double-breasted Armani suit and over it an Armani camel's hair coat with shoulders that made him appear more muscular than he was; he was wearing shiny black Italian shoes with a heel that made him appear taller than he was; Daddy's hair had been styled and blown dry so that it lifted from his head like something whipped, not lying flat, and not a dull flattish white as it had been but tinted now a pale russet colour; how handsome Daddy was! In the boutiques of Trump Tower Daddy bought me a dark blue velvet coat, and a pale blue angora cloche hat; Daddy bought me pale blue angora gloves; my old coat, my old gloves were discarded – 'Toss 'em, please!' Daddy commanded the sales-women. Daddy bought me a beautiful silk Hermès scarf to wrap around my neck, and Daddy bought me a beautiful white-gold wristwatch studded with tiny emeralds, that had to be made smaller, much smaller, to fit my wrist; Daddy bought me a 'keepsake' gold heart on a thin gold chain, a necklace; Daddy bought for himself a half-dozen beautiful silk neckties imported from Italy, and a kidskin wallet; Daddy bought a cashmere vest sweater for him-self, imported from Scotland; Daddy bought an umbrella, an attaché case, a handsome suitcase, imported from England, all of which he ordered to be delivered to an address in New Jersey; and other items Daddy bought for him-self, and for me. For all these wonderful presents Daddy paid in cash; in bills of large denominations; Daddy no longer used credit cards, he said; he refused to be a cog in the network of government surveillance, he said; they would not catch him in their net; he would not play their ridiculous games. In the Trump Tower there was a café beside a waterfall and Daddy had a glass of wine in the café, though he chose not to sit down at a table; he was too rest-less, he said, to sit down at a table; he was in too much of a hurry. Descending then the escalators to the ground floor, where a cool breeze lifted to touch our heated faces; I was terribly excited in my lovely new clothes, and wearing my lovely jewellery; except for Daddy gripping my hand – 'Care-ful, Princess!' – I would have stumbled at the foot of the escalator. And outside on Fifth Avenue there were so many people, tall rushing rude people who took no notice of me even in my new velvet coat and angora hat, I would have been knocked down on the sidewalk except for Daddy gripping my hand, pro-tecting me. Next we went – we walked – and the limousine followed – to the Museum of Modern Art where again there was a crowd, again I was breath-less riding escalators, I was trapped behind tall people seeing legs, the backs of coats, swinging arms; Daddy lifted me to his shoulder and carried me, and brought me into a large, airy room; a room of unusual proportions; a room not so crowded as the others; there were tears in Daddy's eyes as he held me in his arms – his arms that trembled just slightly – to gaze at an enormous painting – several paintings – broad beautiful dreamy-blue paintings of a pond, and waterlilies; Daddy told me that these paintings were by a very great French artist named 'Mon-ay' and that there was magic in them; he told me that these paintings made him comprehend his own soul, or what his soul had been meant to be; for as soon as you left the presence of such beauty, you were lost in the crowd; you were devoured by the crowd; it would be charged against you that it was your own fault but in fact – 'They don't let you be good, Princess. The more you have, the more they want from you. They eat you alive. Cannibals.'

When we left the museum, the snowflakes had ceased to fall. In the busy Manhattan streets there was no memory of them now. A bright harsh sun shone down almost vertically between the tall buildings but everywhere else was shadow, without colour, and cold.

By late afternoon Daddy and I had shopped at Tiffany & Co, and Bergdorf Goodman, and Saks, and Bloomingdale's; we had purchased beautiful expensive items to be delivered to us at an address in New Jersey – 'On the far side of the River Styx.' One purchase, at Steuben on Fifth Avenue, was a foot-high glass sculpture that might have been a woman, or an angel, or a wide-winged bird; it shone with light, so that you could almost not see it; Daddy laughed saying, 'The Ice Queen! – exactly'; and so this present was sent to Momma at 31 Central Park South. As we walked through the great glittering stores Daddy held my hand so that I would not be lost from him; these great stores, Daddy said, were the cathedrals of America; they were the shrines and reliquaries and catacombs of America; if you could not be happy in such stores, you could not be happy anywhere; you could not be a true American. And Daddy recited stories to me, some of these were fairy tales he'd read to me when I'd been a little little girl, a baby; when Daddy had lived with Momma and me, the three of us in a brownstone house with our own front door, and no doorman and no elevators; on our ground-floor windows there were curving iron bars, so that no one could break in; there were electronic devices of all kinds, so that no one could break in; our house had two trees at the curb, and these, too, were protected by curving iron bars; we lived in a narrow, quiet street a half-block from a huge, important building – the Metropolitan Museum of Art; when Daddy had been on television sometimes, and his photograph in the papers; they would say I knew nothing about this, I was too young to know, but I did; I knew. Just as I knew it was strange for Daddy to be paying for our presents with cash from his wallet, and out of thick-stuffed envelopes in his inside coat pockets; it was strange, for no one else paid in such a way; and others stared at him; stared at him as if memorising him – the vigour of his voice and his shining face and his knowledge that he, and I, who was his daughter, were set off from the dull, dreary ordinariness of the rest of the world; they stared, they were envious of us, though smiling, always smiling, if Daddy glanced at them, or spoke with them. For such was Daddy's power.

I was dazed with exhaustion; I was feverish; I could not have said how long Daddy and I had been shopping, on our Saturday adventure; yet I loved it, that strangers observed us, and remarked how pretty I was; and to Daddy sometimes they would say *Your face is familiar, are you on TV?* But Daddy just laughed and kept moving for there was no time to spare that day.

Out on the street, one of the wide, windy avenues, Daddy hailed a cab like any other pedestrian. When had he dismissed the limousine? – I couldn't remember. It was a bumpy, jolting ride. The rear seat was torn. There was no heat. In the rearview mirror a pair of liquidy black eyes regarded Daddy with silent contempt. Daddy fumbled paying the fare, a $50 bill slipped from his fingers – 'Keep the change, driver, and thanks!' Yet even then the eyes did not smile at us, these were not eyes to be purchased.

We were in a dark, tiny wine cellar on 47th Street near Seventh Avenue where Daddy ordered a carafe of red wine for himself and a soft drink for me and where he could make telephone calls in a private room at the rear; I fell asleep, and when I woke up there was Daddy standing by our table, too restless to sit; his face was rubbery, and looked stretched; his hair had fallen, and lay in damp strands against his forehead; globules of sweat like oily pearls ran down his cheeks. He smiled with his mouth saying, 'There you are, Princess! Up and at 'em.' For already it was time to leave, and more than time. Daddy had learned from an aide the bad news, the news he'd been expecting. But shielding me from it of course. For only much later – years later – would I learn that, that afternoon, a warrant for Daddy's arrest had been issued by the Manhattan district attorney's office; by some of the very people for whom, until a few months ago, Daddy had worked. It would be charged against him that as a prosecuting attorney Daddy had misused the powers of his office, he had solicited and accepted bribes, he had committed perjury upon numerous occasions, he had falsely informed upon certain persons under investigation by the district attorney's office, he had blackmailed others, he had embezzled funds... such charges were made against Daddy, such lies concocted by his enemies who had been jealous of him for many years and wanted him defeated, destroyed. One day I would learn that New York City Police detectives had come to Daddy's apartment (on East 92nd Street and

First Avenue) to arrest him and of course hadn't found him; they'd gone to 31 Central Park South and of course hadn't found him; Momma told them Daddy had taken me to the Bronx Zoo, or in any case that had been his plan; Momma told them that Daddy would be bringing me back home at 5.30pm, or in any case he'd promised to do so; if they waited for him in the lobby downstairs would they please please not arrest him in front of his daughter, Momma begged. Yet policemen were sent to the Bronx Zoo to search for Daddy there; a manhunt for Daddy at the Bronx Zoo! – how Daddy would have laughed. And now an alert was out in Manhattan for Daddy, he was a 'wanted' man, but already Daddy had shrewdly purchased a new coat in Saks, a London Fog trench coat the shade of damp stone, and made arrangements for the store to deliver his camel's hair coat to the New Jersey address; already Daddy had purchased a grey fedora hat, and he'd exchanged his amber-tinted sunglasses for darker glasses, with heavy black plastic frames; he'd purchased a knotty gnarled cane, imported from Australia, and walked now with a limp – I stared at him, almost I didn't recognise him, and Daddy laughed at me. In the Shamrock Pub on Ninth Avenue and 39th Street he'd engaged a youngish blonde woman with hair braided in cornrows to accompany us while he made several other stops; the blonde woman had a glaring-bright face like a billboard; her eyes were ringed in black and lingered on me – 'What a sweet, pretty little girl! And what a pretty coat and hat!' – but she knew not to ask questions. She walked with me gripping my hand in the angora glove pretending she was my momma and I was her little girl, and Daddy behind hobbling on his cane; shrewdly a few yards behind so it would not have seemed (if anyone was watching) that Daddy was with us; this was a game we were playing, Daddy said; it was a game that made me excited, and nervous; I was laughing and couldn't stop; the blonde woman scolded me – 'Shhh! Your Daddy will be angry.' And a little later the blonde woman was gone.

Always in Manhattan, on the street I wonder if I'll see her again. *Excuse me* I will cry out *do you remember? That day, that hour?* But it's been years.

So exhausted! Daddy scolded me carrying me out of the taxi, into the lobby of the Hotel Pierre; a beautiful old hotel on Fifth Avenue and 61st Street, across from Central Park; Daddy booked a suite for us on the sixteenth floor; you could look from a window to see the apartment building on Central Park South where Momma and I lived; but none of that was very real to me now; it wasn't real to me that I had a Momma, but only a Daddy. And once we were inside the suite Daddy bolted the door and slid the chain lock in place. There were two TVs and Daddy turned them both on. He turned on the ventilator fans in all the rooms. He took the telephone receivers off their hooks. With a tiny key he unlocked the mini-bar and broke open a little bottle of whiskey and poured it into a glass and quickly drank. He was breathing hard, his eyes moving swiftly in their sockets yet without focus. 'Princess! Get up *please*. Don't disappoint your Daddy *please*.' I was lying on the floor, rolling my head from side to side. But I wasn't crying. Daddy found a can of sweetened apple juice in the mini-bar and poured it into a glass and added something from another little bottle and gave it to me saying, 'Princess, this is a magic potion. Drink!' I touched my lips to the glass but there was a bitter taste. Daddy said, 'Princess, you must obey your Daddy.' And so I did. A hot hurting sensation spread in my mouth and throat and I started to choke and Daddy pressed the palm of his hand over my mouth to quiet me; it was then I remembered how long ago when I'd been a silly little baby Daddy had pressed the palm of his hand over my mouth to quiet me. I was sickish now, and I was frightened; but I was happy, too; I was drunk with happiness from all we'd done that day, Daddy and me; for I had never had so many presents before; I had never understood how special I was, before; and afterward when they asked if I'd been afraid of my Daddy I would say no! no I hadn't been! not for a minute! I love my Daddy I would say, and my Daddy loves me. Daddy was sitting on the edge of the big bed, drinking; his head lowered almost to his knees. He was muttering to himself like he was alone – 'Fuckers! Wouldn't let me be good. Now you want to eat my heart. But not *me*.' Later I was wakened to something loud on the TV. Except it was a pounding at the door. And men's voices calling 'Police! Open up, Mr —' – saying Daddy's name as I'd never heard it before. And Daddy was on his feet, Daddy had his arm around me. Daddy was excited and angry and he had a gun in his hand – I knew it was a gun, I'd seen pictures of guns! – this was bluish-black and shiny, with a short barrel – and he was waving the gun as if the men on the other side of the door could see him; there was a film of sweat on his face catching the light, like facets of diamonds; I had never seen my Daddy so furious calling to the policemen – 'I've got my little girl here, my daughter – and I've got a gun.' But they were pounding at the door; they were breaking down the door; Daddy fired the gun into the air and pulled me into another room where the TV was loud but there were no lights; Daddy pushed me down, panting; the two of us on the carpet, panting. I was too scared to cry, and I started to wet my pants; in the other room the policemen were calling to Daddy to surrender his weapon, not to hurt anyone but to surrender his weapon and come with them now; and Daddy was sobbing shouting 'I'll use it, I'm not afraid – I'm not going to prison – I can't! – I can't do it! – I've got my little girl here, you understand?' – and the policemen were on the other side of the doorway but wouldn't show themselves saying to Daddy he didn't want to hurt his daughter, of course he didn't want to hurt his daughter; he didn't want to hurt himself, or anyone; he should surrender his weapon now, and come along quietly with the officers; he would speak with his lawyer; he would be all right; and Daddy was cursing, and Daddy was crying, and Daddy was crawling on his hands and knees on the carpet trying to hold me, and the gun; we were crouched in the farthest darkest corner of the room by the heating unit; the ventilator fan was throbbing; Daddy was hugging me and crying, his breath was hot on my face; I tried to push out of Daddy's arms but Daddy was too strong calling me Princess! Little Princess! saying I knew he loved me didn't I. The magic potion had made me sleepy and sickish, it was hard for me to stay awake. By now I had wetted my panties, my legs were damp and chafed. A man was talking to Daddy in a loud clear voice like a TV voice and Daddy was listening or seemed to be listening and sometimes Daddy would reply and sometimes not; how much time passed like this, how many hours – I didn't know; not until years later would I learn it had been an hour and twelve minutes but at the time I hadn't any idea, I wasn't always awake. The voices kept on and on; men's voices; one of them saying repeatedly, 'Mr —, surrender your weapon, will you? Toss it where we can see it, will you?' and Daddy wiped his face on his shirt sleeve, Daddy's face was streaked with tears like something melting set too near a fire, and still the voice said, calmly, so loud it seemed to come from everywhere at once, 'Mr —, you're not a man to harm a little girl, we know you, you're a good man, you're not a man to harm anyone,' and suddenly Daddy said, 'Yes! Yes that's right.' And Daddy kissed me on the side of the face and said, 'Goodbye, Princess!' in a high, happy voice; and pushed me away from him; and Daddy placed the barrel of the gun deep inside his mouth. And Daddy pulled the trigger.

So it ended. It always ends. But don't tell me there isn't happiness. It exists, it's there. You just have to find it, and you have to keep it, if you can. It won't last, but it's there.

SEXUAL PERVERSITY IN NEW YORK

Steve Grant

When Harvey Roast went to New York they told him the violence would kill him. But it was the sex, it was always the sex. They actually try and rob you at the fucking airport, Winston from accounts had said. The cab drivers don't speak English, don't know where they're going, carry guns and, when they get robbed, they get their eyes gouged out, offered Debrah from classifieds. But at least you can persuade them to let you smoke in them, she added for reassurance. Try it anywhere else and you'll be castrated with a blunt coffee spoon. The thing about the yobs, he heard from Dunblane, one of the reps who'd claimed to have lived 'in the States' for a twelve-month period, is that they really are extremely bloody hard, Harvey old mate, old feller me lad, they really do look like they've just stepped out of the ring after going ten rounds with Mike Tyson. They all look like Mike Tyson. Except for the ones who look like Spike Lee, they're even worse, they carry switchblades, or they do martial arts, or they use drain-scourer to clean out people's insides. Even Harvey's mother-in-law chipped in: under Grand Central Station there are whole tribes of nomadic winos and derelicts who survive by killing and eating rats that are the size of cats, by doing battle with cockroaches and giant spiders, and alligators and iguanas and... It didn't really help that his mother-in-law was now as nutty as Mr Rochester's first wife. Bellamy, his immediate superior, put the tin lid on it: you've seen that film, *The Warriors*, right? Gangs clash by night across the subway system? Walter Hill, you seen it, right? Pure fucking realism, old mate, pure fucking realism... And remember, always look down. Don't look them in the eye, people are crazy there, really crazy, whirling-dervish crazy, seeing-through-walls crazy.

But when Harvey got to JFK, he found no muggers, no diminutive black men clutching Sanilav canisters with intent to maim, no Tyson lookalikes, unless you counted the large and cheerful customs man who complimented him on his American name. ('No actually I was named after an Australian cricketer called Neil... no, forget it, thank you so much, er, André.') He found a stretch limousine, in the compartment behind the driver there was a small black fridge, a pair of vintage champagne magnums, a 12-inch television and a selection of sushi on a bed of ice. 'Violence is bullshit,' said Maurice, his driver.

'Just don't go near Mount Morris Park, night or day, stay out of the Bronx and don't order a black and tan in a Mick bar. You'll survive.' Maurice told him that he used to work in LA, same kinda job, ferrying movie stars about. 'That Belushi guy, I took him to the Chateau Marmont the time he checked out for good, know what I mean?' Harvey decided that Maurice was probably full of shit, but at least he knew the way.

And there was the car, which was a beauty. Harvey thought of the last time he'd seen an interior like this: it was a porn film over at best friend FitzGerald's. Two girls, a Wall Street high-roller and a chauffeur built like a prize bull, had got up to all sorts in just such a rig. Moisturising cream, a white dildo, a silk cord, a bowler hat, he remembered curiously. The women looked gorgeous. The men looked smug. He was sure it was New York, but doubted whether the locations had been thoroughly scouted.

'Do you know that Paraguayan revolutionary proverb?' asked Maurice, who was a Jew, not Jewish mind, a Jew. Harvey was distracted by his notes for the meeting at the Royalton with Toys 'R' Us, a big one, notes he could have digested on the plane if he hadn't been so busy digesting the beef stroganoff and the blue-label Vladivar vodka. 'I beg your pardon,' he muttered. Maurice actually wore a fucking admiral's cap. 'Paraguayan proverb. In times of war, every hole is a trench. Naaaargggggghh.' Maurice let out one of those Kalashnikov laughs. I should have turned on the TV, Harvey thought, too late. 'Every hole is a trench. Geddit. Hole, pussy, trench, hole, pussy, trench.'

'Are you talking about sex?' Harvey enquired. Who did this Yank think he was, Arthur Miller? 'I'm happily married, thank you'. 'But she ain't here, is she?' the driver laughed. 'This is a hot town, buddy, this is a hot town. This ain't England, this is New York, and you're at war, buddy, and this is the biggest fucking trench you will ever see. Naaaaargggggghh.' Oh sure, Harvey thought. No sex, we're British. He wanted to tell the driver that the Limeys had come a long way, so to speak, that London had sex-shops of its own, and women who could suck a billiard ball through a length of garden hose, and could do things with a cup of tea and a rack of ice cubes that no Big Apple Tart could ever come close to, so to speak, and that English women who also happened to be Swedish, Australian, Thai, Sudanese, Bahamian, Spanish, Serbian, and even American, were some of the best he'd ever come across, so to speak. But he didn't. All he said was: 'You've got a point.'

*

Roast got an electric shock when he opened the door of his hotel suite somewhere level with Mount Everest on Sixth and 46th Street. He'd mention it at the lobby desk but seemed to have been beaten to the bleat by a diminutive and super-irate African who was babbling something about 'CIA bastards' (two days later, the same man would ask Roast if an ornamental structure in the Frederick of Prussia Lounge was a fireplace, but that's neither here nor there). The nice lady at the desk explained that the 'mild tingling effect' was caused by static from 'floorsurfaces' and could be avoided by wiping one's hands up and down on wood. She suggested the door, or, presumably if he was leaving and had just indulged in a vigorous bout of running-on-the-spot, the TV set. 'CIA bastards,' Roast muttered as he returned to the elevator, where the numbers of floors danced before his eyes like configurations in an impromptu lottery draw, before the whole thing clinged to a halt. Five minutes later in his room he had given up on the TV; 38 channels and most of them showing commercials, ads for all kinds of home medical treatments. Are you worried about bowel cancer? What kind of question was that? He headed for the pristine toilet and bathroom, complete with whirlpool, steam-proof wall-phone and 12-inch TV. He looked at the colour of his shit, hhhm, must have been that Burgundy he had on the plane, or was it still gushing its way through bodily customs and excise. Anyway, it wasn't excrement in the proper sense, more like misshapen sludge pats. And the smell. Indescribable. He hadn't gagged on the like of it since that night on the Bass when the smell of his own shit had made him vomit.

Maurice rang the number from a call box on Broadway across the road from the Lincoln Center where he had once held an Oscar statuette and later fallen asleep on a tour of the library. A voice answered: 'The young lady does Sex, French, Greek, Fellatio, Cunnilingus, Sixty-nine… it's forty dollars for the half-hour, one hundred dollars for the full hour, anything else you can discuss with the young lady in private.' He always liked to hear Dolores saying it; the Grand Central announcer's voice, the strange emphases on 'Sixty-NINE' and 'FULL hour', the suggestion that there was anything else to discuss, although he knew that there was. One perverted bastard, a teacher at Juiliard would you believe, had once resquested that one of the girls lie on the bed with her butt pointing at the ceiling and her head buried in the pillow. After ten minutes she realised he'd gone, but not before crapping in her purse. 'Dolly. It's Mo!' 'Hey, Mo, what's up?' Mo had taken Dolores under his wing since Jack had perished in the armed robbery, which had been so awful, so disgusting, so sheerly and wantonly brutal that it even made the inside front page of the *News*; the lowlife in question had done it for change; then after stealing the change they had made him get out of the cab and beat up on him, before shooting him through both eyes. It turned out that they were Haitians, voodoo cats, and the eye stuff was down to this crazy idea that the killer's image was planted on the eyeball after death. Jack should never have taken the fare, but he was that kind of guy, tough, resolute, easygoing, with a pit-bull's worth of confidence even after being thrown out of the trucking business for an excess of honesty. Jack had made a real go of it as a yellow-cab man, then this had to happen, and Dolores, his younger sister by three years, had tried to take over the job herself but had buckled at the first sign of trouble, the first scumbag, the first loudmouth, the first sex pest. Instead Dolores had started booking calls for an escort agency based in Queens, the Shangrila, a job she had acquired with ease through the family connections with the sex trade acquired by ferrying hookers to their clients. Maurice wasn't at all happy with this arrangement, but she got tips, the girls were mostly okay because if they fucked up they were out, and the kickbacks were carried out of the premises. 'There's this Limey guy right, shy, guilty, married, bored, nervous, first time in New York, wants some company, doesn't want to get laid, sells soft toys, has a big day tomorrow, wants to relax, wants to see a ball game, wants someone to take him, explain what's going on, you don't even have to fuck him if you don't want to. It's a class gig, why waste it on the girls, the guy's talking big bucks, a thousand for a few hours' work, and maybe no extra innings.'

Harvey Roast sat in Katz's Deli on Houston staring at the most enormous sandwich he had ever seen. To his left two waiters, if you could call them that, were scrapping over where which customers sat, literally fighting like two very angry footballers who'd momentarily forgotten the code of 'handbags at five paces'. In the basement, an extremely skinny and wizened old man was beating off by the washbasins; as seemed inevitable, his dick was the size of a baby's arm and his expression beatific as if to say, 'Hey, would you want to do anything else on a day like this?' Outside in the street, two black men were lobbing empty bottles in the direction of passing vehicles.

'Send a salami to your boy in the army.' Dolores had mentioned this place, it was a Jewish institution she said, hangout of mobsters and poets, she said. Now he was contemplating this gargantuan slab of rye bread, salt beef, cheese and sauerkraut, the dill the size of the basement man's cock, and wandering what had happened to his career. The baseball had gone well: he'd been underdressed of course, it became cold very quickly, and even though she'd recommended they buy seats in the very upper tier, he'd nearly been hit by a wild swing on two occasions. All round him, braying pubescent Mets fans had invaded his space, had leapt with gloves in their hand to catch the pill as it sped upwards and towards him like some overweight bullet thudding through space.

'Jesus Christ, I could have lost a fucking eye!' Harvey had exclaimed, then apologised as Dolores glared, stared and then went slightly peculiar on him. Was it the bad language, surely she wasn't religious? They had left the game in the eighth inning, which was important said Dolores, it wasn't 'innings', there was no 's', 'not like cricket' Harvey had offered, wondering whether he should tell her about being named after Neil Harvey, the stylish Australian left-hander who had toured with Bradman's all-conquerors the year he'd been born. He didn't; he doubted if Dolores knew or cared very much about cricket, although her enthusiasm for baseball was undoubted. She'd never explained pinch-hitting or bases on balls to him. They took the train from the stadium back to Grand Central, then he suggested dinner. She picked some grossly expensive Louisiana-style restaurant, all gumbo, charred meats, catfish, mint juleps, love-seats, eager waitresses in ante-bellum costume. He hadn't told her about his wife, she hadn't asked him about his wife. 'Is it true half the men in New York are gay?' he asked. She laughed and lit up a Camel Light; he wasn't sure but she might have been blowing smoke in his face. She told him about some of the girls at work. One of them, an extremely tall and skinny redhead had been hired by a rich movie producer who lived in the upper sixties, near to the Carlyle and the Met, real Woody Allen territory full of people walking dogs by the dozen. She had been asked to strip, kneel on all fours with her back to the fireplace. Then the guy had brought in a beautifully groomed Afghan hound, the colour of vanilla ice-cream. He had pointed at the woman and shouted: 'So, Anton, ziss iss vot you vill look like if you do not eat your chopped liver and rusks!' He had laughed, surely she was making this up.

He told her about Fitzgerald, his best friend since university, an habitual adulterer who cheated on Penelope, his wife of eighteen years, every time he drew breath, and with any woman who had a pulse it seemed: the students at his college, casuals he met in bars and clubs when he was supposed to be working late, massage parlour girls that he paid by cheque and credit card, so regular was his custom. Even the Italian nanny, who left early one Christmas and didn't return. Of course, he said, Penelope was the last person to know. 'How can you live with yourself,' she'd suddenly asked. 'In what way?' he'd replied, mulling over the devilled scallops. 'Why, the fact that you are conniving at what this guy is doing. Presumably you know this woman, you visit her house, presumably your wife knows this woman, and so because of some crappy concept of male camaraderie you allow this woman to risk disease, to live a lie, to look after this bastard's children while he's screwing their life savings away or balling women young enough to be his daughter who are probably only going with him to get decent grades.' Jesus, this was going badly. 'It's a point of view. But he's a mate.' 'He's a what. A mate? She's his mate, how can you do that to another human being?' 'Look, I'm not doing anything, for…' Jesus, this Maurice, this limo driver, had a lot to answer for. Trust me, she's my sister and would a good Jewish boy introduce you to his sister if she was a ball-buster? Or a tease?

Now he was sitting in Katz's Deli and he couldn't eat, he couldn't go back to his hotel room, couldn't ring his office, couldn't ring Pamela. What could he tell them? That he'd dumped Dolores in the street, had walked fiercely back to his hotel and drunk the entire contents of the mini-bar, give or take the odd tomato juice. He'd fallen asleep and waking at eight-fifteen with a head as thick as marmalade had walked to Times Square, drank a black coffee and decided that he had to do something to ease all the tension before his meeting at ten am. He'd walked furtively into the Xerena Xerena Sex Arena and found it almost deserted and smelling of disinfectant. He'd needed tokens for the cubicles and had found a five-dollar bill which the bored hippy at the reception changed into shiny coins while simultaneously looking at a really foul magazine that was devoted to the tastes of pig-lovers. Roast had glimpsed a picture of an attractive blonde in bed with a full-sized porker. Jesus. Will you still love me when I'm old and grey?

The booth was clean enough and the lock worked; there was a stool fixed to the floor, an even more pronounced smell of floor cleaner, Jesus what a job he thought, and a small television with what seemed to be a bewildering assortment of channels. Only in America. Thankfully it was almost all straight stuff, hard core, co-eds going down on an older man with the languorous intensity of geishas, a frantically fucking woman of mixed racial origins, definitely a screamer, a mature woman going at it by the banisters with her afternoon lover who had a beard and smoked a pipe, a man on a beach giving head to a disgustingly fit and leggy blonde, a gang-bang involving Latino women and WASP adolescents in which the men wore stockings over their heads and all the women taking it keenly in whatever orifice was available. This was different from London; this wasn't Dolores with her talk of moral codes; or Maurice with his bullshit about Belushi; this wasn't his skyscraper hotel where you had to check out hours in advance to make sure of getting out on time; or the Royalton where he had to meet the man from Toys 'R' Us and which seemed to him from a preview skim like the sort of place David Bowie would go to when he died. This was the real thing. He twisted in his seat trying to control his erection and flip the channels with his free hand while keeping an eye out for the change situation. He decided to go with the co-eds, the languorous sucking, the Asian teenager and the Mid-West nymph politely joshing like infants stuck with the same toffee-apple. During the sweet course, Dolores had 'fessed up: about her husband who was a long-term cheat, how the night he'd gone out for the last time she was going to tell him to get the fuck out, and how three men had robbed him and beaten him and then shot out his eyes. He'd been irresistibly reminded of the bit in *Broadway Danny Rose* when Woody Allen asks Mia Farrow if her husband had been blinded by a similar deed. 'No, he was killed, they go right through.' He'd repeated the exchange and that was just about the end of the evening.

Enough of that. He'd done his business in the booth with only two tokens to spare, hoicked up his trousers, steadied himself and left with as little fuss as he could make. But he'd forgotten to look down. In New York, he'd been told, nobody looked up because they threw things from the high buildings and a ten-cent piece would go right though. But he didn't look down. And it finished him. The Toys 'R' Us man wasn't fooled and was very blunt. 'That's jism on your shoes, pal.' Jism? He looked down and saw what was undeniably a Jackson Pollock-style splash of semen scattered over both of his black leather brogues. 'It's frozen yoghurt,' he spluttered. I had some for breakfast and it must have…' 'Frozen yoghurt doesn't make those patterns, pal,' the man went on, like he was talking about strategic bombing or something. What was worse, he called for a second opinion. Roast was out, the contract was out, the cab driver that picked him up outside the Royalton looked an awful lot like Maurice.

SUZIE AND CHOO-CHOO'S DAY IN NEW YORK

Liz Jensen

Click.

Hi, Murray! Welcome home! *(Pause.)* Say, I'm feeling kinda shy now. *(Pause.)* Actually, just kidding there, Murray. Suzie Hagan, shy? And the moon is made of Roquefort cheese, right? Well Murray. Here we are. I speak, you listen. That's the deal here. *(Long pause. The sound of a cigarette being lit and smoke exhaled.)*

So where's Choo-Choo? I guess that's the billion-dollar question you're asking at this moment. Were you calling her name before you even opened the door of the apartment? *Hi, Choo! Hi, Choochie! Daddy's home!*

That would be kinda poignant.

How long before you found my little note on the coffee table, Murray? About one minute, max, I figured. Plus another ten seconds to put the cassette in the machine?

(The sound of a drink being sipped.)

So here we are. Together, and like, *not* together. You'd better sit down, Murray. Go settle in your orthopaedic chair. You suffer from executive back tension, right? I'm empathising with you here. So sit. It's kinda crazy, but I can't tell you about what happened to Choo-Choo unless I know your butt and spine are real comfortable.

(Pause.)

There's no nice way of putting this, Murray. I guess we cue the mournful music here. If I were more of a technical kind of person, I'd've tried to incorporate a bit of mixing into this tape, but in the end I just thought fuck it, tell it to him straight.

So here goes, Murray: your beloved companion is dead.

(Pause.)

I left that little pause, there, Murray, for it to sink in. All those questions that must be crowding your poor brain, Murray! Who? When? Where? What? Why? How? Believe it or not, Murray, I once began a course on how to be a journalist. That's where I learned about the five Ws and the H. I guess we could say that the H is the most complicated part of this story, Murray.

(Pause.)

Do help yourself to a cigarette, by the way. They're on that piece of hardwood furniture that I guess you'd call your buffet. (By the way, Murray: you sure have good taste.) I bought you menthols. I pictured you as a menthol smoker, I don't know why. You get these things in your head – *Murray Kaplan, the owner of this charming East Side apartment and this beautiful buffet, is a menthol smoker* – and they stay there. Go ahead; light up.

(Pause.)

The part about how I came to look after this place for a week, you already know. The friend-of-a-friend connection, right? The rest you'd never guess in a zillion years. So I'll just 'storyboard' it for you, shall I? I always wanted to get into advertising myself. Do you enjoy it, Murray, as a career? I would. If you said to me – Suze, have you ever thought about getting a job in advertising? I'd say, no hesitation, well thanks, Murray, I'll start, like, *yesterday*!

(Pause.)

Actually – here comes a confession – I'm not completely sure what a storyboard is. I just kinda like the sound of it. Like a story but with pictures in a sort of sequence, right? Or am I way off the mark? I'm calling this one 'Suzie and Choo-Choo's Day in New York'.

(Pause.)

I watched a whole shit-load of TV, Murray, as a kid. To like escape from stuff? Anyway, New York was a place on TV for me till now. I must've watched *New York, New York* a hundred times. Call me a sucker for clichés, but Liza Minelli just really got my imagination working away there. Red stilettoes, fur coats, no panties kinda image. *If you can make it there you'll make it anywhere*, right? *Start spreadin' the news.* Then you'd see all this stuff about Andy Warhol, and street violence, and Woody Allen, and Harlem, and Wall Street, and you'd think: hey, we're talking about one big fucked-up can of worms here!

Hey, Murray: I can hear you saying, *get on with it, Suze. You're veering off the storyboard! Tell me how Choo-Choo died! Who the fuck killed my dog?* No kidding; I really can.

(Pause.)

That pause was just to irritate you, Murray.

(Pause. Sound of drink being sipped. Exhalation of smoke.)

Hey. I got a real lip-smacking proposition for ya. Shall we gaze out of your apartment window together at that classic, world-famous Manhattan skyline? Like, now? Yes! Rise from your chair and look out across those wild inky-twinkling city lights, Murray!

(Long pause.)

You there? You standing at the window? Hey. *(Pause.)* Feel the throb of that great pulse, Murray. *(Pause.)* And see the sky darken.

(Pause.)

I am trying to evoke something here, Murray, with this image. *(Pause.)* Gotham means *goat-town*, Murray, according to my guide-book, because everyone's insane, and descended from a creature with a cloven hoof.

Chew on that, Murray, while I go get another drink.

(Long pause.)

Right, Murray, let's take 'Suzie and Choo-Choo's Day in New York' from the top. The storyboard thing, Murray, goes like this: a friend of a friend asks a blonde Californian woman, via the friend's friend, to look after his apartment and his Pyrenean Wolf Hound on East 63rd Street while he is off filming a feminine hygiene commercial in Key West. Coming from Fresno, the raisin capital of the world ('Raisinville', to its many cynical detractors), she isn't going to turn down an offer of a week in the Big Apple lightly. Especially not just after she's come out of rehab. The owner of the apartment (that's you, Murray, in case you're feeling kinda confused), he leaves in the morning, and my flight from LA arrives in the afternoon; I'm supposed to pick up the keys from the janitor and take Choo-Choo out for her Needs (that's what it says in the letter you left me, Murray, cringe at the memory if you will: her Needs) as soon as I arrive. Then – RELAX AND ENJOY! Says the letter.

(Pause. Rustling of paper.)

It also says, and I'm quoting to you verbatim now because I happen to have it in front of me:

NO LOUD MUSIC, NO FRIED ONIONS IN APARTMENT. (Hey. Would I fry onions?)

TWICE-DAILY WALKS: TAKE LEASH AND POOPER-SCOOPER (cringe, Murray!); DISPOSE OF DOO-DOO (cringe again, Murray!) IN COURTESY TOILETTES.

PUT TRASH OUT ON THURSDAYS AND SATURDAYS. ALUMINIUM RECYCLING WEDNESDAY 10AM.

KEY TO COMMUNAL GYM WITH JANITOR.

PS – NB: JANITOR CROSS-DRESSER.

The mind boggled a bit there, Murray.

(Pause.)

Hey, let's go for a little cameo of this woman now, Murray, this Suzie Hagan who has taken over your apartment while you're filming your tasteful crotch shots in Florida. Not bad-looking, though a close inspection reveals that she's over forty. And not nearly as sophisticated and glamorous as our mutual friend-of-a-friend made out she was on the phone. It's a kind of Chinese Whispers thing. I get transformed from Suze Hagan, formerly Jurgensen, formerly Lee, formerly Underwood, now single again, failure, just out of rehab, into a San Franciscan academic. *Right!*

(Long pause.)

Yeah. Guess that's the cameo over.

(Pause.)

The first thing that happens when Suzie's shown the way to the apartment by the janitor – hey, a man dressing as himself, Murray, or a woman in drag? You didn't specify the original sex – the first thing that happens to our heroine, a bit spaced-out after her long flight from San Francisco, changing at St Louis – she's barely turned the key in the lock, she's barely set foot in the apartment for Chrissakes – the first thing is, there's a scuffle.

Woah! It's, like, the Hound of the Baskervilles?

'Down, Choo-Choo!' yells the janitor. Then retreats. 'See ya, lady!' It's an ambivalent voice, so Suze is still none the wiser on the gender issue here.

(Pause.)

Yeah. *Down*, Choo-Choo. Choo-Choo is supposed to be female, but she's all over Suzie Hagan. Virtually raping her. So I guess sexual confusion reigns supreme on our storyboard for a moment, Murray. The cross-dressing janitor followed by the lesbian bestiality scene, right?

(Pause.)

Now a kinda backstory thing for you here, Murray: Suzie doesn't like dogs, they scare her, 'cos there was one once bit her on the thigh back in Fresno. She's still got the scar, she shows it to the men she sleeps with as a kind of *après*-sex peep show. And sometimes, get this, Murray, kinda in return, they let her hunt for their vasectomy scars, if they have them, and sometimes even if they haven't, if you can picture that, Murray? But she wasn't saying that to the friend of the friend, was she? About not liking dogs. The deal was, she'd feed Choochie and take her walkies. So here's Choo-Choo slobbering and yelping, like Lassie does when there's an emergency, like she might in fact be transmitting the words 'full' and 'bladder' on her doggie psychic frequency. *Needs*, you call them, right?

I'll be honest here, Murray: Suzie tries to ignore it at first. Pats Choochie gingerly on the head, then starts snooping about the place – I'm only human, Murray – checking things out. *Nice* ornaments, Murray. Real tasteful *buffet*. *Good*-sized TV. *Classy* clothes. I'm guessing here, but are all the valuables in the safe?

(Pause.)

Can I freshen your drink for you there, Suzie? Why, sure, thank you.

(Sound of drink being poured).

Then, Murray, somewhere between her third and fourth highball, Suzie starts feeling kinda mad at the dog. She'd been looking forward to relaxing, getting used to the apartment, getting high, watching a little TV – but this Choo-Choo creature's getting real insistent. Won't let her alone. Keeps licking her, and sniffing her pussy, and all that stuff that makes you want to chuck your drink in its face – not that you would, of course. Or if you did, you'd make sure to get the carpet valeted when you left, at a total cost of fifty-nine dollars, not cheap. Anyway, there obviously won't be any peace here until Choo-Choo has had her walkies, you don't need to be a canine psychologist to spot that.

Right!

So I say, 'Okay, Choochie. Walkies. We're going to see the sights of New York. Statue of Liberty. The Empire State. Starting at Central Park.' I figured she'd recognise the word *park*. Central Park is *the world's most famous urban oasis*, according to the guidebook. It's just a few blocks away. Suzie's fantasised about this, in rehab in Fresno. Taking a dog for a walk, and maybe meeting a cute guy, in *the world's most famous urban oasis*.

Catching the *touristo* vibes, Choo-Choo goes and fetches her own leash, and indicates the pooper-scooper, a cross between a shovel and a mousetrap.

'I'm not taking that,' says Suzie.

Hey. She takes it.

(Pause.)

We've gone *exterior* on the storyboard now, Murray. We're *outside*. Well, we walk up East Sixty-Third, and we cross Fifth Avenue, and we enter Central Park at someplace called Grand Army Plaza, according to *el mappo*. So far, so okay, though it's kinda *hot*, and kinda *crowded*. In Central Park, Suzie absorbs various New York phenomena, Murray. Grimy old trees, exposed human flesh, Nikes, personal stereo systems, a whole shit-load of airplanes crossing, like, *let's get the fuck outa this crazy place, man!* She watches some potato-chip wrappers whirling about in the wind for a while. That sure is nice. She checks out the asses on the Roller-bladers, and judges them, pound for pound, to be way inferior to their West Coast equivalents. Too bad, Suze.

(Pause.)

When I go to the supermarket back in Fresno, Murray, this thing happens, like the shopping trolley always wheels me directly to the cookie aisle. And then heads for the booze? It's the same with Choo-Choo; I'm being dragged along against my will here. In the direction of the canine equivalent of carbohydrate and alcohol. Yeah: other dogs and their shit. You got it!

And the attraction is mutual; the creature's butt is, like, a *magnet*.

(Pause.)

Okay, Murray: I can hear you getting agitated here. I can hear you yelling at me, *How did she die? How did she fucking die, man?* Patience, Murray. I'm getting there.

It's near this big clutch of trees that's like a lunchtime kissing and groping area for humans, that Choo-Choo starts limping. Actually, if we're being precise here, it's then that Choo-Choo's limp is pointed out by a fellow dog-walker. It's a little old lady, expensive clothes. She's got this Chihuahua. I don't like Chihuahuas. There was one I met back in Fresno, tried to mate with my artificial fur handbag, and left a smear of an unspeakably gross substance on it.

'Your dog has a syringe stuck in her paw,' she says.

(Long pause.)

So now Choo-Choo has AIDS, right?

I know, Murray. It's hard. I'm empathising here. But I figured you'd want to know the truth. All of it.

'There's an excellent veterinary surgeon on West Forty-Five and Tenth. Number 1202. You go right along there and he'll fix her up.' She seemed not to be lying to me. I've got so that I can spot that in people.

'You have insurance?' she called after me.

I was sure you did, Murray. Your apartment looks like it belongs to the type of guy who has pet insurance.

(Pause.)

So what happened to my fucking *street-map*, Murray? What happened to *el mappo*? Did it drop out of my handbag while I was wiping off some imaginary Chihuahua-spunk? *Christ* knows. This is, like, *not my day* so far. Anyway, somewhere along the way to this veterinary place, I get like *seriously* lost. West Forty-Five and Tenth, the little old lady said. I have strong instincts, Murray, and normally my sense of direction is just absolutely top-notch, like I always *just know* where north is? So although I didn't have *el mappo*, I figured, New York is on a grid system, right. So if that's north, then the surgery is like, *thattaway*.

Hey. Next thing I know it, we're on Broadway! Start spreadin' the news! I'd've liked to linger, Murray, but Choo-Choo's limp is getting real bad, and I'm focusing on getting her to the pooch doc before the HIV works itself into her bloodstream. She's starting to make these whimpering noises.

(Pause.)

She's way too heavy to carry, and so we're slowing down to, like, maybe a fraction of one mile per hour here. And looking at the street-signs, I notice that we're suddenly into the thirties instead of the forties, I don't know how, and now there's this road bum's started showing an interest. He kinda wheedles, this guy.

'I can see it's urgent, what you're doing,' he says. 'Has anyone ever told you that you have a great ass?'

Actually, he was cute enough for me not to be appalled by this. I give him a dollar bill and some change. Hey. I'm on vacation.

(Pause.)

It sure was a hot day. I stopped to buy a 7-Up on this big piece of sidewalk that was kinda crawling with humanity.

'Where is this place?' I ask the street bum. He's been following me.

'Times Square,' he says. Major disappointment, Murray. It's not even a square, man. It's just a stupid *intersection*.

(Pause.)

Hey, d'you know what Suzie's job is, back in Fresno? We're back in storyboard mode now, by the way, Murray. This is a flashbacky thing, for you to reflect on while Chooch and I are leaving Times Square, in the wrong direction as it turns out, with the street bum still in tow.

(Pause.)

So what's our heroine's job, Murray? Can you guess? She hasn't got one, Murray. She's unemployed. I was a high-school teacher, but there was a, like, socio-sexual-stroke-discipline-stroke-authority-stroke-competence problem. I was thinking about this problem, which involved a particularly cute and well-developed eighth-grader, who taught me some interesting stuff, when, get this: Choo-Choo gets hit by a car.

Hey, am I having bad luck or *what*?

(Pause.)

Drunk driver. I'll swear to it. He just came screeching up.

Storyboard here, Murray: Suzie didn't hesitate. She threw herself in front of the dog to protect it from –

(Pause.)

No, I didn't actually. I'm not stupid. I know guys who just cruise the streets of Fresno all day long waiting for jaywalkers. But hey. I did the next best thing; I pulled her back on to the sidewalk. Choo-Choo's still alive at this point, Murray; a bit dizzy, maybe. But I figure, 'Let's think positively here, Suze; we were on our way to the doc's *anyway*. Might as well capitalise on that pet insurance.'

Choo-Choo's obviously real relieved to be alive, because she opens her bowel at this point, and I get to discover the hydraulics of the pooper-scooper, which turns out to be a real cool gadget.

The street bum's still stalking me, in a kinda half-hearted way, so I pay him another two bucks to help me load Choochie into this shopping trolley that's like abandoned on the sidewalk. We're in the Garment District now. Loads of rich-bitch mannequins and coat-hangers and stuff. No-one tries to help us or anything. The trolley's kinda rusty, and one wheel's all skewed. Choo-Choo sure is heavy, but she's not whimpering any more. It's like she knows she's in safe hands, right? Her eyes have grown real big.

(Pause.)

I'm feeling the need for a cup of espresso at this point, Murray, so I start wheeling her into the nearest place, it's called Gracie's, on West Thirty-something Street, but the waitress, she says *no dogs allowed*, in that kinda real rude East Coast bitch way, like I owe her a favour, or something? So we leave Choo-Choo outside in the trolley. *We* is me and the street bum, *Armando*. I was feeling generous. So I let him talk, and paid for his coffee. Then we switched to highballs and he told me his life story. Italian. Five marriages. Dreams of going to Florida, and starting over? I kinda empathised with him, but only up to a point, because I suspected he was a loser. While I was listening to all this, and wondering whether to take him back to the apartment, Murray, and screw him silly, because I'm on vacation, there's this dog-fight develops outside.

(Pause.)

It's Choo-Choo being attacked by an Alsatian. He's actually in the trolley with her there, if you can picture that, Murray. And he's kinda trying to hump her, but she's not responding. I guess you'd call it a rape scene. I stare through the window. There's something about seeing an act of violence through a window, or through sunglasses, or on TV, that kinda distances you from it a bit. Especially if you've just done a line of coke in the john? Do you find that, Murray? But even so, I'm like, flabbergasted. There's a crowd gathered on the street to watch. No one's doing anything to stop it.

New York really is the cruellest place on earth, Murray. It sure put me off the idea of taking Armando home.

(Pause.)

So what happens next? Oh yeah, the Alsatian shoots his bolt, and he's off, and the crowd disperses, and I finish my coffee, and the street bum says he's got an appointment, and he's gotta go, so me and Chooch head off for the veterinary surgeon's again. She's not looking real happy at this point. I still had this completely fixed idea that the Forties were like, *thattaway*, but we still managed to get lost. *Totally*. Like, *again?* It's real hot. And like, *clammy*. And I swear to God, we were suddenly like the only pedestrians in the whole of New York. Try getting a cab when you need one, right? So on we go, until suddenly the trolley wheel finally gives out, the skewed one. No shit, Murray. It was like some dopey cartoon. Except it was for real, and the dog was dying. I could see it in her eyes.

Gee, those *eyes*, Murray. You should've seen them. They were, like, *huge*. Like she was trying to tell me something?

(Pause.)

And hey. Get this. *I suddenly realised what she was saying to me*, Murray, with those big eyes!

(Pause.)

She was saying: 'Take me to see the Statue of Liberty before I go, Suze!' I swear to God, Murray, it was like a telepathic thing. Coke can do that for you, right – like open up all these channels of communication? So suddenly I just, like, *knew*. Hey. This was one cool dog.

So I try my cab-hailing thing again, and – this is fate, I think, right – there's one stops just like that.

(Long pause. Sounds of drink being freshened and cigarette lit.)

Right, we're in the cab now. Here's a piece of dialogue for you, Murray. 'Where to, lady?' (That's the cab-driver. I can't do the accent.)

'Statue of Liberty.' (That's me.) 'My dog has to see it before she dies. It's like a deathbed wish?'

'Statue of Liberty's on an island, lady. You mean you want to go to it, like to take photographs of you and the dog next to it, or ya just want to *see* it, from a distance?'

'How much to go there?'

'You *can't* go there, lady. Not in a cab. You take the ferry. I can take you to the ferry, but it'll cost ya. And dogs is extra.' He says *dogs* like there's an extra vowel in it?

'No expense spared,' I say.

'What are you on, lady? How much you got?' He's sounding kinda suspicious at this point. When I tell him I've only got ten bucks, 'cos I gave the other four to Armando the street bum, he gets real mean. He says, 'It smells like shit in here, lady. Did you step in some dog shit?'

When I tell him the pooper-scooper's full, he gets like *real mad*, and swings the cab round and starts driving in another direction, and says if I don't give him my ten bucks, he'll call the cops.

'I'm dropping you at the station, lady,' he yells at me. 'Best thing you can do, is get yourself a train ticket back to wherever the fuck you came from!'

New York's a real friendly place for tourists, right? I tell him he can shove his fucking Goat-town right up his ass.

(Long pause.)

I guess Choochie realised at that point, that we weren't going to make it to the Statue. I like to think that she forgave me for that, Murray. Do you think she would've done? I just had, like, this feeling that she didn't mind not seeing it, in the end.

(Pause.)

So the cab driver threw us out. And by Grand Central Station, Murray, she lay down and died.

(Pause.)

You know, Murray, they say if you dissect the retina of an animal, or a human, you will see imprinted on the little biological tissue screen – *the mind's eye* – the last thing it saw before it died. I've often wondered why they don't use this trick to solve murder cases. Especially when the victim has that horrified look on their face, like they've seen the murderer. Maybe it's an idea I could patent, and make some money from?

(Pause.)

The Big Apple murdered your dog, Murray. If you dissect her eye, you'll see Central Park, and overlaid on that, Times Square, and all those mean streets in the Garment District. You'll see Gracie's Café. You'll see Grand Central Station. And you'll see, like, a little map of Hell's Kitchen on the internal mirrors of her appalled and now sightless orbs, Murray. Manhattan: murderer. That's how I figure it, anyways. It's kinda an existential thing, if you can get that, Murray?

(Pause.)

I figured you'd want the body, Murray. I figured I owed you that. So I did this neat thing. I've got this nylon travel bag, Murray, that kinda folds real small and you can carry it in your purse? For shopping? Well the kid ain't dumb. I stuffed her inside, and just kinda *dragged* her home. I didn't have the choice, because I was imagining there was like, this whole network of cops following me, making sure I didn't dump the body and start a hygiene risk. She sure was heavy. It took me two hours, Murray. *Two hours.*

Don't say I never do anything for ya!

(Pause.)

Just kidding there.

When I finally reach the apartment block, the janitor comes out. I tell him what's happened, and he says oh my God, lady, what the fuck are you on, just like the cab driver, and carries her up in the bag himself, 'cos he was real attached to that dog, he says. He says *dog* like the driver did, with that extra vowel? I thought for a minute they were the same person!

(Pause.)

Nothing's for free, right, Murray? 'Any items of clothing you could spare, there, lady?' he asks me, when we've dealt with Choochie. ''Cos you and me, we're about the same size.'

Yeah, in his dreams! I give him a bra and this hokey old skirt I don't like any more.

(Pause.)

I stayed in after that, as you can imagine. I'd had it up to *here* – I'm pointing to my throat now, Murray – I'd had it up to *here* with New York. So I just ordered pizzas and stuff, and watched TV. And hey, d'you know what they were running, the second day? Only *New York, New York*, with Liza Minelli!

Hey, that was a cool coincidence.

I've had a great time, Murray, since I abandoned the idea of doing any sightseeing. I figured, just before I left, which is like, now, that I'd do you a cassette, explaining what happened to old Chooch. Murray, I hope I've managed to answer the five Ws and the H for you.

(Pause.)

You know, it's kinda weird, but get this: I'm actually kinda grateful that I had that experience! It was, like, a real adventure? Sure is something to tell the folks back home!

What did you do in Goat-town, Suze?

I took a Pyrenean Wolf Hound to see the Statue of Liberty but it died before we got there. Only in New York, right?

(Pause.)

Rest in peace, Choo-Choo. Oh, yeah: you might like to go see her now, Murray. To, like, say goodbye? She's in the freezer. We cleared a space by the pizzas.

(Pause.)

Well, I guess that's it. I guess we've seen the last frame of the 'Suzie and Choo-Choo's Day in New York' storyboard. Sure hope the feminine hygiene commercial worked out, Murray. I do envy you your job. Hope we get to meet in the flesh sometime. Who knows what might happen? Yo! Like, East meets West, right?

Bye Murray. And thanks for everything.

Click.

OCCUPATIONAL HAZARDS

Thomas Beller

Harriet stood in front of her building, watering the petunias. It was July and the whole block was in bloom. It was a leafy, tree-lined block in the West Village and she had lived on it for thirty-four years. She and her husband Casey had been the bohemians of the law firm where he had worked. They had raised two children there, a boy and a girl, but they were grown up, and now it was just Harriet and Casey and the tenants. She and her husband rented out three small studio apartments and one larger apartment on the top floor to keep the cash flowing.

The arrangement had worked out well. One of their tenants had been there twenty years, and spent most of the time in another city. The man on the top floor was an architect, and was doing wonderful remodelling with his own money. The building was a Federalist era structure, and the architect had unearthed a gas meter made of lead that looked as though it ought to be in a museum. It was like a work of art. The other two tenants were relatively new. One was a very quiet graduate student, Laurie, who kept her place immaculate. The other was a computer expert of some kind named Ned. Once, when in his apartment with the Con Edison man, her husband Casey had seen what he thought was cocaine in a little pile on Ned's desk. 'I'm pretty sure that's what it was,' said Casey. 'But he seems solid.'

Ned was approaching her now, walking down the block with the buoyant, distracted gait he had. He was not her ideal tenant. She preferred quiet girls like Laurie. But in recent years she had come to notice that Casey spent more and more time up in his third floor office taking any opportunity to chat with the tenants as they went up and down the stairs, particularly the female tenants. So she acquiesced to this young man. The fact that he was in computers made him seem vaguely stable. And she liked the idea of men in the building, with Casey getting old.

Ned stopped before her now, wearing shorts and a T-shirt. When he had interviewed with her and her husband he wore a suit and presented himself with such immaculate care. He continued to dress fastidiously, though a bit more informally, for the first few months of his tenancy, but in the ensuing year had become a bit more slovenly, and Harriet often wondered if he had merely put on a show for them or if his life had changed in some meaningful way. She hoped it was the former. She didn't want drama on the upper floors.

Harriet smiled at Ned as he approached. He looked at her, hesitated, and said, 'Those Petunias look great! Those are some great-looking petunias.' They both stared down at them for a moment. They were purple and white. Then he went into the house and bounded up the wooden stairs with big heavy strides. She flinched a little with each thud, as though the old wooden staircase was a part of her.

The pigeons were cooing softly on the ledge outside Ned's bathroom window. He stood in the balmy stillness of his apartment, trying to relax. He wondered if Harriet would be downstairs when his guests arrived. The very thought came under criticism: they are not *guests*, he told himself. The pigeons continued to coo. He stepped out of the bright light of the main room into the dark cavernous interior of the bathroom, lit only by a dim window, heavily frosted and with small wire octagonals built into the glass. It looked out on to an alley and provided the room's meagre light. It was on the other side of this small window that the pigeons had made their home.

The pigeons were the subject of a long-running debate. Part of him thought they were lovely and soothing, their cooing the sound of courtship, of small living things seeking refuge in the big city, and he was happy they had made his little ledge a home. Another part of him, however, took a colder view. They were flying vermin. They symbolised disorder and dirt. Now, faintly outlined against the window's frosted glass, were the silhouettes of two pigeon heads, bobbing slightly.

Ned designed Web pages for the Internet. Few people really understood what, exactly, this meant. Therefore everyone respected it. They assumed, since it had to do with computers, that it must be valid and well paying, and for several years it was. But the sense of limitless growth had tapered off. First the sense of it tapered off, then the fact of it. And now he was in a bind. To contemplate the dilemma sent shudders through him and made him feel sick. He thought of himself as a designer, as an artist, and his great specialty was clean lines, orderly visual arrangements. He recoiled at mess. And yet he was consumed with a sense of unravelling.

He stepped back into his apartment. It was immaculate. At times like this he loved his apartment with a weird passion – its stillness, its prettiness, the *oldness* of the place and the sense of containment. The phone, which had rung so frantically all of the previous evening and again starting at eight that morning, had been unplugged. A sense of peace had come over him.

That morning Ned had culled several names – all female – from a long list of messages left the previous night and that morning. He had been amused and a little horrified to note the thrill of power he felt while scanning the voices. There was an unpleasant anarchy to his little thrill. He didn't like anarchy.

Edith was first. She looked around at his apartment with big round eyes and then she turned and looked at Ned, as though he were another item of furniture in the company of which she was thinking of spending a month.

Ned couldn't bear to look into her eyes and looked instead at her hair. Edith had so much thick black hair that he started having visions of it accumulating in his apartment like hay. His small pretty studio apartment would be like a barnyard full of bales of Edith's thick black hair. This was unfair, he knew. Other than the hair she was perfect. She was a polite soft-spoken girl from Wisconsin who had just moved to New York and was looking for a job. She had recently graduated college. She seemed neat and fastidious. If you are renting your apartment out for a month, you want a neat and fastidious person.

The etiquette, he had been informed by his friend Alfred, was first come first serve, provided you liked and trusted the person to sleep in your bed, walk on your floors, eat off your plates, sit on your toilet and generally *live and breathe* in your apartment. If they had a cheque, you were advised to take it. Unless, of course, you had reservations about their character, their hygiene, their sanity, or, most importantly, their solvency. Was too much hair a legitimate reservation?

Fortunately, Edith started getting a sad look in her eyes about five minutes into the conversation, as though she had developed fine sensors for rejection, and was getting a signal. She left saying she had to think about it. 'I've seen so many apartments,' she said wearily. Casey and Harriet would have liked her, he thought. But he sighed with relief after she closed the door. Only later did he wonder if perhaps there was something strange about his apartment, or about him, that had prompted her to keep away.

Ned was very concerned about what Casey and Harriet would think of his renting out his place for August. He sympathised with their fierce sense of propriety. He sometimes saw Casey standing out front on the sidewalk and staring at his building with the grim pride of someone looking at an old boat that was still floating. The building was more or less his life at this point.

Casey was a retired lawyer. He had been prosperous enough to buy a brownstone in Greenwich Village thirty-four years ago, but something about the gratitude and relief with which he accepted the rent cheque each month suggested that he had not been overwhelmingly shrewd with his money.

He was a thin man, with pale, papery skin and cheeks that became faintly pink when it was cold. His hair was white and sprung out from his head, except when he made an effort to comb it back. He liked small talk. Casey was a menace of small talk. He kept an office up on the third floor, and haunted the stairways like a ghost. His office door stood just at the top of the stairs and when he was in residence he left the door ajar. It didn't provide a view of the whole room, just the vestibule area, but that was enough to get the idea of the room's character – books and papers stacked in precarious piles, the chaos of someone drowning in their own history.

The building was Casey's passion. If some unsuspecting city inspector slapped a ticket on the building's front door for one of the million or so infractions that hover threateningly over the small building owner – a trash can that has strayed too far from its appointed spot on the sidewalk, for example – then Casey would rally in a flurry of litigious energy and take the thing to court. He loved this sort of thing. The whole saga – the ticket, the error of the ticketer, Casey's plans for going to court and the results of the court case (always, miraculously, favourable) – were recounted by Casey to anyone he could find. And given his office at the top of the stairs, all of the building's tenants were at his mercy. Ned wondered what the new tenant would make of Casey, and he wondered what Casey would make of her. He felt he was pimping for Casey, providing him with a little fresh blood into which he could sink his friendly, vampiric teeth. For this small favour surely Casey would leave him alone, let him have his tenant, and work out his financial difficulties in peace. Ned possessed an irrational fear that Casey and Harriet would ask him to leave. It was irrational because they showed no signs of disliking him. But he had come to see his apartment as a little jewel in a crown that was losing jewels left and right.

Arlene was black. Grasping this fact was a horrible moment. Ned stuck his head out of his window to shout 'Up! Up!' which is what he had to do when he had a visitor. The intercom was broken – he didn't want to bother Casey about fixing it – so first he had to get his guest's attention by yelling, then drop a key tied to a piece of wood down four flights on to the sidewalk.

Arlene stepped back and looked up. She had a smile that traversed four flights with ease. He threw the key out the window, waited for the wooden stick to smack against the pavement and then brought his head back into the enclosure of his apartment. His first thought was: she didn't sound black on the phone.

He could hear her faint footsteps on the wooden stairs, getting louder with each step. Right away a voice within him said: 'She gets the place. No discussion, no debate. To not give her the place is to admit you are a racist scumbag.'

To this outburst of propriety came: 'Maybe you *are* a racist scumbag!'

Arlene's steps grew louder on the stairs. They paused on his floor. There were two doors there, and she wouldn't know which was his. He went to open the door and she stood in the doorway, about to knock. From four flights up he had sensed her youth, but her beauty nearly knocked him back. Her skin had a youthful glow. She wore jeans and a tight striped halter top from which her breasts protruded like headlights on an old fifties sedan. The laces to one of her sneakers were undone and they clacked lightly on his wood floor. She seemed not to care.

'Hi!' she said when she came in, a little breathless from her climb. 'Nice to meet you.' They shook hands, exchanged some facts veiled in conversation: she was from LA, in town for the summer, classes at NYU and, by the brightness of her smile, fun.

Ned showed her around the apartment. It was one room. Therefore showing her around the apartment meant standing in one place, throwing out his hand, and saying, 'Here it is!'

'Oh,' she said, smiling, taking it in. 'It's nice.'

'It's a nice place to live,' Ned said. He shot a look at Arlene. She was nodding her head vaguely. She didn't seem too impressed, but it was hard to tell beneath her good cheer. He looked back at the room. There were some framed drawings on the wall. No matter how many times he straightened them, every time he regarded them closely they seemed to be askance. In this respect they were in keeping with the building itself.

'It's a funky place, it has a lot of character,' she said.

'A very nice girl,' said the good crowd within. 'Don't you remember reading that article in the *Times* about evil racist realtors directing black families away from white neighbourhoods and getting all misty-eyed at how mean the world could be? Now is your chance to put politics into practice!'

But it wasn't so simple. He thought of Casey and Harriet. He wondered what they would make of Arlene. Would she play loud music? Would she do it on his bed?

'Let's not skirt the issue,' spoke the voice of probity, reason, integrity, and decency. 'You're reluctant to rent to her because she is black.'

This was not a crisis he expected. This whole process was meant to occupy a small space of time and expend only a little mental energy. He hadn't expected an internal referendum on his own decency. Subletting was meant to be a small detail among larger and more pressing details in his life. It was a detail he wished to not think about. He had a month in the country with his girlfriend, Layla, ahead of him.

Like his apartment, Ned had come to see Layla as a luxury that was almost beyond his means to keep. They had planned a lovely month in a house that belonged to Layla's friend's mother, who felt guilty that it was going to be unused. This anonymous woman's generosity was allowing Ned to turn a small profit.

He tried to think of it as an act of thrift. Why should he let his apartment go unused for a month? And yet beneath this thin rationalisation lay an absolute wreck of a freelance assignment, and an even deeper tremor of financial fear. For months he had coasted on the assumption that the deal would go through, and it was meant to sustain him for the better part of a year. But the deal had fallen through. It was a horrible, mysterious, and inexplicable event, like the floor of a bathroom giving way while you stood there taking a leisurely piss. His credit card bills, which he had previously been shrugging off, began to seem alarming, insurmountable, punitive. To make matters worse, his girlfriend, Layla, had not a financial care in the world, and he was trying to prevent infecting the relationship with his anxiety. He could live the unstructured life of a millionaire because he was a freelancer. She could live the unstructured life of a millionaire because she was a millionaire. To go along with her beautiful and evocative self were two beautiful and evocative words:

Trust.

Fund.

Each was a flower stem from which bloomed a hundred different petals of meaning, all of them lovely.

To stare directly at a potential tenant was to be reminded of the sudden shambles of his professional life and this increasingly discordant aspect of his relationship with Layla. He thought that he would simply give it to Arlene and get it over with. He would get a tenant and a good conscience in the bargain. But then he imagined her with a black man. He glanced over at his bed. Then he imagined her on the staircase with her black boyfriend, the two of them gasping a little as Casey emerged from the doorway at the top of the stairs like a ghost, pale as a sheet with his purple, wine-stained mouth, teetering drunk at nine at night. The image of Arlene on the stairs was much more disturbing than Arlene in his bed.

Arlene turned to him and said, 'It's really nice. I mean, I think it would be perfect for me being here for a month. And I had this awful nightmare, or rather I'm having this awful nightmare right now because I had arranged to rent a room in this apartment without having seen it, I did it on the phone, you know? But the people are just so... unpleasant.' She gave him a big smile, as though he could relate to the word 'unpleasant'.

Ned sensed some sort of punch line, some agenda, but couldn't discern it until it was plainly before him. He pined for Alfred, his consultant, his friend. Alfred knew how to handle these things.

'But the thing is,' she continued with a big smile, as though she were inviting him to her birthday party, 'it's just a bit, I mean... Could the price be a little less?'

'Well,' he said. 'The price is, you know...'

The issue of supply and demand was a touchy one. He stared at Arlene, her open face, and thought – who needs who?

'I'll tell you what,' he said. He hesitated before continuing. Their eyes met, neither entirely comfortable. It was an awkward moment for both of them, and Ned flagrantly let a few beats pass before continuing, savouring this sudden unexpected intimacy. 'I'll have to think about it. The price in the paper is more or less the price.'

He realised that he was afraid she would concede the point right away, pull out a cheque, and want to close the deal. She didn't.

'All right. I have to look at a couple more places, but I'll have my mother call you anyway,' she said. 'As a reference.' She moved out the door and out of his life with the same buoyant easiness with which she had entered. He thought of men catcalling after her on the street, and felt a pang of indignation on her behalf. How he would like to protect her! But then another voice from within spoke up and said, 'Oh shut up, you asshole. You're glad she didn't take it.'

Ned immediately called Alfred, who was serving as a kind of consultant on the sublet issue. Alfred was both an expert on the strange world of Manhattan real estate and a victim of its consuming power. He had lived in a tiny studio apartment on Houston Street, six flights up a dank grey walk-up, for three years. He had no immediate plans to move. And yet every week he scanned the classifieds in the *Voice*, sometimes in the *Times*, and occasionally made visits to look at apartments, as though he were seriously considering a move.

Alfred liked to look. He was a real estate voyeur. He liked the frisson of commerce and possibility, and he liked looking at other interiors into which he might shoehorn his possessions and his life.

Alfred's rationale for his constant, gratuitous and essentially masochistic state of perpetual looking at apartments was that he was staying mentally nimble. 'People move in somewhere,' he told Ned, 'and think they'll stay for a year. Then, boom, the next thing you know a decade goes by. Like that. Ten years in the same dinky little place they didn't even like that much to begin with.'

Alfred lived in a dinky little place he didn't like that much to begin with. His two windows faced South, in the direction of Little Italy, which was Alfred's favourite neighbourhood. He liked to say he lived in Little Italy, but at a slightly cheaper price, since he was technically across the street.

Alfred's apartment obsession had resulted in Ned finding his own apartment without lifting a finger. One day he announced to Alfred that he was thinking of moving, and a little while later Alfred started talking about this amazing studio in a pretty little building that he was thinking about taking. Alfred sometimes deliberated moving; it was necessary to do so to justify all the looking. But after a few days he decided it was too far west, too far away from the little food stores that sold fresh cheese and pasta and the Chinese vegetable stands that he liked, and too far from work, and just not the right place for him. Ned went, took one look at the place, said he wanted it, and got it. Not a single scrunched-up line of classified advertising had to be read.

It was Alfred who had helped Ned formulate the tersely worded description that was to run in the back pages of the *Village Voice*: 128 characters, including spaces and punctuation. What care he had put into its phrasing: 'Big beautiful sunny studio. w/vu. tree lined blk. Safe. Hrdwd fl. Month of Aug.'

'But it's not that big,' Ned had said when Alfred told him to use that word.

'You have to speak the language,' replied Alfred.

Alfred spoke the language. He had internalised the commercial language of Manhattan real estate. Ned once had a dream in which Alfred spoke to him about his girlfriend. 'Her pussy is like a co-op,' Alfred said in the dream. 'I own it, but the maintenance is a killer.' Ned awoke from this dream in a state of bemused perplexity. Alfred hadn't had a girlfriend in years.

The *Village Voice* hit the stands Tuesday evening. Ned had gone out to dinner that night. When he returned his machine was blinking madly. He listened to voice after voice announce itself and fathomed, for an instant, the undulating ocean of life out there. He was briefly connected to the tide of rootless aspiration that washed in and out of New York every day. The sense of having something that others wanted gave him a perverse rush, but after about ten messages he began to feel depressed. Every voice registered the strain of artifice. They wanted to make a good impression. Some people were candid about this. Some of the women, especially, allowed their voice to get a bit silky and flirtatious. After the first few messages, he simply fast-forwarded past the male voices. If he could help it at all, he would avoid renting to a man. He alone could pee in his shower.

'This is turning into a nightmare,' Ned said right away when Alfred picked up the phone. The traditional civilising gesture of introducing oneself on the phone went unheeded in their relationship. It was one of the tacit acts of fealty that they displayed to one another – voice, tone, and diction were introduction enough. 'I'm in an unexpected moral quandary,' said Ned.

'You're always in an unexpected moral quandary,' said Alfred.

'You're always saying *always*,' replied Ned. 'You speak in absolutes. You've never had to stand around in your apartment renting to a black woman.'

'Never is an absolute,' said Alfred. Alfred worked as an assistant to a high level movie agent. He was not just a secretary, he had real responsibilities, and made real money. But he was partly a secretary, and spent his days with a phone headset strapped to his head. Ned had visited him at work once, and thought he looked like an astronaut.

'This is serious. Her mother is going to call me.'

'I would have no problem renting to a nigger,' said Alfred.

Ned, abiding by the rhythm of the conversation, opened his mouth as though to say something, but nothing came out.

'Just kidding,' inserted Alfred.

'Mr Enlightenment,' said Ned. Alfred often made jokes like that, slung around racist slander in every direction, as though to say the most explosively inappropriate words was to somehow diffuse them. But this was the subtle sensitive interpretation. The much more obvious interpretation was that Alfred liked saying the word 'nigger'.

HOMAS BELLER

'Come on, don't get pious with me,' said Alfred.

'I'm not getting pious. You can say anything you want. It's not my problem. If you want to say… If you want to say that word on the phone, fine. It's very abstract. It's just at the moment I am having this pressing sort of dilemma in which…'

'You don't want a black girl fucking in your bed?'

'Sometimes I wonder if a friendship in which the common ground is all that is bad about each person is a friendship worth having.'

'You want to break up?' Alfred was in fine form. He had the cheerful agitation that made him entertaining to be around. This sort of low grade hostility was much better than his other mode, when he simply dissolved into a sulk, was besieged by numerous migraine headaches, and couldn't get out of bed except to crawl to work.

'I'm serious,' said Ned. 'This is a serious issue. I'm worried about what the landlords will think of me subletting anyway. And if suddenly there is this black person roaming around on the stairs, who knows what they'll do.'

'Is she cute?'

'Stunning.'

'Rent it.'

'She says her mother will vouch for her,' said Ned. 'Is a mother a reference?'

Kyra arrived with a silver spoon in her mouth. She walked straight to his bed and sat down. She sat perched like a bird at the edge of his bed, scantily clad in tank top, shorts and prim white sneakers. She looked like someone who went on long, anxiety-purging runs. She was blonde and very thin. She looked like the sort of girl Casey would have a crush on immediately; he would haunt his study for hours and ambush her on the stairs to tell her about the new changes in the recycling schedule, and then, just when she thought she could continue home, he would segue into some arcane bit of historical minutia about the building itself, and she would have to stand there another five minutes.

With Edith he had a muted little scene, with Arlene he had a conversation, but with Kyra, it was obvious, there would be an interview. She had a hierarchical atmosphere about her. Also, the bed was a little higher than his chair, so she was looking down at him. She wore the blank appraising expression of someone looking across a desk at a job applicant.

Though she was blonde and pretty, she was not attractive. Had she been languorous and relaxed, she would have seemed like a movie star or a model, but there was something rather contorted and pretzel-like about her; she possessed a school marmish reproach.

The one contradiction to all this was the spoon, her use of which was sexual to the point of being obscene. She spent most of the interview waving it around like a baton while she spoke. Whenever she wasn't talking she put it in her mouth, nibbled its tip, pressed it between her lips, or submerged it entirely in her mouth and sucked it like a lollipop. It was weird.

Finally, Ned couldn't take it any more and said, 'What's with the spoon?'

'I was eating yogurt on the way over here,' Kyra said. 'And I took this spoon from my house. I live just a few blocks away.' She gestured with the spoon in the general direction of where she lived and, when she finished the sentence, put the tip in her mouth and bit gently with her top and bottom front teeth, as though getting started on a kinky sort of blow job.

'I see,' said Ned. 'I thought it might be a style thing. Like you know how there was that trend when all these people were walking around with these big candy-coloured pacifiers in their mouth? I thought maybe now it was spoons.'

Kyra took a long pensive suck on her spoon, and then removed it. 'No,' she said. 'It's not a trend. It's blueberry yogurt. I ate it on the way over here.'

'Oh,' said Ned. He paused, a little exhausted by the sight of Kyra sitting on the edge of his bed. She explained to Ned that she was a freelance fashion stylist, that she worked a lot, that if someone wanted to reach her they usually called her beeper first, and that she was breaking up with her boyfriend of two years and needed some space. She said she needed some space right away, which is why she was interested in subletting his apartment for a month before she found more permanent digs. She said this in a brisk matter-of-fact tone and immediately, before he could ask anything else, asked him a question.

'Where are you going to be for the month?'

'Out in the country. I'm taking a kind of vacation, I guess, though I can always work. I'm in design, computers, the Internet, you know, so I can take that with me.'

She nodded pensively, tapping the spoon against her lips. 'Where exactly? I mean, what part of the country?'

'The Adirondacks. Way upstate.'

'How many hours?' She was feigning curiosity but there was something more urgent about her questions. She held the round back of the spoon against her lips with delicate fingers.

'I don't know,' said Ned. 'I've never been. I guess four or five or something.'

Kyra tapped the spoon against her lips rapidly now, like it was a lie detector detecting a lie. Then it stopped tapping. She looked around the room.

'You keep your apartment very clean, for a guy. Most straight guys don't keep their places so neat.'

'Thank you,' he said. 'Actually it's not that clean. I mean, it could be cleaner.' He thought of the fifty bucks he had spent on a maid to come in and achieve a degree of immaculateness that he, on his own, could never match. She had done something so magnificent to his toilet bowl that he had been reluctant, at first, to use it for its assigned purpose.

'It's very clean,' she continued. 'I mean, some guys are more clean than others. You're clean.'

'Thank you. I presume you're clean too. I mean, you look clean.'

'Is there an extra set of keys?'

'Of course, and I'll give you the mail box key too. You can throw the letters on the shelf above the…'

'But I mean, I was looking at the locks and, you know.'

'The locks are good. It's a very safe building in a very safe neighbourhood. I wouldn't worry about anything getting stolen.'

'But the point is, the locks are no good if someone has the keys to them.' She put the spoon in her mouth all the way. Ned had really been enjoying this business with the spoon, but now there was a strange bit of agitation rising in her voice that made him apprehensive.

'No one has the keys but you and me.'

'That's my point. You'll have a set of keys.'

'Of course I'll have a set of keys.'

'But how do I know you're not going to show up in the middle of the night?'

'I'm not going to show up in the middle of the night. I'll be in the middle of the woods or something.'

'How do I know you're safe?'

'I presume the woods are safe. Except for bear, but I don't really think…'

'I mean how do I know *I'm* safe with *you*?'

'You don't have to worry about that. I promise you, I'm not going to come down from the woods and come crashing in here in the middle of the night. If I had to get something I'd call.' He said this in a rush, as though he was in trouble, and then caught himself and stopped talking, the indignation being stronger for having arrived late. 'Wait a second here,' he said, in a new, combative tone of voice. 'What are you saying?'

'It's just that if you have a set of...'

'Look, use your judgment. Do I look like someone who is going to sublet his apartment so he can come crashing in and rape his tenant in the middle of the night? That's what you're talking about, isn't it? You're telling me you're worried I'll attack you sexually, that this is some sex scam. Is it because I haven't shaved for a couple of days? Or is it something else.'

'No, listen it's not like that,' she said, for the first time dropping her posture of authority, dropping the defensive shield of her spoon to her side, and opening up in expression and posture.

'I mean who is interviewing who here?'

'I'm just trying to be...'

'I'm the one who is supposed to be checking up on your references, making sure you don't sell all my furniture while I'm away or something. And instead I'm getting this message that you like the apartment but you think I might want to rape you or something...'

'I'm sorry!' Kyra shouted. The room became silent. She seemed really distraught all of a sudden. Ned suddenly felt a strange bond with her. They were in a weird kind of transit. She was someone who needed to rent a place for just a month, and he was someone who needed to sublet his place for just a month – positions of approximately equal vulnerability.

He stared at her and felt a pang of horror that perhaps something awful had once happened to her, that she had been attacked or raped. For a fleeting moment he wanted to ask about it, but was sufficiently in the grip of his senses to keep quiet on the matter. 'This is just something I've been advised to ask about,' she said at last. 'You don't know who is out there.'

'It's true,' said Ned, in a quiet reconciling voice. 'It's weird out there. I'm in the same position. You should hear the people on my machine.'

They sat there uncomfortably for a moment, unsure whether this little outburst was the basis of some kind of friendship and camaraderie or just some weird thing that one wants to forget as soon as possible, like some unpleasant street scene one witnesses by accident. Eventually Kyra said that she liked the apartment but wanted to think about it. Ned took this to mean No, and felt a bit sad. He showed her to the door. They said good-bye in that musical, lighthearted way that friends do after they've had a cup of coffee.

It was quiet in his apartment and he felt her absence. He surveyed its small, pretty space, its white walls and wood floors. Small pleasant sounds of civilian life drifted up from the street. He stuck his head out the window and looked down. Harriet was gone. The petunias bristled with good health. It's weird out there, he thought, and then felt a pang of guilt at how Kyra might have received this bit of banal wisdom. She was on the verge of being single again for the first time in two years. Maybe she was just hysterical at the prospect of sex with strangers.

He went to the bathroom to pee. He was just about to pull down his fly when he heard an outburst of screeching, accompanied by percussive scraping sounds, that made him instinctively flinch. A pigeon fight was taking place on his ledge. Against the grey glow of the window their silhouettes pecked at each other with vicious muscular neck movements, their voices screeched abrasively, their wings fluttered violently. One pigeon flew off from the ledge, then came back like a kamikaze fighter, and the pecking and screaming continued. Ned zipped up his fly, stared wide-eyed at the shadow play, and retreated to the bright daylight of the apartment, where the sound was more distant, less immediate.

He hoped the classified ad was still working its magic. He pictured a clean decent woman sitting in a cafe with pen in hand, circling his number and going to the phone. He tried to picture the perfect tenant, her cleanliness, her quiet aura, but all his images of perfection were just absences. She wouldn't be this, she wouldn't be that. His imagination was consumed with thoughts of vacancy, empty spaces, omissions. He stood there thinking until he realised that the pigeon fight had subsided, and he was standing in silence. Cautiously, he peered back into the bathroom. The outline of two pigeons was visible in the window. Two faint grey shapes, their heads bobbing a little, gently cooing as though nothing had happened. They had somehow made peace.

PERSONAL HISTORY
Brooke Auchincloss

'Yes I'm from New York,' I say shifting my drink to my other hand.

My great grandparents came to New York from Scotland at the turn of the century. I like to imagine them on the deck of a great steamer ship, standing tall against the bracing winds. The woman is six months pregnant and delicate but strong with masses of stringy red hair piled haphazardly on her head. A few strands of sea-soaked hair hang in front of her piercing green eyes; she pulls her crocheted shawl tighter around her broad shoulders and gazes out at the endless sea. When the ship finally docks she and her husband fight their way on to the gangway and push themselves through the crowd and into the new world.

In actual fact my great grandparents were wealthy thread merchants. They probably had their own state room and a carriage to meet them at the other end of the voyage. My great grandmother would have been driven from the ship to a large brownstone on the Upper East Side where tea was served by uniformed maids in a large drawing room by a fire. A large and decaying aunt in one corner of the room would have ordered the lamps lit at 4.30pm sharp.

In the morning my great grandfather would put on his morning coat and taking his cane from the hall stand he'd walk to the corner where he would read the papers and smoke at a gentlemen's club behind cut-glass windows. Later when my grandfather was born he would wear sailor's outfits from a men's outfitters and the maiden aunts would allow him to sit in the parlour when company arrived – but he would have to sit perfectly still.

In the mornings the street outside the house would be full of the sound of fruit sellers and dairy maids singing their wares. My grandfather would lean out of the window and look both ways up and down the cobbled avenue then he would descend the four flights of stairs to the kitchen and talk to the maids as they ironed dollar bills for his great aunt.

When my grandfather married my grandmother they lived on Fifth Avenue and my grandmother had her picture in *Harper's*. One night my grandfather helped wheel the *Spirit of St Louis* through the sleeping streets of New York to Madison Square Garden for an exhibition. I love to think of him pushing the giant silver body of the plane past sleeping stone skyscrapers in the moonlight.

While my grandfather worked at the stock exchange my grandmother went out. She wore elegant silk slip gowns and fur wraps and attended gay functions where she danced on moonlit roof terraces above Central Park with men in starched white bow ties. Then they moved out of the city.

When my father was in college he attended debutante balls in the big hotels in Midtown. Once he strode along the white line in the middle of Fifth Avenue in the early hours of the morning in white tie and tails as the sun rose.

I was born in a hospital above FDR Drive and came home to a small apartment on the Upper West Side with big art and small furniture. My parents wore bell bottoms and taught me to walk up stairs in the park on Riverside Drive. My mother had big bouffant hair and wore lipstick. Then she had long brown braids and sandals. My father grew a moustache and they moved out of the city.

When I moved back to New York I was sixteen and I lived in a flat in Spanish Harlem. The windows were covered with metal screens and the walls were painted blood red. If you flicked on the lights at night you could see hundreds of frantic cockroaches running for cover. At night I'd lie on my mattress on the floor and listen to the traffic and sirens and loud Latin music. I worked for a film company and I had an affair with a museum guard whose father was in the Mafia. He'd only seen him once and his father had slapped him across the face so that the men he was with would think the boy was a messenger, not his son. We went to Studio 54 and danced the hustle under the flashing lights.

I left New York for London when I was eighteen and now we see each other only at Christmas time when New York is white and red and green. I sit in the window of my sister's apartment watching the snow float down in big white puffs. Across Broadway there's a Korean shop that has no doors because it never closes. I love to watch people struggling over the muddy sludge of the gutter up on to the hard white curb then down to the slippery sidewalk before leaving their footprints in the snow.

'Ah, New York,' he says in an accent that reeks of Cambridge. 'I hate it. It's so new, so superficial.'

DOVES IN THE CIRCLE
Michael Moorcock

Situated between Church Street and Broadway, several blocks from Houston Street, just below Canal Street, *Houston Circle* is entered via Houston Alley from the North, and *Lispenard, Walker* and *Franklin Streets* from the West. The only approach from the South and East is via *Courtland Alley*. Houston Circle was known as *Indian Circle* or *South Green* until about 1820. It was populated predominantly by Irish, English and, later, Jewish people and today has a poor reputation. The circle itself, forming a green, now an open market, had some claims to antiquity. Aboriginal settlements have occupied the spot for about five hundred years and early travellers report finding non-indigenous standing stones, remarkably like those erected by the Ancient Britons. The *Kakatanawas*, whom early explorers first encountered, spoke a distinctive Iroquois dialect and were of a high standard of civilisation. Captain Adriaen Block reported encountering the tribe in 1612. Their village was built around a stone circle 'whych is their *Kirke*'. When, under the Dutch, Fort Amsterdam was established nearby, there was no attempt to move the tribe which seems to have become so quickly absorbed into the dominant culture that it took no part in the bloody Indian War of 1643-5 and had completely disappeared by 1680. Although of considerable architectural and historical interest, because of its location and reputation Houston Circle has not attracted redevelopment and its buildings, some of which date from the 18th century, are in poor repair. Today the Circle is best known for 'The Three Sisters', which comprise the Catholic Church of *St Mary the Widow* (one of Huntingdon Begg's earliest commissions), the Greek Orthodox Church of *St Sophia* and the Orthodox Jewish Synagogue which stand side by side at the East end, close to *Doyle's Ale House*, built in 1780 and still in the same family. Next door to this is *Doyle's Hotel* (1879), whose tariff reflects its standards. Crossed by the Elevated Railway, which destroys the old village atmosphere, and generally neglected now, the Circle should be visited in daylight hours and in the company of other visitors. *Subway*: White Street IRT. *Elevated*: 6th Ave El at Church Street. *Streetcar*: B & 7th Ave, B'way & Church.
  - *New York: A Traveller's Guide*. RP Downes, Charles Kelly, London 1924.

1.

If there is such a thing as unearned innocence, then America has it, said Barry Quinn mysteriously lifting his straight glass to the flag and downing the last of Corny Doyle's passable porter. Oh, there you go again, says Corny, turning to a less contentious customer and grinning to show he saw several viewpoints. Brown as a tinker, he stood behind his glaring pumps in his white shirtsleeves, his skin glowing with the bar work, polishing up some silver-ware with all the habitual concentration of the rosary.

Everyone in the pub had an idea that Corny was out of sorts. They thought, perhaps, he would rather not have seen Father McQueeny there in his regular spot. These days the old priest carried an aura of desolation with him so that even when he joined a toast he seemed to address the dead. He had never been popular and his church had always chilled you but he had once enjoyed a certain authority in the parish. Now the Bishop had sent a new man down and McQueeny was evidently retired but wasn't admitting it. There'd always been more faith and Christian charity in Doyle's, Barry Quinn said, than could ever be found in that damned church. Apart from a few impenetrable writers in the architectural journals, no one had ever liked it. It was altogether too modern and Spanish-looking.

Sometimes, said Barry Quinn putting down his glass in the copper stand for a refill, there was so much goodwill in Doyle's Ale House he felt like he was taking his pleasure at the benign heart of the world. And who was to say that Houston Circle, with its profound history, the site of the oldest settlement on Manhattan, was not a centre of conscious grace and mystery like Camelot or Holy Island or Dublin, or possibly London? You could find all the inspiration you needed here. And you got an excellent confessional. Why freeze your bones talking to McQueeny in the box when you might as well talk to him over in that booth. Should you want to.

The fact was that nobody wanted anything at all to do with the old horror. There were a few funny rumours about him. Nobody was exactly sure what Father McQueeny had been caught doing, but it must have been bad enough for the Church to step in. And he'd had some sort of nasty secretive surgery. Mavis Byrne and her friends believed the Bishop made him have it. A popular rumour was that the Church castrated him for diddling little boys. He would not answer if you asked him. He was rarely asked. Most of the time people tended to forget he was there. Sometimes they talked about him in his hearing. He never objected.

She's crossed the road now, look. Corny pointed through the big, gold-lettered green window of the pub to where his daughter walked purposefully between the wrought-iron gates of what was nowadays called Houston Park on the maps and Houston Green by the realtors.

She's walking up the path. Straight as an arrow. He was proud of her. Her character was so different from his own. She had all her mother's virtues. But he was more afraid of Kate than he had ever been of his absconded spouse.

Will you look at that? Father McQueeny's bloody eyes stared with cold reminiscence over the rim of his glass. She is about to ask Mr Terry a direct question.

He's bending an ear, says Barry Quinn, bothered by the priest's commentary, as if a fly interrupted him. He seems to be almost smiling. Look at her coaxing a bit of warmth out of that grim old mug. And at the same time she's getting the info she needs, like a bee taking pollen.

Father McQueeny runs his odd-coloured tongue around his lips and says, shrouded safe in his inaudibility, his invisibility: What a practical and down-to-earth little creature she is. She was always that. What a proper little madam, eh? She must have the truth, however dull. She will not allow us our speculations. She is going to ruin all our fancies!

His almost formless body undulates to the bar, settles over a stool and seems to coagulate on it. Without much hope of a quick response, he signals for a short and a pint. Unobserved by them, he consoles himself in the possession of some pathetic and unwholesome secret. He marvels at the depths of his own depravity, but now he believes it is his self-loathing which keeps him alive. And while he is alive, he cannot go to hell.

2.

'Well,' says Kate Doyle to Mr Terry McLear, 'I've been sent out and I beg your pardon but I am a kind of deputation from the whole Circle, or at least that part of it represented by my dad's customers, come to ask if what you're putting up is a platform on which you intend to sit, to make, it's supposed, a political statement of some kind? Or is it religious ? Like a pole?'

And when she has finished her speech, she takes one step back from him. She folds her dark expectant hands before her on the apron of her uniform. There is a silence, emphasised by the distant, constant noise of the surrounding city. Framed by her bobbed black hair, her little pink oval face has that expression of sardonic good humour, that hint of self-mockery, which attracted his affection many years ago. She is the picture of determined patience, and she makes Mr Terry smile.

'Is that what people are saying these days, is it? And they think I'd sit up there in this weather?' He speaks the musical, old-fashioned convent-educated, precisely pronounced English he learned in Dublin. He'd rather die than make a contraction or split an infinitive. He glares up at the grey, Atlantic

sky. Laughing helplessly at the image of himself on a pole he stretches
hard-worn fingers towards her to show he means no mockery or rudeness
to herself. His white hair rises in a halo. His big old head grows redder, his
mouth rapidly opening and closing as his mirth engulfs him. He gasps. His
pale blue eyes, too weak for such powerful emotions, water joyfully. Kate
Doyle suspects a hint of senile dementia. She'll be sorry to see him lose his
mind, it is such a good one, and so kind. He never really understood how often
his company had saved her from despair.

Mr Terry lifts the long thick dowel on to his sweat-shirted shoulder. 'Would
you care to give me a hand, Katey?'

She helps him steady it upright in the special hole he had prepared. The
seasoned pine dowel is some four inches in diameter and eight feet tall. The
hole is about two feet deep. Yesterday, from the big bar, they had all watched
him pour in the concrete.

The shrubbery, trees and turf of the Circle nowadays wind neatly up to a
little grass-grown central hillock. On this the City has placed two ornamental benches. Popular legend has it that an Indian chief rests underneath,
together with his treasure.

When Mr Terry was first seen measuring up the mound, they thought of
the ancient redman. They had been certain, when he had started to dig, that
McLear had wind of gold.

All Doyle's regulars had seized enthusiastically on this new topic. Corny
Doyle was especially glad of it. Sales rose considerably when there was a bit
of speculative stimulus amongst the customers, like a sensational murder or
a political scandal or a sporting occasion.

Katey knew they would all be standing looking out now, watching her and
waiting. They had promised to rescue her if he became unpleasant. Not that
she expected anything like that. She was the only local that Mr Terry would
have anything to do with. He never would talk to most people. After his wife
died he was barely civil if you wished him 'good morning'. His argument was
that he had never enjoyed company much until he met her and now precious
little other company satisfied him in comparison. Neither did he have anything to do with the Church. He'd distanced himself a bit from Katey when
she started working with the Poor Clares. This was the first time she'd
approached him in two years. She's grateful to them for making her come but
sorry that it took the insistence of a bunch of feckless boozers to get her here.

'So,' she says, 'I'm glad I've cheered you up. And if that's all I've achieved, that's good enough for today, I'm sure. Can you tell me nothing about your pole?'

'I have a permit for it,' he says. 'All square and official.' He pauses and watches the Sears delivery truck which has been droning round the Circle for the last fifteen minutes, seeking an exit. Slumped over his wheel, peering about for signs, the driver looks desperate.

'Nothing else?'

'Only that the pole is the start of it.' He's enjoying himself. That heartens her.

'And you won't be doing some sort of black magic with the poor old Indian's bones?'

'Magic, maybe,' he says, 'but not a bit black, Katey. Just the opposite, you will see.'

'Well, then,' she says, 'then I'll go back and tell them you're putting up a radio aerial.'

'Tell them what you like,' he says. 'Whatever you like.'

'If I don't tell them something, they'll be on at me to come out again,' she says.

'You would not be unwelcome,' he says, 'or averse, I am sure, to a cup of tea.' And gravely he tips that big head homeward, towards his brownstone basement on the far side of the Circle.

'Fine,' she says, 'but I'll come on my own when I do and not as a messenger. Good afternoon to you, Mr Terry.'

He lifts an invisible hat. 'It was a great pleasure to talk with you again, Katey.'

She's forgotten how that little smile of his so frequently cheers her up.

3.

'Okay, Katey, so what's the story?' says Father McQueeny wearing his professional cheer like an old shroud, as ill-smelling and threadbare as his clerical black. The only life on him is his sweat, his winking veins. The best the regulars have for him these days is their pity, the occasional drink. He has no standing at all with the Church or the community. But, since Father Walsh died, that secret little smirk of his always chills her. Knowing that he can still frighten her is probably all that keeps the old shit alive. And since that knowledge actually informs the expression which causes her fear, she is directly feeding him what he wants. She has yet to work out a way to break the cycle. Years before, in her best attempt, she almost succeeded.

To the others, the priest remains inaudible, invisible. 'Did he come out with it, Katey,' says Corny Doyle, his black eyes and hair glinting like pitch, his near-fleshless body and head looking as artificially weathered as those shiny, smoked hams in Belladonna's. 'Come on, Kate. There's real money riding on this now.'

'He did not tell me,' she says. She turns her back on Father McQueeny but she cannot control a shudder as she smiles from behind the bar where she has been helping out since Christmas, because of Bridget's pneumonia. She takes hold of the decorated china pump-handle and turns to her patient customer. 'Two pints of Murphy's was it, Mr Gold?'

'You're an angel,' says Mr Gold. 'Well, Corny, the book, now how's it running?' He is such a plump, jolly man. You would never take him for a pawnbroker. And it must be admitted he is not a natural profiteer. Mr Gold carries his pints carefully to the little table in the alcove, where Becky, his secretary, waits for him. Ageless, she is her own work of art. He dotes on her. If it wasn't for her he would be a ruined man. They'll be going out this evening. You can smell her perm and her Chantilly from here. A little less noise and you could probably hear her mascara flake.

'Radio aerial's still number one, Mr Gold,' says Katey. Her father's attention has gone elsewhere, to some fine moment of sport on the box. He shares his rowdy triumph with his fellow aficionados. He turns back to her, panting. 'That was amazing,' he says.

Kate Doyle calls him over with her finger. He knows better than to hesitate. 'What?' he blusters. 'What? There's nothing wrong with those glasses. I told you it's the dishwasher.'

Her whisper is sharp as a needle in his wincing ear. She asks him why, after all she's spoken perfectly plainly to him, he is still letting that nasty old man into the pub?

'Oh, come on, Katey,' he says, 'where else can the poor devil go? He's a stranger in his own church these days.'

'He deserves nothing less,' she says. 'And I'll remind you, Dad, of my original terms. I'm off for a walk now and you can run the bloody pub yourself.'

'Oh, no!' He is mortified. He casts yearning eyes back towards the television. He looks like some benighted sinner in the picture books who has lost the salvation of Christ. 'Don't do this to me, Kate.'

'I might be back when he's gone,' she says. 'But I'm not making any promises.'

Every so often she has to let him know he is going too far. Getting her father to work was a full-time job for her mother but she's not going to waste her own life on that non-starter. He's already lost the hotel next door to his debts. Most of the money Kate allows him goes in some form of gambling. Those customers who lend him money soon discover how she refuses to honour his IOUs. He's lucky these days to be able to coax an extra dollar or two out of the till, usually by short-changing a stranger.

'We'll lose business if you go, Kate,' he hisses. 'Why cut off your nose to spite your face.'

'I'll cut off *your* nose, you old fool, if you don't set it to that grindstone right now,' she says. She hates sounding like her mother. Furiously, she snatches on her coat and scarf. 'I'll be back when you get him out of here.' She knows Father McQueeny's horrible eyes are still feeding off her through the pub's cultivated gloom.

'See you later, Katey, dear,' her father trills as he places professional fingers on his bar and a smile falls across his face. 'Now, then, Mrs Byrne, a half of Guinness, is it, darling?'

4.

The Circle was going up. There were all kinds of well-heeled people coming in. You could tell by the brass door-knockers and the window-boxes, the dark green paint. With the odd *boutique* and *croisanterie*, these were the traditional signs of gentrification. Taking down the last pylons of the ugly elevated had helped, along with the hippies who in the sixties and seventies had made such a success of the little park, which now had a playground and somewhere for the dogs to go. It was lovely in the summer.

It was quiet, too, since they had put in the one-way system. Now the only strange vehicles were those which thought they could still make a short cut and wound up whining round until, defeated, they left the way they had entered. You had to go up to Canal Street to get a cab. They wouldn't come any further than that. There were legends of drivers who had never returned.

This recent development had increased the sense of the Circle's uniqueness, a zone of relative tranquillity in one of the noisiest parts of New York City. Up to now they had been protected from a full-scale yuppie invasion by the nearby federal housing. Yet nobody from the projects had ever bothered the Circle. They thought of the place as their own, something they aspired to, something to protect. It was astonishing the affection local people felt for the place, especially the park, which was the best-kept in the city.

She was on her brisk way, of course, to take Mr Terry McLear up on his invitation but she was not going there directly for all to see. Neither was she sure what she'd have to say to him when she saw him. She simply felt it was time they had one of their old chats.

Under a chilly sky, she walked quickly along the central path of the park. Eight paths led to the middle these days, like the arms of a compass, and there had been some talk of putting a sundial on the knoll, where Mr Terry had now laid his discreet foundations. She paused to look at the smooth concrete of his deep, narrow hole. A flag, perhaps? Something that simple? But this was not a man to fly a flag at the best of times. And even the heaviest banner did not need so sturdy a pole. However, she was beginning to get a notion. A bit of a memory from a conversation of theirs a good few years ago now. Ah, she thought, it's about birds, I bet.

Certain some of her customers would still be watching her, she took the northern path and left the park to cross directly over to Houston Alley, where her uncle had his little toy soldier shop where he painted everything himself and where, next door, the Italian shoe-repairer worked in his window. They would not be there much longer now that the real estate people had christened the neighbourhood 'Houston Village'. Already the bar had had a sniff from Starbuck's. Up at the far end of the alley the street looked busy. She thought about going back, but told herself she was a fool.

The traffic in Canal Street was unusually dense and a crew-cut girl in big boots had to help her when she almost fell into the street, shoved aside by some thrusting Wall Street stockman in a vast raincoat which might have sheltered half the Australian outback. She thought she recognised him as the boy who had moved in to Number 91 a few weeks ago and she had been about to say hello.

She was glad to get back into the quietness of the Circle, going round into Church Street and then through Walker Street which would bring her out only a couple of houses from Mr Terry's place.

She was still a little shaken but had collected herself by the time she reached the row of brownstones. Number 27 was in the middle and his flat was in the basement. She went carefully down the iron steps to his area. It was as smartly kept up as always, with the flower baskets properly stocked and his miniature greenhouse raising tomatoes in their gro-bags. And he was still neat and clean. No obvious slipping of standards, no signs of senile decay. She took hold of the old black lion knocker and rapped twice against the dented plate. That same vast echo came back, as if she stood at the door to infinity.

He was slow as Christmas unbolting it all and opening up. Then everything happened at once. Pulling back the door he embraced her and kicked it shut at the same time. The apartment was suddenly very silent. 'Well,' he said, 'it has been such a long time. All my fault, too. I have had a chance to pull myself together and here I am.'

'That sounds like a point for God for a change.' She knew all the teachers had been anarchists or pagans or something equally silly in that school of his. She stared around at the familiar things, the copper and the oak and the big ornamental iron stove which once heated the whole building. 'You're still dusting better than a woman. And polishing.'

'She had high standards,' he says. 'I could not rise to them when she was alive, but now it seems only fair to try to live up to them. You would not believe what a slob I used to be.'

'You never told me,' she says.

'That is right. There is quite a bit I have not told you,' he says.

'And us so close once,' she says.

'We were good friends,' he agreed. 'The best of company. I am an idiot, Kate. But I do not think either of us realised I was in a sort of shock for years. I was afraid of our closeness, do you see? In the end.'

'I believe I might have mentioned that.' She went to put the kettle on. Filling it from his deep old-fashioned stone sink with its great brass faucets she carried it with both hands to the stove while he got out the teacakes and the toasting forks. He must have bought them only today from Van Beek's Bakery on Canal, the knowing old devil, and put them in the icebox. They were still almost warm. She fitted one to the fork. 'It doesn't exactly take Sigmund Freud to work that out. But you made your decisions, Mr Terry. And it is my general rule to abide by such decisions until the party involved decides to change. Which in my experience generally happens at the proper time.'

'Oh, so you have had lots of these relationships, have you, Kate?'

She laughed.

5.

'I was sixteen when I first saw her. In the Circle there she was, coming out of Number Ten, where the drycleaners is now. I said to myself, that is whom I am going to marry. And that was what I did. We used to sing quite a bit, duets together. She was a much better and sweeter singer than I, and she was smarter, as well.' Mr Terry looks into the fire and slowly turns his teacake against the glare. 'What a little old snob I was in those days, thinking myself better than anyone, coming back from Dublin with an education. But she liked me anyway and was what I needed to take me down a peg or two. My father thought she was an angel. He spoke often of the grandchildren he would care for. But both he and she died before that event could become any sort of reality. And I grew very sorry for myself, Kate. In those first days, when we were having our chats, I was selfish.'

'Oh, yes,' she says, 'but you were more than that. You couldn't help being more than that. That's one of the things hardest to realise about ourselves sometimes. Even in your morbid moments you often showed me how to get a grip on things. By example, you might say. You cannot help but be a good man, Mr Terry. A protector, I think, rather than a predator.'

'I do not know about that.'

'But I do,' she says.

'Anyway,' he flips a teacake on to the warming plate, 'we had no children and so the McLears have no heirs.'

'It's a shame,' she says, 'but not a tragedy, surely?' For an instant it flashes through her head, Oh, no, he doesn't want me to have his bloody babies, does he?

'Not in any ordinary sense, I quite agree. But you see there is an inheritance that goes along with that. Something which must be remembered accurately and passed down by word of mouth. It is our family tradition and has been so for quite a time.'

'My goodness,' she says. 'You're Brian Boru's rightful successor to the high throne of Erin, is that it?' With deft economy she butters their teacakes.

He takes some jelly from the dish and lays it lightly on top. 'Oh, these are good, eh?'

When they are drinking their last possible cup of Assam he says very soberly: 'Would you let me share this secret, Kate. I have no one else.'

'Not a crime, is it, or something nasty?' she begs.

'Certainly not!' He falls silent. She can sense him withdrawing and laughs at his response. He sighs.

'Then get on with it,' she says. 'Give me a taste of it, for I'm a busy woman.'

'The story does not involve the Irish much,' he says. 'Most of the Celts involved were from southern England, which was called Britannia in those days, by the Romans.'

'Ancient history!' she cries. 'How long, Mr Terry, is your story?'

'Not very long,' he says.

'Well,' she says, 'I will come back another time to hear it.' She glances at her watch. 'If I don't go now I'll miss my program.'

As he helps her on with her coat she says: 'I have a very low tolerance for history. It is hard for me to see how most of it relates to the here and now.'

'This will mean something to you, I think, Kate.'

They exchange light kisses upon the cheek. There is a new warmth between them which she welcomes.

'Make it scones tomorrow,' she says. 'Those big juicy ones they do, with the raisins in them, and I will hear your secret. We'll have Darjeeling, too. I'll bring some if you don't have any.'

'I have plenty,' he says.

'Bye, bye for now,' she says.

6.

'All the goodness is in the marrow!' declares Mrs Byrne, waving her bones at the other customers, 'but these days the young people all turn their noses up at it.'

'That's not the problem at all, Mavis. The plain truth is you're a bloody noisy eater,' says Corny Doyle, backing up the other diners' complaints. 'And you've had one too many now. You had better go home.'

With her toothless mouth she sucks at her mutton.

'They don't know what they're missing, do they, Mavis?' says Father McQueeny from where he sits panting in a booth.

'And you can fuck off, you old pervert.' Mavis rises with dignity and sails towards the ladies'. She has her standards.

'Well, Kate, how's the weather out there?' says Father McQueeny.

'Oh, you are here at last, Kate. It seems Father McQueeny's been locked out of his digs.' In other circumstances Corny's expression of pleading anxiety would be funny.

'That doesn't concern me,' she says, coming down the stairs. 'I just popped in for something. I have told you what I want, Dad.' She is carrying her little bag.

He rushes after her, whispering and pleading. 'What can I do?'

'I have told you what you can do.'

She looks back into the shadows. She knows he is staring at her. Often she thinks it is not exactly him that she fears, only what is in him. What sense does that make? Does she fear his memories and secrets? Of course Father Walsh, her confessor, had heard what had happened and what she had done and she had been absolved. What was more, the Church, by some means of its own, had discovered at least part of the truth and taken steps to curb him. They had sent Father Declan down to St Mary's. He was a tough old bugger but wholesome as they come. McQueeny was supposed to assist Declan who had found no use for him. However, since Father Walsh died, McQueeny revelled in their hideous secret, constantly hanging around the pub even before she started working there, haunting her, threatening to tell the world how he had come by his horrid surgery.

She is not particularly desperate about it. Sooner or later she knows her father will knuckle down and bar the old devil. It must be only a matter of time before the priest's liver kills him. She's never wished anyone dead in her life, save him, and her hatred of him is such that she fears for her own soul over it.

This time she goes directly across the park to Mr Terry McLear's. It might look as if she plans to spend the night there but she does not care. Her true intention is to return eventually to her own flat in Delaware Court and wait until her father calls. She gives it twenty-four hours from the moment she stepped out of the pub.

But when she lifts the lion's head and lets it fall there is no reply. She waits. She climbs back up the steps. She looks into the park. She is about to go down again when an old chequer cab pulls up and out of its yellow and black depths comes Mr Terry McLear with various bags and bundles. 'Oh what luck!' he declares. 'Just when I needed you, Kate.'

She helps him get the stuff out of the cab and down into his den. He removes his coat. He opens the door into his workshop and switches on a light. 'I was not expecting you back today.'

'Circumstances gave me the opportunity.' She squints at the bags. 'Who is Happy the Hammer?'

'Look on the other side. It is Stadtler's Hardware. Their mascot. Just the last bits I needed.'

'Is it a bird house of some kind that you are building?' she asks.

'And so you are adding telepathy to your list of extraordinary qualities, are you, Katey?' He grins. 'Did I ever mention this to you?'

'You might have done. Is it pigeons?'

'God bless you, Katey.' He pulls a bunch of small dowels out of a bag and puts it on top of some bits of plywood. 'I must have told you the story.'

'Not much of a secret, then,' she says.

'This is not the secret, though I suppose it has something to do with it. There used to be dovecotes here, Katey, years ago. And that is all I am building. Have you not noticed the little doves about?'

'I can't say I have.'

'Little mourning doves,' he says. 'Brown and cream. Like a kind of delicate pigeon.'

'Well,' she says, 'I suppose for the non-expert they'd be lost in the crowd.'

'Maybe, but I think you would know them when I pointed them out. The City believes me, anyhow, and is anxious to have them back. And it is not costing them a penny. The whole thing is a matter of fifty dollars and a bit of time. An old-fashioned dovecote, Katey. There are lots of accounts of the dovecotes, when this was more or less an independent village.'

'So you're building a little house for the doves,' she says. 'That will be nice for them.'

'A little house, is it? More a bloody great hotel.' Mr Terry erupts with sudden pride. 'Come on, Kate. I will take you back to look.'

7.

She admires him turning the wood this way and that against the whirling lathe he controls with a foot pedal.

'It is a wonderful smell,' she says, 'the smell of shavings.' She peers with casual curiosity at his small, tightly organised workshop. Tools, timber, electrical bits and pieces, nails, screws and hooks are neatly stowed on racks and narrow shelves. She inspects the white-painted sides of the near-completed bird-house. In the room, it seems massive, almost large enough to hold a child. She runs her fingers over the neatly ridged openings, the perfect joints. Everything has been finished to the highest standard, as if for the most demanding human occupation. 'When did they first put up the dovecotes?'

'Nobody knows. The Indians had them when the first explorers arrived from Holland and France. There are sketches of them in old books. Some accounts call the tribe that lived here "the Dove Keepers". The Iroquois respected them as equals and called them the Ga-geh-ta-o-no, the People of the Circle. But the phrase also means People of the Belt.

'The Talking Belts, the "wampum" records of the Six Nations, are invested with mystical meanings. Perhaps our tribe were the Federation's record keepers. They were a handsome, wealthy, civilised people, apparently, who were happy to meet and trade with the newcomers. The famous Captain Block was their admirer and spoke of a large stone circle surrounding their dovecotes. He believed that these standing stones, which were remarkably like early European examples, enclosed their holy place and that the doves represented the spirit they worshipped.

'Other accounts mention the stones, but there is some suspicion that the writers simply repeated Block's observations. Occasionally modern construction work reveals some of the granite, alien rock driven into the native limestone like a knife, and there's a suspicion the rock was used as part of a later stockade. The only Jesuit records make no mention of the stones but concentrate on the remarkable similarity of Kakatanawa (as the Europeans called them) myths to early forms of Christianity.'

'I have heard as much myself,' she agrees, more interested than she expected. 'What happened to the Indians?'

'Nothing dramatic. They were simply and painlessly absorbed, mainly through intermarriage and mostly with the Irish. It would not have been difficult for them, since they still had a considerable amount of blood in common. By 1720 this was a thriving little township, built around the green. It still had its dovecotes. The stones were gone, re-used in walls of all kinds. The Kakatanawa were living in ordinary houses and intermarrying. In those days it was not fashionable to claim native ancestry. But you see the Kakatanawa were hardly natives. They resembled many of the more advanced Iroquois peoples and spoke an Iroquois dialect, but their tradition had it that their ancestors came from the other side of the Atlantic.'

'Where did you read all this?' she asks in some bewilderment.

'It is not conventionally recorded,' he says. 'But this is my secret.'

And he told her of Trinovante Celts, part of the Boudicca uprising of 69 AD, who had used all their wealth to buy an old Roman trading ship with the intention of escaping the Emperor's cruel justice and sailing to Ireland. They were not navigators but good fortune eventually took them to these shores where they built a settlement. They chose Manhattan for the same reason as everyone else, because it commanded a good position on the river, had good harbours and could be easily defended.

They built their village inland and put a stockade around it, pretty much the same as the villages they had left behind. Then they sent the ship back with news and to fetch more settlers and supplies. They never heard of it again. The ship was in fact wrecked off Cornwall, probably somewhere near St Ives, but there were survivors and the story remained alive amongst the Celts, even as they succumbed to Roman civilisation.

When, some hundreds of years later, the Roman legions were withdrawn and the Saxon pirates started bringing their families over, further bands of desperate Celts fled for Ireland and the land beyond, which they had named Hy Braseal. One other galley reached Manhattan and discovered a people more Senecan than Celtic.

This second wave of Celtic immigrants were the educated Christian stone-raisers, Romanised astronomers and mystics, who brought new wisdom to their distant cousins and were doubtless not generally welcomed for it. For whatever reasons, however, they were never attacked by other tribes. Even the stern Iroquois, the Romans of these parts, never threatened them, although they were nominally subject to Hiawatha's Federation. By the time the Dutch arrived, the dominant Iroquois culture had again absorbed the Celts, but they retained certain traditions, stories and a few artefacts. Most of these appear to have been sold amongst the Indians and travelled widely through the north-east. They gave rise to certain rumours of Celtic civilisations (notably the Welsh) established in America.

'But the Kakatanawa spoke with the same eloquence and wore the finery and fashions of the Federation. Their particular origin-legend was not remarkable. Other tribes had far more dramatic conceptions, involving spectacular miracles and wildly original plots. So nobody took much notice of us and so we have survived.'

'Us?' says Kate Doyle. 'We?'

'You,' he says, 'represent the third wave of Celtic settlement of the Circle during the nineteenth and twentieth centuries. And I represent the first and second. I am genuinely, Katey, and it is embarrassing to say so, the Last of the Kakatanawas. That was why my father looked forward to an heir, as did I. I suppose I was not up to the burden, or I would have married again.'

'You'd be a fool to marry just for the sake of some old legend,' she says. 'A woman deserves more respect than that.'

'I agree.' He returns to his work. Now he's putting the fine little touches to the dowels, the decorations. It's a wonder to watch him.

'Do you have a feathered headdress and everything? A peace-pipe and a tomahawk?' Her mockery has hardly any scepticism in it.

'Go over to that box just there and take out what is in it,' he says, concentrating on the wood.

She obeys him.

It is a little modern copper box with a Celtic motif in the lid. Inside is an old dull coin. She picks it up between wary fingers and fishes it out, turning it to try to read the faint letters of the inscription. 'It's Constantine,' she says. 'A Roman coin.'

'The first Christian Emperor. That coin has been in New York, in our family, Katey, since the sixth century. It is pure gold. It is what is left of our treasure.'

'It must be worth a fortune,' she says.

'Not much of one. The condition is poor, you see. And I am sworn never to reveal its provenance. But it is certainly worth a bit more than the gold alone. Anyway, that is it. It is yours, together with the secret.'

'I don't want it,' she says, 'can't we bury it?'

'Secrets should not be buried,' he said, 'but kept.'

'Well, speak for yourself,' she says. 'There are some secrets best buried.'

While he worked on, she told him about Father McQueeny. He turned the wood more and more slowly as he listened. The priest's favourite joke that always made him laugh was 'Little girls should be screwed and not heard'. With her father's half-hearted compliance, the old wretch had enjoyed all his pleasures on her until one day when she was seventeen she had taken his penis in her mouth and, as she had planned, bitten down like a terrier. He had torn her hair out and almost broken her arm before he fainted.

'And I did not get all the way through. You would not believe how horrible it feels – like the worst sort of gristle in your mouth and all the blood and nasty crunching, slippery stuff. At first, at least, everything in you makes you want to stop. I was very sick afterwards, as you can imagine, and just able to dial 911 before I left him there. He almost died of losing so much blood. I hadn't expected it to spurt so hard. I almost drowned. I suppose if I had thought about it I should have anticipated that. And had a piece of string ready, or something. Anyway, it stopped his business. I was never reported. And I don't know how confessors get the news out, but the Church isn't taking any chances with him, so all he has now are his memories.'

'Oh, dear,' says Mr Terry gravely. 'Now there is a secret to share.'

'It's the only one I have,' she said. 'It seemed fair to reciprocate.'

8.

Two days later, side by side, they stand looking up at his magnificent bird-house, complete at last. He's studied romantic old plans from the turn of the century, so it has a touch or two of the Charles Rennie Mackintosh about it in its white austerity, its sweeping gables. There are seven fretworked entrances and eight beautifully turned perches, black as ebony, following the lines of the park's paths. He's positioned and prepared the cote exactly as instructed in Tiffany's *Modern Gardens* of 1892 and has laid his seed and corn carefully. At her request, and without much reluctance, he's buried the Roman coin in the pole's foundation. Now we must be patient, he says. And wait. As he speaks a whickering comes from above and a small dove, fawn and pale grey, settles for a moment upon the gleaming roof, then takes fright when she sees them.

'What a pretty thing. I will soon have to get back to my flat,' she says. 'My father will be going frantic by now. I put the machine on, but if I know him he'll be too proud to leave a message.'

'Of course.' He stoops to pick up a delicately coloured wing feather. It has a thousand shades of rose, beige, pink and grey. 'I will be glad to come with you if you want anything done.'

'I'll be all right,' she says. But he falls in beside her.

As they turn their backs on the great bird-house three noisy mourning doves land on the perches as if they have been anticipating this moment for a hundred and fifty years. The sense of celebration, of relief, is so tangible it suffuses Kate Doyle and Mr Terry McLear even as they walk away.

'This calls for a cup of coffee,' says Mr Terry McLear. 'Shall we go to Belladonna's?'

They are smiling when Father McQueeny, evicted at last, comes labouring towards them along the path from the pub and pauses, suddenly gasping for his familiar fix, as if she has turned up in the nick of time to save his life.

'Good morning, Katey, dear.' His eyes begin to fill with powerful memories. He speaks lovingly to her. 'And Terry McLear, how are you?'

'Not bad thanks, Father,' says Mr Terry, looking him over.

'And when shall we be seeing you in church, Terry?' The priest is used to people coming back to the faith as their options begin to disappear.

'Oh, soon enough, Father, I hope. By the way, how is Mary's last supper doing? How is the little hot dog?' And he points.

It is a direct and fierce attack. Father McQueeny folds before it. 'Oh, you swore!' he says to her.

She tries to speak but she cannot. Instead she finds herself laughing in the old wretch's face, watching him die, his secret, his sustenance lost for ever. He knows at once, of course, that his final power has gone. His cold eyes stare furiously into inevitable reality as his soul goes at last to the devil. It will be no more than a day or two before they bury him.

'Well,' says Katey, 'we must be getting on.'

'Goodbye, Father,' says Mr Terry McLear, putting his feather in his white hair and grinning like a fool.

When they look back the priest has disappeared, doubtless scuttling after some mirage of salvation. But the dovecote is alive with birds. It must have a dozen on it already, bobbing around in the little doorways, pecking up the seed. They glance around with equanimity. You would think they had always been here. The distant noise of New York's traffic is muffled by their excited voices, as if old friends meeting after years. There is an air of approving recognition about their voices.

'They like the house. Now we must see if, when they have eaten the food, they will stay.' Mr Terry McLear links a proud arm with his companion. 'I never expected it to happen so quickly. It was as if they were waiting to come home. It is a positive miracle.'

Amused, she looks up at him. 'Come on now, a grown man like you with tears in his eyes!

'After all, Mr Terry.' She takes his arm as they continue down the path towards Houston Alley. 'You must never forget your honour as the Last of the Kakatanawas.'

'You do not believe a word of it, do you, Kate?' he says.

'I do,' she says. 'Every word, in fact. It's just that I cannot fathom why you people went to so much trouble to keep it dark.'

'Oh, you know all right, Kate,' says Mr Terry McLear, pausing to look back at the flocking doves. 'Sometimes secrecy is our only means of holding on to what we value.'

Whistling, she escorts him out of the Circle.

DANIEL'S SKYLINE
Christopher Burns

I kept all my son's work from the day when he first went to school. At the bottom of his wardrobe in his bedroom there is a cardboard box with wallet files: tucked into each file are drawings, mementoes, school reports, pieces he has written. Photographs, like some of his old clothes, are kept separately.

He is the only person I have done this for. Only a few traces remain of my husband – a handful of wedding and holiday shots, our marriage certificate, our decree absolute. An archivist would discover only fragments of my married life; most of the evidence has been deliberately destroyed. With Daniel it is different. For him, an entire biography could be constructed from what I have collected and retained. I even handed in some of his work as evidence, thinking it might do him good with his assessors.

Before visiting Daniel this afternoon I looked again at some of the folders. I found it distressing. I sat with the contents fanned out around me, achingly aware that each clumsy image, each badly written word was from a time beyond recovery. The future, whatever it will be, can only be tighter, darker.

Just before puberty Daniel wrote an essay. It took him a long time to write. He visited the library by himself and noted down details which he transcribed exactly. I did not discourage him; neither did his teachers. We were all pleased to see him take such an interest. And besides, at the time, it did not seem that a boyish fascination would become a lifelong obsession.

The essay reads like this –

New York is the greatest city in the world and the tallest. It is made of skyscrapers. The skyscrapers reach so high they scrape the sky. Everybody looks like ants. They run around. The skyscrapers are hundreds and hundreds and hundreds of feet high. When I grow up I will live in New York. I will have a house on top of the tallest skyscraper. I will never go back to the ground. There is the Chrysler Building. There is the World Trade Center the highest skyscraper it is 1378 feet high. There is the Empire State. There is the United Nations building it is glass and steel. There is the Seagram building it is smoky glass and aluminium. When I am on the top of my skyscraper I will see over the whole wide wide world and never never go back to the ground where I was born.

He signed it with his name, house number, street, and the name of an English city. I still live at the same address.

My son never became sensitive about his childish work. He had no need. It differs only slightly from work he produced later. Much of this is written notebooks which are kept on a shelf in his bedroom. He has not slept in that room for some time, but I have changed nothing. Like the keeper of a shrine, all I do is maintain it.

The room is postered with New York sights of the most recognisable kind – the Statue of Liberty, the Brooklyn Bridge, Central Park and, most of all, skyscrapers. The risen skyline flattens itself against Daniel's walls. In the high summer shots the buildings are hard-edged, windows etched deep by the angle of illumination; in autumn a thin bronze veneer coats the verticals and reflective surfaces glare in the sunset. Perhaps most magically of all, at two in the morning the city is massed blackness and geometric constellations, as if a god had scissored the night sky, folded it into uprights, and stacked it shoulder to shoulder around the brakelight-ribboned streets.

Daniel's books are undisturbed, too. Most of these are picture guides to the city. And there are several videos, some of which he has watched over and over. I have sat with him while he compulsively rewound tapes and viewed favourite sequences again and again, as if they held secrets which only repeated study would make clear.

On the inside of the door he has pinned the postcards that his father has sent – no more than one a year, always with a hackneyed tourist image of the USA on the picture side and an uncomplicated greeting on the other.

For a while Daniel's father lived in New York; later, he sent postcards from other parts of the country. I never knew his address until now.

He left me before his son was two years old, before Daniel's condition was confirmed. I was pleased to see him go; I don't want to meet him ever again. I always wished he would stop sending the cards. Once or twice I intercepted them and tore them up, but conscience made me hand over the later ones.

I sometimes wonder if the early postcards, simplistically garish and welcoming as they were, were the keystones for Daniel's fantasy and obsession. I don't think he wants to meet his father; he has no interest in him. It is the city that fills his imagination.

Daniel has never been to New York. I don't expect he will ever go. Neither will I.

The assessment centre lies on the very outskirts of a town fifty miles away from our home. Beyond its high unscalable walls a featureless range of grain recedes across vanished fields whose hedges were grubbed up before I was born.

A few weeks ago, when Daniel was first sent here, I stood in an interview room on the upper storey and gazed through the smoked glass. I pretended to be absorbed by a distant farmhouse and a solitary line of elms, but in reality I saw little. I hoped that the angry trembling in my limbs was not visible, although for several minutes I could not control it. When I had composed myself and turned back, I realised that the only impression I had retained of the view was of an immensity of sky.

I had complained that Daniel was being assessed too far away from where he lived. No one actually dismissed me, but they were urbane, aloof, uncaring. Distance from home was hardly a relevant factor, I was told. And besides, one possible result of the investigation was that my son would be placed in a prison even further away. After all, the courts had found him guilty. The reasonableness of that statement, and the emphasis on the word *guilty*, as if no other verdict had been possible, made something lurch inside me.

This morning it was different. There were only the two of us in a booth. We were separated from other visitors by shields of thick glass, but warders stood at the end of the long room and cameras with filming lights bright as fake rubies were trained on us all the time.

We sat at either side of a table that resembled an interrogation bench. The table top was grimy and smooth. I thought of the dozens, hundreds of other mothers and sons who must have talked across the same horizontal barrier.

I reached out and tried to take Daniel's hand, but he moved it away from me. I asked him how he was. He did not answer. Instead he ignored the question and stared to one side, apparently taking in nothing.

He was far too young to be in such a place, I thought; no matter what his chronological age, he was far too young.

'You have to take care of yourself,' I said. 'Living here like this must be very hard for you.'

Daniel jerked his head, caught my gaze for a fraction of a second, and then looked away again. 'Home,' he said.

'But it's not home, Daniel. Not our home. And not the other one that you've lived in. You're among friends there. This is completely different. There are people here who are going to help decide what happens to you.'

Suddenly he became preoccupied with his fingers, and began to interlace them as if he had just discovered a new trick. I watched him for a while. Big though Daniel was, I wanted to pick him up, take him home, comb his hair and brush his teeth and make sure he was dressed properly. No one was doing that for him now. True, he'd attempted all of these things, but ineffectively. His hair was parted in two uneven swatches separated by a ragged line, his breath smelled, and he had been issued with clothing that was too big. The collar of his shirt was so wide that it made his neck appear thin and his head too large. He looked so out of place, so vulnerable, that I had to concentrate hard so that tears would not come to my eyes. He hated to see me cry.

'Can't you get someone to help you?' I asked.

'What?'

'You know, with combing your hair and things like that.'

'I'm a man. A grown man. There's, uh, no need. Not for that.'

I nodded. 'Right. So. So what's happened to you over the past few days? Have they been testing you every day?'

'Yes, that's right. Every day. I think.'

He still could not look at me. I was used to this. Daniel never held a gaze. He was incapable of it.

'Listen,' he said suddenly, and cocked his head. As he listened to a noise I could not hear, small tremors ran through him and made his head sway.

'I can't hear anything,' I confessed.

He raised a hand and extended one finger as if in admonition, but I wondered if he was pointing upwards. I strained my ears to listen. In common with others who shared his condition, Daniel had excellent hearing. All that I could detect were the low mumbling of others talking in the shielded room and a few indistinguishable muffled noises from elsewhere in the building.

'Boeing,' he said with a smirk. 'New York flight.'

Of course, there was no way he could know where the plane was going, but I thought it certain that he could hear it, and possible that he could identify it. I was very still and tried not to breathe for a few seconds. Then I believed that I could detect a distant engine murmur, far, far away – but it may have been a wish to hear, nothing more.

'It might not be going to New York. It might not even be going to America,' I said.

Daniel nodded vigorously and struck the edge of the table several times with his fingers. 'Heathrow to Kennedy. On the regular schedule. The distance is 3475 miles from central London to, uh, the *Daily News* building.'

'Right,' I agreed. Any resistance to such determination was merely token.

'The plane I take.'

'One day.'

'Soon. I'll take it soon.'

'There are a few things that have to be sorted out here first, Daniel.'

There was a pause. I knew he would ignore me.

'That's why they're keeping you here,' I went on. 'The people who are interviewing you, the people doing all those tests, all those measurements, they're doctors.'

'Yes. Right.'

'Clinical psychologists. Men and women who are trying to find out what kind of person you are. Whether or not you're dangerous. Whether or not you can be trusted to live in the outside world.'

Petulantly, Daniel arched away in a half-spasm.

'I'm doing my best to help,' I said. 'I've told them what a good son you always were, how I've always been proud of you, how you'd never hurt anyone. I always said that; that you'd never hurt anyone. But my word isn't enough. They won't just believe me. They want to do their own tests, reach their own conclusion. What they decide –'

'I'll take it soon,' Daniel interrupted, his hand drumming irregularly on the side of the desk. 'Sooner than, uh, than anyone thinks.'

I knew he meant the New York flight.

'Maybe one day,' I said. 'When this is all over.'

His eyes rolled upwards as he tilted his head toward the ceiling. I knew he was listening for another plane, or any kind of distraction, but that he could not hear anything.

'They believe her, you know,' I said cautiously.

Apart from a quiver in one arm, he did not move.

'I don't think you meant to do anything. I'm sure you were just curious.'

A look of concentration invaded Daniel's face, as if he were willing a plane into existence.

'I know you didn't mean to hurt her,' I continued. 'I don't think you *did* hurt her. She panicked, that's all.'

'No more,' he said sharply. It was a demand that we stop discussing something he found unpleasant and unsettling. Throughout his life he had been liable to fly into a rage if forced to confront a consequence of his own problems.

'You have to talk about this, Daniel.'

He said nothing.

'You have to tell the doctors that you'd never been with a girl before, that you didn't know what was going on.'

Still no reaction.

'You have to convince them that you just wanted to see what she looked like, that was all. You've never seen a girl without clothes before, have you?'

I do not know if he shook his head or nodded.

'They have to be convinced that you were just a couple of adolescents. If things had been different it would all have passed off quite normally, just like it does like for most people. Just like it did for me and your father.'

And for the first time for years I thought of those few minutes with the man I had married – the ridiculous, unsettling festival lights that played on the side of our hotel; the reeling shouts of visitors celebrating in the streets outside; the humiliating, intertwining rhythm of breath and bedsprings that I was sure would permeate the building; and, at the moment when I longed most sharply for escape, the sound of a single-engine aircraft flying tourists on a half-hour trip along the holiday coast. When he had finished he lay on top of me and gave a little snigger of self-congratulation. I stared at the ceiling, listening to the engine fade, and knew that everything had changed.

Daniel had been conceived on that very night. For several months, I thought he was my rescuer.

'No more,' he repeated, this time in an agitated manner. His hand twisted and leaped on the table like a landed fish.

'If you can't talk to me about it,' I asked, 'who can you talk to?'

Daniel turned in his seat. I thought he was about to stand up and leave. I spoke his name quickly, and reached out to touch his hand. He pulled it away.

'You must be very careful what you say,' I insisted. 'You must convince everyone that you didn't mean any harm.'

'I didn't harm her. I didn't.'

'I know it, Daniel.'

'I was just –' And he stopped and moved his upper body again.

'Curious,' I repeated.

'Curious,' he echoed. 'Yes. That's right. Was just, uh, curious.'

I had imagined the scene many times. At the back of the home there was a large conservatory where tropical plants grew beneath a high glass roof. I visited it once or twice; Daniel had taken me. Everyone loved the plants, I had been assured; their shapes, variety and colours made a visit to the conservatory both stimulating and therapeutic. But the humidity had taken my breath, and the jungle of greenery had been so thick that there was a feeling of threat about the place.

It was in here that Daniel had assaulted the girl.

Even now it was impossible to find out what had really happened. Not much, I suspected; some fumbling, a little exposure, perhaps some extended touching. But nothing violent, nothing threatening, nothing invasive. The girl hadn't become distressed until afterwards, and by then Daniel himself was upset and tearful.

'What made you stop?' I asked, although I already knew the answer. Like his intellect and his character, Daniel's sexuality would never fully develop. To him it would always be a puzzle, a mild pleasure, perhaps even a threat, but never a fulfilment.

'I didn't stop,' he said.

I waited.

'*Didn't* stop,' he insisted. 'I wanted to, uh, to go on. That's what should happen. You should go on.'

'She stopped you?'

'She, uh, didn't like me. No. Ugly, she said. She said I was ugly. Me. She said I frightened her.'

He looked at me for a moment. For a second he was a young man, rejected, hurt, possibly vengeful. He was just like the rest of us.

And then I saw in his eyes, quite clearly, that he was beginning to make his escape, and that nothing I said would bring him back.

'I'll not take her,' he said decisively, turning away again.

I shook my head. 'No, don't.'

'I'll go on my own. To New York.'

'Yes. You do that.'

'Bank of Manhattan, 927 feet. Chrysler Building, 925 feet with 185 feet spire on top. It's taller.'

'That's right.'

'Empire State. Built 1931. 102 floors. 1250 feet high. So big you can see mile after mile after mile. As big as that.'

'That's right.'

'World Trade Center. Twin towers. 1966 to 1976. 110 floors. 1350 feet. All in New York. Every, uh, every one of them. Nothing but skyscrapers. I'm going to live there. Soon. You know that. Yes, you know that. Hundreds, hundreds of feet high. On the very top. Watch the sun go down and people in the streets tiny as ants. I'll be happy there.'

'Yes Daniel,' I agreed; 'on the very top.'

I am in Daniel's room, sitting on the floor. A letter lies beside me on the carpet. Outside it is dusk.

When I arrived home the letter was behind the front door. Although I have not opened it, I recognise the handwriting. It is from the man I once married. It is postmarked New York. And it is addressed to Daniel.

I am sitting in a kind of museum. All around me are the displays – dramatic, changeless, chosen. The television swims with images; they are black and white, high contrast, grainy. I look at the screen and then around the room.

Everything here is a guess at reality, a chance, a dream. It is not a re-creation, not a representation, but a work of fiction. Whatever the letter says I know that it, too, will be an invention.

Often I wonder if our entire lives are governed, not by what is real, but by what we are able to imagine.

I have seen the film many times – the arrival at the island, the sacrifice, the monster touching his prize with a tenderness so clumsy that it may be mistaken for an attack.

I take one of Daniel's notebooks down from its shelf. Laboriously, exhaustively, he has copied down fact after fact about his city – materials, dates, addresses, tonnages, dimensions. I leaf through the notebook, ignoring the letter at my feet.

Tormented beyond endurance, driven by something he can never be capable of explaining, the monster scales the vertical walls. An excited crowd gathers in the street below and gasps in horror when he plucks the girl from her room.

As he heads ever higher, the girl clasped tenderly in his fist, single-engine aircraft fly over the risen skyline. Moment by moment, building by building, they close in on him as he reaches for the summit.

THE NEW ZOO
Rikki Ducornet

Recent upheavals at the Bronx Zoo have been so extreme rumour insists the park exists only in the minds of the mad. What follows proposes a reasonable explanation for vagabond myths and is intended to help the potential visitor overcome his terror of new forms – still open to elaboration – that have spontaneously regenerated a necropolis. Now more than ever the Zoo is that 'ocean of life' its founders imagined. I should add that at this stage of the park's history, it is irrelevant to the Board if the solution to the problem was as extravagant as it was illegal.

In the first decade of the new century, lethal strains of rogue prions scoured the Zoo of animals, many of them very rare and obtained through the tireless industry of friends. Scoundrels and thieves, too, are essential to a world class zoo, and this fact, admitted by the Board after decades of denial, had much to do with the acceptance and adoption of the current situation, as did the Board's worsening eschatological mood, and the unique personalities of our president, Mrs Ditmars Beerbower, and the astonishing Ms Few Seconds.

After the plagues, the Zoo was empty for several years. Little by little squatters arrived to claim first the small mammal house, then the bear dens. When summer came and a night watchman saw young people thrashing about in the otter pools, he contacted the president of the Executive Committee, Mrs Ditmars Beerbower, who, along with members of the Zoological Society and the Board of Managers, met with the squatters in the Administration Building at Baird Court. (Those who suggested we inform the city police were reminded by our president that the Society had assumed control of the grounds on July 1, 1898, and that the lands continued to belong to the Society. 'Therefore,' Mrs Ditmars Beerbower said in those unarguable tones we have come to admire, 'this is *not* city business. This is *our* business.')

The squatters responded to the civil treatment they received and seduced us with the Event precipitated by Ms Few Seconds who, marvellous in her mane of green hair and tattooed pinafore, explained with unexpected eloquence the diaspora of the floating population.

'We have come via the Bronx Park transit,' she began, 'Lenox Avenue,

Bradbury Bridge and the Third Avenue Elevated. Some of us were already living at Fordham Station from which the north-west entrance to the park is but a half-mile distant. Some came up to the open manhole three blocks south of the Croton entrance. We have survived cut-rate narcotics, the Immigration Service, dumpster food, the City Planning Commission, voodoo, assault weapons, the epidemic of the winter of 2016, evangelists and the NYPD.'

'Some of us abandoned middle-class neighbourhoods,' Few Seconds continued, 'others luxury condominiums, others the subways. We have come singly or in groups from Union City and Central Park, the Devil's Kitchen and the Flatlands. We had fled Hackensack, Little Italy, Flushing and Rockaway Beach. Some of us were living in coolers at LaGuardia, others in the heating vents at Yankee Stadium. Somebody survived in Bloomingdale's by sleeping upright in a coat rack; another camped in the General Theological Seminary's latrine. A junkie lived in Morningside Cemetery disguised as a corpse, and a queen shared a dog house on Utopia Parkway. We've come from all over New York and we are still coming.'

Few Seconds is a beautiful specimen of animal vitality and she is eloquent, too. She explained that if the tribes were partial to piercings (her own nipples twinkled with stolen gems) they put their collective foot down on clitoridectomies and foot binding.

'Nor do we condone the sacrifice of fingers and tongues,' she continued, flashing teeth stained with betel. 'We feel no need for expiation, for guilt and punishment. *We are not demented!*' The tribes cheered at this. When they had quieted down, Mrs Ditmars Beerbower said with conviction:

'You are Free Spirits.'

'Yes!' Few Seconds agreed. 'But we know there is no freedom without responsibility.' She explained she had been a philosophy major at Rutgers and had dropped out when Humanities was bought up by the Soft Drink Industry and the Presidential Campaign.

'Tell us more,' said our Treasurer, pouring Few Seconds a Pisco Sour. 'What *rules* you?'

'Mutability,' Few Seconds replied without hesitation, 'and Beauty.'

We learned that the tribes are fluid and defined by families of forms characterised and elaborated by, for example, true and fictive horns, sham wings, stilts, hoops of fire, wickerwork, holographic *peshwaz*, big bottoms, battery-powered tails, false noses and turbans – and by colours: red moleskin and mud is a popular disguise, as is birch bark, gold paint and indigo *espadrilles*. Few Seconds said that because she is currently green she has chosen to live in Parrot Hall:

'Tomorrow I may be covered with fur and join the Neo Berbers of Otter Pond,' she smiled, dazzling us. 'Skin colour and gender are rarely an issue although the Blue Hermaphrodites of Tortoise Yard insist gender matters *to them*.'

'The tribes are vegetarian,' Few Seconds' current companion Blue Niles added. 'Our furs are acrylic and should a vital organ fail we refuse animal replacement parts.'

'Life ends in Death,' Few Seconds said simply. The entire company – squatters, Board members and Friends of the Zoo – nodded sadly and spontaneously observed a minute of silence, some crouching cat-like and others standing erect on tiptoe like birds about to take flight.

In the New Zoo, history and the solar year have succumbed to the whims of fashion.

'Like astronomers,' Few Seconds smiled, 'we believe in *appearances*.'

'Surfaces are *surfaces*.' Blue Niles agreed, languorously caressing his own azure skin. 'We wish to be simultaneously gorgeous and unpredictable.'

'The instant,' Few Seconds added, 'is all.'

Creatures of the moment, the lives of the tribes are punctuated by makeovers and those events or 'pulses' during which they 'self signal'.

'That's when we get to "strut our alchemy"!' Hi Fever, a lovely semi-salamander, explained. The tribes believe psychology is a branch of aesthetics and eros the 'main event'.

'Everything's Eros!' Few Seconds told us. 'Our justification for this sensuous levity is that *there is no God*.'

'In their beauty and total atheism,' Mrs Ditmars Beerbower concluded, addressing the Board, 'they are very like the animals they have come to replace.' She then removed her blouse revealing to our surprise and pleasure a beautiful scarlet brassière trimmed with *faux* egret. 'To the Aviary!' she cried, strutting alchemy to demonstrate her support of the tribes. All of us found ourselves swept up in the instant, crying: 'To the Aviary!' And, once we were there, 'NO OPTICAL CONCESSIONS EVER!' The tribes passed out props.

Now let us explore the fabulous continent which was once the Bronx Zoo:

1. Arriving at the East 182nd Street entrance, we pick up a safe-conduct pass – those small red plastic cones some keep in a pocket but most tend to worry

between tongue and teeth. Making a sharp turn to the right, we pass the Antelope Barns currently inhabited by the Topiary Tribes (fine specimens of proud, indolent and swaggering fops whose hair is coaxed up stainless steel rods screwed to their skulls). Bearing left we descend into the valley of Bronx Lake. The approach is narrow and steep and we must negotiate a succession of treacherous steps. Very possibly our descent will be animated by an improvised fair: acrobat priests will, for a feverish glance, cast astrological charts or, in the cool of the evening, rouge the visitor's lips. The plain, when we reach it at last, is spare and crusted with salt; it is wise to bring water along as the walk to Agassiz Lake is arduous. However, more often than not, a campfire enlivens the distance. We approach it, the pass held between our teeth, and, our identity assured, are offered thimble-sized cups of Turkish coffee and some excellent hashish. Throughout the summer, days at a time may be spent in this section of the park in rambles and rides. (Donkeys are available at many major sites, and on occasion curtained palanquins. No fixed hour is posted for closing; throughout the park the absence of clocks is striking, as is the lack of money machines and public telephones. Public baths are plentiful, however.)

2. We choose the Bronxdale entrance. Passing the psilocybin gardens on the left, we follow Few Seconds' Path for a full mile. The path, edged by a brass railing carved with rampant phalli, conveys us to Linnaeus Point from where we may admire the Boat People of Agassiz Lake, a settlement of Marsh Avatars and the oyster beds and oyster roasts of New Jersey. If we follow the path to the bottom of the gorge, we will see the remains of the Pelham Avenue Trolley System. The trolley has not been replaced since the time of the Great Flood, but express steamers leave for the Bronxdale exit subway terminus periodically, and they all serve milk and honey. While waiting we may dig for clams with the Cope Lake tribes, purchase a burnoose in the colourful souks above Agassiz Falls, or sip sherbets made with ice from the Catskill Mountains. Wandering self-signers garlanded in saffron knots and little else haunt this section of the park, and it is here, beneath the charming painted canopies that the New Zoo's anniversary is celebrated always unexpectedly. For several weeks after, the air smells of myrrh.

3. The Cope Lake Exit is invariably wet and must at all costs be avoided in months of rain. Wearing galoshes, continue south several miles to Hunt's

Point where the Beerbower Geyser – a ·jet of scalding water rising into the air at the rate of 4,000 gallons a minute – greets the astonished visitor. If the wind is good, climb aboard one of the 9th Street wheelbarrows – all equipped with sails – and head for the Croton Reservoir. Here admire the swarms of carp: each wears a ring in its nose. The strata are much dislocated and the disturbing forces have left the entire area in confusion. The plain from 39th Street to Battery Park is covered with efflorescences of salt and even fossil amber. This gives way in Brooklyn to a weary waste of sand. On clear nights Fez may be seen gleaming just over the horizon.

4. Finally, the Flatbush entrance leads us into some of the most curious geological and libidinal areas of the park. Here the East River, always the scene of adventures and miracles, has forced a passage through the granite barrier of Greater Old Manhattan, creating a series of falls and revealing the grottoes of Grand Central Station. Rumour has it that these grottoes, known for their erotic illuminations and the massive new World Tantric Temple Complex – lead directly to the storage rooms of the Holography Museum and so may explain the quantity of first-class illusions available in the souks. With any luck, visitors to the Temple Complex will be ambushed and tenderly ravished.

From the cliffs on both sides of the Union Square Ravine, cascades fall into the Harlem River. Behind this veil of green water the All Aquaria Acrobats beckon us and, as in a dream, we enter willingly into their uniquely irresistible morphogenetic fields for a brief, regenerating holiday – from which we emerge reeking of love, our fingers and mouths stained with betelnut and keef, hungry as bears, frisky as mares and, as the lights go up on Broadway, ready for *anything*.

– for Karen Elizabeth Gordon

ELEVATOR MAN
Edward Fox

As he awaited the day he and his wife Violet would move from North Carolina to New York, Bill luxuriated in nostalgia for the city of his birth. They were moving because Bill had got a job offer from a bank in New York, with a high enough salary to make it worthwhile for them to move, and to be able to live in Manhattan, even if their new apartment would probably be the size of one of the rooms in the big comfortable house they had been living in down south, in their leafy college town. Bill, who had left New York as a child and had never been back, leapt at the chance to live once again in the city of his happiest days, and of his ancestors, and which also happened to be, according to cosmologists and anyone with any sense, the centre of the universe. Violet, who was the leader of the local modern dance ensemble, liked the idea too, for her own important reason: it would be a chance for her to move out of the small pond in which she was far too big a marine vertebrate, and migrate on to land to advance her evolution into a serious choreographer. Her daydreams glowed with the moonlit vision of the draughty dance lofts of SoHo, the sweatshops of the avant-garde.

In his vigil of anticipation, Bill meditated on the city's virtues. Does the water still run clear from the Croton aqueduct, down from the crystal-clear lakes of the Catskills (he mused), purer than Perrier, so abundant you can let it run while brushing your teeth? And does the black-vested Greek coffee-shop waiter still give you a glass of it with ice the instant you sit down? And every few years is there still a shortage, and brushing your teeth with the water running is illegal, for a while? Or one of the nineteenth-century cast-iron mains pipes breaks, and water bursts out, flooding a neighbourhood, closing the streets. New York is the most old-fashioned city in America, with its own cast-iron ways of doing things that have not been replaced since the last century. Yet in New York City, instead of having a lake at your door, or a field of corn, you have infinity itself, mathematically expressed: the grid of streets expanding northward forever, and less obviously sideways as well, giving you little shocks as you discover the unimagined Tenth, Eleventh, Twelfth Avenues. The extremes are inconceivable, yet they exist, even if you never see them. And up at the farthest tip of Manhattan, the edge of the world, there is virgin forest...

Bill was too much of a Yankee for North Carolina, anyway. He wore his checked shirts ironed, so their loud geometry suggested Mondrian rather than the logging camp. He also spoke too fast, and in twenty years had never let his vowels dilate in the southern humidity. Nor did he ever see the point of southern charm and languid good manners. A tight, tense character had been built into him in the course of a childhood in a small New York apartment a long way from the ground, with no easy way to get out, no grass, and just a television to play with. A clenched, ironic paranoia was his default condition.

Before long, he was back in the Byzantium of his longings. Bill and Violet rented an apartment on the Upper West Side, off Broadway. Their old house was made of wood, had several big sunny rooms, and a porch with a sofa on it, and was cheap. Their one-bedroom apartment in New York cost $1,450 a month, and the place had been painted so many times that the walls seemed to be caked in icing sugar. Every time a tenant left, the landlord applied a new layer of chalky white paint, and every new painting further obliterated physical detail: the light-switches were visible only as slight rectangular bulges near the door-frames; the electric sockets were two tiny mouse-like eyes in the skirting boards. The bathroom had small black-and-white hexagonal tiles on the floor, and big, chunky porcelain fixtures. On the sink, the faucet marked with an H issued cold water; hot water came from an unmarked faucet that was larger than the other one. The bathtub had a shower head that produced a jet of water so dense and powerful it could make you buckle at the knees if you weren't ready for it. No horizontal was an even plane; no vertical was true: the floors were warped and the doorways askew. Thick iron heating pipes ran from floor to ceiling in each room. At night they made a rattling noise that sounded like a devil was pouring ball bearings down them from the roof. The radiators hissed violently, and sputtered boiling water. Together these infernal devices made the place so hot they had to keep the windows open day and night, even though it was January. You couldn't turn the heat down. But Bill loved the apartment because it was typical of the neighbourhood. It was the kind of apartment Dustin Hoffman lived in in *Marathon Man*.

The fabric of the city fascinated Bill. He surprised himself with how much he remembered about the place, and quickly adopted the role of amateur urban historian. When out walking together, they couldn't pass a manhole cover without Bill stopping to look at it and giving Violet a little lecture. Violet was amused by his delight with every particular of life in New York, and she too was excited to be experiencing it herself for the first time. She too found it marvellous. She loved the roar the city made at night, at once exciting and soothing, the twinkling particles of mica in the sidewalks, and novel things like having cold sesame noodles from a Szechwan restaurant delivered to your apartment by a waiter on a bicycle. They were very happy. Bill was working at the bank, and Violet was beginning to establish contacts in the dance world, so in their first weeks they would often meet downtown in the evenings, in a bar or restaurant that Violet had spotted during the day in TriBeCa or SoHo.

Bill especially loved the elevators, those mysterious vertical gondolas, without which the skyline of New York, and human life within it, would be impossible. Among the many fascinating things about them was that each one was different: they were as numerous and infinitely various as snowflakes. For the elevator in their building he developed a particular homely affection. It had dark wooden walls, a key pattern decoration around the ceiling, and a varnished metal operating panel with adhesive metal numbers stuck beside the buttons. Some of these numbers had fallen off. (Despite the rent they were paying, everything in this building looked like hell.) The elevator moved very slowly, and whirred and clanked ceaselessly. Bill and Violet would lie in bed and hear it moving through the night, through the dark, sooty elevator shaft, which reached down to the centre of the earth, it seemed, deep through the bedrock of Manhattan. Their apartment was on the tenth floor of a building which had eighteen floors, seventeen if you didn't count the thirteenth floor, which for occult reasons didn't exist.

Bill developed the habit, when doing laundry in the washing machines in the basement, of opening the door to the room which housed the elevator's controller mechanism, a metal cupboard full of electrical switches and wires, and gazing at it in wonder. Alóne in the dark, dusty room, it would spray sparks and issue sinister clicks as it sent the elevator up and down the shaft. It was a very old system, and he would lose track of the time he spent watching it. It seemed to be imitating a living thing.

· 'If the elevator gets stuck,' he told Violet one evening, as he was bringing in a basket of clean clothes, 'there's a telephone in it you can use to call for help. It reminds me of a story by Edgar Allan Poe, in which a man installs a bell in his tomb because he's afraid of being buried alive.'

'Why are you so interested in elevators?' she said. It was the first time she had ever felt impatient with his interests.

He was lost for an answer, unable to state that one of his strongest memories – not the clearest, since it was much obscured by time and worn down by decades of psychic gnawing – was of being trapped in an elevator during the Blackout of 1966, when the whole of the north-eastern United States lost electric power, because of the failure of a piece of electrical switching equipment the size and complexity of a toaster up near the Canadian border. He sat on the floor in the pitch dark with his father until the superintendent of the building forced open the doors and led them out, lighting their way with a flashlight. The car had stopped between floors and his father had to climb up on to the floor and lift Bill out.

Instead of answering, he said, after a moment, 'Did you know that the ropes are twenty times stronger than they need to be? *Twenty times.*'

'No, I didn't,' she said, in a clear tone of disgust. He looked at her sheepishly and said no more about elevators. He was afraid of boring her.

At first, being in New York put the wind in Violet's sails. She auditioned for three different companies, and two of them called back a few days later to offer her a part. She was having the newcomer's good luck: the results one gets in New York when one is new to the place, and full of delight at just being there, as opposed to where one used to be, and consequently full of enthusiasm and fresh insights. This produces a sense of boundless opportunity, and an irresistible momentum of success. The newcomer's amazement with the city helped her get up in the morning, although their apartment was dark and got no direct sunlight. Bill's fascination with its ancient fabric fitted into her adventure of discovery.

One night Violet went into the bathroom, turned on the light, and saw a cockroach the size of a Buick nibbling at the blue crust around the rim of her toothpaste tube. She came to realise – to her horror – that if you let your gaze come to rest anywhere in the apartment, after a few minutes one of these translucent leathery monsters would scuttle into view. She mentioned it to Bill. He just shrugged. A side of him she hadn't known before was coming into view. Normally he would have sought to comfort her. Now he seemed not to care.

'This is New York,' he explained. 'There are cockroaches here. You just get used to it. Every couple of months the exterminator will come and blast the whole building with poisonous smoke. The bugs go away for a while, and then they come back, and that's how it is. You just accept it.'

'But they're filthy and they carry diseases!' Violet said.

'That's true,' Bill allowed, with a curious blankness. This was a shock to

Violet, because Bill had always been so fastidious about keeping things clean. Now he was accepting something he would never have accepted before. He seemed practically to *like* the damn cockroaches.

All she could think of saying was, 'I don't understand you,' and turned over and went to sleep.

A few days later, Bill came home from work, got into the elevator, and finding himself alone inside it, instead of getting out at the tenth floor, rode all the way to the top of the building. There were no apartments on the eighteenth floor, only a small landing with a door that led out on to the roof. The steel door was not locked, but it was stiff. He pushed hard against it with his shoulder, and it opened with a loud creak against a wedge of snow. The action felt magical and transgressive. Going out on to the roof was something he remembered being forbidden to do as a child.

The snow on the roof was hard and pristine and glowed a twilit blue. He trod slowly across it, savouring the crunching sound of each step. The dark grey winter sky was heavy with the potential of another snowfall. No stars were visible, not a single heavenly body, but it was dimly suffused with the light it had absorbed from the city. The roar of the city, of furnaces, trains, and distant sirens, rose up all around him. Bill could see the looming silhouette of the building's water tower ahead of him to his left. He approached it and stood under it for a few minutes, until the cold penetrated his overcoat and scarf and forced him to move. He looked down over the low wall that surrounded the roof, defying his feeling of vertigo, and watched the traffic streaming up and down Broadway. He felt himself spreading through the city like a mist.

The steel door was still open. He shut it behind him and pressed the button for the elevator, and waited for it on the small landing. It seemed to take for ever to arrive, although he could hear it wheezing and grinding down below, moving up and down between the lower floors.

When the elevator at last arrived, and the doors opened, Bill stepped inside and pressed the button for the tenth floor. The doors closed behind him, but the elevator did not move. He pressed the button again, harder this time, but there was still no response. He leaned into it, feeling with his fingertip for a connection that might make the car obey his wishes, and when that didn't work either, he stabbed at the button half a dozen times. Having exhausted all the possible ways of pressing the button, without success, he leaned his back against the wall, slid down to the floor, and sat.

It was not an unpleasant way to pass the time, so he settled down to wait. Bill noticed the emergency intercom in its framed box on the wall above the operating panel, but it never occurred to him to use it. Rescue would come in due course, he thought. There was no point rushing things. He had been here before. He remembered the building his grandmother had lived in on the East Side. It was a very old, very grand building, and there had been an elevator man named Arnold who wore a peaked cap and a uniform, and operated the elevator using a handle that moved in a curved slot. It was unlike modern elevators in that you could actually control it, that is, make it go faster and slower. Arnold's skill, when conveying passengers to their destination floors, was to be able to go up fast, and then decelerate gently and evenly to align the floor of the elevator car with the floor on to which the passenger would step. Then he would rattle open an inner gate, and close it behind him after the passengers had disembarked. His grandmother used to send Arnold on errands, to deliver her used detective novels to a friend, a retired humourist, on the sixth floor. She used to play cards with a group of old ladies on Tuesday nights, one of whom was called Bobby and wore a visor. Bill smiled as he remembered how his grandmother loved sports and gambling, and would regularly go to the races at Aqueduct until she got too old to do so, after which she would place her bets by telephone with a bookie, which was illegal. She wept when the boxer Rocky Marciano died, and still called Kennedy Airport Idlewild.

The time passed blissfully. Bill may have fallen asleep for a while, because this reverie was followed by a kind of vision, in which he felt himself bodily transported to a large, crowded banqueting room in the nineteenth century. Its dark mahogany walls, embellished with a carved classical frieze around the ceiling, resembled the dark walls of the elevator that enclosed him. The room was full of men, dining fabulously, making a mirthful racket of booming talk and raucous laughter. The long table was covered with dishes and glasses, and decorated with little American flags. In the centre was a mass of orchids and lilies.

The clamour was pierced by the clink of a knife against a wine glass, persistently seeking to make itself heard. The hubbub subsided, and a bearded man in formal attire stood up and began to speak. He held in his hand a telegram; it was from, he boomed, the president of the United States, Theodore Roosevelt, conveying his congratulations and good wishes and sending his regrets at his being unable to attend its annual dinner. He then offered a toast, in honour of a distinguished secretary of the society who was lately deceased.

The address was fulsome and florid. *He was truly one of nature's noblemen – and a brilliant luminary in the constellation of his country*, the speaker declaimed. *He was a man of sound comprehension, fruitful mind, and high-toned feeling – and his whole career is an excellent example of the intense personal efforts of members of the Friendly Sons to aid their suffering countrymen. We hail him with triumph...* As the speech proceeded, Bill felt the vinous warmth of the attentive, convivial gathering. The words blurred, with only the cadences sounding in Bill's mind, yet he felt moved to tears by the rhetoric.

When the superintendent arrived and forced open the doors, and found Bill inside, with tears streaming down his face, he was purple with anger. 'What you been doing?' he demanded, blaming Bill for the elevator's malfunction. Of course, Bill had done nothing, and protested his innocence, but the super blamed him anyway. Bill was disoriented by this: it wasn't in the script. He stood up, composed himself, stretched, and stammered out an incoherent explanation to Violet about what had happened. He had been in the elevator for two hours. They went out to an Italian restaurant in the neighbourhood and had linguini with red clam sauce.

In the restaurant, Bill was in good spirits, elated to the point of being a bit manic, Violet thought.

'What happened to you?' she asked, in a pointed, puzzled tone.

'It got stuck. So I waited,' he said; but Violet was still waiting for an answer.

'I had a kind of vision. First I was in my grandmother's apartment on the East Side. Then I was at a dinner of the society my great-grandfather belonged to. It was like walking into the past. It all felt completely real.' He shivered. They finished a bottle of chianti and walked home in a relaxed and cheerful mood.

That night he dreamed that he was alone in a cabin in Alaska in winter, snowed in with a stock of supplies: a drum of Quaker Oats, a can of coffee, and piles of canned food. He felt confined, enclosed, but somehow, the next day, at peace. It was a strange dream: the sense of confinement was accompanied by an equal sensation of abundance. At work the next day, he daydreamed of hermits' cells in desert caves, or on inaccessible mountain crags in Tibet.

A few days later, Bill came home from work, skipping about with excitement. He had found a book in a secondhand bookstore, a thick frayed volume entitled *Elevator Engineering: Maintenance and Design*. He waved it like a trophy. 'This book is the *bible* of vertical transportation,' he said proudly, holding it with two hands. Violet picked it up and flicked through it. To her dismay, she saw that it was an engineering manual, full of tables of numbers and mathematical formulae.

That Saturday, the elevator broke again, and Bill was again trapped inside it. This time it clearly wasn't an accident. He had somehow managed to disable the mechanism, and stall the elevator between floors, provoking four hours of angry complaints from other residents of the building. The superintendent was unable to open the doors of the elevator, and had to call the Fire Department. The firemen found Bill curled up asleep on the floor, wearing Otis Elevator Company overalls. They mistook him for an engineer who had fallen asleep on the job.

THE FORTUNE-TELLER
Elisa Segrave

He goes into the dark yellow room, feeling like an uprooted tropical plant. He left Florida only yesterday. The previous occupant has placed the bed the wrong way round; the head sticking out into the room. The black cleaning lady in her pink overall explains that the girl had a phobia about sleeping with her head close to the wall. A punk singer killed his girlfriend in the hotel a couple of months ago. Ralph read about it in the papers.

This afternoon in mid-December, Ralph lies on the bed thinking about an older man he met on the beach in Key West, a professor. He took Ralph out to dinner on his nineteenth birthday. He had very long, silvery-black eyelashes and taught English at a college in Georgia. He seemed cultivated and well-read but then, as Ralph was eating the lobster the professor insisted he should have on his birthday, the older man remarked casually that he often heard voices from Outer Space. Afterwards, he asked if he could come up Ralph's room on Duval Street but Ralph excused himself, saying the hotel manager wouldn't like it. The voices from Outer Space and the professor's long eyelashes – he wondered if he was wearing mascara – made him uneasy.

Two days later Ralph left. As he climbed on to the Greyhound bus for the long ride to Miami along the Keys, he regretted going. Now, he isn't even sure why he's come to New York, except to pass time, because he doesn't want to go home. Ever since October, when he left home in Chicago, he's been running, but he still isn't sure what he's running from. It might be from the shock of his father's death last summer – heart attack – or of his mother's subsequent collapse – since his father's death she's started drinking again and fallen over twice, first breaking a leg, then an arm. Or maybe he's running from a failed love affair with a young woman he met last spring in Racine, or from his younger brother Jay's decline into drink and drugs.

He came to New York in October, two months ago, with money his father had left him. He stayed in the city only three days – each morning he sat in a coffee-shop alone wondering why he was there. (One morning he saw Lilian Hellman in there; he didn't dare speak to her.) He went north to Buffalo to visit a friend then in early November he flew south to Key West, half in search of the young woman with whom he'd had the love affair. The last time they'd met, in summer in Chicago, he'd told her he might go down to Florida in November.

'Great! I have a fantasy that I'll come walking up the beach in Key West on your birthday and there you'll be, strolling over the sand to meet me.'

He pretended to himself, for several weeks, even up to his birthday and after, that she'd really meant it.

Now it's nearly Christmas. There's this nagging feeling that there's something wrong. His money has almost run out. He doesn't know what to do next. He dropped out of college last summer. He knows he's not tough enough to get a job in New York. He doesn't want to go home but he guesses he'll have to, for Christmas. His mother and Jay are expecting him.

He can't afford more than two nights in this hotel so he calls up an old school friend who's moved to Washington with his young wife and arranges to stay in the tiny apartment they've kept, on West 10th Street. Why's he spinning out his stay, he asks himself again, after arranging this. He doesn't even like New York. He's running, running, with a feeling of dread, but he still doesn't know why. He doesn't want to go home.

New York has its Christmas lights on; there's the big Christmas tree outside the Rockefeller Center, but he can't appreciate these niceties. When he was ten, he, his parents and Jay, eight, spent a night in the Plaza Hotel. He and Jay were taken to FAO Schwartz nearby where they were each allowed to choose a toy. Jay chose a gun which shot out ping-pong balls very fast. Ralph chose a complicated Meccano set. That afternoon their father took them in a horse-drawn carriage through Central Park while their mother shopped in Saks. Jay was cute then, with floppy blond hair and vivid blue eyes, inherited from their Swedish mother. Ralph remembers the multi-coloured jacket Jay wore, turquoise, purple and gold. He remembers the way Jay followed him anxiously along the icy paths in Central Park, while their father stood still, absorbed in the skaters on the pond. He and his brother were very close. But now he can't relate to Jay's despair. It's too frightening. The empty bottles in his brother's bedroom are like something out of a melodrama. Jay's still only sixteen. Now the Plaza Hotel is out of their reach. Ralph wouldn't feel comfortable even in the lobby. The hotel on West 23rd Street, where Dylan Thomas died, is more suitable. But he doesn't feel at home there either. All the time the feeling of dread, of heaviness, is behind and in front of him, but he still can't name its source.

The next morning he takes the Lexington Avenue subway uptown, to see about his air ticket home. He plans to land at O'Hare airport on Christmas Eve, at the last possible moment, to celebrate Christmas. His mom and Jay are his closest relations but when he's with them he feels panicky. They're addicts, dependent on alcohol and drugs. (His mother's on librium, or was when he last heard.) They don't want to admit it or do anything about it. He should feel sorry for his mother, now a widow, but he hates her self-pity. If he gets too involved with her and her grief, he will be enslaved. He resents the way that some of her close women friends hint that her drinking is caused by him and his brother. He's dropped out of college and Jay's been in trouble since the age of fourteen, for being found with cocaine and for selling it to other local teenagers. Is it surprising that lovely blonde widowed Mrs Willard drinks? That's what her friends think.

After coming out of the airline office, Ralph walks a little way south and finds himself in Lexington Avenue next to a Chinese laundry. He sees a notice advertising a fortune-teller. He turns in, goes up two flights of stairs and knocks.

A youngish woman with glossy black hair and sharp dark eyes sits in a small pink room, a lit crucifix behind her. On a shelf are two small statues of the Virgin Mary, one black. On a low table is a bigger statue – Jesus, a foot high, arms outstretched, halo fixed to his head, his red Sacred Heart exposed and glowing. (Ralph's mother, a non-Catholic, always said that these exposed Sacred Hearts reminded her of butcher's meat).

Ralph and Jay were brought up Catholic by their half-French father. These religious statues are therefore reassuring to Ralph at first, but then, as he sits down to face the fortune-teller on her red velvet cushion, they begin to seem creepy and vulgar – totems from a more primitive world.

The fortune-teller is probably Puerto Rican. He extends his two palms to her. He says nothing but she, looking at him with her dark eyes, immediately voices the fear, the dread which he still can't name. Something terrible is going to happen, very soon. She can stop it, but only if he comes back, as soon as possible, tomorrow, or even better this afternoon, with more money, which he must hand over to her so that she can offer *many many* prayers to avert this disaster. These extra prayers will cost two hundred dollars. It's up to him.

Shocked, he says he'll decide later. He hands her thirty dollars, her regular fee, and takes the subway downtown. The girl sitting opposite him is engrossed in a book called *You Will Not Die*. When the train stops at 42nd Street she notices him staring.

'I have a terrible fear of death,' she explains. 'I work as a doctor's reception-ist. I see a lot of sick people. I would do anything to live, even till over a hun-dred. Even if I was ill and in pain. Even if I had to make a deal with the Devil.'

She tells him how interesting the book is, how, in it, past lives and near-death experiences are recounted by those whose hearts stopped temporarily and who then came back to live for several more years. (Pity that didn't happen to his father.) She mentions a Jewish girlfriend who went on holiday to Venice or Vienna – she can't remember which – and found herself in a place which had once been a ghetto. This friend had 'an incredibly strong feeling' that she'd lived in that very ghetto several centuries earlier.

It seems absurd that this robust young woman in her bright purple coat with a fur collar should be afraid of death. Ralph wonders if she is exagger-ating, to make herself seem interesting. He nearly tells her about the fortune-teller and even thinks of asking her advice, but then they arrive at his stop. He gets off and she stays on the train.

'Stay well! Stay warm!' she shouts, waving at him through the window.

Back in the hotel three black girl students are chattering happily in the lobby. Their camaraderie makes him feel more isolated. In his room, he starts writing a letter to Jay, warning him that a Danish guy whom he met in Key West might turn up in Chicago. 'Please be friendly and offer him a bed if he calls before I arrive,' he writes. He's aware that by writing this letter he's try-ing to persuade himself that his brother is still capable of behaving in a nor-mal and hospitable manner. Actually Ralph isn't sure. Maybe Jay just stays in his room all day now drinking. He decides not to send the letter after all.

He keeps thinking of the fortune-teller and wondering what he should do. If he pays her two hundred dollars he'll have to leave New York at once; that would be the last of his father's money. She's blackmailing him; he knows that. He would discount the whole thing, except that she picked up so accurately his feeling of dread. Now he can't be free of it, or of her.

He's only ever been to one fortune-teller before in his life, and that was on First Avenue when he was sixteen and in town for a pop concert with Jay. They had wandered into a basement bar to drink beer, trying to be grown-up. The barman had refused them drinks, but the fortune-teller had been sitting alone at a little table in the corner.

'Why don't you like yourself, child?' he had heard her ask Jay at once, glancing at his palm. 'If someone gave you a silver spoon you'd dash it to the ground.'

Now he realises that that old lady, with her grey hair and Brooklyn accent, was kind compared to the young woman on Lexington Avenue with her sharp dark eyes and her creepy religious statues with their double messages.

He calls Jan, the aunt of a friend from college. He's only met her once. Jan's from Bulgaria. She invites Ralph at once to a Hannukah celebration that evening, in the garment district where she lives with her husband, an Israeli doctor.

He walks over there. The huge loft is full of life-size female figures, carved in wood. The living people in the room are also all women, which he finds disconcerting. First there is Jan, who has lived in New York for ten years and now wants to emigrate with her husband to Israel. Her brother lives in Tel Aviv. Jan is tall, with big hips, greying wavy hair and a moustache. She could be thought masculine, but seems unconscious of it. Like the other women from Eastern Europe whom he has met, Jan seems warm, strong and maternal, very unlike his own mother, who's fragile, elegant and child-like. Jan is very physical. Even now, as she stands by the stove, she is entwined with a blonde, pale-skinned woman, with hair scraped back and bags under her eyes, her face pudgy like a potato. Both of them are doing the cooking.

Opposite him at the table – he is offered a glass of juice – is a woman with a heavy dark face who at first looks bad-tempered. She is Spanish. Then there is another lady with cropped grey hair and a lined face in a long green dress who complains because he gives her a limp handshake 'like a fish'. This complaint makes him wary of her for the rest of the evening.

At last another man arrives. It is David, Jan's husband. After shaking hands, he goes to sleep behind a screen. He is a sculptor – the wooden figures are his – but also a doctor in Harlem, and is exhausted after work. He is short, with a huge head and large blue eyes behind glasses. He isn't as gregarious as his wife and when Ralph, shaking hands, tells him politely that he is excited about coming to the Hannukah, David replies: 'It's no big deal.'

Then the blonde woman's husband comes, carrying something he has made for the celebration, a candle-holder with eight holes. Everyone praises this piece of handiwork. The man who made it is a poet. Ralph thinks he looks beaten-down and submissive.

They all wait for the food. Ralph is asked some questions about Chicago, which he finds boring. The Spanish woman remarks that she's glad she doesn't have to cook tonight; for once she will let others wait on her.

The Hannukah speciality is potato cakes, called by a Yiddish name which

Ralph can't understand. While Jan and her blonde friend are making them, a disturbed man arrives. To Ralph, this man is a typical New Yorker, because of his cynicism, his extreme nervous energy and his veneer of sophistication. He says he is a furniture designer but finds it impossible to make a living here. He criticises the rich businessman he is working for at the moment, boasting that when this employer told him off for taking too long, he stopped work altogether.

'He *loved* it!'

The furniture designer tosses his head and looks extremely gay.

He is good-looking, with large grey eyes and a bony face. (Ralph thinks that he and the furniture designer look rather alike. Has anyone else noticed this?) The furniture designer keeps referring to his ex-mother-in-law, who, he says, hates him. He seems attracted to the rock-like bullish quality of the Spanish woman, who announces that she has lived without a husband for twenty years in a New York apartment, bringing up her two children alone. Although she's been so long away from her country, or perhaps because of this, she speaks lovingly of Spain as a place with better food, more sun and a more human way of life. When her children are grown up, she says, she will go back there. She describes her village near Seville, surrounded by orange trees.

Whenever the furniture designer addresses her, she looks puzzled and knits her brows, in an attempt to understand. He talks about sex, saying he doesn't think that women have the same problems as men; they can go without it for a very long time.

The Spanish woman shrugs: 'I don't see what's so complicated. You eat, sleep, make love. It's as simple as that.'

She continues: 'I go to my office and I stay in my apartment, so no harm comes to me. That's my life.'

She discusses her children. Her son did some modelling as a boy but now as a teenager he has problems with older men trying to seduce him. She has tried to bring up her children well, according to her Catholic religion, but they're both very selfish, she sighs. Her son is a Sagittarian.

The interior decorator, in a silky voice, begins to talk about astrology, trying to impress her with his knowledge of the movements of different planets and how they affect character. But she looks more puzzled than ever, and keep nodding and knitting her brows, especially when he congratulates her on her sex appeal, saying, 'Your come-on with men is terrific!'

He goes into the bathroom and Ralph sees him through the open door, looking at himself surreptitiously in the mirror. He's very vain. The Spanish woman winks at Ralph as if to say, 'What a child he is – like you, like all men!'

Meanwhile, the woman who had said Ralph's handshake was like a fish, who is an old Bulgarian actress, complains that she has backache. She moans, and the furniture designer rushes out of the bathroom, unzips her dress and begins to massage her back. They are obviously old friends.

Another woman, who arrived late, stands by the kitchen table and begins declaiming what Hannukah means. She has just read about it in a book. But she takes so long and seems so confused that no one understands her. At last Jan breaks in and begins explaining the significance of the eight candles in the candle-holder. Even this explanation is confusing for someone who doesn't know it already. Jan says it refers to the persecution of the Jews, when they had to hide in a cave and had only oil enough for one lamp. They had to remain hidden for eight days and by a miracle the oil increased and they were able to have a lamp each of those days.

Ralph likes the certainty of religion. He wishes he was like the Spanish woman. He understands why the furniture designer feels so attracted to her. She makes him feel safe.

Ralph imagines her living in her apartment, a tiny island of security. She might as well be in Spain now, except she wouldn't earn so much money. Is her present secluded, limited existence the kind of life that New York imposes on its more fearful citizens?

He's always felt very alone here, ever since he first came alone, aged seventeen, for one summer, to work in a hotel where his mother's cousin was manager. The way the city was laid out, like a piece of toast on a grill, unnerved him. He feels more at home downtown but even now he perceives New York as harsh, masculine; he feels no more important here than a bit of dust.

At midnight his host, the doctor, takes Ralph down on to the street and directs him towards the subway. Ralph's unfamiliar with this stop. He'll have to cross town and change trains twice. He has the impression that, by directing him to this deserted subway at midnight, David's testing him. Will Ralph stand up to the dangers of the city that David and his wife face daily? Obediently, Ralph says goodbye and descends the steps. He is alone on the platform. Everywhere on the walls are jagged graffiti like wire – electric-blue, yellow, parrot-green, blood-red, black. The designs are meaningless to him and alien – the marks of the jungle. He doesn't even know which direction he's headed and there's no one to ask. He's already forgotten what David said.

Safe from the doctor's scrutiny, he goes back up the steps on to the street and hails a cab. Five dollars to his hotel.

In bed, he wishes he'd asked the Spanish woman's opinion of the fortune-teller. Surely, she'd have told him not to hand over the two hundred dollars. She's an old-fashioned Catholic and the Catholic church forbids dabbling in the occult.

Next morning, he despises himself for even considering handing over so much money to a stranger, who is surely a charlatan. The young woman probably picked up on his fear by telepathy. This is how she makes a living. Maybe she really does have second sight that something dreadful is going to happen, but how could she affect the turn of events? Anyway, she has no right to take advantage of other people's tragedies.

Ralph packs his suitcase, pays at the desk and takes a cab to West 10th Street. The driver thinks he said West End Avenue and starts driving up-town. 'Speak English, kid', he says rudely, when Ralph remonstrates. He can hardly speak a word himself.

In the tiny flat are written instructions about putting bleach down the plug-hole of the sink to stop cockroaches. Ralph feels more isolated here than in the hotel, and more desperate.

Peter, his friend from Buffalo, arrived in New York last night on the Greyhound. He is staying in a tiny borrowed apartment on the lower East Side. Almost at once he is involved in a drama with a man in the flat below, who breaks in the first night looking for drugs. The next day, Peter moves to a hostel near Ralph. Ralph didn't think there was anywhere so cheap to stay in the Village. It's one step above a place for down-and-outs. As a teen-ager, Peter went to a private school in New England. In New York, with no money, and no drive, he could be on the street at once. It's not difficult here to go down.

Ralph goes to meet Peter in the Lion's Head, on West Ninth Street. This is the kind of place Peter loves, a basement bar like a dark womb where he can sit all day, nursing a couple of beers. He's a typical Cancerian man, afraid of engaging with life. Ralph likes him but Peter's timidity in this city upsets him. He realises that Peter reminds him of his brother. Ralph doesn't tell him about the fortune-teller. He doesn't want to look a fool. He's still mulling over what to do. He returns to the flat, leaving Peter in the bar.

The flat is so tiny that it's like sitting in the cockpit of an aeroplane. Across the road is a club for gay men. Ralph wishes momentarily that he was gay;

then at least there would be a safe community who would welcome him. He wouldn't feel so alone. Or maybe this thought is naive and romantic.

He checks his money again. If he pays the fortune-teller what she asks, he will definitely have to go home. But what is he doing anyway here, except killing time? Why is he hanging on?

That afternoon, he takes a subway up the West side. He gets out and walks along 57th Street, along the south side of Central Park, towards Fifth Avenue. Just here, in front of the Plaza Hotel, where he came yesterday, is surely one of the most elegant parts of New York. He watches the horse-drawn carriages, their drivers waiting for out-of-towners. It seems a long time ago that he and his father and Jay went in one. He will never experience anything like that again. His father's dead. Stretching north towards Harlem is the rest of the park with its enormous grey boulders. He almost expects to see bears coming out from behind those rocks. He marvels at the mixture of elegance and savagery in this city.

He arrives at the fortune-teller's building. He goes up the two flights of stairs and hears the murmuring of voices. She's with someone. He sits on a wicker chair on the landing. Above him, in a little altar, is another statue of the Virgin, two candles burning beside her. He remembers a story his mother told him, of how once, outside the Palmer House Hotel in Chicago when she had got off the airport bus, she had met a young Spanish woman looking for a cab and crying. When his mother asked what was wrong, the young woman said she hadn't finished some sewing she was supposed to have done and that the Virgin Mary would be very angry with her.

'Surely the Virgin, who is so sweet and kind, would not be angry?' said his mother, soothing the poor young woman. She had got into a cab with her and helped her find her hostel. Now he hardly ever sees this aspect of his mother.

There's the sound of a chair scraping. The door opens and a very thin man comes out. His face is emaciated, like a figure in an El Greco painting. He has huge pale blue eyes, sparse hair and a fearful expression. He edges past Ralph and down the stairs.

The fortune-teller's face lights up with surprise – and pleasure – when she sees Ralph. Maybe this unguarded pleasure is what forces him into an instant decision. She had given up on him, he realises. What a fool he is to come back! He goes right in and stands opposite her. Today the fortune-teller is wearing a soft black shawl covered with tiny stars. Her eyes are sharper than ever. She indicates to him to sit, but he doesn't.

'I've decided not to give you the extra money. If the awful thing's going to happen, it's going to happen,' he announces defiantly.

The fortune-teller opens her mouth to argue but he turns and walks out, down the staircase. He's proud of himself. He rushes down Lexington Avenue very fast in a bitter wind, stopping once to buy a plant for his mother, dark green with black stripes. He will buy something for Jay later, probably a book, and a tape for Jay's birthday, which is on Christmas Eve.

'That's the zebra plant,' says the elderly black assistant, wrapping the plant in paper. The kindness in the old man's voice disarms Ralph. He walks on, more calmly, to 42nd Street, where, outside the New York Public Library, a young man with a pony-tail asks: 'Want to score a lid?' He shakes his head.

Later he and Peter have a pizza in the Village. Peter again seems vulnerable and confused. He says he might get a job as a gardener in a park. Maybe he'll move to Montreal. Ralph can't help him.

Making that decision about the money has, after all, not given him any relief. Now all the time the sense of nagging worry, of foreboding, engulfs him. He can't throw it off. He feels lonely again in the tiny flat on West 10th Street. He doesn't like walking back there. The flat, so cosy when his newly married friends lived in it, now seems horribly cut-off. The grey Hudson River that he can see out of the window makes him feel desolate. As a last gesture to Florida, to the sun, to another life, he buys a card of a handsome tiger in a bright green jungle and posts it to the professor in Key West. He's there, with his long eyelashes, till January.

Ralph takes the plane to Chicago on Christmas Eve. He has the zebra plant for his mother and a book for Jay – a biography of Dylan Thomas – but couldn't find a suitable tape.

There, at his mother's, he hears. His brother was found hanging in the garage that afternoon. It was Jay's seventeenth birthday.

At the funeral, Ralph stands beside his mother in her black fur coat. He thinks he can detect a faint smell of wine under her perfume. He feels sorry for her but as he flings earth on to his brother's grave – the priest signals to him to do this – he thinks longingly of the dark, bullish woman he met at the Hannukah. He is sure that she will keep her promise. She will eventually go back to Spain, to her orange trees, to a more human way of life. He wishes he could go with her.

LITTLE TALES OF NEW YORK

Lynne Tillman

1.

There was a man who loved his dog. The dog was as loyal as the day was long. But the man had a hard life and the only good thing in it was his dog. So he threw himself off the lower level of the Queensboro Bridge, into the East River. He held his dog in his arms. The dog was discovered in the river tugging at the man's body. He was trying to carry his master to shore. But the man was dead, and the dog was placed in a shelter.

2.

There was a discontented woman who discovered at sixteen that she was adopted. She was relieved, because she'd always been dissatisfied with her parents. The woman spent twenty years searching for her birth mother. Finally she found her, and they were reunited on Staten Island. But the woman was disappointed in her birth mother, who died shortly afterward. And for the rest of her life she regretted having looked for her.

3.

There were two teenaged brothers who loved snakes. They kept a 13-foot Burmese python in the Bronx project where they lived. They hoped to make careers out of caring for reptiles. But one day, when one of the brothers was about to feed the snake a live chicken, the python mistook the brother for prey. The brother was found lying face down in a pool of his own blood in the hallway of the apartment building. The snake was still coiled around his midriff and back. Their mother had asked her sons to get rid of the python, but she recognised her son's passion for reptiles. 'He loved animals,' she said. 'He went to the zoo all the time.'

4.

There was a man from Queens who had a big appetite. He held the record as the world champion hot-dog eater. But 320-pound 'Animal', as he was called, was dethroned by 144-pound Hirofumi Nakajima, Japan's top eating champ. Nakajima set a new world record at Nathan's Famous on Coney

Island – twenty-three and a half franks in twelve minutes. The fallen champ said of the new champ: 'When I first saw how small he was, I was ready to pick up a copy of the *Daily News* and read while I was eating. But he was on his game.'

5.

There was a Bronx man who was found dead in a vacant lot. He'd been stabbed many times. The killers had even tried to cut out his heart. The man had been sleeping in the lot, though his home was near by. Detectives have no suspect and have appealed to the public for help in solving the heartless slaying.

6.

There was a determined wife who stayed home and took care of the children. But her husband was cheap. He didn't give her enough household money. She argued with him and grew to hate him. One day she met a young man and fell in love. For a while she was furtively happy. Then she and her lover went to a hitman and arranged to have her husband murdered, for $10,000. She saved her meagre household allowance. Her husband also fell in love with someone else and went to the same hitman to murder his wife. Both plots were foiled, and the miserable pair went to jail.

7.

There was a woman who wanted to be skinny. She ate not fat or starch. She kept no food in her loft. Her eyes grew big in her head. She stared hungrily at friends as they ate their food. One day she disappeared. It's said she wasted away.

8.

There was a man whose wife left him. They had four children. He didn't want the divorce, but she did. He tried to get her back and pleaded, but she said no, never. And she expected him to help support their kids. He became more and more enraged and frustrated. So he phoned her one day and arranged to take the whole family for a drive. He planted a bomb in his car and it exploded. He murdered them and himself with one blast. 'HE WAS EVIL,' the *New York Post* headline screamed. 'Love rage drove dad to blow up his family.'

9.

There was a young woman on Wall Street who worked her way up the ladder. Many people in her company envied her, but she had her boss's approval. Then one day her boss died, and she was fired.

10.

There was a sweet little girl from Queens. When her mother loved her, she thought her daughter was good enough to eat. When her mother hated her, she thought her daughter was the devil. One day, at the school cafeteria where she worked, the mother placed the little girl in the oven. She set the temperature to 425 degrees. School employees quickly removed the girl. But the girl went to the hospital with second-degree burns all over her body.

11.

There were two brothers in the Bronx who had a strict mother. She was religious and made them study hard. The older brother hated her. He wanted to kill her. He asked his younger brother to help him. He was going to use a crossbow and arrow. The brothers argued. The younger one refused to do it. So the older brother shot him with the crossbow and arrow. The arrow lodged in his neck, but he survived. 'He did get seriously injured,' said a detective, 'but he had God with him.' Their forgiving mother expressed no vengeful feelings toward her older son. The mother was just 'trying to cope with the tragedy of having one son in the hospital and the other in custody,' the police said.

12.

There was a security guard who was bored at work. Georgevitch walked around a vast Manhattan office building six nights a week. One dull night he called an oldies' radio station and requested a song: 'Secret Agent Man'. Georgevitch gave his name and the name and address of the building he guarded. It happened that a police officer was listening to the same oldies' programme. When he heard the security guard's unusual name, he remembered it. He also remembered that Georgevitch was wanted for petty larceny and cheque-forging and that he'd once been arrested for impersonating an officer. Later that same night, Georgevitch was picked up and taken to jail. If he'd known a cop was listening he wouldn't have given his name, he said, but he was going crazy watching the cleaning people.

13.

There was a man who was very jealous. After his lover of 21 years broke up with him, he shadowed her, followed her everywhere. She was afraid of him and carried a protection order against him in her pocket. When the jealous man stabbed her to death in a subway station, the protection order was still in her pocket. The man fled. His Brooklyn neighbours said he'd been bragging he'd do it and escape, that he had a plane ticket to Miami. One neighbour said, 'When he got out of jail for violating the first protection order, he dyed his hair. It was red, a crazy colour.' Another believes he was contemplating suicide. 'But he wants somebody else to do it. Since he lost his mother, he'd say, "I wish somebody would kill me." He's not well.' His terrified daughter fears that she and her grandmother are next, and the police are protecting them. Cops form a 'protective shield' around the two whenever they walk the murdered woman's grey poodle, Boy Boy.

14.

There was a young club woman who liked to drink blood. She met a man who had advertised his 'wish to become a donor to a female vampire'. It was love at first bite. Now they happily nibble and suck each other's necks. They trust each other to be forever free of disease and think they're ageless. 'Drinking blood's very intimate,' the young woman says. 'And I like pain to a certain degree.'

ASLEEP IN WOLF'S CLOTHING

Jonathan Carroll

Look at this hat. The worst, right? You wouldn't be caught dead in it, right? Whoops, maybe I shouldn't say that, seeing as how where I find myself at this point in time.

I found it in a two-dollar bin on 14th Street. You know, down where all those cheap-o stores are lined up like fifty-year-old whores, selling everything you don't want. T-shirts that say 'Yes, I *am* Elvis', toy robots, twenty-dollar stereos.

But I was in this mood, you know? It was a nice day out. Mary and I'd been in bed all morning, doing the black act... like that. So we're walking down 14th, trying to figure out what movie to see. Suddenly I spot this ug-ly-fuck-in' hat in a two-dollar bin. I pick it up with two fingers like the thing is radio-active or got cooties. I say to Mary, who can go along with a joke better than anyone, 'Waddya think of me in this?' She walks back and forth with her hand on her hip, checking me out like I was the Mona Lisa or something. Finally she says 'You look like a big plate of ham and eggs when I'm hungry, baby. That hat is *you*.' But you know, she was kidding. If she really meant what she was saying, I would've punched her out because that hat wouldn't look good on anything that *breathed*, believe me.

I start posing like a model. Mary's laughing, and it's turning into the best day of the year. 'I'm buying this.'

'Good idea.' She's laughing so hard, she puts her hand over her big kissy mouth and I love her more than ever.

So I go into the store and put it on the counter in front of the Oriental guy there. The place smells strange. Like smells you never had in your nose until that minute? That's what weirds me out in this city when I'm around the Orientals or the Arabs or any of the others. The Greeks are okay. The only thing they ever do is buy up luncheonettes and change the names to the Sparta or Athens or Zeus and serve their coffee in blue and white cups with pictures of Greek statues on them. The food stays the same. Corned beef hash. Burgers.

But with the others, even though they've lived here for years, you go into their places and it's like you're back in the old country. Or on some other fucking planet. Star Trek stuff. I went into one Arab store once and every goddamned person in there was wearing a white robe over their heads.

Not only do things smell different in these places, they got calendars on the walls with nutty writing, the kids are sitting in the corners eating weird food, and a lot of them got that blank look in their eyes like they're either stoned or fish. You know what I mean?

I guess it's natural, but look, you come to a new country, especially America, you should adapt to the place now that you're living here. If it was so great in I-rak, why not stay there? I mean, falafel's okay, but don't say you're American if you're eating that shit three times a day, or with chopsticks or something.

So I go in to pay for the ugly hat and Wing Ting behind the counter barks out 'Two Dah-luh' like a Pekinese dog. Like I couldn't read the sign outside. Now remember, I'm probably the only idiot in the whole city of New York who'd be willing to give up two bucks for this head horror. But when he says it like that, like I was a bum or was going to rob him, I'm instantly pissed off. That little midget in his Michael Jackson T-shirt and the crap he's selling in that store: big pink dolls, Martin Luther King paintings on velvet, gold plastic gondola boats holding clocks that aren't working... He should've been down on his chinky knees praying at my altar, thanking me for giving up my two Dah-luh for his hat. But no, he wasn't doing that. His voice was sounding like I'd stole his two dollars and he wanted it back.

The whole thing started as a joke. We're out for our walk. I see the hat, Mary gets into it, we're laughing...

But now I'm angry. I should've walked out and just kept going, but this guy was pissing on my paradise and I didn't like that. So I take out the money and drop it on the counter. One of the bills catches a breeze and floats down to the floor on his side. He doesn't move.

'I want a receipt.'

'What?'

'I want a receipt for my two dollars.'

'No receipt. You go now.'

There's where I could've gone World War Three but hey, this man had already taken up way too much of my life. That's what Mary always says – don't let them take any more of your life than you have to – and she's right. So instead, I tell the guy Va fongoo and walk out with my new hat.

As I'm going, I realise I want her to see me in it when I come out the door, so I put it on just as I'm getting to the street. But two things happen right at the same time. The first is, I don't see Mary. I'm looking up and down the street but she's nowhere. Mary's as dependable as they come. She's got her bad sides, but this isn't one of them. She tells you she'll be there at ten, she's there on the dot. She says it's because she's Sagittarius. But this time she's *not* there, whereas a minute ago she was standing right there. Strange.

While I'm looking around, I notice this big black Cadillac limo parked out in front. Thing's nine miles long. The back door is open and a black guy in a chauffeur's suit is standing by it with his hand on the door. He's looking at me and smiling. I don't pay much attention because I'm thinking where's Mary.

Then I hear 'It's him! Oh my God! It's *him!*'

I'm looking to the left and this comes from the right and by the time I turn my head, these three *very* foxy-looking Latino girls are rushing up to me.

'I don't believe it! I don't believe it! It's Rickie! Aaaugh!'

'Hi, uh –'

'Oooo, I gotta kiss you. Please please, can I kiss you? I love you, Rickie!'

'*What?*'

Now, the one who wants to kiss me is like a seven and I'm thinking, you wanna kiss me, I'm up for it. But her friend, who's at least a nine, shoves seven out of the way and grabs me around the neck and takes first shot. I mean, she pushes her tongue into my mouth like an electric plug into a socket. I'm so shocked I'm just standing there, helpless. Sort of. The kiss is all over my face and it's nice, but her tongue is as big as a truck and I can't breathe.

'Hey, hey, that's enough. Leave him alone!' The chauffeur grabs nine and pulls her off me, really rough. But she doesn't mind because even held back, she's looking at me with steam in her eyes. The third girl who's pretty damned nice too tries to come up, but the chauffeur is right there and blocks her off. While he's keeping her back, he says to me over his shoulder 'I think we have to get out of here, sir. We're going to have a riot in a minute.'

I don't know what the hell's going on, but it's all nice so I don't know what to do. Where's Mary? Why're these girls going nuts? Where am I supposed to go with this guy? Most of all, why me? Who do they think I am to be giving me such a treatment?

This friend of mine, Dave Pell, was walking down the street one day when a guy came up and asked for his autograph. Dave's quick and went along with it, but signed his own name and handed it back. The guy looked at it and got angry. 'Come on, write your real name.' Dave says that *is*. The guy says no it isn't, you're Elton John. Dave looks a little like Elton, but only in the dark at three in the morning, but that's not what this *shadrul* thinks. By the end of the thing, the two of them are screaming at each other and Dave's an inch away from giving the guy big pain.

I'm thinking this is the same thing, mistaken identity, so as the chauffeur is pushing me towards his car and the girls are all yelling Stay with us! I yell at them 'Who do you think I am?'

'Rickie!'

'Rickie, we love you!'

'I wanna have your baby!' Nine said this. Number nine's screaming she wants to have my baby on 14th Street in the middle of the day.

'Rickie Prousek!'

I was almost into the car when one of them shouted that. I stopped. That's me – Rickie Prousek. If they knew my name, they hadn't made any mistake. They wanted to kiss *me*. Why?

Before I could ask, the chauffeur's pushing me into the back of this fuckin' limo the size of a 747 and since I don't have my balance I just go forward. But soon as I'm seated in there, the girls are pressing up against my window, kissing it all over the place and leaving these big red smudges. Now get this – one of the girls yanks up her halter top and shoves her chee-chees against the window. Beautiful. I'm going nuts. Get me some of that, but it's too late – the driver jams away from the curb and I'm looking through the back window at the nicest set I've seen since last month's *Penthouse*.

'Did you see that?' I caught the driver's eye in the rearview mirror and he smiled.

'I did, sir.'

'I don't know what the hell is going on here.'

He just gave a little laugh and looked back at the road.

'I walk out of that store and suddenly all this comes down.' I don't know whether I'm talking to him or me. The truth is, I'm kind of nuts at the moment. 'And by the way, where're we going?'

'To the book signing, sir. It'll be quite a scene there too. I've heard they've been lining up all morning.'

'What book signing?'

He just kept chuckling like wasn't I the funny one but didn't say anything more. But it isn't every day you get to ride in a limo and I thought what the hell, go with the flow and see what happens.

Anyway, there were things to look at in the car. There's this mini fridge and a telephone and a TV with a built-in video. Everything's this kind of dark blue and reminds me of all the times I've watched limos pass by and tried to look inside through the tinted windows at who's in there.

'So this is a limo, eh?' I open the fridge and there's everything you'd ever want to drink riding around New York with your head up your ass, not knowin' what's going on. I reach in and take out a bottle of beer. Dos Equis, no less. I open it up and sit back.

The guy takes a left on Park Ave and floors it. The city's passing by and I'm drinking my beer and why not? I'm thinking I wish about a hundred people I know could see me now. Hey, Mr Osborne, remember in ninth grade when you told me I wouldn't amount to nothing? Well, check out old Rickie now, gliding uptown in his black limo, you little faggot. Or Tanya and her snooty fucking attitude. Wanna ride in my limo, Tanya? How about a glass of Chivas to smooth you out? Hah!

Then it hits me – Mary! Mary set this whole thing up. Like a surprise or something. 'Hey, excuse me?' The driver looks in the rearview again. I say 'Did Mary do this? I mean, did Mary DeFazio arrange for you and all?'

He shrugs and goes on smiling. I wish he'd do a little less of that and more explaining. But that's got to be it. It's not my birthday, but as I said, that woman can pull off a joke better than anybody so maybe this is one of her crazy brainstorms. But why isn't she here to enjoy it with me? And what about the girls back there? She didn't arrange for that flash job, that's for sure. I don't call her Queen Jealousy for nothing.

We tool along in silence for a while and then he takes a few lefts and rights and pulls up in front of a store. There's a few hundred people standing out in front of it and there are so many that they've got cops out there keeping order.

Soon as the crowd sees our car stop, they come forward. I don't know what's going on but figure I'd just better sit tight till someone gives me the word on what to do.

The driver gets out and comes around to open my door. He smiles in and offers me a hand but I don't need no hand to get out of a car, so I do it myself.

Nuts. The whole world out there goes nuts. Rickie! Rickie! All of them are screaming and yelling and rushing forward and even with everything that's been going on in the last hour, it takes me a few seconds to realise they're screaming at me – Rickie, not some other one. They're here for *me*.

Before I get a chance to react, two cops come up on my sides and grab hold of my arms. They start pushing me towards the door of this bookstore, but it's not easy because the mob is all around us.

'Rickie! We love you!'

'I'm your greatest fan!'

'Rickie, sign my book. It's for my mother. She's dying!'

'Sign my head, Rickie. I got my hair cut like this just so you could sign my head!'

'Rickie, this is for you!' This big fat chick like a lineman for the Jets is pushing forward and she's holding this huge purple cake. It's as big as a toilet seat and across the top of it it says 'Rickie Prousek Fan Club' in yellow squiggly letters.

'Get back!' one cop yells and stiff-arms the fat chick so hard that her cake goes flying. But I don't see where because they're jamming me into that store and there's nothing I can do but keep moving.

Once inside, the crowd is even bigger but the cops get me through to this little table where there's this stack of books about a mile high. The manager of the store is a smoky-looking blonde and she's looking at me like I could scratch every itch she has.

'Mr Prousek, it's such an honour.' She shakes my hand and hers is so soft and warm I want to curl up inside it and take a nap.

But there's no time. Everybody's churning around and howling to get started. So I do what they tell me and sit down at the table with all the books on it. Before I'm crushed to death by the mob, I just get a second to take a look at the cover. On it is this big colour picture of me smiling, under the title '"Immortal Me" by Rickie Prousek.'

To tell you the truth, I don't like to read and the idea of me writing a book is about as far away as fuckin' Antarctica, but what was I supposed to do, tell them you got the wrong Rick? Don't think so.

They give me this fat black magic marker and the crush starts.

'Could you sign it to Leo Specht, sir? In German, "Specht" means woodpecker. Did you know that?'

I look up at this guy. 'Izzat right?' I write 'Hiya Leo. Love Rickie' on the cover of his book and hand it back. The owner says 'Ooo, you signed the *cover*, what a novel idea.'

'Please sign "I love Diana".'

'Sign "To my dear friend, Ed. I'll always remember the cinnamon toast", please.'

'What? Why would I sign *that*? What toast? I don't know you!' As soon as I say that, the guy looks like he's going to cry. Then he apologises. Do you believe it?

It goes on like that till my hand is shaking. People come up with ten books but two's the limit. The good-looking blonde stands right next to me and watches over everything like a hawk. She keeps asking if I'd like anything to drink or eat. What I really want is a cigarette, but you can tell this is definitely a smoke-free zone, so l don't say anything.

Just when I'm starting to get really tired, the fat woman with the purple cake comes up, looking like she just crawled out of a Stephen King swamp. I mean she's fat anyway, right? But now I see where that cake went when the cop sent it flying – all over her front. I mean, she's smeared with purple frosting and chocolate cake, her hair looks like she stuck her finger in an electric socket, and to top it off, she's got a look in her eye that scares the shit out of me. She's holding one of my books, but even that's smeared with purple.

'I've been waiting for three days. You have to sign my book!'

'Sure. Waddya want me to say in it?'

But she squeezes it up to her chest like I was trying to steal it away. 'No, you don't understand! You have to sign it to *me*!'

'Okay, I –'

'TO ME!' she screams out and the whole fucking place stops dead. Then before I know what's going on, she's shoving the table aside and coming at me. The cops try to get between us but it's no good. Too late. She's here already and grabbing hold of me by the front of my shirt. 'You have to sign it to me, to Violet! You have to sign it –'

The cops jump her and wrestle her down, but she's no small thing, plus she's still got hold of my shirt and she's so big, there's nothing I can do.

Well, that's not true. For a while there's nothing I can do, but when she pulls me in and I'm sure she's going to kiss me, I gave her a quick left hook that rang her fuckin' bell, believe me. Then the blonde from the store hit her over the head with a big mother stapler and down goes the purple whale.

'That's it! I'm outta here! Game over.' I push for the door and even though the crowd's still thick as ten hands in one pocket, they let me through. But they're still screaming and yelling and grabbing at me. Rickeeeeeeee!

Luckily the car's right out in front, motor running and the door's open, thank God. Soon's I'm in, the door slams and we're off again. I look through the back window and everybody's wavin', for Christ's sake!

'What the hell was *that?*'

The driver's shaking his head. 'Terrible. Terrible. They promised they would have good security. That shouldn't have happened.'

I was about to say something, but at that moment I looked at the floor and saw my two-dollar hat lying there. That started me thinking and I said to the guy 'Who am I?'

'You're Mr Prousek.'

'Yeah, that's right. But who am I? I mean, why am I so famous?'

'Why?'

'That's right, *why?* Let me tell you something. This morning I walk into a store to buy a hat and when I come out, my girlfriend's gone, but I got a limo waiting and girls goin' ape for me. Then you take me here and some purple nutcase tries to rape me with a book. So that's what I'm saying – why am I suddenly so famous? What'd I do?'

He smiles again but it's not so big this time and I can tell he's confused. Maybe he thinks I'm pulling his leg or testing him about something. But I can tell from the look in his eye my question makes him real nervous.

'I'm serious. What'd I do? I sure didn't write that book. So what else am I famous for?'

'I don't think I understand the question, sir. Everyone knows why you're famous. You –'

BAM! He ploughs right into this big yellow Ryder rental truck stopped at the light in front of us. Two soul brothers jump out, combined total weight ten thousand pounds of mean-looking black flesh. And that's not all – they got on various T-shirts that advertise the fact they hate every white person on the planet. The bigger one is in a Louis Farrakhan 'Million Man March' shirt and is holding a silver baseball bat in his hand which itself is the size of a grapefruit.

My driver gets out and I can see the whole thing going south. The brothers check out this Oreo in his chauffeur's suit and they think 'What you drivin' Whitey around for, Fool?'

And that's exactly what it looks like for a while. They're lookin' mighty pissed off at my chauffeur for hitting them and now everyone's gesturing around with their arms, trying to make their points. The guy with the bat's not saying much, but he's tapping the damned thing against his leg like he's ready to start whompin' any minute now. After a while the other one – who's wearing an 'It's a Black Thing' shirt and got on nasty-looking camouflage pants – goes back to the truck and is back a minute later with what looks very much to me like a piece, thank you very much.

Now I know what's up because the chauffeur comes over to the car and knocks on the window for me to open up. He's gone over. He's turning me loose to his brothers so they don't kick his ass too in the bargain.

So I'm thinking Fuck *you*, Bro! Let 'em try and get in here!

He shakes his head like I don't understand, but I understand just fine. Then the guy with the piece comes over and leaning down on my side, smiles and shows me it's not a gun. It's a camera!

He yells out at me 'Can we take a picture?'

Next thing I know, I'm standing in the middle of First Avenue with 'Black Thing' on one side and Baseball Bat on the other and we're all smiling at the chauffeur holding the camera.

Which draws another crowd. Seems like the whole city of New York has been waiting for me all day. Every time I show my face now I'm flooded with people.

'It's Rickie Prousek! Holy Christ!'

'Rickie! Oh God!'

'No way!'

'*Way!*'

I'd had enough of that for one day, so I jump back in the car and tell the driver to get going.

We peel out but two blocks later, even before I got a chance to get an answer from him about who the hell I was, he pulls up in front of a restaurant called Secrets.

'What's this?'

He looks at his watch and breathes a sigh of relief. 'We're just in time for your luncheon date. I didn't think we'd make it.'

'In here? I know this place. I saw it on "Entertainment Tonight". This is like the hoity-toitiest place in town.'

'You'd better hurry, sir. You'll be late.'

Now you gotta remember I went out that morning planning on a movie and maybe a bite to eat somewhere after. Now here I am supposed to be going into Mel Gibson's favourite place. I look down at my clothes, not like I forgot what I was wearing or anything, but just checking. I mean, after everything else that happened today, maybe my fairy godmother changed me from a pumpkin into a princess or something when I wasn't looking. But no such luck. I'm still in my jeans and sweatshirt.

First I think, now what? But then, hey, I'm Rickie, everybody thinks I'm famous. I get to do anything I want and that gives me the courage to pick up my two-dollar hat and waltz right into the place like I owned it.

Inside it looks like a garage, you know? It's, like, cinder blocks and white paint. But the people in there make up for the no-frills look. They're either beautiful or rich-looking and then two feet away from me is Jay Leno! I'm stunned, but not so stunned not to notice people are staring at me too. They're smiling and nodding like not only do I belong there with the likes of Jay, but they've been waiting to see me.

'You bum! I've been here half an hour.'

The voice isn't anything special so I don't think she's talking to me. Then I feel this really sharp pinch in the middle of my back. I whip around because there's nothing I hate more than a pinch.

Madonna. I swear to God, it's Madonna there and she's looking at me. 'Where have you *been*, Rickie?'

I was pretty angry when I left an hour later. The lunch was good, I mean the food was, but I'd give you back the lunch. All she did was talk about herself. I didn't get a word in edgewise. I mean, she talked the *whole* time. About ten times I wanted to ask her how she knew me, why I was famous, all those types of questions. But once she started talking about Madonna, there wasn't any air left in the room. Like a Virgin, my ass.

When I get out on the street, I can still hear her voice whanging away in my head. I ate too much, I gotta headache and I still haven't found out what I did to get here.

And then the limo wasn't there! I'm standing out on the street like an idiot wondering where's the car. Then I think maybe it's gone 'cause I just imagined all this. I'm running through all my maybes, confused, angry, weirded out of my socks and not having one idea about what I'm supposed to do next.

I look around and see a phone booth. A light goes off in my head. Mary! Give her a call and she can tell you the secret. The only good idea I've had all day. I go over to it, fish a quarter out of my pocket (Madonna paid for lunch), and call her number.

'Hello?'

It's her! I'd know that voice on the moon.

'Mary? Honey?'

'Who is this?'

'It's me. Rick.'

'Rick who?'

'Come on, cut it out. You know, your boyfriend, Rickie Prousek?'

'Oh yeah, right. Real funny, and I'm Meryl Streep.' Click.

She hung up! And I didn't have another quarter. I'm standing there saying every curse I know in the world when suddenly the door to the booth bangs open into me from behind. What the… I turn to whoever's out there, ready to kick their ass, but when I see who it is, I stop fast.

It's me. And not only is it me, it's three me's. And one of them has a gun.

'Get out of the booth, Rickie.'

'Look, hey –'

'Get out of the booth or I'll shoot you right here.' He points the gun at me and giggles like a girl. So do the others. Then I get a better look at them and they're not really me. At first you'd think they were, but even though they got the hair gelled back like mine and other things, none of them *really* looks like me. They're like those bad Elvis impersonators. You know what I mean? The ones who've got the hair and the sideburns and the spangly suits, but one look and you start to laugh at the pathetic fucks for even trying to look like the King.

One of these guys is about a foot shorter than me, one's a foot taller and the other is a fucking Arab. The one with the gun, naturally. But you don't say no to a gun so I open the door, real slow.

'It's him, it's really him. You were right, Hassan!'

'Of course it's him. All right, don't do anything funny, Rickie. Just walk out and get in the cab.'

Down the street a ways is a yellow cab parked. I walk in front while Hassan-Rickie comes up right behind me. Every few steps he gives me a poke with the gun. The others are a few feet behind us. It's a normal cab, but on the bumper is a sticker that says 'My Heart Beats for Dachshunds'.

'Get in.'

What was I supposed to do? I climb in. Hassan gets in next to me while the other two fakes get up front. When we're all settled, the little guy pulls away from the curb real slow like the world's safest driver.

'What's going on?'

Nobody says anything for about twenty blocks until the passenger up front says 'Could I see your hat?'

I didn't even know I was wearing it by then, but I took it off and handed it over. He put it on and suddenly all three of them are laughing like maniacs.

'We did it! We stole him.'

I don't say a word.

We drive way uptown till we're like in Riverdale. Then we're out of the car and walking into a beat-up apartment building. The three of them are talking to each other but I got nothing to say.

We go up a few flights and then one of them gets out some keys and opens a door. They point me to go in first.

I take one look and whistle. Not only are there six dachshund dogs in there, just kind of rambling around. Six dogs in an apartment! *Plus* the whole goddamned place is ten thousand pictures of me. Magazine pictures too, not any snapshots or anything. There are Rickie dolls on one shelf, at least ten copies of 'Immortal Me', a lifesize dummy made up to look like me and wearing the same clothes all of us are wearing… It was a shrine to Rickie Prousek.

'Sit down.'

There's a ratty green couch in the middle of the room and I sit. Two of them plop down on either side of me and the other on the floor in front of us. All the dogs go up to him and kind of cuddle around. Nobody says a word for I don't know how long. I sure don't have anything to say. The room's like a cemetery, except for the dogs snuffling and scratching.

The Rickie who's wearing my hat finally says 'We're sorry we brought you here, but we had to.'

I just nod, trying to be cool and get some thoughts together in my head.

'We're your greatest fans.'

I look around that ka-ka room and say 'Looks like it'.

'We've been following your career for years.'

'Yeah well, then *you* can tell me why I'm so famous. What'd I do to, you know, get here?'

They all think I'm joking.

'No, I'm serious. Please, willya tell me what I did to be so famous? I really want to know.'

The guy with the gun shakes his head, but big Rickie says 'I paid a thousand dollars for your ice skates at a celebrity auction last year.'

'Yeah well, you got robbed because I don't skate.'

He immediately pulls back like I hit him. 'You don't have to be rude.'

Hassan says 'You don't understand how important you are to us. We brought you here because…'

'... Because we have to talk to you,' little Rickie blurts out. 'You've got to tell us how you did it. The *real* truth. We've all read your book, sure, but we know most of the media stuff is lies or exaggerations. We needed you here, alone, so we could talk quietly and, you know, *connect*.'

'Connect *what*? I don't know!' I'm cheesed to the max and start to get up. Enough of this. But gun guy tells me to sit back down. 'I don't know nothin'! I wish I did!'

Like they were all reading each other's minds, the three of them stand up like they were one person. I'm on the couch staring up at three me's and the looks on their faces were not have-a-nice-day.

'You'll tell us, or you're not getting out of here alive. Do you understand? You may think you're so big and famous and we're nothing, but not today, Rickie. We got you and you're not moving till –'

'But I just –'

Hassan bent down and put the barrel against my forehead. 'No more bullshit.' His voice was ice cold; like my father's when I was a kid and I'd done something really wrong.

The little guy sat down right next to me. He reached over and put his hand on top of mine. That more than anything sent a chill up my spine. 'We know everything we could find out. But we want to hear the truth from *you*. Now's your chance to tell the real story, Rickie. Why don't you start at the very beginning. We've got all the time in the world.'

LOOKING FOR BOLIVAR

Christopher Fowler

There are a number of ways you can change your life in a week.

You can fall in love with the wrong person. Career-switch from banking to wicker repair. Experience religious conversion. Get caught shoplifting. Change your barber. Undergo an epiphanal moment when you realise that you'll never drive through Rio in an open-top Mercedes unless you stop spending your weekends drifting around the shops looking at things you don't really want. What I mean is, at some point you either realise who you are and act toward the grain of your personality, no matter how unpalatable that might turn out to be, or you end up in a kind of bitter emotional cul-de-sac that eventually leads to you machine-gunning thirty people dead in McDonald's.

I saw this ad once for running shoes or CDs that said 'Whoever you are, be someone else.' I was twenty-four when I realised I could no longer imagine being someone else, and decided to make a change before it was too late. I moved from London to New York, and ended up looking for Bolivar.

As a child I was sickly, timid, sensible. Rejected by other kids, adored by adults. 'So grown-up!' my aunt would marvel, pinching my face between her fingers as if reaching a decision on curtain material. I left college with unimpressive credentials and was employed in the customer relations department of Barclays Bank, a job with an interest factor equivalent to staring at mud. To spend an evening in the pub with my colleagues was to grasp a sense of the infinite.

I rented a dingy flat in north London. 'It's not a lower-ground,' my estate agent-brother informed me, 'it's a basement. I should know.' I failed to meet the Right Girl. 'Plenty of time for that,' said my mother, who had a mouth designed for holding pins, 'after you've done some hard work.' When the possibility of a transfer came up I took it without quite knowing why, although shifting from such a domineering family to a place where my nearest relative would be several thousand miles away seemed the sensible thing to do.

Maybe I was sick of living in a city that looked like a fishtank whose owner had forgotten to change its water. Maybe I went to New York because the streets were wide and the light was high, because the wind swept in from the sea, because at night the town looked like Stromboli's fairground – how many reasons could there be?

On the day I left, I found myself at the departure gate surrounded by relatives vying with each other to impart advice. I boarded the flight with a head full of rules and lectures, and forgot them all before we landed.

The big things about New York were over-familiar before I'd even seen them. Vertiginous chromium avenues and yellow cabs were so instantly commonplace that they were rendered curiously unimpressive. Rather, I remember being struck by ground-level details. The colours of old Manhattan, faded reds and browns, interiors painted a dingy shade of ochre peculiar to the city. Those little iron hoops that bordered all the trees. Racks of vegetables sprayed with water. Basketball courts on the street. Smelly subway gratings through which could be heard the distant thunder of trains. Vending machines chained to the ground, but trusting you enough to take just one newspaper.

The bank rented me an apartment in Hoboken. My first mistake was to lease a flat where the bedroom window was situated above a bus stop. I had no idea people would actually sit on the bench below all night long, talking and playing ghetto blasters. I wasn't about to go down and ask men with grey cotton hoods protruding over leather jackets to turn the music down.

After six weeks I was desperate. I am a light sleeper at the best of times, but this was impossible; I arrived at Union Square each morning lurching into work like a zombie. Finally I arranged to break the lease and move to another apartment in a quieter neighbourhood, but there was a shortfall between the dates of about a week, when I would have nowhere to stay.

One evening in early June I went out with some people from the bank. They were more conservative in conversation than their London counterparts, but spoke frankly of their careers and finances – subjects we tend to regard as slightly taboo. They were sending off a teller named Dean Stanowicz, who was leaving under some kind of cloud nobody wanted to talk about. We went to this little Jewish restaurant and they gave him a gaudy iced cake, a tradition for every staff birthday, anniversary and wedding. For some reason I found myself explaining my housing problem to Dean, and he told me about a woman he knew who owned an apartment on West 44th Street. It seemed this woman – I couldn't decide how the two of them were related – was going into hospital for a hip operation, and she needed someone to take care of her apartment for a week. It was perfect. Our dates matched exactly. Her name was Mary Amity, which sounded friendly.

Until then it hadn't occurred to me that people lived in the centre of Manhattan. On Saturday morning I arrived at the front door of Miss Amity's building carrying a bag of clothes, a bulky set of keys and a page of scribbled instructions. Dean was supposed to have taken me around the place on Friday evening, but didn't seem very reliable. I had called his home number, but his message service was switched on. I don't know what I was expecting to find inside that tall terraced house with brown window frames and black railings. I had not yet been invited inside an American home – my colleagues worked hard and kept to themselves, valuing their privacy and guarding it accordingly. I suspected they considered me unfriendly, and back then perhaps I was.

A deep brown hallway – that colour again – smelled of freshly polished boots and led to four gloomy flights of stairs. At the top of these, a firetruck-red front door sported three hard-to-open locks. The keys weren't marked, and the elimination process took me twenty minutes. I resolved to label them before I attempted to regain entry. I was a tidy man, and liked labelling things.

Inside, a narrow hall led to a disproportionately enormous lounge that smelled strongly of cigarettes. There were dozens of scruffy plants dotted in between comfortable pieces of furniture, and as many stacks of books. In the corner was an easel with an odd half-finished painting of what appeared to be a three-legged cow, or an overweight hairless cat, on it. There were a number of seventies' new age items scattered about, including a blue glass bong and several sets of redundant wind chimes. Miss Amity had been admitted to hospital two days earlier, so I had the place to myself, or so I thought. No sooner had I set my bag down when a man in white overalls wandered out of the kitchen with a mug of tea in his hands, real PG Tips tea, not those perfumed things on strings you get in New York cafés.

'Hi,' he said amiably, 'do you know if there's a toy store around here?'

Thrown, I shrugged. 'I'm new in town. I don't know where everything is yet.'

'See, I gotta get my kid this troop-carrier spaceship for his birthday and I ain't got time to get to FAO Schwartz. Sixty bucks for something that'll be broke in a week. Crazy, huh? Makes me wish a bunch of real mean aliens would turn up and blast the shit outta the place just so kids would stop wanting models of 'em.'

I wasn't in the mood to conduct a conversation about spaceships with a total stranger when I had been expecting to be left in peace on my own. Just then, an extraordinary clanging noise started up in the next room.

'I'm Charles,' I shouted, holding out my hand and hoping for some reciprocal information.

'And I'm Carlos. Hey, Chuck.' He slapped my fingers.

'Charles, actually.'

'You the guy looking after the joint while the lady of the house is away?'

'Yes, but I don't know – I mean – I wasn't expecting anyone else to be here.'

He looked amazed. 'You mean Dean didn't say anything about me and Raoul?' He aimed a paint-spattered thumb back at the kitchen. 'Raoul's in there trying to get the wastepipe loose.'

'Not a word.'

'You want some tea?' He filled a mug from a large brown pot and returned with it. 'Miss Amity's kind of like the mother Dean never had. When he found out she'd have to go into hospital and miss her birthday, he arranged for us to come in and rebuild her bathroom, kind of a surprise for her when she comes out, so if she calls, don't say nothing about it. She's got this old bath that ain't plumbed in right, and the tiles are all cracked, so we're putting in a load of new stuff.'

'Then why does she need someone to look after the place if you're here?'

'Because we're only gonna be here a couple days, and Bolivar gets lonely.' Skittering in across the polished floorboards came a bulky brindle bull terrier with a grinning mouth that looked wider than his body. He was wearing a broad leather collar studded with spikes, the kind of dog that looks like he's owned by the manager of a bar. I stepped back, alarmed. As a child, I'd had a bad experience with such an animal.

'Nobody said anything about a dog.'

'Hey, he's no trouble. Eats anything, waits till he gets outside to piss, spends most of the day snoring and farting. Not like a dog at all. More like an intelligent pygmy with a big appetite.'

The bedroom was filled with dusty velvet swagging and framed photographs crammed onto unstable tables. Miss Amity appeared to be a sparky, photogenic woman in her early fifties, well-preserved, compact, her hair a range of different colours from copper to blonde. She was strangely beautiful, in the way that very kind people eventually become. She seemed to attend a lot of charity events, and across the years had been photographed with an unlikely range of guests, including a couple of mayors, Zsa Zsa Gabor, Joe DiMaggio, Sylvia Miles, Joey Buttofuoco and someone who looked like – but surely couldn't be – Malcolm X. There was also a picture of a man dressed as a giant carrot.

She wore a lot of junk jewellery – the room looked like a dumping ground for Mardi Gras beads. It wasn't tidy, or very clean. Nor was the rest of the apartment. The refrigerator contained mostly items past their sell-by dates. There was something growing in a Tupperware tub, and a half-chewed plate of lasagna had a kind of pubic mould springing from it. While I was unpacking, Raoul wandered in chewing a chicken leg. He transferred the grease from his hand to his thigh and slapped his fingers against mine. 'Yo – Chaz, how ya doin'?'

'Er, Charles, actually.'

'Listen, you got no hot water tonight.'

'Great.'

'We're not plumbers.'

'I'm sorry?'

'You don't have to be all hoity-toity with us. We're not plumbers, we're just helpin', out, okay?'

I didn't wish to appear stuffy but they both seemed over-familiar, with me, and with the apartment. Carlos was sitting with his legs hanging over an armchair watching NBA highlights on cable. Raoul was chugging a beer in the bathroom, hammering on the pipes again. Wandering uncomfortably from room to room, I announced that I was going to take the dog for a walk.

'A word of advice,' called Raoul. 'Let him lead you. He'll go the route Mary always takes him. Bolivar knows the way, okay?' Bolivar stared at me knowingly, then rolled back on his haunches and began licking his absurdly protuberant testicles. I slipped the heavy chain around his muscular neck and seconds later was dragged out to the stairs.

Ron's Lucky Silver Dollar Bar & Grill did not possess a grill, although there was a giant silver dollar in the window above a hand-painted sign that read SUBS & GYROS. Where I came from, a giro was a cheque. I asked the barman if he was Ron.

'Nope. Ron's dead. He ate a bad scallop. Not here, somewhere else. I'm Bill.'

'Charles.'

'What can I get you, Chuck?'

'I don't really – the dog pulled me in here.' I pointed at my feet. Bill leaned over the bar. 'It just – wouldn't stop pulling.'

'Hey, that's Bolivar! Hey boy!' The dog hoisted itself clumsily onto its hind legs and began scuttling back and forth with its tongue lolling out. Bill poured two shots from a bottle with a lot of signatures on it. He raised his glass. Not wishing to seem rude, I drank with him. The shot tasted like chillis mixed with liquid soap. I noticed that Ron had arms like a weightlifter, or someone who'd been in prison. His biceps were as big as his head. He had a tattoo of a scorpion stinging itself.

'So where's Mary?'

'She's in the hospital. I'm apartment-sitting for her.'

'She comes in most nights. Her son, Randy, used to work here.'

'He was a barman?'

'Well now, that's not for me to say. Randy operated for himself, kind of a one-man business.' Ron suddenly found something to do behind his bar. A crease of concentration ran across his forehead. Then he brightened. 'But you're welcome here any time. No friend of Mary's will ever be a stranger in the Lucky Dollar.' He grasped my hand warmly, grinding several bones to powder.

When I returned to the apartment, Raoul and Carlos had gone, locking up behind them. It took me ages to open the door again. They had left behind the remains of their dinner. I was washing their plates in cold water when the phone rang.

'Hey, Mary,' yelled a woman's voice. 'I have the armadillo. Do you realise Dan had to bring it in the back of his car from Tucson?'

'This is Charles,' I replied patiently.

'Oh. I must have the wrong –'

'This is Miss Amity's apartment.'

'Then who the hell are you?'

I explained. It was something I was obviously going to be doing a lot.

'Shit. Look, I'm gonna have to bring this damned thing around because it's making a hole in its box. You're Jewish, right?'

'How can you tell? Did you say an armadillo?'

'I can spot a nice Jewish boy like an eagle can see lambs in a canyon. Are you married? Don't answer. I'll be there in twenty minutes. No, don't thank me, just pour me a drink. Whisky, rocks, Jim Beam if there's any left.'

I replaced the receiver, puzzled.

'Mary paints,' said Melissa, setting her glass onto a paper coaster I'd found. She stifled a giggle.

'What's funny?' I asked.

'She'd get a kick seeing you put down coasters. She's not that kind of person.'

'What do you mean? What kind of person?'

'You know, like Tony Randall in *The Odd Couple*. She lets her drinks leave little rings on the table.' Melissa crossed long, jean-clad legs. 'She likes to paint animals, but it's tough painting at the zoo with so many people around, so I told my brother to get her something. Well, he drove up from Tucson to see me, and he brought this.' She pointed to the armadillo. It was scratching around in a corner of its straw-filled box. The creature was about a foot long, and had funny bristling ears. It looked mechanical, hardly a living creature at all. 'I can't keep it in my apartment because I have cats.'

'What about Bolivar?' I asked. The dog was whining in the kitchen, scrabbling at the door.

'Oh, he'll be fine. You take good care of him, he's Mary's pride and joy. The armadillo can look after itself, trust me. It's nocturnal, and that's when it'll try to dig its way out. I've left it a box of insects and vegetables. You just top it up with broccoli and cockroaches. But tell me about you, you adorable thing. You're English, single obviously.' She sat back and waited for me to talk.

Melissa originally came from Kansas, 'The Dorothy State', as she drily referred to it. She was as thin and brown as well-worn leather, her bony wrists covered in fat gold ropes, someone who'd had a hard life and then found money. I liked her from the first, which was just as well because she out-stayed her welcome and got completely drunk. When I tried to get her to the door, she made a grab for my balls. 'Mary would like you,' she announced, 'but you need to get out more. Put that adorable face in the sun.'

I had to give the cab driver an extra ten dollars to take her. But that night I had my first decent eight-hour sleep in weeks.

The next morning was Sunday. I had a hangover, and was looking forward to a lie-in. There was a smell in the apartment beneath the ground-in cigarette smoke that I associated with my own childhood. It took me a while to realise that it was dampness, something I didn't associate with American homes, yet it made me feel comfortable and secure. Burrowing back into the blankets, my rest was interrupted by the front door slamming. I figured Carlos and Raoul were back, but then I heard different voices.

'*Xanadu*'s fabulous. Olivia Newton-John as a Greek muse, all lip gloss and roller skates? It's been waiting fifteen years to be recognised as a classic, but the world is still not ready. You can learn so much about hair maintenance watching her.'

I pulled myself out of bed and opened the curtains. The day was warm and wet, the sidewalk empty and every bit as Sundayish as a residential English backstreet. The sky had a dead, exhausted look. I listened to the lounge.

'Donald loses all his dates because of his terrible taste in movies,' said another voice. 'Just as they're starting to get along fine, he drags them off to see a double bill of something like *Grease 2* and *Yentl*.'

Making sure my pyjamas were not exposing anything, I ventured out of the bedroom. There were three strangers in the kitchen making coffee. A muscular young man in a black nylon T-shirt, a slender Asian boy wearing rather a lot of makeup for this time of the morning and an attractive, overweight girl with dyed black hair. They seemed as surprised to see me as I was them.

'Oh my God, we woke the maid,' cried the Max Factored one. 'Who are you, honey? Did you know you got no hot water?'

'I'm Charles,' I explained. 'Yes, I did know. I'm looking after Miss Amity's apartment for her.'

'Well, Charlene, I'm sorry we woke you but Mary never mentioned anyone was staying here.'

'That's okay. I should be getting up anyway. Who are you?'

'Donald.' Mr Black T-shirt thumbed his chest. 'That's Jaffe, and Val's the female, gynaecologically speaking. Jaffe's still undergoing some kind of sexual identity crisis but the men are rooting for him, so he may get through it with just a few mascara burns. Your armadillo has escaped.'

Jaffe was wearing an extraordinary badge on his jacket, little pieces of broken mirror, an old Andrew Logan design from the eighties, and it kept catching the light, shimmying specks onto the nicotined ceiling like a disco ball. I saw that the armadillo was trying to dig its way out through the kitchen cabinets, away from the light. Fascinated, Bolivar was taking gentle snaps at the creature, as if trying to cradle it in his enormous jaws. I wanted to separate them, but I'd never touched an armadillo before.

'You can join us for brunch if you like,' Donald offered. 'We'll be discussing the movie career of Brad Pitt in depth, and you may wish to contribute something to that. Are you from Harvard or something? You have a funny accent.'

'I'm English,' I said apologetically, as you do. I wanted to ask why he had access to Mary's apartment, but could find no way of phrasing the question politely. At my feet the dog was whimpering in frustration and the armadillo was noisily butting its head against the units.

'So, Charlita, you going to join us for a glass of second-rate champagne and a Spanish meal presented between slices of cantaloupe?' asked Jaffe.

'Thank you for the offer,' I replied, offended, 'but I have things to do.'

'He's so polite. I *love* it.'

'We're old friends of Mary's,' Val took the trouble to explain. 'We always come by on a Sunday. She reads our tarot, then arranges my astrological week. I can't go out of the house without it.'

'Well, she won't be able to do it for you today.'

'She already did.' Val held up a scroll of paper. 'She left it out for me. What star-sign are you?'

'I don't believe in the stars,' I said testily. 'You have your own door keys for the apartment?'

Jaffe was defensive. 'Mary gives her keys to everyone. Don't think you're special.'

'What's she like?' I asked Val.

'Mary? A sweetie. Prickly as a cactus, soft as a pear. Bad at keeping secrets. Her parents were imprisoned by the Nazis. She's had a wild life. Come with us, we'll tell you all about her.'

'No, really, thank you, I can't.'

'Your choice. You're gonna miss the dish.'

Laughing, they left. I don't know why I refused their offer. Their over-friendliness unnerved me. In such situations I invariably retreated. After they had gone I wandered about the apartment wondering if I should clean it. I decided to wait until the bathroom was finished. The shower stall was filled with weird oils, dried flowers and glycerine soaps, none of which smelled very pleasant. Even in here there were buckled photographs taped on the walls. She seemed to have so many friends. I had virtually none. Bolivar was whining for a walk, and I was just about to take him when the telephone rang.

'Is that you, Charles?'

'Yes, it is,' I replied, instinctively knowing that this was Mary Amity.

'How are you settling in, dear?'

'Very well, thanks. I just wondered – forgive me for asking – how many people have you given your front door keys to?'

'I've never really counted. I could probably work it out. Do you need to know?'

'No, I was just thinking about security.'

'Darling, I have nothing worth stealing. My most precious possessions are all inside my head. Although if a woman called Sheryl-Ann tries to let herself in, you must stop her.'

'How do I do that?'

'Just put your foot against the door until you can get the chain on, that's what I always do. Then call the super. You'll recognise her easily, she looks like a hooker but I swear I had no idea she was when I gave her the keys. How is my Bolivar?'

'He's fine. He's – fine.' I looked down at Bolivar, who was trying to choke himself to death on the lead, torn between conflicting desires to torment the armadillo and get out on the street. 'How are you?'

'Thank you for asking. So polite. I've had the operation, I just have to lie here and heal. Take good care of him, won't you? Don't let him overeat. He'll eat absolutely anything. He ate a shovel once. Give me your work number, just in case.' She didn't explain in case of what, but I gave it to her. I was a guest in her apartment, after all.

'I wasn't able to get hold of Dean,' I explained. 'He was going to show me where everything was.'

'You're a big boy, you can find things out for yourself, can't you? You won't be hearing from Dean for a while. He's gone away.'

'Oh? He didn't tell me he was going –'

'Well, the truth is he's starting a jail sentence. It's not his fault. He's a good boy who's had some bad luck. Take my dog for a walk, will you? He likes walks.'

'Hey, Bolivar, c'mere you big hunk of muscle!' screamed the waitress, pulling Bolivar's front paws up on her apron. It seemed unhygienic. This time, the dog had stopped sharply on a corner three streets from the apartment, then dragged me into a coffee shop called Manny's Freshly Brewed Sip 'N' Go. The waitress, a slender, pretty Puerto Rican girl with smoky eyes, butted heads with the dog, then dropped him back down.

'I'm Maria. Listen, the manager'll piss blood if he sees the dog in here.' She laughed carelessly. 'The health board already hate him. They closed us down in '95 for having mice in the pan racks.'

'You know Miss Amity?'

'Oh sure. She used to teach tap over at this crummy little studio on West 46th. I wanted to be a dancer, but I really wasn't good enough.'

'Was she a dancer, then?'

'Once, long ago, out in Hollywood. Chorus stuff. Way before she took her accountancy exams and married that maniac, that crazy pianist.'

'She was married to a pianist?'

'Her second husband. The first one shot himself, but then I guess he had a good reason. Not that the pianist turned out any better. That was all before my time. Mary was sub-leasing the studio from this guy who turned out to be some kind of gangster. He ran a luggage shop near the Marriott that was a front for a gambling syndicate, one of these places that sold suitcases, statues of Jesus and flick-knives, and had old Turkish guys in the back playing cards. He had to get out of town quick, and robbed the studio while everyone was in the tap class. Cleaned the place out of wallets, purses, jewellery, took all Mary's savings from the apartment. But he didn't get out in time, and they cut one of his feet off. The right, I think. Sure slowed him down. Mary says it made him a better person. She's always in trouble, one of those people, y'know? You wanna make sure you don't get caught up. It has a way of enveloping everyone. It's because she has this instinct, she knows stuff about people and sometimes they don't like it. You ready for a coffee?'

On the way home I met another half-dozen people who were acquainted with Bolivar and Mary Amity. A Greek couple in a dry-cleaners. Two old ladies in ratty fur coats who finished each other's sentences. A thin horse-faced man in a floor-length plastic slicker. A cop. I would have expected this sort of thing in an English country village, but it did not seem possible that one woman could be so well known in such a cosmopolitan neighbourhood. From each of them I gleaned another curious piece of information about my hostess, but they confused my picture of her instead of clarifying it. The cop mentioned her recent divorce from 'that writer, the guy who caused all that trouble at Rockaway Beach'. Was this the pianist, or someone else? The couple in the dry-cleaners professed themselves glad that Mary had gotten her eyesight back. The horse-faced man asked me if she still had 'the singing hen'.

I returned to the apartment half-expecting to find another stranger sitting in the lounge, but for once it was empty, and I could concentrate on going through the figures I needed to prepare for work the following morning. Or I would have been able to, had the armadillo not clawed them all to pieces and pissed on them. It took me the rest of the day to put everything right, during which time I fielded over a dozen phone calls from borderline-crazies asking for Mary. Apparently she ran some kind of astrology hotline on her other number Sunday evenings. I don't know the details but I think there was some kind of gambling element involved because one guy asked if he could put thirty dollars on Saturn. Deciding to set her voicemail in future, I finally got to bed just before one, having first locked the rewritten papers safely inside my briefcase.

Sleep did not come easily. My head was full of questions. Why had Mary's first husband killed himself? Why was the second one a maniac? Why was Dean in jail? Why couldn't I just ignore all this stuff and quietly get on with my own life?

On Monday, Bolivar had to stay behind in the apartment while I went to work, but Raoul and Carlos arrived just as I was leaving.

'Yo! The Chuckster!' bellowed Carlos. 'The new tub is arriving today. Gonna be some banging.'

'That's fine,' I said, relieved. 'Do your worst. I won't be here.' I stopped in the doorway. 'As a matter of interest, how do you know Miss Amity?'

She had helped the pair out of some difficulty when they were little more than schoolkids, in trouble with the law. Carlos now worked for a security firm and Raoul was a hot-diver. That is, he explained, he was paid to jump into radioactive water at power plants, in order to fix things. 'It hasn't done a hell of a lot for my sperm-count and my pants glow in the dark,' he laughed, 'but the money's good.'

The great thing about the location of Mary's apartment was its proximity to the bank. I could be there in a few minutes, not that I particularly wanted to. It wasn't a very interesting job. That evening I was back by five thirty, and returned to find the front door standing wide open. Carlos was on the floor doing something intricate with spanners. His portable cassette recorder was playing a mutilated tape of mariachi music.

'You know the front door's been left wide open?'

'Raoul, I asked you to shut it, man.'

'Where's the dog?' I asked.

'You didn't take him to work with you?'

They looked from one to the other, then back at me.

I asked the neighbours. I walked the streets. I reported the loss to the police. Bolivar was nowhere to be found. He could have left the apartment at any time during the day. By ten o'clock I was in a state of panic, but there was nothing to do except return home and see if he had managed to find his way back.

There was no sign of him. I fed the armadillo, which by this time was making the kitchen smell strange, and went to bed, if not to sleep.

When I awoke the following morning to find yet another stranger in the apartment, I was glad to have someone to talk to. He was a very large black man named Gregor, and was washing his underpants in the kitchen sink.

'You have something wrong with your water.'

'What are you doing?' I asked.

'Your basement washer-dryer is being overhauled and I couldn't get in the bathroom, there's pipes an' shit everywhere,' he explained.

'I mean, what are you doing here in this apartment?' I noticed an aggressive tone in my voice that I could have sworn wasn't normally there.

'See, Mary lets me use her utility room because mine is full of hookers.' He wrung out an enormous pair of Calvin Klein Y-fronts and draped them over a radiator. 'They work the street a block down from here, right outside my building, and we have a deal with them to be off the sidewalk by seven in the morning, when our kids start getting up, but in return they get to wash all their stuff in the utility room, and I don't want to be sharing a drum with all their split-crotch shit. So Mary gave me her –'

'– apartment keys. I understand. I'm Charles. You want some coffee?'

'Sure thing, Charlie,' he said gratefully. 'I hope I'm not putting you to trouble or nothing.'

'Oh, it's no trouble,' I said wearily, reaching for the coffee pot.

I could hardly concentrate on work that day, I was so worried. There had been no word about Bolivar, and I wondered how long a dog could survive by itself on the streets of Manhattan. He was wearing a collar, but to my knowledge there was no address on it. I called the police again, but finding a lost dog came a pretty long way down their list of things to do today. I resolved to leave work early and continue trawling the streets. Naturally, by five o'clock it was raining so hard that you couldn't see more than the blurred red tail-lights of the nearest retreating cab.

By eight o'clock, soaked through and in despair, I ended up back at the apartment. I had just managed to get the door open when the telephone rang.

'Oh, I'm so glad you're there,' said Mary. 'I tried you at work but they said you'd gone for the evening. I spoke to a nice young lady named Barbara. Such a nice voice. She broke up with her boyfriend, did you know?'

'No, I didn't know that.'

'You should talk to her. A good soul, but lonely. When she's not with someone she puts on weight. You can tell just by listening.'

'Yes, she's very nice,' I agreed, pulling off my wet raincoat. 'I was just taking the dog for a walk.'

'In this terrible weather? Oh, you didn't have to do that. Put him on, will you? Let me hear him.'

I desperately looked around. 'He can't come to the phone right now. He's eating.'

'He'll come when he hears my voice. Bolivar!' She began shouting his name over and over. I hoped she was in a private room. With no other choice available, I was forced to impersonate the bull terrier. I interspersed ragged breathy gasps with some swallows of saliva.

'Good boy! Good boy! Put Charles back on now.'

I wiped my mouth. 'Hello, Miss Amity.'

'Oh call me Mary, everyone does. I just wanted to thank you for being so kind to me, Charles. Lying here in hospital you start worrying about all sorts of things, and it's such a comfort knowing that someone responsible is taking care of my precious baby.'

Fifteen minutes later I was in Ron's Lucky Silver Dollar Bar & Grill, chugging back beers and telling the barman my problem. I had to tell someone.

'I've let the poor woman down, Bill. She allowed me to stay in her home, not because she needed someone to look after the place but because this guy I know told her I needed somewhere to stay for a week. She trusted me out of the goodness of her heart. I see that now. But I let her down. I lost her prized possession, her best friend! How could I do that? How could I be so irresponsible?'

'Strictly speaking it wasn't your fault,' said Bill, flicking something out of a beermug. 'The builders, they should have kept the front door shut.'

'You don't understand. It's a matter of good faith.'

At the other end of the bar, one of the patrons switched on the wall TV. *Lady and the Tramp* was showing. The film had just reached the part where the unclaimed dog in the pound was walking the last mile to the gas chamber. All the other dogs were howling as it went to its lonely death.

'Hey, turn that thing off!' shouted Bill. 'Jeez, sorry about that, Chuck.'

'How am I going to tell her, Bill? I mean, Dean would be able to break it to her gently, but he had to go to jail.'

'I know about that.'

'You do?'

'Sure. He comes in here with Mary.'

'Why is he going to jail?'

'He used to do a little – freelancing – for Mary.' He seemed reluctant to broach the subject.

'Oh? Was he handling her accounting work?' I knew she'd sat accountancy exams, and Dean was a teller, after all. The thought crossed my mind that they had been caught working some kind of financial scam together, and that Mary was not in hospital at all but with him in jail.

'No,' replied Bill, 'dancing.'

'What do you mean?'

'She has this entertainment company that supplies dancers to office parties, you know the kind of thing, sexy girls coming out of cakes, stuff like that. Meter maids, nurses who strip, all above-board and legit. And she has some guys who take their clothes off. Well, Dean owed some money and needed to get cash fast. She persuaded Dean to earn it by doing this act where he was dressed as a cop, and he'd turn up in some chick's office and tell them they were under arrest, and they'd ask why, and he'd say for breaking men's hearts, and then he'd whip out his tape deck and play *Stop! In the Name of Love!* and strip down to a sequinned jockstrap.'

'So why was he arrested?' I asked.

'He was coming out of the Flatiron Building after a birthday appointment and saw somebody being mugged. Well, he was still in uniform, and saw this guy off, but get this, the victim reported him for not being a real cop. And it turned out this wasn't the first time he'd used his outfit in public. They found him guilty of impersonating a police officer. That's taken very seriously around here.' He saw my mug was empty. 'Let me fill that for ya?'

I sat in the apartment, staring at the spot where Bolivar had spent his evenings happily assaulting the armadillo. When he wagged his tail, his entire body flexed back and forth like a single muscle, a grin on legs. I missed him.

Mary owned the fattest telephone book I had ever seen, but as I only knew the first names of her friends I couldn't find any of them listed within its pages. Raoul and Carlos had finished the bathroom and gone, leaving a bunch of red roses behind in the sink, and the armadillo, which seemed to have discovered a prisoner-of-war method of getting out of its box and back in before I got home, had eaten the piece of paper bearing the number of Carlos's mobile phone. I was trying to figure out my next move when the telephone rang.

This time it was Donald. Apparently, Mary had rung him and asked him to call me. I hadn't liked his attitude the other morning, but now he seemed a lot friendlier. Still, it seemed odd that he should call. I decided to break the news to him about losing Bolivar. He told me that the first thing I needed to do was duplicate a stack of posters and staple them on telephone poles around the neighbourhood.

'You think it's wise putting Miss Amity's number on them?'

'You worry too much, anyone ever point that out to you? Listen, it's easy, I'll help if you want.'

My first instinct, the one that came all too naturally, was to say no. Nobody in our family ever accepted help of any kind. Then I thought, this is crazy, and accepted his offer. That evening we put up nearly a hundred posters. The rain didn't stop for a second, but it was fun walking around the backstreets, past the glowing restaurant windows, talking to someone so alien that everything we spoke of began from opposite points of view. We didn't find Bolivar but at least I had done something positive, and that felt good.

The next day was Wednesday. Mary was due out of hospital on Friday. She called again that evening, and this time I managed to avoid bringing the dog to the telephone for a conversation. She wanted to know about my parents, and I had to admit I found it easier talking to someone I had never met.

'Families. They mean well but they're blind,' she said.

'I miss my dad.'

'Of course you do. I come from a very big family. My father planned to bring us here for many years, but by the time we finally reached New York there were only a few of us left. So I made the city my family. It was the most logical thing to do. A little assimilation is good for you. How's my doggie?'

'Uh, he's fine. He's in the kitchen, eating.'

'Then I won't disturb him. And I won't keep you from your evening. Nurse Ratchett is about to come around with my knockout pills. I hide them down the side of the bed. It drives her nuts. What birth sign are you?'

'Pisces.'

'Ah.' I could hear her smile. 'That would explain it.'

The rain had stopped. The street glittered and beckoned. As a European I find it impossible to watch American network TV because of the commercials, so after a quarter-hour of fidgety channel-hopping I headed back outside. I tried to imagine where Bolivar might have gone, but the dog knew so many stores and bars in the neighbourhood I had no idea where to start. He had a better social life than me. Deliberately ignoring my boss's advice – 'If you have to walk in New York, pick a destination and home in on it like a Cruise missile' – I wandered aimlessly for half an hour, then headed back to the apartment.

On the front steps I collided with Melissa, who was coming out of the building.

'I left you a Dutch apple cake. I baked too much for myself. You need more flesh. Oh, and I topped up the armadillo's box with some cabbage leaves and a mouse. Manny can get them for you, from his coffee shop.'

I was touched. 'Thanks, Melissa, that's really sweet of you. Do you want to come up for a drin– coffee?'

She waved the offer away. 'No, I can't stop. Besides, you already have a visitor.'

'Who?' I'd been hoping for a quiet night.

'I didn't catch his name but he looks like one of Mary's emotional cripples. She does this course, this therapy thing. Did you know she's a qualified therapist? By the way, this came off.' She put the top of the bathroom's hot-water tap in my hand.

'No, I didn't,' I replied, pocketing the faucet. 'If someone told me she was a freelance lion-tamer, it wouldn't surprise me.' Wondering who or what I was in for now, I ventured upstairs.

'Bad luck doesn't make you a loser. Do I look like a loser to you? No, you give me respect, 'cause what you see is a chick-magnet, a pretty sharp guy. Not a loser.'

He wore Raybans on top of his head, silver-backed Cuban heels and a blue tropical shirt covered in marlins. Slick-black hair, a hula-girl tattoo on his forearm, jiggling above a diamante watch 'with a rock so big it could choke a fucking horse'. He was settled in the armchair I had come to think of as Carlos's chair, nursing a large whisky. He seemed edgy and anxious to get something off his chest, and I wasn't about to argue. For all I knew he was carrying a gun. He looked the type, only more weasally, like if he shot someone it would be because the safety catch had accidentally come off.

'Yeah. So. I got this debt around my neck from some stuff I'd picked up in the Keys. Not drugs, man, everyone thinks drugs in Florida but this was a shipment of French silverware, like cutlery and saltcellars and stuff, I figured from some Louisiana family. And I can't get rid of it because, get this, it's too valuable. I called Mary and at first she told me to return it, like I could just waltz back and cancel the deal.'

I could sense it was going to be a long night, and that I wouldn't like whatever it was this guy was working toward, so I poured myself a whisky. I never used to drink.

'She already knew what I was holding 'cause she'd seen it on the news – the *national* news – on account of the silverware once belonged to some French bigwig or something. Now a guy in Harlem called Dolphin Eddie is offering me a cash deal so low it's a fucking offence to nature, but I figure okay, I won't make a profit but it'll wipe the slate on my debts.' He held up his glass. 'Can I get another one of these?'

'Look here, Mr –'

'Randy. Randy Amity. This is my mother's apartment. I'm her only kid. I guess you think that's weird, considering how many times she's been married, but something went wrong with her tubes after she had me. You're Chuck, right?'

Now I saw the family resemblance. God, she must have been disappointed.

'Anyways, I'm leaving the stuff here.'

'Here?' I exploded. 'Are you crazy? Where is it?'

'Relax.' Randy sat forward and drained his drink. 'It's safely stashed away.'

'What if your mother finds out? Good Lord, she could get hurt.'

'I don't think so. It was her idea. I was just gonna to stop by, stash the silverware for a couple of nights and take a bath, but the hot-water faucet is missing.'

'Can I at least see this – merchandise?'

'Sure.' He reached beneath the armchair and pulled up a large inlaid gold and blue leather case. Inside the silk-sewn lid was a brass panel faced in dense scrollwork. I tipped the case to the light and read the owner's name. *Donatien-Alphonse-François, Comte De –*

My jaw dropped. 'You mean to tell me you stole the cutlery of the Marquis De Sade?' I asked, appalled. 'Do you have any idea how valuable this stuff is?' The carvings on the bone-handled fish-knives, in particular, were outrageous.

'What can I tell you?' shrugged Randy. 'I'm the black sheep of the family. Only Mama loves me, even though she won't introduce me to her friends.'

'You don't look like her.'

'That's good. I guess I'm more like my pa.'

'Which one of her husbands is that?'

'The one she didn't marry,' he replied thoughtfully.

Just then, the door buzzer went and we both flew into a panic, shovelling the knives and forks back into the canteen like a pair of kids caught smoking dope in their bedroom. Randy stowed the case and signalled the all-clear, and I answered the door to find myself looking at a very frail elderly man in a ratty cardigan, holding a ficus tree almost as tall as himself.

'I want you should give this to Mary,' he said, shouting at the top of his voice. 'I don't want it no more. It ain't the plant, it's the money.'

'I – what? Wait.' I held up my hand. I didn't want him to repeat what he had said. He was extremely deaf and possibly half-blind, for he seemed to be addressing a spot several feet above my head.

'The tree, it's full of money,' he bellowed. 'I don't want it no more.'

I looked back at Randy, who was hiding behind the couch. He gave a puzzled 'Wassamatta?' look.

'I want you should give this to Mary,' the old man repeated. I felt like asking him why he hadn't used his keys like everyone else. 'I'm not crazy or nothing. You're looking at me like I'm crazy.'

'I'm sorry, I don't mean to,' I apologised. 'I'll give her the plant.' I wanted him to put it down before he fell down.

'It's her damn plant anyway. She lends her plants to people. I'm in her Thursday night group. Every week since my wife died. Exploring the Senses. I told her I was depressed and she gave me the plant, but she stuck money in the pot, like this way I won't think it's charity or a handout or nothin', but I saw through her, so I'm bring it back. There's sixty dollars there and you can tell her I ain't touched a damn penny.' He thrust the battered tree into my arms and started off for the stairs. How he ever got up them in the first place I'll never know.

'An' tell her from me,' he yelled, looking back over his shoulder, 'that's a great plant she has there. Tell her it did the trick.'

Much to my relief, Randy left at midnight. He was staying at his ex-girl-friend's mother's house in Queens. From the way he was talking, I had a suspicion that he might be sleeping with her. He promised me the cutlery would only remain in the apartment for a few days, but I knew that someone with eyes like a starving boa constrictor would be capable of telling anything to anyone.

I put the ficus in with the other plants, made myself a coffee and sat by the window for a while. The room seemed oddly silent now. For the first time in ages I thought about sharing my life with someone. No one in particular, just someone.

On Thursday I called the police again, with no luck. Miss Amity was due home the next evening, and I dreaded to think what I would say to her. I played back her messages; the usual assortment of normality-impaired individuals, someone asking her about selling a speedboat – she seemed to be acting as the middleman in a deal – someone else wanting to know if you could put a copyright on planets and sell them as brand-names.

Someone had also been in the apartment. I could smell cigar smoke. There was a squashed-out butt in the sink, and a pair of half-empty coffee cups beside the sofa. Worse still, it looked to me as though they had made love on the bed. The covers were rumpled and the room smelled stale and faintly perfumy. There was a time, just a few days ago, when the discovery would have shocked me, but my accumulated indirect knowledge of Miss Amity told me something about these new occupants. That, trapped perhaps in love-less relationships, they had fallen for each other and were unable to meet any-where else, so she had allowed them to use the apartment for their trysts.

When Miss Amity called, I told her my suspicions.

'Damn,' she cried, 'that filthy whore has been dragging her johns in again. I warned you about Sheryl-Ann. Once I came home and found some poor businessman tied naked to a chair with duct-tape. It took hours to get it all off because he was so hairy. A nice man. I had to lend him cab fare because she took his wallet. His wife couldn't see they had a problem. Listen, I must tell you my news. Barbara has a date. Aren't you pleased for her?'

She never waited for you to catch up. 'Who are we talking about now?'

'Oh, Charles! The girl in your office. I fixed her up with my cousin Joel. He owns a chain of hardware stores. Is two a chain? He's taking her dancing. Isn't that great? Do you like mariachi music?'

She seemed to be moving in circles around me, making waves, brushing against the lives of others. This was beyond my experience. 'I'm very glad for her,' I replied. 'How did you –'

'If somebody calls about a speedboat, don't talk to them. I checked it out, and I get the feeling it was not acquired legally, if you know what I mean.'

I took Friday afternoon off. I was so nervous about Miss Amity coming home, I wanted some time to myself to figure out how to handle it. She called from the hospital at four to say she was just leaving. At half past, there was another call.

'Guess what?' shouted Donald, out of breath. 'We found the dog.'

I leapt out of the armchair. 'My God, Miss Amity's due back any minute. Where is he?'

'In your building. He's been there the whole time. Mrs Beckerman's been looking after him. He stays with her whenever Mary goes out of town.'

'Why on earth didn't she bring him back?'

'I guess she thought she was meant to look after him, what with Mary in the hospital. She called me to ask when Mary was getting out. Ground floor, apartment 1b. Go get 'im.'

'Donald, you are a lifesaver.'

'So buy me a drink sometime, Mr Snooty Englishman.'

'Tomorrow,' I promised. 'Tomorrow night.'

'Deal.'

The other line rang. I switched across and answered. 'Hello?'

'It's me, Mary. I stopped to get some groceries on the way. Listen, I can't get in. I don't seem to have my keys. You will be there, won't you?'

'Of course. I'm looking forward to meeting you.'

'Did you get the dog back from Mrs Beckerman?'

'You mean – you knew?'

'That you'd lost him? Of course I knew. From the moment you performed that ridiculous impersonation over the phone.'

'But if you knew, you must have had an idea where Bolivar had gone.'

'Well, of course,' she replied.

'Then why didn't you tell me?'

'I would have thought that was obvious. I wanted you to spend some time with Donald. Charles, I have something to tell you. I was talking to your mother earlier and –'

'My mother? My mother in England?'

'You have another?'

'How did you get her number?'

'Barbara found it in your address book. She's seeing Joel Saturday. I hope they get on. They're the same height; it's a start. I called your mother because I wanted to ask her something, that's all. She thinks an awful lot of you. We talked for quite a while, her and me, and one thing led to another, and I accidentally let slip –'

The other line rang.

'There's another call.'

'I have a feeling that'll be her now. Don't be mad.'

'Hold on.'

I gingerly switched to the other line.

'Mary Amity tells me you're gay,' said my mother. I nearly dropped the phone. Regaining my composure, I switched lines back.

'I didn't mean to out you,' said Miss Amity apologetically, 'I wasn't sure you even knew yourself, but it was obvious to me. Families. We shock and disappoint each other, but there's still love. Look at Randy. Pour a drink. Brandy is good. Talk to your ma, don't fight, just run with it, she's fine. I'll be there soon.'

I talked to my mother.

I collected the dog.

I waited for Mary.

But Mary Amity never arrived. We never did meet.

She hadn't been in the hospital for a hip operation. The doctors had removed a tumour. She didn't want to worry people. In the cab she developed a cramp and asked the driver to take her back. She died a few minutes after being re-admitted.

She was the only person who ever got my name right.

I no longer work at the bank. I have an apartment of my own now, a modest place in Brooklyn. Two floors up, with four rooms, one bull terrier and far too many sets of keys.

HEART PROBLEMS
Cris Mazza

In May, when Neil Artell called, she could tell he was different. He was the first one with a specific deadline – for a contest held by a SoHo photography club every spring. Not that it was impossible he could *also* be a sicko, but maybe a sicko with more potential to really be *worth* something. And not just because of the contest.

This year's contest had been a month or so ago, he hadn't won a placement, he said, and he was going to do several series on the same theme over the next six months then enter the best set. Loralee was his first try. 'Then, for sure, *I'll* be the best one,' she said, smiling, which of course he couldn't see through the phone.

She'd changed her classified ad again. It said *Very fresh female model for private sessions, no questions*. Neil said, 'Does this, uh, mean *you* don't ask questions or, uh, *I'm* not allowed to?'

'It means whatever we want it to mean.'

'Okay... Well, okay, of course I do need to know what... uh, how much you weigh. I know that's such a rude question. Let me, uh, explain. I wanted to use... um... my daughter for this series. But... naturally that wouldn't be... appropriate.'

Loralee was on her stomach on the tangled, unmade bed. The sheets had that limp, damp feeling. Dale was at work. He'd left complaining of tightness in his chest. Loralee held the phone between shoulder and neck and cleaned her fingernails. She could hear the potential cash cow breathing – not panting, just breathing loud, like someone who's asleep. She didn't know yet that he had an overbite and couldn't close his mouth all the way.

'Uh, you wouldn't, by any chance, um... weigh under 100?' he asked.

'You guessed it.'

'Good, and... well, the reason... My daughter's 14 now. I wanted to do something like this last year, not *exactly* this same thing, but... you know, never did. Well, now... um, my wife and I are separated...'

Loralee rolled to her back, heartbeat like a boomerang, gazing at nothing in particular through bands of sun striping the usual floating dust. The sun only hit this window, at the most, twenty minutes a day. 'I think I understand what you're looking for,' she said. 'I think you won't be disappointed.' No one and no mirror looking back at her to let her know if she was smiling or sneering.

A shower, quick shampoo, then the thorough body shave that took, sometimes, until there was no hot water left. As usual, when they didn't ask for a particular type of apparel, she wore only three articles of clothing: plain white underwear, tank top, and sweatpants she'd lifted from the locker room on her last day of high school, the school's name on one leg now badly fading so she only washed them in cold water and wore them only to sessions. She should've taken more than one pair. But five years ago, who could know?

Neil Artell's building was a yellow-brick walk-up in Brooklyn. Furnished studio and one-bedroom apartments, the kind with plaid drapes, dark brown shaggy carpet with cigarette burns and dark stains where the shag is matted, phony wood grain plastic coffee tables, one bluish brownish tweedy sofa with cushions squished to about half the thickness they'd started, all the lights installed into the ceiling or mounted on the walls with thick bumpy amber glass covering the light bulb, and certain walls like cardboard where you'd swear the nails your neighbours pound in to hang pictures will come poking out on your side so you could hang a picture on the same nail – those were the walls added when big family-sized apartments were broken down into studios and one-bedrooms – the other walls were cold, yellowed plaster, with the smell of onions that were fried next door 20 years ago just now making its way through. The studio's bathroom had been changed into a darkroom, the main area was set up with professional lights and reflectors and large white backdrops blocking one wall because it had a fold-down bed. The kitchen nook had a curtain drawn across it. Neil said she could change her clothes there. There was no TV but he had a portable radio and was listening to a Mets game. Someone next door was watching cartoons. Someone was frying bacon. A voice buzzed upstairs. A baby cried, somewhere far away. Something with an old crackly voice screamed *be quiet* about ten times in a row before Loralee realised it was a parrot.

It didn't take long to get rid of sweat pants, tank top and underwear. On the counter beside the sink, where a toaster or coffeepot might be, there was just a travel kit filled with slightly used make-up; a hand mirror hung on a nail on the wall; and, dangling from one of the cupboard knobs, a brand new white terrycloth robe which Loralee put on before coming out of the kitchen. Neil was using a meter to test the light from different angles, so Loralee went and sat on the stool which was almost surrounded by the three white back-drops. Then Neil went over to where the camera was set up on a tripod.

'Let's, uh, have a look,' he said, smiling. There was that overbite. He was also mostly bald with some wispy, thin colourless hair and hazy brownish-blondish eyes. Loralee eased the robe off her shoulders, let it fall around the stool like a tablecloth. Her feet perched on one of the stool's rungs, knees together, hands on her thighs, back straight, chin up. She could feel the cool metal on her shaved twat, imagined her lips making a kiss print on the seat.

'You're… uh… pretty close to what I, uh… had in mind.' He stopped to blush. 'I mean, I hung up on a few girls after they answered the phone, I could tell they were… you know. I had this idea for a series… the maturity of youth, you know? Does it sound cliché? My daughter… god, they grow up fast. Scares me.'

'Why?' Loralee put the robe over her shoulders again.

'Last time I saw her without clothes… she was a girl, a child. Now… well, I can't *imagine* her being any different, but of course I know she *is*. You don't want to hear this.'

Loralee smiled. 'You started paying ten minutes ago. The time's yours to… do whatever you want.'

Neil closed his mouth over his teeth, it seemed, with some effort required. The cartoon next door ended with the Loony Tunes theme song, then an advertisement for Transformers with a voice-of-doom announcer, but the words too boomy to understand. The parrot shrieked, *Hey dummy!*

Neil said, 'I didn't like her to wear so much make up… but… why don't we have you go ahead and put some on. Use… a lot… especially, um, on your eyes. I've got some stuff in there. See, then, after a while, I'll smear it like you've been crying.'

'Sounds like fun.'

'I… uh… don't know your name yet.'

'Oh. Yeah. It's LeeAnn. Just LeeAnn. You know, like Cher.'

While she was back in the kitchenette, she asked, 'So your kid is 14? When I was 14 I looked like a little boy.'

'Well, uh,' he chuckled, 'um… now you look like…'

'A little girl!' she giggled. Some footsteps stumped overhead and a stereo started playing Donna Summer.

In the make-up kit she found black eyeliner so she used it over and under each eye, then black mascara and purple eye shadow – the choices were purple, powder blue or light green. Instead of red or pink, she also used the purple lipstick, the colour of a bruise, and matching nail polish on her fingers and toes. 'I'm not real good at putting this stuff on, I don't have a lotta practice.'

'That's OK. Perfect, in fact.'

'I mean, my hand's kinda shaky with this eyeliner brush.'

'Are you... uh... frightened?'

'Huh?' She paused behind the curtain. She could hear him breathing again, but it still wasn't like panting, just breathing through his mouth. 'Oh,' her voice went higher. 'No... what's there to be scared of? I'm always, like, excited before a session.' Loralee came back into the studio. She wasn't wearing the robe. 'Okay?'

'Uh... oh, yeah, that's... perfect.' He turned the baseball game off.

The studio was fairly warm. 'You might want to put a sweater on,' she said. She opened the window behind one of the backdrops, then stood, concealed from his view, and let cool air rush in at her. Her nipples became erect. She'd used rouge on them too.

Hi there, be quiet! the parrot shouted.

Neil kept having to go into the kitchen to warm his hands over a burner on the stove. He rolled his own film on a larger spool, so he never had to stop to reload the camera. They used the stool in some of the shots, in others she sat on the floor with a checkerboard, playing an imaginary game, biting the tip of one finger on one hand while her other hand pushed a checker with a single purple-fingernailed finger.

Then he used an eyedropper to create the tear-streaked make-up. He carefully held just her shoulder while she tipped her head back and he hovered over her to put the drops of water on her eyes. She could smell the sheen of sweat on her skin, a damp pungency but not dirty, and she goose-bumped when a breeze wafted in the window, bringing the fragrance of lighter fluid. Someone had lit a barbecue on their fire escape. An engine revved over and over outside, then died with a little cough. Donna Summer wailed her ass off upstairs. The parrot trying to drown her out, *Hey dummy, Hi there, Be quiet.* Loralee was trying not to laugh or smile. Before he'd started shooting, Neil had said, rather ceremoniously, without stuttering, 'What shows on a girl's face when she's alone? Think about that. You're alone. No one around to keep telling you that you're grown up enough now or that you're not nearly so.'

He also didn't stammer when he gave instructions. He had a couple of pillows and a white quilt for the last few shots. She lay on her stomach on the quilt, folded hands across the pillows, facing him, knees bent and feet in the air over her butt. Then she put the quilt over her head like an Indian blanket and sat cross-legged. She curled on the rumpled quilt and hugged a pillow. Then finally lay on her back with knees bent and legs spread, the quilt over the middle of her body and pillows propping her head up so the camera could see her face above the shadows between her knees.

'Whoops,' Neil said, 'I, uh… forgot your break.'

'That's okay,' Loralee smiled and stretched, arching her back off the floor. Neil went into the darkroom for a moment; she heard the toilet flush before he came back.

'Is that it?' she asked.

'I think so.' He shut the window. 'You must be cold.'

'I'm never cold during a session.' She was still lying on one of the pillows, on her side, the other pillow between her thighs, the quilt trailing across her, but not covering her tits. The cartoon next door only had music and explosions. A kid yelled that he wanted juice while the parrot squawked noises that weren't words. A real person said, 'Be quiet!'

'I won't turn off the lights yet,' Neil said. 'It'll warm up the room faster.' He took the camera off the tripod and put it in a case, then came back with her robe and held it out for her to put on. He looked her right in the eyes and didn't drop his gaze when she looked back. Without smiling, she stood, leaving the quilt on the floor. She turned so her back was to him, so he could put the robe on her shoulders. While he did, she turned slightly and brushed his hand with one nipple.

'Uh… sorry,' he said. He was motionless.

Loralee smiled, but she wasn't facing him so of course he didn't see it. Zings of hot pulsations began inside her, as though she could hear them, like a heart monitor telling her she was alive. She thought about a glass contraption Dale's parents had given her for her birthday, shaped like an hourglass but with four compartments instead of two, and filled with a blue liquid instead of sand. When you held it in your hand at the bottom, the blue liquid started bubbling and spurting upward into the other chambers. That's what *she* felt like, that glass contraption filled with weird blue liquid. She could hear him breathing through his mouth, and when the breathing paused she knew he'd closed his lips over his teeth to swallow, then he resumed breathing. A cartoon war came through the wall, with chattering mouse-voices manning the explosives. The ceiling throbbed with disco music. Loralee laughed and turned to face him, the robe still open in front. 'You've got yourself a 24-hour-a-day nightclub here, you can boogie any time you want!' She began a little dance, not moving nearly as much as she would if actually at a club. The parrot cried *Hey dummy!*

'C'mon, it's, like, an insane asylum discotheque, let's try out some crazy moves!'

'I don't dance,' he said, watching her. It was hard to tell if he was smiling, the way he had to breathe with his mouth open.

She took his wrists. 'Here, c'mon, I'll help you. Oh wait, you've got shoes and I'm barefoot, I don't want my toes squashed. How about I ride on your feet.' Standing on her toes on the tips of his leather oxfords, she swayed side to side slightly, letting her weight shift foot to foot, until he also began rocking one foot to the other, side to side. 'That's good.' She was still holding his wrists, and his hands hung half open, palms up, as though balancing two grapefruit while he swayed back and forth. The robe fell backwards off her shoulders when she shimmied. Naturally her tits didn't bob, they were only about the size of half a tennis ball each. But pointier than that.

A phone rang and the music above them stopped. A vacuum cleaner droned on one side. Little girl voices sang about *My Little Pony*. With four small, quick steps, Loralee switched her feet so she was still standing on his shoes, but they were now facing the same direction. As she slowly arched her back, she raised her arms, still holding his wrists, and her tits homed right into his cupped hands. She continued to arch, relax and arch her lower back, just enough to move her nipples against the palms of his hands. Then his hands moved by themselves, like gathering cotton, all five fingers coming together to pull her nipples before closing over the whole tit again. Guts on fire, Loralee gradually let her knees buckle until she was kneeling on the quilt, and, like a dance, Neil stayed behind her, lowering himself with her, his hands cupping her tits the whole way.

He kissed her neck. She could actually feel teeth on her skin. Her guts maintained the disco beat, added the flashing neon lights embedded in disco floors. Steaks were charbroiling on the barbecue outside. Someone had the same baseball game on a radio somewhere outside, loud, so they could hear it over the revving engine. Kids shrieked and laughed out on the sidewalk. She relaxed back against his chest, but he suddenly stood and backed away. 'No… I'm not sure I… I didn't intend…'

Still on the floor on her knees, she turned and caught one of his hands before he was out of reach. She held just his index finger. Except for being on her knees, she was upright. She could feel the dried, sticky mascara that had run from her eyes, and the cakey purple lipstick still on her mouth. She looked him in the eye steadily while his gaze met hers, fell, met hers again, dropped, came back, fell again. She stroked his index finger with her thumb. A kid made a siren noise with his voice, fading around the side of the building, then getting louder again as he circled around to the front. The TV next door had changed to a car race with announcers shouting over the hysterical howling motors. Loralee's voice was a petite, ugly sing-song, 'What's the matter?'

'I... uh... I'm not sure... I...' Maybe he laughed, or gasped. She was still stroking his finger with her thumb.

'Show me how,' she said, seeing him through the blobs of mascara around her eyes. 'C'mon, we did the youth part, now the maturity.'

'My theme is... uh, you know... *premature* maturity.'

'But,' she unzipped his slacks, 'does being premature keep the maturity from being hot and... impatient?' She tugged on his finger and brought him back down to his knees on the quilt while he, with his free hand, took his half soft cock out of his pants. An adult voice, probably female, barked out a string of demands. A kid threw a fit, stomping feet, voice squealing, rising to shrieks. Then a slap, then crying. Loralee released Neil's finger and settled on to her back, reaching over her head to pull one of the pillows under her neck. He followed, but propped himself on all fours over her, not touching her any-where, not even his dick which looked like it might retreat on its own back into his pants and boxers.

She said, 'Shouldn't my raging hormones be affecting you more than this?'

It did start to grow when she held it and touched her tits with it, back and forth, then rubbed it on her stomach, played in her bellybutton for a moment. He stayed propped up on his arms hovering over her. She had to writhe around to get the various parts of herself close enough to stroke his cock against. She'd never had to do anything like this before. Why now? Maybe he *wasn't* the big one, potential cash cow, but it seemed too late to decide that *now*. By then she was sliding it back and forth in her slit, and finally with a soft sound in his chest, he pushed it all the way in, and she could lie still and rest while he thrusted. She was suddenly exhausted. He touched the adrenaline pooled in her stomach with every push, but the hotspot was smaller and smaller, like he was removing it, bailing it out every time he went in. After a while the feeling she was most aware of was razor burn in her crotch. He opened his mouth as though to scream when he finished, but no sound came out. His tongue looked very small and pulled back into his mouth. His eyes were shut so tight she couldn't even see his eyelids, just a bunch of wrinkles, like an empty eye socket.

Neil fumbled in the pocket of his pants, handed her a handkerchief. She took it, looked at it, dropped her hand to her side, still holding it. Neil still hadn't pulled away. He just waited until his dick dwindled on its own and wasn't even big enough to be in her any more. Then he stood up.

Loralee wiped her crotch with his handkerchief, went into the bathroom to throw it away, but it was too dark. She couldn't find the trash can, hit her shins on the toilet, so she dropped the handkerchief into the bowl. She turned and strips of film hanging from a line tickled her face like spiders, like the bathroom was a kiddie Halloween haunted house. She could be the ghoul.

Neil was sitting slumped on the stool. 'I think I'm having a heart attack.'

'The world is full of weak hearts, isn't it?' she said. Then added, 'It isn't aerobic exercise.' She sounded downright nasty. She couldn't feel her pulse, couldn't find it in her wrist, quickly pressed both hands to her throat until she found the tired throb. She sighed and went to the kitchen to get dressed. Again, it didn't take long to put on underwear, sweatpants and tank top.

He was silent. Then his voice was right behind her. She whirled around, but he was still on the other side of the curtain. 'You okay? Need anything?'

'A million bucks,' she said, didn't think it was loud enough for him to hear. She watched the curtain move a little as though he was leaning against it. She looked at the gaudy make-up she'd used, put the lipstick and nailpolish into her purse.

'I don't have that much,' he said with a wimpy chuckle. 'But, I... I mean...'

'How much d'you have on you?'

'Uh... a hundred... fifty. That okay?'

'Sure.' Every word clipped. 'That's for the session.'

'Oh.' Air went out of him like a punctured life raft.

The kid outside was still doing the siren, still running around the building. Someone shouted a greeting, a car idled in the street. A dog barked. The siren passed the front windows. 'You don't want anyone to, you know, *know* about this, do you?'

'What do you mean? I... you *asked* me... you asked me to...'

'Who's gonna know that?' She rubbed her eyes with a paper towel. Crumbs of mascara rained on to the counter top.

'Pardon?'

'And besides,' staring at the smeared black on the paper towel, 'how'm *I* supposed to know what's best for me. *You're* supposed to know better. You know, I may have the bodily functions of a woman, but… aren't girls my age too young… to decide?'

'Oh god,' he moaned. 'I have two-fifty. I… I have my weekly… um, child support payment.'

'Perfect.' With another paper towel she wiped her lips. But in the hand mirror, it still looked like she'd just had a grape popsicle.

When she came out of the kitchen, the money was already stacked neatly on a coffee table which had been shoved right next to the front door to make room for the session. Neil's back was to her. As he reached to turn off the last umbrella light, he tipped his head and wiped an eye on his shoulder. She crept out before he turned around.

The sky had become overcast. She could smell a cake baking as she went down the stairs. The kid doing the siren was gone, or else he was one of the two boys throwing pebbles at toy dump trucks in the gutter. The parrot was out on a fire escape. *Be quiet!* it screamed. *Hi there!*

SHRINKING
Elizabeth Young

Really, it makes you go mental, I mean crazy straitjacket lobotomy mental. During much of the past year here in New York I was convinced that my whole face was a nineteenth-century sanatorium for rich hypochondriacs. I, as ruling quack, would entice them to their rooms, situated around my eyes or nose or whatever. Then I'd convince them that they were well poorly, with something vague like a twisted colon. They were going to need months of expensive treatment, stretching on the rack, enemas by the gallon, sadistic osteopathic pounding. It was all just an excuse for me to pick and hack at my formerly perfectly OK complexion. I'd spend hours – days, months – fantasising about all these people and their lives while I gouged away with tweezers or needles, talking aloud, drooling occasionally while blood pooled here and there on my ruined face. That is exactly the sort of thing crack can do to you. A lot of people get that impulse to attack their skin. It's quite well known – goes right back to the old days when coke and speed users used to get to believing that there were insects crawling around under their skin and they had to get them out. But only crack can transport you so far away you don't know what the fuck is going on any more. Well. That is not quite right. The fact that I made it so I was aware that my imaginary clinic patients were being conned and that there was nothing whatsoever wrong with them shows that I did have a grasp of the real situation. You don't become a different personality on drugs like they would have you believe, you can't hide from yourself completely while taking them. Really you know everything. You just don't want to.

It is *so* bizarre, that stuff. I mean, 'crack', what a name, just like some ad-agency invented it and chances are they did. 'Crack! The finalist in the Final Solution!'; or 'Genocide is tough – we're with you on that. But new 'CRACK' keeps hands and consciences clean. The humane way to do business today!!'.

I know you have already dismissed me as some druggy no-hoper with charred synapses who cannot possibly be taken seriously – but just give me a minute. I've been thinking about it, see and it just totally does not compute. Like, straight off, what the fuck is crack anyway? No one is quite sure. It is supposed to be cocaine hydroxide, the smokeable base left after the cocaine hydrochloride – the powdered, smoking, shoot-up sort has been treated with an alkali (bicarbonate, ammonia) to form an insoluble precipitate. But I made my own free-base for years and smoked it in a pipe and it wasn't really the same as crack. Free-base got you very high, it lasted longer, it often had a floaty, dreamy effect and you moved very slowly as if underwater even as your heart rate shot up. Sure it could have a nasty, obsessive, paranoid edge and the come-down was bad and then you wanted more. But mainly it was heaven and didn't fuck up your physical health and you could still function if you didn't do it 24-7. People say the powder was just better quality back then.

Crack by contrast is a fucking horrible drug. But it's so addictive that even if you can't stand it you find yourself walking, like some sort of brain-implant zombie, back down to the corner, or calling your guy on his mobile. It's cheap right, ten dollars a hit here, ten quid in London, but you wanna buy a few rocks at once, so it mounts up. The first hit of the day sends you as high as Mr Spock but only for a few seconds. But unless you wait an hour or two it's a waste sucking more, it doesn't really work, don't ask me why and anyway you never believe that so you keep doing it all day. The come-down is twisty and weird and you do the usual crawling around in case you've missed some, picking up bits of cat litter from the carpet and smoking them. You usually get a terrible headache. And a truly nasty earache that persists for days even if you don't use any. And it fucks up your eyesight. Whether you smoke it with ash or not it screws up your lungs and soon you can't walk far. You don't wanna eat, you don't wanna fuck, you don't wanna look after yourself or brush your hair or clean up or see anyone or have a life; you can't work. You're in some parallel universe with your obsessive compulsions and fantasies, focused only on the next rock. It strips you away to nothing and you don't care. Big-time users sometimes have strokes. Or bits of you get paralysed. And you get all raggy and scabby and you can't go out if you still have a room and your hair is snarled up and exploding and sticky, full of old tortoiseshell combs and slides you've forgotten about, real deep down in the mess. And you hate the rock because it makes you insane but you just can't stop doing it. Sucking on the devil's dick. Ha! Right.

The rock is poison. And who do they give it to? The black guys. They control the business and they use it and suffer from it. So, perhaps it is not too crazy to think that suppose those assholes who believe America is being raped, pinned down, legs apart, while an endless queue of illiterate, fatherless, homicidal, dope-crazed gang-bangers take turns to violate her – just suppose these patriotic Christians, these fundamentalists, or bankers, or CIA or Rockefellers or Illuminati or Mafia or whatever fucking conspiracy-cluster-fuck actually runs things – suppose they all got together and said 'Eugenics is a dirty word now, too many goddamn liberals around, we can't just gas all those diseased no-hopers and their mongrel babies, six-month-old thugs in high-tops can take down an old lady no problem, so let's get them to off themselves. Hey we're not heartless – give 'em a buzz at the same time – it's easy, so easy like giving candy to a baby and it'll be bringing us those tax-free dollars too – call Merck now, call Lilly and order a super-addictive, grind-you-to-death drug.

I could scream, right now. Imagine having that sort of dribble in your head all the time. Imagine trying to keep a life together and think straight while there is an implant in your head forcing you to fuck tubercular street dealers, their pricks leaking purulent yellow goo for a hit on a pipe that makes you feel totally nervous and unhinged anyway. Well that is what it's like for me. I never know when – bang, crash – Cassie will be back in charge, and I'll wink out like a kid's night-light – and she'll be trolling the clubs in those skanky clothes. I can be washing my hair and thinking about my job applications and zap! I'll come back half-way to Red Hook in some dirt-bomb dive with shampoo dripping down my neck and a stinky T-shirt that has 'If I Want To Listen To An Asshole I'll Fart' on it, plus a ripped, chiffon mini-skirt, no knickers, no bra – and then *I'm* supposed to hustle us out and get home – from places which haven't seen a checker cab in twenty years. And then how am I supposed to pay for it? Get Cassie back to give the driver a blow-job I suppose…

Okay. I mustn't get carried away like that… Stay cool, take your time, you are going to get better now, Rhonda always says. I'm Alice. Rhonda is my therapist. She is so great. She has completely changed my life – well she has *given* me my life. Before there was only Cassie. My illness is Multiple Personality Disorder. It is in *DSM* 4 now. I am an alter personality. In fact, so far I am Cassie's *only* alter personality but I keep hoping more will emerge – there are people in group who have up to a hundred alters and sometimes I feel a bit stupid with only one alternative personality but all these things take time, Rhonda says. I mean I wouldn't want *too* many… Anyway, I didn't even know I existed until I saw Rhonda, well not in this sense of having a name and a separate personality. Alter personalities are created in childhood when there is huge trauma and the mind splits into different parts, or personalities, to protect itself. Sometimes such personalities can communicate with each other in various ways – sometimes they don't even know they exist and the core personality just loses time when an alter has taken over. Cassie would lose time all the time, because that was when I was looking after things for her –

Shut up shut up shut up you demented piece of New Age psychogabble gabble brain slime – this has – like, gone just too far – into total bullshit psychoDisney trainwreck personality time. This 'Alice' doesn't bloody exist. I should know. She is an aspect of my personality I have always known about. We all have different sides to us – facets? Right. This person is just the part of me that is more together and sensible and knows when I am fucking up – like nearly all the time – and tries to talk me into being responsible and get a job and stuff. Everyone has these balancing bits – some of you is rational and some irrational – and if you didn't have a way of keeping a balance you'd be fucking totally mental, *long go-o-o-ne*. And socially, if much of your personality is – well, kind of extreme, like mine, you'd be well fucking dead. So there. That's it, that's all she wrote. Until that money-vampire, that cultist clinician Rhonda Bellamy gets hold of me and starts talking to one bit of me like it is a separate person. She has totally fucked with my head and tried to brainwash me. These Yanks are so fucking enthusiastic and gullible. Whatever their way of life they want to conform to it absolutely and have everyone think exactly the same way they do. Whether it's a self-styled Satanist or a stock-broker they've got their little map of appropriate behaviour and they are not going to deviate from it one tiny inch.

In therapy circles the multiple personality deal is the ne plus ultra of the moment. Every head-doc wants them as patients because it can take *for ever* to – ahem – introduce the alter personalities to each other and re-integrate them into one healthy, happy psyche. And meanwhile the – client – is really ill and the insurance pays out, they have to now it's in *DSM* 4. Great scam – eh? Get all the loonies on one big bandwagon and keep collecting their fares. Oh and guess what? These patients need lots and lots of hospital time and group therapy. Do they ever get better? Perhaps Eve has only one face now, although I doubt it. No one is wholly consistent. No, they don't get better. Think of it this way – suppose the Jackson Five never existed – they were just alter parts of Michael so they could deal with their father. Finally they get absorbed into the core personality – the famously well-balanced Michael Jackson. Ha-bloody-ha. As for this losing time schtick – sure I lose time. I even waste time. Can anyone remember everything they've done, 'specially on drugs? Hardly. Do people never do things on impulse and then wonder why and then forget all about it? Like once I was offered this job on a newspaper back in London, so I must have applied and all. I lasted about two weeks; the more they got to know me, the more discouraged they felt, I guess. So I walked out. And then, just before I left London I got a place at this really famous, big-time art school to do a sort of post-grad/post-dip thing in mixed media and cultural studies and I got all these awards for living and tuition and all so I must have done something right but then I thought 'Fuck it – if I don't go and live in NY now I never will, I won't get round to it and then I'll be too old or too dead.' So I did a last scam for money and fucked off.

And what a great idea that was. Cassie chucks aside this incredible award and her whole future – *my* whole future, not to mention Ajuna, the sweetest guy in the world – and she drags me over here to live out some druggy, death-trip daydream that is pointless and dated and adolescent and stupid. I love London. It's strange and orderly and beautiful. You can get on with your life there. It's sophisticated and anonymous. I know now that I didn't want to leave. But Cassie gets Ajuna's mother who is American to sort out an apartment just south of St Mark's Square – this couple who need cat-sitters for their poor, de-clawed miniature pedigrees (no one de-claws in England, it's too cruel) and the little mites are so overbred they can't breathe and sound like they have asthma. Then Cassie figures she'll pay some guy to marry her but of course she doesn't need to, they are queuing up, so she picks the richest, some preppie airhead from Darien, and afterwards she vanishes and he is going 'Like – what happened?' Cassie can be really lucky. It was always me who got screwed – oh no! That's not funny! That's sick! Mustn't cry… lose… another contact… lens…

Oh God. It's the poor-abused-rape-and-tortured-victim me again. Ignore her. Look, everyone has doubts about doing something radical with their life – particularly about seeing something through to the end, something which part of you knows is fucking horribly self-destructive. You don't have to have a whole separate little Barbie doll in your head to debate the wisdom of leaving your country and a guy who is your best friend even if he does want to be a whole lot more. I had to come here, right? And I looked after those squash-faced, little cream-puff kitties OK. And then I was able to stay with guys who wanted me – Destry and Tyrone and Kingdom and Jones the Tie. I don't really remember the marriage bit I was so out of it but at least I have citizenship. I had a job in a top book-store – on Broadway, the one with literally miles of second-hand. It was dead good. I was still using gear like in London and you can function but I learned in about five seconds the old truism, the smack in London is great and the coke shite but it's the other way round here. The smack here is completely organised by the mob and cut to nothing, 0.005%, I'd say – these people are not even addicted. Not at all. It's all in their minds. And they sell it in the weirdest way – in these balloons? Exactly like kid's party balloons but not blown up except these drug balloons are miniatures! If you blew them up they'd be about the size of a thumb. I kept wondering – is there a factory somewhere that makes these things? And so I got to using rock more often, more than in London. And then I got arrested for shop-lifting in this dinky design store off Fifth Avenue, I'd only taken some toothpicks with handles full of water and glitter stars, I wanted to use them for hair-pins in my top-knot along with my chopsticks. There were a couple of other things too. They had some excellent toys – teensy juke-box rings and earrings with all those zany-shiny colours and teeny buttons and turntable correct and even minute 45s; they were so incredibly cute. I've always loved miniatures, doll's house champagne bottles, even kitty-kats. And court was just like the movies with all these hysterical people shouting in Spanish and I had a real public defender with a wet moustache and when this little dust-up settled I was fined and had to enrol in a methadone programme (yawn) and seek therapy. (After all they couldn't unmarry me from Endicott Cabot Peabody Lowell VII or whatever he was called.) Things were getting kind of smashed up and I lacked the green poultice (dollars, turd-brain!) but the methadone dump (they have *orange* methadone!) supplies free fucked-up persons for would-be quacks to practice on so that is how I came into the smooth hands of Ms Bellamy, the wicked witch of the West Side. She's not even a bloody doctor, probably got a mail-order counselling diploma from Juarez. Think standard Noo Yawk whine softened by Southern Lady Sympathy Syrup background. 'And just whah… do you hafta be… so host-ial, Cassandra?' Because lady, you hate me and you are trying to get rid of me, that's why.

Come *on*. Rhonda does *not* hate you Cassie, and you know it. She just wants to stop you destroying yourself. She wants you to see why you're doing it.

I know why I'm doing it. I've always known. Fuck off. Aneeee-ways, as they say here, it wasn't too bad at first. Like we were just chatting and I was wishing she didn't have so many Georgia O'Keefe and Frida Kahlo prints, they both painted such sick pictures but in a sneaky way like honesty was all they cared about, and I was wondering how she could afford so much jade and I'm trying to tell her about the god-awful tedium of growing up in a clunky Forties vicarage in Sussex and she's ready to get misty-eyed – the old fraud – about the English countryside. And I have to put her straight about how there is no countryside now, there's silos and silage and fertiliser plants and industrial parks and farm-machinery storage and abattoirs and factory-farms and no animals unless they are well dead. And in the vicarage it was like time had stopped one late summer afternoon. How still it was. How empty. Even the dog looked stuffed, lying in a shaft of sunlight in the hall. And Dad frozen in his study, in his jerky cableknit fisherman's jersey ordered from the *Observer* newspaper, writing a sermon with a fountain pen on what looked like cheap loo-paper (onionskin, it was called) on a leather-trimmed blotter, pretending he was Matthew Arnold or some prat like that. And Ma frozen in the kitchen, the Aga cold and the room dark, looking out at next-door farmer's mud and barbed wire as if she expected Squirrel Nutkin to appear and wondering why she was so depressed and the Librium didn't work any more.

'So you were lonely. Their only chiy-uld?' Ma Bellamy coos.

I was adopted. Me and my brother Eddie. But he died. I don't want to get into that right now, OK? I said *no*!

Yackety-yackety. Why don't I just shut up? But I have to go back there and she's all 'Y'know, you're such a verra clevah girl; why do you feel you have to act so dumb?' Cunning bitch, flattering cunt. She made me get really stupid and I didn't even know. Anyway, she's saying, to me, you got away, you got out, you went to London. (Yeh and became a big, fucking druggy mess.) So, she wants to know, how did I end up here?

'In this crap room, you mean?' She smiles. But she knows she's not going to get much more out of me and she wants to hypnotise me. I don't care. She does some sort of standard eyelids-heavy, count-down shit and I hear her murmur something like 'high eye-roll' and I go to sleep for a minute, then wake up. I feel just the same.

'Let's try again, Cassie. How come you're here in New York?'

I don't really want to tell her this. It's too personal. But unfortunately I try.

When I was a kid, my favourite character in kids' books was a girl called Pippi Longstocking. And it was just because she wore black tights or leggings all the time. I think they were Swedish books. I'd never seen anyone wear black tights. She looked cool. And it was like I recognised really early that I could never have a normal life. I was always going to have to be some sort of dumb-ass bohemian, 'cept I didn't think it was dumb then. It was foredoomed, fore-told. And as I read more and more I felt that the coolest place all during this century was New York. Lots of British kids felt like that. It's quite normal. So I got into having more and more fantasies about New York; I felt like I was here all along. I was hanging out in Greenwich Village round the time of the Great War. I was smoking opium down Mott Street – lying on a wood-en bunk in the warm pit on an icy night, easing down my stockings and grimy garters to rub at the red indentations on my upper thighs, thankfully breath-ing in the blessed fumes of Fook Yuen (Fountain of Happiness) yen pock – a dollar a draw or a quarter a pin-head – watch the boy perform the sacrament, heating the dope over the yen dong, the lamp, while the shadows loom and jump on the basement walls... I knew all the words to 'Willie the Weeper' and 'Cocaine Bill and Morphine Sue'. I can still sing those songs – 'Cocaine Bill and Morphine Sue – were walkin' down the avenoo... Honey take a (sniff), honey take a (sniff)...' oh and 'the shit was so thick it made Dracula sick, three snorts of that air made vet junkies kick... but they sucked and farted, fucked and parted, true freaks to the bitter end...' And doing crimes here was always – these awesome characters – way back in the mid-nineteenth cen-tury; gangs like the Plug Uglies and the Shirt Tails down around Five Points and I'd pretend I was in the Dead Rabbits gang with Hell-Cat Maggie who wore false fingernails made of brass for scratching flesh to pieces and her teeth were filed into little sharp points for tearing people's faces off. Down round Corlear's Hook and Hell's Kitchen there were all these dives so dan-gerous that God-fearing citizens would shit to think of them – Cat Alley, the Lava Pit, the Tub of Blood – spawning grifters and shysters and banco artists, second-storey men, gun-molls and gangsters and lushes and hypos, hopheads, yeggs, sirens, dames – a seducer's vocabulary never heard in the Home Counties. And then the century turns and I'd be in Greenwich Village and would run into characters like Elsa von Freytag-Loringhaven, the Baronin – world-class eccentric, she adored William Carlos Williams and flung open her ratty fur coat to flaunt herself naked at him. She shaved her head and polished it and painted it purple and wore postage stamps on her cheeks; her face was powdered bright yellow, her lipstick black – she wore silver tea immersion balls and stuffed birds for jewellery. She had spoons hanging from her hats. One hat was a coal scuttle, another a birthday cake with all the candles on.

And I would have an affair with Djuna Barnes who was doing her journalism then and we would lie in her room in the summer heat, her white muslin curtain very clean and not moving, and look at her wooden painted carnival horse although she got that later in Paris and her eyelids were heavy and green and shiny and her language was baroque; she called her left tit 'Redlero' and her right tit 'Kedler' – well that is what her grandmother named them and then she went to Berlin and took coke. And there were wars churning up the Atlantic but all the most incredible people still came to New York, Duchamp and Max Ernst and – oh, now I'm clicking across Grand Central Station in a Chanel suit and heels like diamond-tipped daggers with a crocodile case full of mob money, after Prohibition provided all those career opportunities in crime, and then later I had black cotton or Mexican skirts splashed with puce flowers with huge elasticated belts and cute sandals and plum toenail varnish and I was a free spirit like Diane di Prima or Joan Vollmer and knew Burroughs and Huncke and Lucien Carr and Leroi Jones back when... and it all just went on and on and on. Unbelievable! The Factory and the Sixties silver tarnish and varnish, and Edie Sedgwick, seventh heaven – 'oh it isn't fair/how her ermine hair/turned men around...' – and now some things were in my own lifetime too, Warhol the man-machine with the white straw-wig and empty Ray-Bans and the fifteen-minute suicidal boygirls with that mother-of-pearl translucent junkie skin and waterfall hair... and the siren-call gets louder and louder and the drums beat harder and the feedback smashes my eardrums at the Dom and Studio 54 and Max's and CBGB's and it goes on and on, faster and faster like a spaceship that's lost control and outzipped the speed of light and will flash on for ever – the punk boys, beautiful as Narcissus with their adze cheekbones and pinned pupils and ribs you can count and endless legs in black trousers so tight you can't get them over their heels – Richard Hell and Tom Verlaine, oh, you know, Mapplethorpe, horses, horses, horses... and on, money and clubs and awesome writers; dark, shady Jewish girls with hair like spilt ink who've had affairs with everybody, and tough, dykey writers with orange crew-cuts, abstract tattoos, branding, scarification and piercings that catch on your buttons when you try and kiss her, and black poets with long, waving fingers and tiny wooden beads in braids and names like jewels, and pushy performance artists trying to outdo each other and critics steeped in venom – a zillion ways to be cool, a zillion ways to die – everything ever imagined has been done here – how could I not come here? Britain has been gobbling up the scraps for years –

I paused for breath – suckin' in the rock can do that, you just drone on. Fuck it. I shut up.

Rhonda stretched, her no-colour eyes gleaming behind huge Lois Lane specs. She looked amused. Patronising. Well, fuck her too.

'It seems kinda ironic to me,' she spoke slowly 'that someone should come here in pursuit of all the things that Americans have been seeking in the old world for so long. Decadence, art. Freedom. Self-actualisation. Corruption, decay, sophistication.'

'Look, you get all those things in any capital city now – *apocalipsis yah!* I didn't have to come here for that stuff. Each city has its own style, that's all. I was just always – er, magnetised by this one. Perhaps – duh – I was here in a previous incarnation. Sure. *And* New York got more and more important down this century till it was like, top city. Everyone wants to come here. People come here for their dreams. They still believe in them here, they still think they can come true. They know everywhere else in the world is locked down tight, all sewn up – one way or another. But here is always open wide – like a screaming mouth.'

Now she'd got me talking again Rhonda Shit-stirrer was no-way going to back off.

'Screaming mouth... incarnation... hmmm... Where did you learn all this about a far-away city?'

'Books. I read all the time when I was a kid. We weren't far from London. I got weird books there.'

'Why did you feel the need to absent yourself from your childhood?'

'Dunno. Bored.'

And so endeth the first lesson where Rhonda drew blood. But I had to go back if I didn't want to violate the court order. At that point she didn't bother me too much. I was kind of interested. Tiny, delicate bones in her wrists. Emerald rings. Very tall. Her skin beige-ish and gleamy. Her face slightly pouched, like a chipmunk. Her hair was silver-blonde, obviously long because she always had it battened down tight with grips and combs and chunks of tortoiseshell. Dull, expensive, designer clothes. Beige, sand, taupe, they flowed and swayed. Rich bitch taste. Married rich, I guessed. Some internist at Mount Sinai – no, an Ob-Gyn. No wonder she preferred to see me at her house and not in that scummy clinic. Perhaps she fancied me! ... Perhaps? ... she did? ... I have these skinny, pipe-cleaner legs and 'cause I couldn't smoke I would wind and unwind them round the chair. And I'd see her rain-coloured eyes following the pattern on my old Pucci print leggings until they would lock on the spot where the twisting colours slipped into the shadow of a skirt no longer than a wide silk ribbon.

So the next time Rhonda seems to feel there has been some kind of a big breakthrough and after her dopey hypnotising routine again, she is all over me like grubs on a corpse. Why couldn't I recall my childhood in any detail? Why was I always reading back then? Did I ever lose time? What was the pain I took drugs to suppress? Did I know how ill I was? A homeless, jobless crackhead and I maintained I didn't need therapy? Had I heard of denial? (Yawn.) Blah-de-blah… Had I ever read a book called *The Courage to Heal*?

That was too much.

'Certainly *not*.'

Why was so I so vehement? Was there something about the book that threatened me?

'I'm threatened by bad writing.'

Rhonda went all pink around the nose. I must have hurt her baby. I felt almost sorry for her. I said in a gentler voice:

'OK, OK. Perhaps it's not that shitty. I'll try and take a look, huh?' Rhonda was quivering like a dog that has scented spilt blood.

'Who am I talking to?'

'Me.'

'What part of you?'

'I was just trying to be a bit polite. A bit nicer.'

'Let's give this "nicer" you a name, shall we?'

'Oh, puh-lease.'

'Call it anything – a number, an adjective. It will help. I promise.'

'Oh Jesus.'

But she went on and on, bullying, chivvying, entreating, saying it was standard therapeutic technique and I should at least give it a try, she believed I needed help whatever I said and I was getting really tired. Eventually I said, 'Go on then. Call it "Alice".'

And that was that. I just sort of gave up. 'Alice' talked. 'Alice' wondered if she had been sexually abused as a child (who hasn't wondered?). *No*, she couldn't remember but she thought it might come back. She had nightmares in which her mouth got stuffed with more and more food, then garbage and then shit and she couldn't swallow any of it. Rhonda was very happy. 'Alice' agrees to attend Rhonda's Recovered Memory Group. 'Alice' is happy to keep a journal, participate in guided imagery, dream work, body work, art therapy, hypnosis, rage work. 'Alice' is a histrionic prima donna.

When I get out of there I am raging. I hurl my leather jacket round my shoulders and walk about twenty blocks downtown with the snow-flakes hitting my face and soaking through my trainers and I don't even notice. I am so angry.

I let that fucking Rhonda get away with it! Christ – Americans. You're nothing in this country unless your grandfather buggered you for Satan before you could crawl. And then you spent your entire childhood in some half-baked intergenerational Satanic cult being routinely walled up in coffins with starving rats and snakes. Or you're sacrificing babies with a razor-sharp athame or servicing queues of high-ranking Masons in B-movie robes all longing to pee in your mouth or violate you with sink plungers. No wonder nobody gets any education. And then after puberty you're either breeding for Satan or undergoing inept abortions for Him and meanwhile you do your SATs and go to the Senior Prom and you forget completely that your Mom is a High Priestess with a tendency to stalk about in leather corsets brandishing raw cow's hearts studded with nails and bake amanita muscaria mushrooms into the chocolate chip cookies. Yeah! Very likely!

Look, Cassie – don't exaggerate. No one's suggesting any of that.

They will. I mean, you will…

No, I don't think so. Cassie, you had a bizarre childhood and you can't remember it. Well, you weren't there. You kept reading. Suppose Rhonda has a point? After all, even you agree you have wondered about sexual abuse. What is wrong with giving your most reasonable, amenable aspect a name? It might clarify things.

Fucking Rhonda. She's one of those therapy cultists who see sexual abuse everywhere. You can bet all her patients are multiple personalities. She makes them be.

Give her a chance. She's just doing her job. She might be right, Cassie. Look how incredibly fucked up your adult life has been. Anyway – just *suppose*, while you were doing all that reading, another aspect of you was actually there, living everything?

Cassie and I argued like that, back and forth, in the snow, but in the end that is how it turned out. I started having flashbacks with Rhonda and in group very soon. The nightmares were of forced fellatio when I was a little kid. I'm sure I will recover more images. With the support of the others I learned that Dad had abused me for years. Cassie escaped into books, lucky her, and I suffered for her all those years but I was crushed and Cassie grew stronger. Eventually I vanished, except I was still always trying to help Cassie, who naturally was unconsciously affected by our experiences. Now *I'm* getting courage and Rhonda says we'll integrate but we'll have to go into hospital. Then I'll go back home to London and tell Ajuna how I feel about him. And go to college. And get a job. And get married. And all that. Why despise it? That is so elitist…

Oh bollocks! What a fuckin' insufferable prig. Dad was too lazy to lift a double gin, let alone a gym-slip. I'm *never* going back to London. I belong here. Ajuna's a good friend, sure, but I'd rather marry the Pope. *Fuck*, fuck. Rhonda has driven me purely insane.

The memories just kept flooding back. I think Mum might have done something too, but I can't get that clear. Still – what with Dad being a vicar I'm getting some very disturbing feelings about the church and the hymnals and the robes…

I knew it! I knew it! It'll be full-scale Satanism next with Farmer-George-Next-Door and Darren-From-the-Pub and Doctor-Horrocks-from-the-Big-House all staggering butt-naked round the churchyard in the driving sleet of an English November night, stopping off to throw a fuck into the vicar's infant daughter and plunge a pig-sticker through some gypsy's kid on the font, before going off for a fish supper at the chippie.

I've got to stop her.

Someday Cassie will get my memories too. Then she won't want to be like she is – all self-destructive. She'll want an ordinary, peaceful life too. I understand so much now. If you think you were abused you were whether you were or not. Also I have learnt something really important. I am the core personality, the original. Cassie is the alter, created to protect me and let me survive. She was never meant to take over like this. She is a fuck-up. With all the support I'm getting, things are moving fast. I've got a pretty room now, in the apartment of one of the Adult Survivors from group, Althea. It is a safe building, midtown with a porter – and a striped awning! Althea and I talk a lot and run in the park. I've got a part-time job doing PR and organisational work for another Adult Survivors group, a very influential one. They are very vocal against the False Memory Syndrome Foundation. I help put out the newsletter too. Cassie still runs off a lot and does drugs but everybody is very understanding when I don't turn up or something. They know it's only a matter of time. As soon as there is a place on Rhonda's supervisor's ward I'll check into hospital for detox and heavy-duty MPD therapy. It is lucky I was able to organise us for long enough to take out medical insurance when we got married here. I don't seem to hear Cassie so much now. She used to go on and on, druggie babble. And her personality is – was – kind of extreme and overpowering. I think she is getting discouraged. There are so many of us Adult Survivors and we are always there for each other and we are getting so strong. Soon I'll be myself again.

… It's true I've been feeling kind of lost lately but it is nothing to do with 'Alice' and all that witch-hunt nonsense. If part of me is weak enough to fall for that twisty psycho-think, well – let 'her' get on with it for now. I'm tuning out. In fact I've got to get out. I can't take it, my head full of this shit. Adult Survivors of Incest with so-called recovered memories are just ordinary boring, flaky people who want a simple answer to all the crap that fucks them up – an answer that lets them blame everything on anyone but themselves. It gives them an identity that guarantees knee-jerk kindness and sympathy wherever they go. Wankers. I don't mean to disrespect anyone who has really suffered abuse in childhood – but they usually seem to remember. How could these recovered memory jerks 'forget' all that pervy, intergenerational witch cult hoo-ha? Oh yes – they were 'dissociated'. Well why don't people 'dissociate' from everything hellish – losing parents, fatal accidents, concentration camps, torture, imprisonment? Why do people remember any agonies if they can get out of it and 'dissociate'? It's not even grammatical.

Once Rhonda got the sexual bit between her teeth and her routine agenda going, she spent all her time on 'Alice' and wrote me off. So I have never mentioned what is really bothering me. New York is like an incredible drug. At first it gives you everything but gradually, simultaneously it takes everything away. When I first arrived here and got a cab from the airport to the Port Authority Bus Terminal, I just couldn't believe anywhere could be so much more so than I'd imagined it. It was like seeing all the dreams of the world coming true at once – the rose and silver evening light streaking down the mirrored monoliths; the sudden flashes of clouds and rain and storm and sky between the buildings and the electricity running faster and wilder as the night darkened; lights that ran and trickled and danced and spoke to each other far above the little wet tunnels of streets. The whole place was like every film ever made here happening all at once. You just couldn't watch everything.

Yet, gradually, living here I got the strange feeling that everything that I'd loved, everything that had originally drawn me here was over. Finished. Everyone – ordinary people, anyone – had got cool-looking. You could buy cool. Everyone who'd tried had gone as far as they could. Performance artists had committed suicide on video, GG Allin had stumbled on stage with his wrecked rock band and shit and thrown his turds in the audience and then OD'd, Joe Coleman had bitten the heads off live rats, Orlan had had plastic surgeons graft horns on her head. People had killed for fun and profit and enlightenment. They had tried sorcery and santeria, bestiality, buggery, celibacy. Now there is no farther out to go. No more conventions to be voided or boundaries to be transgressed. No more rebellion – no more adventure – no more wild world. What do you *do* now if you don't want the whole-wheat bread of ordinary, shared human experience or an endless treadmill of second-hand, pointlessly outrageous rituals? Years ago, back in the Sixties, Amanda F in London trepanned herself with an electric drill, punching a hole in the top of her skull to let the pressure out and stay high for ever by opening the third eye. She is fine today but I don't fancy doing that. *So*, what is there? It has all been done. Everything. And now it seems that everyone in New York has decided to fall in love with mediocrity. The pedestrian, the second-rate, the stupid. Low IQ hysteria everywhere, aliens and angels, faeries and feng shui. And all these recovery – survivor – victim groups. And everyone is so fired up on this second-rate shit that it has got to me too. Well, some of me.

Some of it.

So it's not only that soul-sucking Rhonda wants to mash me like a roach and only wants the 'Alice' bit to thrive – but also that I feel at a dead-end. The end of a piece of history. The end of 150 years of Do What Thou Wilt 'cause there is no heaven or hell; the end of the entire sweep of increasingly popular mass hedonism all the way from Baudelaire to Balearic Beat – the ancient, libidinous pleasures of the aristocracy finally peaking in the wholesale, cut-price bohemianism of the Sixties and ending, right here in front of my trainers in TriBeCa, in complete nullity.

That had been me, all the way. Me, with my New York alternative destiny. Me, my soul, my essence. Another ordinary, mass-produced, morbid boho fuck-up. Me with my petty crime and minor perversities, my dope, my uptown rock and coke, my downtown smack and tranx, my sicko scenes and bizarre shit and weird books. Well I might have hit the big No Through Road but I was damned if I was going to let my most minimal and illiterate qualities – my 'Alice' – put me out of business.

Suddenly – it was when I remembered Amanda F's trepanation – I had an idea. The process had been filmed – pretty girl, dark glasses, shaven patch, electric drill, spouting blood, smiles. The movie was still shown. *Cui bono*?

Let's take this slowly, clearly.

What did I want, even now? Actually it was pretty clear. I wanted to stay in New York for ever. I wanted to get rid of 'Alice'. I wanted to ruin Rhonda B. I wanted to be famous. Iconic. I wanted to be part of New York. I belonged here. I knew now that these dreams were doomed, out-dated but they were all I had. All I had ever had. I'd come here because of these dreams, these fantasies and now I must make them come true before my entire identity was assassinated by some devastating psychic lobotomy.

So, I put the old diamond in my nose – it was all hard and crusty with snot but it felt familiar and I moussed my hair and tried to flatten it down to cover my ears against the cold – the black streaks were growing out and the top was all soft and just blonde and I got my big patchwork wool jersey and a long scarf and my biker's jacket and little leather sheath skirt and the thickest black leggings I could find and ankle boots and hooked on my red-tint shades against the glare and Althea scowled as I rushed out the door and ran past the elevator. A blast of wind and snow fell on me like a gang of baby muggers outside but I got to a downtown bus and rode to near Washington Square, drawing all my recent best ideas on the steamy windows. Let them go.

I was going to visit an old friend. From now on I must use pseudonyms but Moebius Franco was just one of this guy's many aliases. He was a filmmaker who produced grind-house horror and sexploitation films for money to finance the horror and sexploitation films he made for art. There wasn't much difference between them except of course the arty ones were slower. He was also rumoured to cross to an even shadier side of the street occasionally, given sufficient inducement.

Moebius was staying in an anonymous mid-price Washington Square tourist hotel. World traveller and world-forsaker, he'd been through ownership – glassy architectural icicles bursting with rotting curios and antiques and so-called art, always with a life-size blonde Barbie doll always floating face down in the pool; he'd lived at the Chelsea and the Château Marmont and he'd had a baroque apartment with curly balconies on Chartres Street, New Orleans and a teeny geodesic dome in New Mexico and it had all run out on him and he didn't care. Once he had been the very image of the avant-garde film-maker about town, with his long, dirty black curls and shades at noon and leather jackets and designer strides and Tiffany's coke-spoons and track-marks on his arms but now there were no style statements left to make. His hair was cut short and carelessly in the brutish non-style of an old mercenary and his specs were untinted and off the rack. He was holding an ordinary can of beer and staring at an ordinary television. Behind him on the bed a naked Asian girl was applying pale blue Hard Candy polish to her toenails. Her name was Hwee Hwee.

I shook the snow out my hair and outlined my project. I said that if he could raise the finance for my proposed movie and film it he could have sole rights and all remuneration. I pointed out that it would be much in demand – firstly stills and key scenes for the world media. Then the US psychoanalytical big-wigs would need a version. And anthropology departments and museums. Then the arty circuit would have to have another, presumably edited version as this would be performance art. Finally the uncut version could be held back as a great rarity, rendered un-copiable and sold for vast sums to, um, selected collectors.

I didn't mention the possible attentions of the law. I also had to lie, in defer-ence to any shards of humanity lingering amongst Moebius's hell-charred synapses. I said that I was I was dying of cirrhosis and had no more than a few weeks and that I would make my wishes quite explicit on camera.

Moebius was a professional yawner but I could tell he was interested. He opened his eyes. He pointed out the central, problematical flaw in my idea and I said I'd hoped he could help with that. Surely he knew someone capable? An anthropologist or, more likely, some witchy-type person with the right books? Obviously he/she'd have to be paid for their labour.

Moebius stood up, revealing truly awful cheapo chino pants. God, he was still making a style statement, I mean an anti-style one.

He stretched. 'Oddly enough,' he said, 'I saw a guy today – that old synchron-icity boogie – who is being pursued by some Caribbeans of desperate mien, brandishing machetes. They think he owes them. He wants to ship out. He might oblige you, Cassie. He was a Westchester Satanist, back in the Seventies. He tried to form a cult called X.Pi.Dite but didn't have the charisma. So he became a performance artist with an all-round post-Crowley act.'

'That Duchamp really finished art,' I said.

'It's a point of view.'

'Yeah, I have more than one.'

'So, I'll let you know. Coupla days?'

I could hear 'Alice' screaming softly somewhere inside,'like a scalped leveret but I told her to shut it bitch, she could run but she couldn't hide.

It was a done deal. The *auteur* bit. The magician took the bait. In cash. This guy Grissom – 'He likes to be called "Magus", someone told me. He's an Ipsipissimus – some shit like that…' – sounded kinda depressing. He was reputedly a pretty cack-handed sorcerer too. I had to meet him to film the first segment at his place for continuity. He lived in a townhouse in the West Seventies with his Mom. Trust fund baby. Soon to be trust fund senior citizen.

Grissom had the whole top floor and it was just what you might expect. Stuffed birds of prey in mid-screaming lunge loomed up. There were Haitian sequinned vévé flags on the walls and a signed bloodied phallus from Mapplethorpe. There was a collection of Austin Osman Spare originals. There were walk-in closets for his bondage gear and robes. I was glad to see he had moths. There were head-high scroll-work iron candle-holders everywhere with decades-old stalactites of thickly intricate yellow wax drooling down the sides. There were skulls – animal and human and sugar – voodoo dolls and impedimenta, sticky santeria altars, mussed up with split rum, stubbed-out cigars and Seven Powers candles. He was insanely eclectic. A library housed his original Crowleyana and scruffy old grimoires with brass hasps. There was some sort of chapel but I didn't go in. There was even a kind of mocked-up autopsy room, with dissecting tables, guttering, trocars and all. Very homely, very tacky – but, in this case very useful. It was all pretty grubby – I suppose he just couldn't get a cleaner to stay…

'Enoch, Enoch,' I said by way of introduction.

'Wha?'

'You're supposed to say "Who's there" and I'll say "Simon Magus" and you go "Simon Magus who?" and I say "Simon Magus a cup of tea". It's an occult knock knock joke. I assume you've studied Enochian mag*ick*.'

'Yes, of course but –'

'Skip it.'

Magus Grissom had obviously gone into magic*ck* because he looked the part. He tossed his lengthy black and grey hair constantly. His nose was aquiline, his cheekbones high, his eyebrows ominous. But middle age and self-indulgence had brought girth to his midriff and paps to his chest. The once-beautiful boy was dewlapped, nervy and balding. Also I don't feel any man over fifty should sport an abundance of ironware punched through their facial flesh. Let alone tattoos of Kali.

We would never be soul-mates but I felt that his persistent, predictable decadence was entirely appropriate.

I got into a chair with more carvings of snakes on it than seemed necessary and said my piece to camera. How I was dying but would not detox or seek treatment as my will to live had been destroyed by the ministrations of Bellamy and her asinine misdiagnosis and general mind-fucking. I was detailed and accusatory.

Now only the finale remained.

Because neither Moebius nor Grissom wanted to get their hands too dirty I'd promised to turn up in the necessary condition. That last morning – it was still cold but the air was bright and blinding with promise the way it can sometimes be in New York. I walked a long way down Fifth Avenue. On West Tenth Street I rang all the bells on a certain door but immediately a doughy lady jerked the door open and started yelling 'No! No again! G'wan, get outta here! More ghouls, more perverts! What's wrong with you people?' And she gave the great oak door a shove but –

I stopped it with both hands.

'I'm sorry ma'am. I don't understand you. I'm a tourist – from England? – and I wanted to see where Mark Twain lived. I'm going on after to Patchin Place to look at where Djuna Barnes and Theodore Dreiser and Eugene O'Neill and John Reed all lived –' I gave her my sweetest smile. The woman looked uncertain and fiddled with a rhinestone brooch at her neck.

'You're a student, I guess?'

I nodded.

'Well then. I oughta say sorry.' She turned and shouted something indistinct into the gloom. 'Just alertin' my neighbour. Can't be too careful. Well. I knew about Mr Twain but not those other folks you mentioned living hereabouts. You can come in out the cold. There's nothing to see here but.'

I was inside, walking across those terrible tiles.

'I'm Ms Stoddard,' the pumpkin lady rambled on. 'I look after the man up-stairs. He's very sick. He's been here a long time. Well, you won't know but ten years back a little girl died here. Beaten to death. And her father a lawyer and her mother a publisher. Both on drugs. They'd adopted her – illegal, ya know? It was a big, big case.' She dropped her voice. 'Poor kid was abused all ways, they say. Oh it's a terrible world.'

I felt dizzy and shivery. I wondered if the haunted apartment upstairs still had a brass eagle on the door. I wondered what it all looked like when Twain would walk in, twirling his cane, and take off his straw hat. I hadn't really wanted to be inside. It was too creepy.

Don't lie, Cassie. You've always been completely morbid. Remember you dragged us round Tompkins Square Park looking for where Daniel Rakowitz butchered some poor dancer? You're a ghoul. I only knew Mark Twain lived here. I had to get us in. You're sick. You're crazy.

Come *on*. Everyone knows about this place – it was so awful. Anyway, why can't I be interested in a writer *and* a crime? Why can't you? Why can't anyone? People are not dualities – good or bad, straight or fucked. They are both, all of them. No one is split into one decent, art-loving law-abiding good woman and a druggy, sick, stupid, bad girl like what Rhonda – and you – would have me believe. It's just not like that. *Ever*. Oh fuck it, I'm putting you down. Right now.

And that was almost the last conversation I ever had with 'Alice'. After that she did almost nothing but scream.

The light in New York is very strange. It comes slicing through the gaps between the buildings at funny angles. It can look like all times of day at once too – pale dawn, bold afternoon, the first brush of twilight dust. The light can be clear and glassy as it bounces off cars, or green and shadowy as it snakes round corners. I walked fast. I could sense smooth, blonde 'Alice' straining to break free and walk off for ever into real life, leaving me a starved, empty shadow, ready for death. No chance.

OK. Now. I am sitting on the pavement near Grissom's house, writing the last bit of this in my notebook. I feel no doubts. I am who I am. I'm doing the right thing.

In a few minutes I'm going to stand up, double over, clutch my stomach and pretend to be very ill. Someone will help and I'll indicate that I only need my medication – a very large prescription bottle for chronic indigestion. Some stranger will feed me what is actually barbiturate powder dissolved in vodka. Moebius and Grissom think I'm committing suicide but – no way! This is an act of affirmation... Won't they be surprised! They'll also learn, eventually, that I wasn't physically ill at all. Well, good for business. The story should unfold, run and run like diarrhoea. She who laughs last...

Three o'clock and all's well if a bit psychedelic round the edges. All went as expected and I'm on the first floor of Grissom's house, waiting for the eleve– lift, to buzz me up past his Psycho Mom in her den. Must write quickly. Feel sick... mustn't spew... great last words? Oh, like Pancho Villa – 'Tell them I said something interesting.' Nice one, Pancho... I – I put this notebook in my pocket & it'll be found sometime soon...

What happened to Eddie, what happened to Eddie?

Cassie, you hurt him really badly in a game and Ma and Pa waited too long to call the doctor.

Why – why they wait?

They didn't want a little boy.

Go 'way, Alice. G'way.

You can't kill me without killing yourself.

Jeez, I know *that*. You were always so dumb... stupid I mean... elevator button 4. Oh no, not now, please – I can hear Rhonda's sickly voice – 'And what was your rea-yul name, Cassandra? When you were a chi-yuld?'

'Alice.'

Elevator up up

~~Moebius~~ Mobe here. That crazy English bitch Cassandra Donner made me promise to write up what happened to 'complete her account' (what account? I guess it'll turn up). She said the artwork would be in three parts – my film, the *objet d'art* and the writing. What the hell. Me, I'm no scribe – I didn't even graduate High School but I'm real smart so I'll just jot this down as best I can. I guess the poor fucked-up kid deserves that much. I hate shrinks anyway.

New York late winter afternoon. Not yet dark. Cassie staggers in and flops onto one of Grissom's black oak church pews. She's wearing silver ankle-boots and a full-length pure-white fake fur coat, kinda beautiful. Underneath just one of those Frenchy lingerie-type silk slips – ivory, peach – I don't know. Loads of lace. Nothing else. You can see everything. She's got legs like Olive Oyl. Natural blonde too. But no tits. Her coat is streaked with yellow vomit and she's got her hands pressed over her mouth. Her pink tinted shades are half falling off. Her hair and fringe are straight and thick as a horse's tail, corn-blonde at the top and then silver and black stripes to her shoulders.

'She's supposed to be dead,' whimpers Lard-Ass Grissom.

Cassie's barely conscious but she summons the will to pull a plastic bag out of the coat pockets and put it over her head and slide down an elastic band to secure it. We can't just sit and watch – that's illegal – depraved indifference or something. So we just leave the camera pointed at her and go into the chapel and Grissom sucks on a few pipes and I smoke some Rasta skunk weed. Then we play chess.

When we go back it's all over and it's a mess. She's shit all down those spindly white legs and on her coat and her face beneath the plastic is all bloated, black and purple and spattered with sick. Her eyes are all red. Some veins must have burst. I zoom in for a few close-ups. Grissom gets the heebie-jeebies big-time, he's practically hysterical. He is a total wuss. I'm taking the Fifth on how much experience of such scenes I've had but I'm worried about him. I need him to straighten out and fly right.

I'm really busy with the camera – this has got to be the high-quality, collector's market stuff and I need him to fix her up and arrange her and generally get everything on display. Eventually – with a few threats – I convince him to get into character and appear on film. Lordy, Lordy. He insists on appearing stark naked – I think he wants to show off the ampallang pierced through the glans of his weenie. He also insists on a face mask – a crude, Mardi Gras overkill, smothered in feathers, pearls and sequins, crowned with a peacock tail, even though I point out that his ass is much better known around town than his face.

Finally, when I've finished filming him pretending to fuck her, this way and that, it's Grissom's big moment. Tsanta time! Naturally he wimps out.

'But you got an embalming room,' I go.

'That's just fantasy stuff. I'll have to go down and get a Sabatier from Mom's kitchen.'

'You *must* have some waterproof sheets? OK. Let's do the show right here.'

Naturally Grissom is a hopeless hacker. He just cannot seem to get Cassie's head off. I can't and won't help him. No way am I appearing on screen. He's sawing madly, sweating buckets, clanking like an ironmonger's in a hurricane and cursing all the time. He seems to be a bit of a misogynist. Still, the movie should be worth zillions in the right places – although I can't think of which bits I'll be able to show publicly except the beginning and end.

Finally by twisting her head round and round he gets the last gristly bits free and it's off. The blood clots surprisingly quickly at the neck.

We have a coffee break. Grissom can't drink with his mask on.

'OK, buddy, this is your big scene now. It's an ancient ritual, isn't it, South America? Did you get the instructions out of those old tomes shackled in bondage in your library?'

'Actually I got all the info off the Internet.'

And fuck me with Ronald McDonald's spatula but he's right. He drags over all these endless screeds of fax print-out and starts blotching them with his bloody fingers.

'Gee, that looks just *awful* on film.'

'Can't be helped. I gotta read as I go along.'

We'll need some really fine mood music on the soundtrack.

Grissom, sitting cross-legged on the black rubber in a pool of blood makes a long slit in the back of Cassie's head and starts trying to detach the skin from the skull. It takes for ever. Then he gets the skin sorta inside out and scrapes the flesh off with a scalpel.

We have a few more drink 'n' drug breaks but I won't let him off the sheet. He's too messy. He puts on some music but it seems he's only got the soundtracks to old Broadway shows. This is hard work.

He has a needle and thread ready and he sews her eyes and lips shut just like in a real movie. Her head looks like a dark balloon that's sorta collapsed. Her hair is all over blood.

'I'll wash it later. I've got some great new conditioner made of peach pits.'

He plops through to the kitchen, leaving bloody foot-prints on the stripped floor-boards, and chucks the head in a casserole on the stove.

'It's gotta cook. And then I gotta cool and heat the cavity over and over and then fire it like pottery. It takes days. So, that's a wrap for you till I show you the result.'

'Lend me a few of your props – let's start with the stuffed raven – and I'll do some *tableaux morts* before rigor sets in. Then fold her into a bag and put her out with the garbage. She's just a little girl.'

We were completely exhausted. It had taken over twelve hours and the stars were out. I left Grissom to clean up, checked he had his passport ready and went out to find a cab.

A few weeks later spring hit Manhattan as if the sky had upended a bucket of sunshine over the embattled city. As Rhonda – now *Dr* – Bellamy swivelled in her leather chair she could see a grimy confetti of pink and white blossom cartwheel against her long, elegant windows. Humming, she sipped her café au lait from the dark green soup-bowl cup and started slitting open mail with her jade sliver. She was tuning out another siren wail when she realised it was her own doorbell.

Her assistant, newly confident and shining, bounced into the room holding a gift-wrapped box.

'Special delivery, Rhonda! The boy says he has to wait for fifteen minutes and then take it on to a gallery or somewhere. I think it's some art for you to look over.'

Rhonda nodded, smiled and started to unwind the peach-coloured lace ribbon, noting the neatly typed address label. She raised her eyebrows at Megan who left the room somewhat less confidently.

The black leather box inside the wrappings appeared a little worn, like an old-fashioned diorama.

One side of the box was made of clear glass so that you could look at the objects within. These were: a standard mock-up of the New York skyline in the background; a little, jokey, pastiche graveyard in the foreground; and at the very front a tiny, shrunken head, its pouting but tightly sewn lips almost touching the glass. As the box tipped, artificial snow swirled about the scene, in a parody of a souvenir.

On top of the box was another neatly typed label. 'The Last Of The Bourgeois Individualists', it read. 'An authentic late 20th century tsanta. Artwork by Magus G. Film produced and directed by Mobe Dick. From an original idea by Cassandra Donner with commentary to follow.'

Rhonda held one hand to her mouth in unconscious imitation of Cassie's final attempt not to vomit. A horrid, nasty hoax? But what *had* happened to Alice, well Cassie? She just seemed to vanish one day.

Rhonda took an antique magnifying glass out of its crocodile skin case and examined the tiny head, no more than a few inches in diameter. It was dark and leathery but artfully made up in Cassie's trademark style – flecks of silver glitter on the eyelids, green mascara, luscious, glistening dark-pink lipstick, despite the awful cruel rigging of the stitches around both the mouth and eyes. The head was a little battered and clumsy, like a child's attempt at papier-mâché but there seemed to be a tiny, ironic smirk on the still-kissable mouth that was utterly characteristic. Miniature versions of some of Cassie's earrings decorated the tiny lobes – dice, an angel, a cat, a bone. Even her nose-stud had been restored – a sequinned fleck. And the hair; from Alice's butter blonde to Cassie's grown-out skunk stripes, well, God, Rhonda could see the roots.

Rhonda could not see the accompanying (edited) video which was obscured by the storm of ivory tissue paper. She was backing away from the table, biting her nails for the first time in years when the delivery boy entered, swept everything up and demanded that she have a nice day.

Her chances of that were very small, I think, but much smaller had she known that photographs of the art-work and copies of the accusatory, but still edited film were currently landing on the desks of every prominent editor and media mogul in America, as well as going to a number of eminent psychiatrists and bureaucrats, including those at the hospital where she and her husband worked.

Cassie was going to stay in New York City for ever.

With many thanks to all the innumerable historians, biographers, critics and others who have written about New York. Special acknowledgments to Patti Smith's Seventh Heaven *(Telegraph Books, 1971),* Djuna *by Andrew Field (University of Texas Press, 1985),* Djuna *by Phillip Herring (Viking 1995), Feral Press and in particular* Low Life *by Luc Sante (Vintage 1992).*

Visit Penguin on the Internet
and browse at your leisure

- ◆ preview sample extracts of our forthcoming books
- ◆ read about your favourite authors
- ◆ investigate over 10,000 titles
- ◆ enter one of our literary quizzes
- ◆ win some fantastic prizes in our competitions
- ◆ e-mail us with your comments and book reviews
- ◆ instantly order any Penguin book

and masses more!

'To be recommended without reservation ... a rich and rewarding on-line experience' – Internet Magazine

www.penguin.co.uk

READ MORE IN PENGUIN

In every corner of the world, on every subject under the sun, Penguin represents quality and variety – the very best in publishing today.

For complete information about books available from Penguin – including Puffins, Penguin Classics and Arkana – and how to order them, write to us at the appropriate address below. Please note that for copyright reasons the selection of books varies from country to country.

In the United Kingdom: Please write to *Dept. EP, Penguin Books Ltd, Bath Road, Harmondsworth, West Drayton, Middlesex UB7 ODA*

In the United States: Please write to *Consumer Sales, Penguin USA, P.O. Box 999, Dept. 17109, Bergenfield, New Jersey 07621-0120*. VISA and MasterCard holders call 1-800-253-6476 to order Penguin titles

In Canada: Please write to *Penguin Books Canada Ltd, 10 Alcorn Avenue, Suite 300, Toronto, Ontario M4V 3B2*

In Australia: Please write to *Penguin Books Australia Ltd, P.O. Box 257, Ringwood, Victoria 3134*

In New Zealand: Please write to *Penguin Books (NZ) Ltd, Private Bag 102902, North Shore Mail Centre, Auckland 10*

In India: Please write to *Penguin Books India Pvt Ltd, 706 Eros Apartments, 56 Nehru Place, New Delhi 110 019*

In the Netherlands: Please write to *Penguin Books Netherlands bv, Postbus 3507, NL-1001 AH Amsterdam*

In Germany: Please write to *Penguin Books Deutschland GmbH, Metzlerstrasse 26, 60594 Frankfurt am Main*

In Spain: Please write to *Penguin Books S. A., Bravo Murillo 19, 1° B, 28015 Madrid*

In Italy: Please write to *Penguin Italia s.r.l., Via Felice Casati 20, I–20124 Milano*

In France: Please write to *Penguin France S. A., 17 rue Lejeune, F–31000 Toulouse*

In Japan: Please write to *Penguin Books Japan, Ishikiribashi Building, 2–5–4, Suido, Bunkyo-ku, Tokyo 112*

In South Africa: Please write to *Longman Penguin Southern Africa (Pty) Ltd, Private Bag X08, Bertsham 2013*

READ MORE IN PENGUIN

A CHOICE OF FICTION

What a Carve Up! Jonathan Coe

'"They're not monsters you know. Not really," says Mortimer Winshaw, heir to desolate Winshaw Towers, of his clan. Oh, but they are, really, real monsters. And Jonathan Coe's novel is, really, something to get excited about ... a big, hilarious, intricate, furious, moving treat of a novel' – *Guardian*

Partial Eclipse Lesley Glaister

Jennifer is in solitary confinement, imprisoned for an undisclosed crime. As she waits for time to pass she reflects on the events that brought her there: her strange home life with an eccentric grandmother and her wild love for Tom, a philandering musician. 'She has an uncomfortable knack of putting her finger on the things we most fear, of exposing the darkness within' – *Sunday Telegraph*

Ireland: Selected Stories William Trevor

'He is a master of understatement, a minimalist, using detail with the delicacy of a man stalking rare butterflies: his characters are not drawn, but pinned down – just one or two precise thrusts and there they are, revealed in all their subtlety of colour' – *Daily Telegraph*

Something to Remember Me By Saul Bellow

Dedicated to Bellow's children and grandchildren, *Something to Remember Me By* tells the wonderfully tender and funny story of a young man's sexual initiation and sexual guilt, one bleak Chicago winter's day in 1933. That story, narrated like a memoir, is collected here with Bellow's acclaimed novellas *The Bellarosa Connection* and *A Theft*.

No One Writes to the Colonel Gabriel García Márquez

In a decaying Colombian town, the Colonel and his ailing wife are living a hand-to-mouth existence, scraping together or borrowing the money for food and medicine. The Colonel's hopes for a better future lie in his rooster, which for him, and indeed the whole town, has become a symbol of defiance in the face of despair ...

READ MORE IN PENGUIN

A CHOICE OF FICTION

An Experiment in Love   Hilary Mantel

It was the year after Chappaquiddick, and all spring Carmel had watery dreams about the disaster. Now she, Karina and Julianne were escaping the dreary north for a London University hall of residence. Awaiting them was a winter of new preoccupations – sex and politics, food and fertility – and a pointless grotesque tragedy of their own.

Jackson's Dilemma   Iris Murdoch

At Penndean, preparations for the marriage of Edward Lannion and Marian Berran are under way. The wedding party is to arrive the day before, and Marian, who loves surprises, will come on the morning of the wedding. But as the guests anticipate the festivities, something shocking happens. 'A work of brilliance' – *Independent on Sunday*

The Vinegar Jar   Berlie Doherty

From childhood on, Rose Doran's life has been one of lovelessness and loneliness. Smooth-talking William abandons her, along with his baby, Edmund. Rose seeks comfort in an unsatisfactory marriage to Gordon. But it is not until she meets Paedric, her mysterious neighbour, that her colourless life is transformed – with disturbing consequences.

Bright Lights, Big City   Jay McInerney

Portraying a week in the life of a young journalist on a *New Yorker*-style magazine, Jay McInerney's debut novel explores hangover days and night life in the apartment blocks and clublands of eighties Manhattan. 'Deadly funny' – Raymond Carver

These Same Long Bones   Gwendolyn M. Parker

Eleven-year-old Mattie died falling from her slide. No one in the prosperous community of Hay-Ti, the 'coloured' section of Durham, North Carolina, is unaffected. 'A thoughtful and generous-hearted novel that shows a life "both blessed and ... hard", sustained by human resilience and always aglow with insoluble mystery' – *The New York Times Book Review*

READ MORE IN PENGUIN

The *Time Out* Book of London Short Stories
Edited by Maria Lexton

Distinctive, daring and defiantly diverse, this is undoubtedly the most exciting collection of original British fiction we are likely to see this side of the millennium.

These twenty-five short stories, which were written especially to mark the twenty-fifth anniversary of *Time Out*, share London as a setting. Just as *Time Out* has faithfully recorded London life in all its varied aspects and pursuits, these stories reflect wildly differing views of the capital. Each tale contributes a singular slant to the city while together they form an explosive exploration of the dangers and delights of London life in the late twentieth century.

The collection contains contributions from some of today's most exciting writers, whose voices echo the diversity of London life. The line-up includes nineties literary laureates Will Self, Adam Thorpe and Hilary Mantel; Brit crime supremos John Milne and Mark Timlin; horror-writers Clive Barker, Christopher Fowler, Kim Newman and Anne Billson; and the inimitable Julie Burchill. With first stories from Nick Hornby and Gordon Burn, this collection is truly representative of the literary talent in Britain today.